T4-ATV-848

VAMPIRE ROYALTY:

The Rebellion

by
Valerie Hoffman

AMERICAN LEGACY™ Books • Washington, DC

AMERICAN
LEGACY™
Books

ISBN 1-886766-45-2

Copyright © 2006 Washington, DC

Published in the United States of America
Publisher:
American Legacy Books
Washington, DC

All rights are reserved. No part of this book may be reproduced,
entered into a retrieval system, nor transmitted in any form by any
means, whether electronic, mechanical, photographic, photocopying,
manual (by hand), digital, video or audio recording, or otherwise; nor
be produced as a derivative work; nor be included on the internet;
nor be performed publicly in any manner without the prior written
consent of the copyright owner. (The exceptions to the preceding
are short quotations within other publications and short passages by
the media. Both must include the credit references of title, author,
and publisher.) To request consent, write to the address or call the
telephone number near the end of this book. Explain the nature of
the proposed usage and include your address and daytime telephone
number.

VAMPIRE ROYALTY:

The Rebellion

Contents

Acknowledgements

I would like to take this opportunity to ac-knowledge and express my appreciation to my husband, Norman Hoffman, for his dedication in helping me to attain my dream of becoming an author.

I also would like to acknowledge all of the staff at American Legacy Books who have helped to turn my dream into a reality.

I would like to express a special appre-ciation to my editor, Donna Howell, who went the extra mile and provided me with invaluable advice.

Dedication

This book is dedicated to my husband, Norm, and to my brother, the real Andrew Gabriel.

BEDLAM

Moans and wails echoed through the upper floor of the old two-story house. Ear-piercing shrieks punctuated the bedlam. The stillness of the first floor offered a striking contrast to the chaos of the upper levels. The first floor's silence abruptly was broken by the tinkle of shattered glass. Immediately, a flurry of white-clad figures converged on the area. Mrs. Brown, the head nurse, was the first to enter the room. An orderly and a student nurse quickly followed her. An elderly woman sat in the center of the waxed wooden floor with her bony legs crossed and her housecoat in disarray. An intense inner fervor contorted her seamed and withered face. Compressing her thin lips, she stared with protruding eyes as she concentrated determinedly on her task.

Inhaling sharply, the intern gazed fixedly at the old woman as she used a shard of glass to saw through the bandages on her wrist. Mrs. Brown shot a quick and sympathetic but stern look at the intern as she signaled for the orderly to restrain the patient. She watched for a moment while the orderly led the old woman back to bed. Satisfied that the situation was under control, she returned her attention to the student.

"Being in a psychiatric facility with real mentally ill patients isn't the same as reading about it in textbooks. Your professors apparently forgot to tell you about one very important practice: Never provide patients with items that can be used as weapons," she reprimanded sternly. "I trust nothing like this will happen again."

The young woman shook her head so vigorously that her cap slipped slightly askew. "Why, she's probably not more than twenty," thought Mrs. Brown, who usually developed a motherly interest in her protégées at some point in their training. Having no children of her own caused her to take a maternal attitude towards the students. Her face softened as she decided to pass on some more advice.

The front door of the converted house opened. Sunlight burst into the hall and temporarily blinded the occupants of the corridor. The sunlight was eclipsed by a shadow as the visitor entered the house. High heels tapped a staccato beat across the wooden floor as the figure approached. The swishing of fabric mixed with a distinctive perfume announced the visitor before the head nurse's eyes adjusted to the light.

"Oh, Miss Parker," the nurse said to the tall slender woman. As the young woman walked towards them, the nurse studied her ensemble of a gray soft suede skirt and jacket with approval. No raggedy jeans and torn t-shirts for this young lady. Miss Parker always was turned out in clean, modest, and fashionable apparel, which unintentionally obtained the head nurse's approval.

Victory Parker paused in the hallway to peer inside the room. She took in the scene and then turned a sympathetic face towards the nurse. "You seem to have your hands full at the moment, Mrs. Brown, so don't worry about showing me to my father. I can find my way."

The graceful girl continued down the hall and disappeared around a corner. Watching her as she walked away, Mrs. Brown explained to the curious nurse, "That was Victory Parker, the daughter of the new director." She leaned forward while continuing confidentially, "She has her eyes set on becoming a Supreme Court justice someday. I wouldn't be at all surprised if she made it, too," she asserted, while beaming as if she were somehow responsible for the goal.

Responding to the student's startled look, she added, "Well, she's due to start law school in a couple of weeks and her father will tell anyone who'll listen about her ambitions."

Both nurses returned to the room and Victory Parker was forgotten as they surveyed the mess. "I'll get a broom and dust pan," offered the student.

THE PATIENT

Victory paused outside of her father's office door. In bold letters, the nameplate spelled out, "Dr. Howard Parker, Director." She traced the inscription with her fingers, while her cobalt blue eyes gazed at the words. Pride rippled through her as she considered her father's professional achievement. Being appointed as the director of St. Mary's Psychiatric Clinic was a very impressive and coveted position. Although small, the hospital was prestigious. As its director, her father was recognized as one of the top psychiatrists in the country.

The hollowness of the triumph hit her like a blow. She fought back a fresh surge of tears. She closed her eyes against the pain, but, when she reopened them, a shadow had fallen across the blue depths. Her mother, recently killed in a car crash, would have been so proud. Closing her mind against the memories, she fixed a smile firmly in place.

Now, she and her father had only each other. Someday, she might be able to bring him enough joy and happiness that he would be able to forget the terrible tragedy that had robbed him of his beloved wife. So far, her efforts had been partially successful. When she had graduated with top honors from one of the most influential schools in the country, her father had expressed pleasure for the first time since the accident. She knew that law school was going to be tougher and she hoped that she would be worthy of her father's confidence.

She smoothed her gray skirt and tugged a rebellious strand of golden hair back into her French braid before knocking on the door.

"Come in," commanded a deep baritone. Victory opened the door, twirled through the entrance, and clicked the door shut. Dr. Howard Parker continued staring intently out of the window while ignoring the intrusion. Victory observed an orderly, who was wheeling one of the patients down the cement walkway leading through the gardens. Unaware of any extraordinary occurrence, she softly cleared her throat. The doctor turned distractedly. A frown of irritation at being interrupted marred his compassionate features. Again, she softly cleared her throat. Recognition dawned and brought the doctor out of his contemplation. Joy spread across his face and warmth lit his blue eyes.

"Victory," he exclaimed, as he covered the distance between them in quick easy strides. "I wasn't expecting you back for another two weeks."

"Oh, Papa, Florida is so stiflingly hot this time of year. I just couldn't stand it a moment longer," she explained, as she gazed into his compassionate features. Despite the recent tragedy that had worn permanent lines around his mouth and forehead, he was still a handsome man. His bearing was still erect and strong, too. There had been a few weeks when she had been really worried. She pushed those thoughts aside as she noticed that he was staring expectantly.

"Laura and I decided we'd had enough, so we took the first flight out this morning. Besides," she added, as her eyes reflected his joy, "I decided that I needed to spend more time with my favorite man before going back to the grindstone," she said, while wrinkling her nose. "Honestly, Dad, I don't think I will ever be finished with school."

She offered the explanation in a breathless rush as an attempt to distract him with talk of school so he wouldn't focus on the prematurely terminated vacation. The holiday had been his idea. He thought that it was a way to make it up to her for losing her mom and having to devote herself to a father who had lost all interest in life. She hadn't wanted to go, but he had insisted. When the job offer came, she decided that it was safe to leave him since he would have a new challenge in his life. However, after a few days, she had been so fretful that the vacation became more of a burden than a treat. So, without any regrets, she had packed her bags and come home.

Howard Parker held his daughter at arm's length. "Well, despite the heat, the Florida sun seems to have agreed with you," he asserted, while examining her rosy cheeks and healthy tan. "I am delighted that you decided to spend more time here before you leave. I hope I can finagle some free time. I've been here a month and, instead of the work easing into a steady routine, there seems to be a constant stream of new challenges."

"You know you love it. Sinking into work up to your ears has always been your thing, Daddy Dearest," she teased. She was pleased that something finally had distracted him from his grief.

Dr. Parker sat down. Victory took a seat on the soft leather sofa across from him and then began regaling her dad with her Floridian exploits. In a remarkably short time, she and her girlhood friend, Laura Warner, had taken Palm Beach by storm. "Hardly surprising," thought her doting father. Both girls were extremely attractive. Their contrasting complexions complimented each other to perfection. His only surprise was that the young men of the county had let them slip through their fingers so easily. "Must be the hot weather that makes Southerners sluggish," he surmised. "Enough about me, Daddy. What have you been up to here? Have you settled into the new house? How do you like your new job? Do you have any interesting cases?"

Her father laughed. "Slow down. You know it's been my lifelong dream to own a home on the Cape and a thriving practice in Boston. So," he responded, as he began ticking off his fingers, "to answer your questions: I've moved into the house, but use it only on weekends and vacations. I bought a condo closer to work. Yes, I like my new job and, yes, I have one patient I would classify as out of the ordinary."

Victory's eyes sparkled with interest. Picking up on what she knew was her dad's most important point, she replied, "You know, Dad, I think I've heard you say that about a patient only twice before."

As Dr. Parker leaned back in his swivel chair and clasped his hands behind his head, his tan jacket opened and revealed a fall print vest of oranges and russet flowers. She grimaced. She remembered the birthday celebration when she proudly had presented him with the vest. It had been the first gift that she had chosen without her mother's guidance. Victory was thankful that her fashion sense had matured since she was ten. She was surprised that he still had the eyesore.

"This patient is by far the most fascinating case I've ever studied. In fact, I've considered writing a paper on his case."

"Really?"

"Yes," the doctor said emphatically. His eyes darkened with an inner glow as he continued. "I've named him Al. Al is short for albino. He was here when I arrived and several strange circumstances surround his case." The doctor leaned forward, placed his hands on his light brown trousers, and pounded his knee for emphasis. "For one thing, he is catatonic."

She gave a strange look to her father. That doesn't sound peculiar for a patient in a mental hospital."

"It isn't, but several of the staff who have worked here for many years report that he has been here longer than they have."

Victory was baffled. Her father obviously attached great significance to this finding. "Dad, I realize I don't know much about psychiatry, but I was under the impression that patients suffering from catatonia could remain in that state indefinitely."

He shook his head and patiently explained. "According to the documentation and witnesses," said her father, pointing out of the window, "the man appeared to be between the ages of 35 and 40 when he arrived. If he has been here for over 20 years, which is what Mrs. Brown insists and his records verify, he would be in his late fifties to early sixties. Right?"

She nodded tolerantly. Despite her confusion, she was happy to see her father being so animated.

"Well," said her father, who was trying to reign in his excitement, "that man still looks to be about 35 years old."

She laughed, but, as she realized that he was serious, her eyes widened and she gasped, "That's impossible! Because he is an albino, maybe his hair doesn't turn gray or maybe his medical condition has slowed down the aging process." Curiosity caused her to glance through the window in the direction that her dad had pointed. Only the top of a blonde head was visible above the back of the wheel chair. Turning back to her father, she quipped, "No wrinkles, either? I know millions of women who would love to know his secret."

A shutter closed over his features and he turned to straighten some papers on his desk. Victory squirmed uncomfortably as she stared at her dad's rigid posture. She knew that he had been offended by her flippancy, so she said in a more sober tone, "I'm sorry, Dad. I didn't mean to make light of your findings. Please tell me what else is strange about him."

Mollified, he continued, "Well, as I mentioned, he is an albino, but, even for someone with a pigment disorder, his reaction to the sun is extraordinary. He burns in the sun." He held up a hand to forestall her comments. "I don't mean he turns red if exposed to the sun for an extended period. I mean the sun burns his skin. His skin actually singes! If he is out for more than a few minutes, he gets blisters that burst and start to bleed. His skin blackens. As difficult as it is to believe, one time after he had been exposed, I went to brush what I thought was some dirt off of his arm and discovered it was ash! After five minutes of sunshine, Al had second-degree burns. That's not all. We treated him for severe sunburn and, the next morning when I came to check on his condition, all trace of the burn was gone. Not just healed," he emphasized," but vanished. If I hadn't seen the skin the previous day, I would never have believed the reports."

Victory was silent. In all of the years that her father had been working in the field, she couldn't remember him ever discussing anything so extraordinary. "It sounds so incredible. It sounds as though you have some sort of medical phenomenon here. Was he in much pain?" she asked, as her eyes strayed back to the window.

He smiled. His compassionate daughter, who couldn't even bear to swat a fly, obviously would be concerned about the patient's suffering. "He didn't show any sign of it, not a flicker of an eyelid or spasm or sound."

"What about relatives? Surely, he must have a history, someone who knew him, some identification?"

"According to his chart and Mrs. Brown's recollection, there was no identification. The local hospitals and police were notified, but no one ever reported a man fitting his description as missing."

Dr. Parker pulled out his gold pocket watch, another gift from his daughter. He briefly consulted the timepiece and then snapped it shut. "Al is due back now. We've been timing his solar tolerance. His resistance appears to be lengthening by a few minutes every few weeks, but we still have to be careful. We have a physician coming to check him later, but I have some free time until then. Why don't you make the rounds with me? I'll introduce you to him. Then, we can have lunch together."

Victory stood and lifted her purse from the edge of the desk. "I'd love to, Dad, but I promised Laura I'd meet her at Faneuil Hall. I'm already running late or I'd take you up on the offer. I stopped by to find out where the condo is so I can drop off my luggage. I will come home for dinner, though, and you can tell me more about this fascinating patient. Maybe you'll have some additional insight after the doctor examines him." A frown tugged at the corners of her mouth as she said, "In all these years, I would expect that several physicians would have thoroughly examined this patient."

Dr. Parker shook his head regretfully. "Since he was unresponsive, it appears that he was left alone after the entrance evaluations. Certainly, there are no notes in his chart to indicate that he was ever examined after the initial tests."

She shook her head sympathetically. "I might be able to come back tomorrow. I must admit that my curiosity is aroused." The doctor scribbled the address on a piece of paper. Stuffing the note into her purse, she looked up into her father's twinkling eyes.

"I hope your legal documents are treated with more respect," he teased, while holding the door for her.

Victory laughed, as she preceded her dad down the hallway. "I don't have any legal documents to worry about, yet."

"Well, it couldn't hurt to become more organized."

She groaned and sidestepped the old argument. "You know, I really like the ambiance of this place. It feels more like a home than an institution. "

Her father laughed, as he placed an arm around her shoulders. "That's because, Darling Daughter, it is a house."

They continued their light bantering as they passed through the main hallway. Their voices reverberated and then faded as they headed towards the front of the house.

NOT QUITE ALIVE

In one of the rooms off of the main hallway, a figure lay motionless and unaware of his surroundings. The comfortable bed, plumped pillows, and pictures of saints strategically placed about the room were neither noticed nor appreciated. The figure lay passively, existing as he had since his arrival: seeing yet blind, conscious yet unthinking, living yet not quite alive.

Awareness infiltrated by degrees. Ever so slowly, a sound penetrated his protective cocoon. Laughter but not just any laughter. The melodious tinkling evoked images and brought forth memories, painful and incomplete, like pieces of a jigsaw puzzle. A scent drifted tantalizingly through the barrier of his blunted senses. At first, it was faint. Then, it was as strong as an unkept promise. Then, once more, it grew faint. The odor enhanced the images and brought them into focus until the pieces of the puzzle began to fall into place.

Fragmented images began to emerge – kaleidoscoping at first, then coalescing into complete scenes. Long-suppressed and half-forgotten memories of him with a woman struggled to the surface. The woman's smile was as bright as the sun and her eyes glittered like jewels. As if it were part of a movie, a scene unfolded on the blank screen of his mind. He and the woman were laughing with abandon, as they tumbled on a grassy lawn. Hopelessly, they became entangled in the woman's long velvet skirt. As he bent over to kiss her, the scene shifted.

Another memory broke through the barrier. He and the woman were sharing a picnic lunch under an elm tree surrounded by green pastures and hillsides covered with wild flowers. She adoringly gazed at him as he presented her with a square velvet box. Upon opening the gift, she felt her face radiating with joy as she slipped the diamond on her hand.

Scenes were bombarding his growing awareness. Another memory sprang to life. He and the woman, who was dressed in a blue velvet riding habit, were racing across the open fields on horseback. Admiration darkened his eyes as he watched the other horse and rider in perfect accord. They blended together as one. Sitting astride, they galloped merrily across a drawbridge and into a cobbled courtyard. Leaping from the saddle, he helped her dismount. He tenderly gazed down at her, stroked her silky hair, and lightly brushed his lips across her mouth. "I love you," he murmured against her hair.

Her eyes reflected her devotion as she gazed up at him. Someone approached and he cursed the intrusion. She chuckled and chatted gaily as they strolled arm-in-arm into the castle.

Now that the dam had burst, the other memories, so long suppressed, flooded in. Eventually, the most painful memories broke the surface. The sunny days and sultry nights were replaced by stormy dissention and frequent fights.

A moan escaped through tight lips as he remembered himself and the woman in conflict – her eyes wide with terror and her face white with shock as she stared in horror at the lifeless body at his feet. Turbulent emotions tore from her and hit him like blows. Feeling her fear while sensing her pain and confusion, he reached out to explain, but she backed away. When he tried to offer reassurance, she became hysterical.

"Marry?" she wailed, as the sound trailed into laughter and then caught on a sob. "We can never marry, never have children, never lead a normal life. Why," she gasped, while glancing down at the corpse with revulsion, as a fountain of tears gushed down her cheeks, "you're not even human!"

Again, he tried to comfort her, but, as he stepped forward, she held up her hand in the ancient sign of protection. Her attempt at banishing him like some evil spirit was futile, but her retreat towards the edge of the walkway brought him up short.

As her eyes widened, he realized his mistake. His hesitation had confirmed his guilt. Behind him came the sound of distant footsteps and echoing laughter. Exasperated and aggravated, he watched as her eyes grew enormous and her face turned ashen.

"Desist," he commanded silently with his fear escalating. The woman appeared close to fainting and he was too far to keep her from falling into the gaping abyss. The barrage abruptly ceased. The air was thick with the sudden silence. Stalemated, he eyed his fiancée, whose hair and gown were billowing behind her in the stiff breeze. The gray sky and distant hills provided a picturesque backdrop that sharpened his awareness of her perilous position. Despite his reservations against force, he could see no other alternative.

Suddenly, she was falling from the parapet. Had she been shoved or had she jumped? He dove after her, but all that he caught was the hem of her gown. The momentum of her fall carried them both over the edge. They were both falling. The air rushed by. The wind pummeled their bodies. The rocks below reached out jagged hands to embrace them.

He had been able to maneuver his body under hers so that he could take the initial impact. His action had been in vain. The crash had proven too much for her. She lay on top of him with her body broken and still. Had he seen love in her eyes in the last moments or had there been only fear and revulsion? He would never know.

Afterward, he had survived, as he knew he must. But, from then on, there was only anguish for what he could never be and self-loathing for what he was. He wandered aimlessly in despair. He refused sustenance and comfort. Finally, in a remote land far from his loss, he collapsed.

He allowed his life force to drain without caring about himself or anyone else. Until today.

REVIVAL

Suddenly, his eyes snapped into focus as awareness penetrated the void. His lips curved slightly. As if waking from a dream, he gave a mental shake. Then, the first conscious sensations struck like hammer blows. Spasms racked his body as it cried out for nourishment. He slowly had been starving to death. Now, every reawakened cell of his emaciated body was crying out for relief. Licking dried and cracked lips, he forced himself to continue lying perfectly still.

Chords on his neck bulged while a thin film of perspiration broke out on his face. He bit down on his lower lip to keep from screaming as another wave of cramps consumed him. Blood seeped into his mouth and he shot up as though electrified. How long had he been here? Too long, judging by the conversation that he overheard. He listened cautiously without giving a sign of his heightened awareness. Only muted murmurs punctuated by an occasional wail from above disturbed the stillness. His perfect night vision penetrated the inky blackness. No one was in the vicinity at the moment, but that could change at any time.

Abruptly, he stood up. With a speed that belied years of inertia, he strode to the closet to reclaim his clothing. Staring at his reflection in the full-length mirror, he grimaced at the picture that he presented. Gaunt, almost to the point of emaciation, he could not remember the last time that his body had received nourishment. The thought evoked elicit images that he quickly quelled. As he continued to gaze at his reflection in the mirror on the closet door, a broad smile split his face. He was sure that he looked no better than a vagabond. Still, the clothing was preferable to an institutional uniform. From a conversation that he had overheard, he knew Doctor Parker had decided that it would be a good idea to allow the patients to keep as many familiar objects as possible – if they were not harmful. This was his attempt at making their transitions less stressful. In his case, the doctor also had thought that reminders of his past eventually might trigger a response. At the time, it had been a vain hope. But, now, as he slipped into his old clothing, he gained a new appreciation for the idea.

Stealthily, he crossed to the window. The iron bars presented little difficulty as he grasped each one and jerked. A slight snap as brittle as a twig cracking accompanied each removal. A gasp from behind caused him to turn around. In the doorway stood a young nurse, her eyes wide, her mouth slack with shock. Seconds ticked by as they stared at each other. Never breaking eye contact, he approached slowly. The girl's eyes widened further, but she could not look away. Her mouth opened and closed, but no sound came out.

He halted inches away. One arm snaked out and pulled the nurse into the room while the other silently pushed the door closed. He considered his options while she gazed fixedly at him. Keeping her quiet wasn't a problem while he was with her, but what could he do to prevent her from sounding the alarm after he had left? The smell of her skin was intoxicating. The warmth of her body strained his resolve. His stomach muscles contracted and black spots danced before his eyes. He started to shake. The nurse's cap slipped slightly askew. He needed to get out of there immediately, but, the moment that he released her, all hell would break loose. Could he bring her with him? He swallowed hard. His gaze desperately swept around the room as the persistent demand for nourishment overwhelmed him. On the verge of succumbing, he lowered his eyes to the sheets. If he could tear them into strips...

A violent cramp tore through him and he doubled over in agony. "What's wrong?" she mumbled, as she slowly shook her head. She was unsure whether she was referring to him or to herself.

Her concern caught his attention and he glanced down at the attractive young woman, still clasped tightly in his embrace. There was a gentle reassurance on his lips. She was beautiful, he realized as she gazed up at him with rounded eyes and partially parted lips.

Jerking away, he suddenly released her. He bolted towards the window while hoping that he would have enough time to get clear of the grounds before she alerted the others. A tug on his coat sleeve pulled him from the window. He jerked free and bolted for the sill.

"Wait," she pleaded, "you'll get hurt. Ouch."

As she cried out, he glanced back. Looking at her was his mistake. Ruby droplets glistened on the jagged steel of the bars. His eyes flicked from the window to the girl. Blood dripped from a long gash on her arm. "That will probably require some stitches," he thought, as he pulled her into his arms.

Wiping his sleeve across his mouth, he balanced on the edge of the window ledge. He surveyed the grounds and became a dark silhouette blending with the darker shadows before fading into the night.

Chapter 1:

The Plastic Politician

Washington, DC, ten years later

"Those are some of the reasons John Callahan and I are your best choices for the next president and vice president of the United States. In the final weeks of the campaign, I hope we can continue to count on your support because we can achieve our dreams only with the allegiance of our constituents. Thank you."

Loud applause and boisterous cheers followed Craven Maxwell as he stepped down from the makeshift podium. Victory Parker watched ambivalently as the elegantly clad figure began to circulate on the arm of Elizabeth Dumont, the hostess of the party and one of the richest women in Washington. The late Mr. Dumont had been a shipping tycoon, who had died at an early age and left a fortune to his young widow. "How convenient for her," Victory thought wryly. She had followed the couple's progress and had read the scandals flaunted by the tabloids. She frowned into her champagne glass. The press had implied that Mr. Dumont had been involved in organized crime. His widow also had been a frequent focus of attention for her torrid love affairs. "How could the campaign managers not advise their candidates against associating with that band?" she wondered. "They probably allowed it because they gave higher campaign contributions."

She sighed. When had she turned so caustic? She decided that it must have happened after she had been offered a position in one of the top law firms in Washington. Innocence and a basic belief in the human species had been liabilities that she had been forced to shed in order to survive in politics.

Curtailing her introspection, she again focused on the couple. Elizabeth Dumont was old enough to be his mother. Yet, she was flirting outrageously with the man who could eventually be second in command of the country. "And he," she thought cynically, "in the interest of the campaign, is encouraging her." Her conclusion soon was confirmed when she intercepted Maxwell as he was rolling his eyes and discreetly gesturing towards the widow. Turning slightly, she caught a petite brunette nodding understandingly, as she giggled into her champagne glass.

Disgusted, she wondered how he could have been so indiscreet. However, after looking around the room, she realized that she had been the only one who had noticed the exchange. She shifted her attention back to the man. With his plastic politician smile fixed firmly in place, Craven Maxwell certainly was charming in his black tie and tails. He was also an eloquent speaker, she admitted grudgingly. Still, if it had not been for her steadfast conviction in his running mate, she never would have considered voting for their ticket. John Callahan was a gentle-looking man who reminded her of her father. He came across as compassionate but firm. He had a love of his country and the people in it. He managed to convey the feeling that he would be a force to reckon with if the need arose. Although his political partner embraced the same views and even proposed many innovative reforms of the criminal justice system, mental health facilities, and medical treatment centers, Victory couldn't banish her uneasiness whenever she watched him on television or saw him in person.

Covertly, she continued to watch the progress of the couple across the crowded room. Mrs. Dumont appeared to be intent on introducing the candidate to everyone in the room. She sipped her champagne while peering over the rim of her glass and then switched her attention to Laura. Victory's lifelong friend was engaged in a lively conversation with a couple of male admirers. Her long black hair rippled and gleamed in the soft light, as she turned from one to the other. "That silver gown really suits her and matches the gray of her eyes," she thought, as she moved to join her friend. Neither Laura nor her companions seemed disturbed by the intrusion. Laura playfully linked her arm through her friend's. "Tory," she said with feigned relief, "you are a godsend. These two gentlemen are arguing about which one will escort me home," she said, amid her tinkling laughter. Victory studied her friend's glittering eyes and bright smile. She groaned inwardly. "I was explaining to them that I already had an escort, but they would not believe me. You see, gentlemen, I can't possibly leave my friend."

Victory eyed the two men warily. She wondered how difficult it would be to extract her friend from the situation without causing a scene. The two men were young, but had the dissipated looks of much older men. She suspected that they were socialites who frequented elite functions. Their demeanors warned that they were used to getting what they wanted. The taller had bright red hair, a long nose, and a smattering of freckles dotting his face. The shorter was a round young man. He had permanently pursed lips and a perspiring forehead that he repeatedly wiped with his handkerchief.

"Well, Ron," said the taller to his companion, "it looks like we don't have to flip a coin, after all. Now, there's one for each of us."

"Yeah, Hank," agreed the one called Ron, who was staring at Victory as if trying to see through her blue lamé gown, "I'll take the blue one and you can have the silver."

Victory shot her friend an irritated glance. What had Laura's perpetual flirting gotten them into this time? Before she could invent a diplomatic excuse, an authoritative voice interceded.

"I'm sorry, fellas, but the ladies have agreed to stay and discuss some volunteer work they promised to do for the campaign."

Surprised, all four turned to stare at Craven Maxwell and their hostess. The vice presidential candidate was grinning affably and was holding out his hand. An awkward silence ensued until Mrs. Dumont hastily made the introductions.

"Please allow me to present Mr. Henry Cartwright and Mr. Ronald Bennett. Of course," she stated coolly, while haughtily nodding towards the women, "you already know Laura Warner and Victory Parker."

They shook hands and spoke briefly of politics until the two younger men excused themselves and disappeared into the crowd.

Victory smiled gratefully. "That was certainly worth two votes."

"It was my pleasure," he responded smoothly, with white teeth flashing. He flashed a wide smile, while his dark eyes probed her with interest. "I couldn't resist coming to the aid of two such beautiful ladies and, at the same time, recruiting two new volunteers."

Victory glanced at Laura out of the corner of her eye. Bantering with gorgeous men was her specialty, but she seemed to be tongue-tied.

Surely, even Laura realized that he wasn't just any gorgeous male, but possibly the next vice president. That was obviously enough to subdue her normally vivacious friend.

After a brief pause, Victory shrugged. "You were serious about volunteering?"

Maxwell soberly nodded his head. For a moment, he looked like the cat that swallowed the canary. Her earlier unease resurfaced. Whenever the full force of his onyx gaze rested on her, she felt as if she were suffocating. The sensation passed. She blinked and glanced around the room to regain her equilibrium. He smiled charmingly. "Quite serious, Miss Parker, especially since I recognize you as the lawyer whose legal skills I've recently admired."

Startled, Victory was seized by an inexplicable panic, but, as their eyes locked, her alarm faded. She enquired politely, "When did you have such an opportunity," she asked. How could she have missed Craven Maxwell in the courtroom, not to mention the accompanying commotion that would have been caused by his presence? This time, his smile seemed predatory. "I was fortunate enough to observe a case in progress as I was waiting to meet an associate at the courthouse earlier this week. Your eloquent defense of the accused was very impressive."

Despite her misgivings, she was intrigued. "Do you remember any specifics about the case?"

"Yes, as I recall, you were defending a middle-aged indigent woman who was accused of petty theft."

Sparks shot from her eyes as she exclaimed indignantly, "You mean that poor woman who was hauled off to jail because she stole some food to feed her starving children? As I told the jury, Mr. Maxwell, I feel very strongly about that issue. When a mother has to steal to feed her family and then is prosecuted as though she had committed a felony, there is something wrong with our criminal justice system."

Pausing to catch her breath, she glanced at her friend. Laura was staring blankly ahead and was seemingly oblivious to the conversation. It would be wise to make their excuses and take her friend home.

"I agree wholeheartedly, Miss Parker," said Maxwell, distracting her, "that is why our ticket supports a broader-based job market and drastic reforms in the prison system. I agree that two years for stealing a loaf of bread is rather harsh, but suppose this woman made stealing her livelihood? I believe that programs could be implemented to give that woman a chance of successful rehabilitation. After her debt to society is paid, she should have a chance to start over without the stigma of a prison record pursuing her throughout her life."

Victory nodded enthusiastically. She might have misjudged this particular politician. He certainly seemed to embrace the same philosophy that she endorsed. In fact, she was beginning to find him quite compelling.

"As long as the program did not apply to those who had committed serious felonies."

"Of course," he agreed, as he smiled enigmatically. After a beat, he continued smoothly, "I would consider it an honor if two women of such caliber and integrity as the two of you would consent to become part of our team."

"What could you possibly know about our character or background?"

He paused, took glasses from a tray, and offered them to the ladies. He took a leisurely sip before replying. "You surely would expect I would have conducted a background check on all potential members of my campaign."

Victory bristled at the invasion of privacy. Her earlier unease resurfaced. She was on the verge of inventing an excuse when he raised his glass. "A toast to our new volunteers. May our association prove both professionally and personally rewarding."

As she lifted her glass, she wondered what she could do. Besides, she really did believe in the party platform and in John Callahan. She also supported Craven Maxwell's reforms. So, why did she feel so uncomfortable? To her surprise and relief, Laura suddenly came to life.

"To our association," she echoed, "When do we start?"

"Report to the campaign headquarters at nine o'clock. Our campaign manager will show you what to do."

"What's wrong with you?" Victory hissed when Craven Maxwell and their hostess had moved on.

Laura shrugged, as one rhinestone strap slipped from her shoulder. She pushed it up and said cheerfully, "I suppose I was overwhelmed by Mr. Maxwell's presence. After all, it's not every day you get to meet the future vice president."

Victory was skeptical. In her capacity as a senator's aid, Laura dealt with many politicians, dignitaries, and very wealthy men. Her friend had even dated some of them, but she left the remark unchallenged.

"Look," said Laura, drawing her attention, "Mr. Cartwright and Mr. Bennett are leaving. Now, we can relax and have some fun."

"Weren't you having fun? You certainly seemed relaxed when I found you," she commented dryly. She watched the two young men leave the mansion. Each escorted a young woman.

"Thank goodness! They found other interests." Her sarcasm was lost on her friend, who did not appear repentant in the least. Victory, more introverted by nature, was content to skirt the crowd and observe. She sighed good-naturedly. Laura, on the other hand, having averted one conflict, was ready to rejoin the festivities. In an hour or so, Victory would be bailing her out of another mess.

"Are they actually the sons of Bill Cartwright and James Bennett?" asked Laura, wrinkling her nose.

Victory raised a cynical eyebrow. "Would they have been invited if they weren't?"

The brunette laughed, as she slipped into the throng and left Victory indulgently shaking her head. To her right, the French doors beckoned invitingly. Beyond, she could make out a balcony with a wrought iron fence gleaming in the moonlight. "A safe haven from the oppressive throng," she thought and gave in to the irresistible urge to escape.

Chapter 2:

The Marquis

Elizabeth Dumont glanced irritably at the butler standing by her elbow, as he proffered the small card. She was sure that everyone whom she had invited to the party had arrived long ago. Gracefully disengaging herself from the group of politicians, she picked up the card. Delicately arched brows lifted, as she hurried after the butler.

A gracious smile was in place by the time that she reached the door. Standing in the entrance was a tall slender man dressed in a dark gray tuxedo. Over his left arm, he carried an overcoat. An umbrella was in his right hand. At the curb, a chauffer stood at attention by the side of a white Rolls Royce. Elizabeth craned her neck to look into the face of the distinguished gentleman. As their eyes met, a flutter of excitement tightened her stomach. His platinum blonde hair was parted on the side and feathered across his forehead. Worn short, it appeared slightly tousled. His aquiline nose drew attention to his sensual lips. Slightly curved, they were thin and firm. Her heart began to beat faster as the socialite imagined those lips set in lines of cruelty or passion. His eyes, however, were what drew and held her attention. They were the most mesmerizing shade of turquoise that she had ever seen. Staring, she felt as if she were drowning in their fathomless depths. Entranced, she continued to gaze fixedly at the man to the point of forgetting her surroundings. Finally, he broke eye contact as he bowed over her hand.

Mrs. Dumont blinked several times and then refocused on her guest. He radiated authority with a casual grace. The air around him crackled with vitality. As he spoke, the rich timbre of his voice was so soothing that the hostess was lulled and had to force herself to concentrate on the actual words.

Smiling graciously, he said, "I hope you will excuse the intrusion, Mrs. Dumont. I realize I am not one of your guests, but my name is Andrew Gabriel, Marquis of Penbrook. I would not consider intruding on your hospitality except I am in search of a relative. I heard I might find him here."

Mrs. Dumont opened her mouth, but no sound emerged. She cleared her throat and then tried again. "You are by no means intruding, Lord Gabriel. I would be honored if you would join my guests. If you will tell me who your relative is, I will send my butler to locate him."

The man inclined his head slightly. "That is most kind of you. I am looking for Craven Maxwell."

The elderly socialite's composure slipped slightly. "You're related to Craven Maxwell?"

His sensual lips twitched in amusement as he again slanted his head.

Mrs. Dumont narrowed her eyes appraisingly. Although she and Craven had known each other for years, he had never mentioned having aristocratic relatives. She considered the possibility that this stranger was a fraud, but dismissed the idea. Everything – from his regal stance and accent to the gold ring bearing his family crest – screamed British aristocracy. She studied his features closely. He did bear a resemblance to the vice presidential candidate. Craven was dark while the marquis was fair. So, at first glance, she had not assimilated the similarities.

The marquis bore her inspection with patience. When their eyes locked again, she blushed. "I'm sorry, Lord Gabriel, but Mr. Maxwell left some minutes ago. However," she continued, while recovering her poise, "any relative of Mr. Maxwell's is welcome. Would you like to join us as we celebrate his future success?"

Andrew opened his mouth to decline and then hesitated. Across the room, he glimpsed a figure in blue stepping through a set of French doors. The image had been so fleeting. Could he have been mistaken? Quickly, he scanned the crowd of elegantly clad people until his eyes fastened on a beautiful brunette in a glittering silver gown. He smiled warmly at the elderly socialite as he accepted her invitation. Signaling the chauffer, he allowed Mrs. Dumont to lead him into the throng.

Several minutes later, he casually strolled onto the balcony and inhaled the intoxicating night air. The scent of the wild flowers mixing with perfume caused an ache in his chest and a long dormant yearning.

He continued to linger in the doorway. Extracting himself from the hostess had proven difficult since she seemed determined to introduce him to practically everyone in the room. After the first dozen backslapping politicians and fawning females, he began to wonder about the wisdom of announcing himself as a relative of the "golden boy." The news seemed to give instant celebrity status to him. "I would have preferred to remain anonymous," he thought wryly, but then realized the absurdity of that desire.

He lost all interest in the procession of wealthy business executives, politicians, and socialites until Mrs. Dumont moved to a group of people that included the brunette in silver. Studying her intently, he listened with interest as Mrs. Dumont introduced him to Laura Warner. Miss Warner was an aid to Senator Daily. She had aspirations of eventually acquiring her own congressional seat. He already knew about her ambitions, but wanted to hear her response. Laura laughed infectiously and forthrightly smiled up at him. She acknowledged the truth of the statement and, at the same time, humbly admitted that she was a long way from her goal. Pleased with the encounter, he toasted her success and then spent several minutes discussing her future plans. During the conversation, the hostess was called away to attend to a minor crisis. Her departure gave Andrew the ideal opportunity. He excused himself from his charming companion and stepped onto the balcony. Suddenly, he felt a tingling sensation. Although the balcony seemed deserted, he sensed her presence. He gazed up at the moon as it drifted behind a bank of dark clouds. The fading light reflected from his hair and radiated a silvery sheen to the strands and an alabaster glow to his skin. Then, a heavy black cloud swallowed the light and cast the terrace into shadow. Silent as a cat, he moved further into the night. His perfect night vision detected a slight movement in the dark. At the other end of the balcony, another set of doors leading to a large ballroom were open. As a band began to play, the strains of a waltz emanated from the room.

Victory leaned against the railing while she enjoyed the muted music. Sipping her champagne, she contemplated the beauty of the full moon as it cast shimmering lights across the garden. Suddenly, a bank of clouds captured it. She sighed. It was time to go back inside and be sociable. Turning, she stepped towards the door, but then stopped. A strangled gasp caught in her throat. Before her stood a man with his back to the open door and his features in shadow. Strange. "I didn't hear him walk up behind me," she thought, as she regained her composure. She merely turned and there he was – tall, dark, and imposing – and was blocking her exit.

"I'm sorry," she stammered, "I thought I was alone and, when I turned, you startled me."

She looked at him expectantly, but he made no move to step aside. Instead, he leisurely lifted his glass to his lips. Victory had the outrageous notion that he was using the action as an excuse to covertly examine her.

"I also thought the balcony was deserted and planned to take in some fresh night air. I am pleased, however, that I was in error."

Listening to the melodious timbre of his voice, Victory detected a British accent. His voice had a soothing resonance. Instinctively, she relaxed. Before she could think of anything to say, he stretched out a hand.

"I am Andrew Gabriel, Marquis of Penbrook, at your service."

Victory held out her own hand, but, instead of a handshake, he pressed it to his lips. "I thought gestures like that died out in the last century," she said. She was surprised and touched. The skin that his lips had brushed still felt warm and tingly. She stared at their clasped hands and felt oddly reluctant to pull away.

He was slow in releasing her. After a long silence, she realized that he was waiting for her to reciprocate. She laughed self-consciously. The sound was soft and musical on the night air and it brought an answering smile to his lips.

"I'm sorry. You must not judge all Americans by my ill manners. My name is Victory Parker. I'm an attorney here in DC."

He gestured to the garden below. "The scenery is breathtaking by moonlight."

Victory turned towards the yard. Her desire to reenter the house was forgotten. "It was," she agreed, while peering into the darkness, "when there was enough moonlight to view it."

He stepped up beside her. As if in answer to her complaint, the moon broke free of the clouds and radiated its silver brilliance. Curiosity aroused Victory, who tilted her head to get the first clear look at her companion. Her eyes widened and she almost gasped aloud. He stood leisurely with one leg propped on the bottom of the railing and his elbow resting on the top, as he silently surveyed her. He was the realization of her dreams. She studied his silver-gold hair, turquoise eyes, sensual lips, and hard jaw. If he had been made-to-order, he could not have been more perfect. Moonbeams danced along his pale skin. When he smiled down at her, Victory felt lightheaded.

A stiff breeze blew and she shivered slightly. Her lamé halter dress was not meant for standing outside in Washington's fall air. The part of her mind that still functioned rationally urged her to go inside, but she could only stand and remain dazed by the classic beauty of the man next to her. A stiff breeze tore through the garden and she shivered again. Before the gooseflesh formed, he settled his jacket over her shoulders. Victory reveled in the coziness of the material and the faint scent of his cologne that was clinging to the lining.

"Forgive me, Miss Parker," he said, while gazing at the captured stars mirrored in her cobalt blue eyes, "for keeping you out in the cold. I would hate to have you catch a chill," he said, as he guided her towards the doors, "As delightful as that blue gown is, it is not designed for warmth."

"Perhaps," she murmured. She was not quite sure to what she had agreed.

Breaking eye contact, he took her arm and escorted her back into the room. The band was starting another waltz as she slipped the jacket from her shoulders. Solemnly, he accepted it. He slid into the jacket with such grace that she was captivated. Again, she berated herself for gawking, but it was as if she were compelled.

The marquis' lips twitched slightly as he stated, "Now that we have shared a balcony and my jacket, I believe I know you well enough to ask you to dance."

They glided across the floor in perfect harmony. Victory was oblivious to everything except the feel of his arm around her waist and his overpowering magnetism. Under the soft lighting of the chandelier, his skin and hair seemed to take on a golden hue. His eyes also appeared darker. An involuntary shiver ran down her spine as he caught and held her gaze. Deeply searching, his eyes probed hers. She had the impression that he was trying to read her mind. Before she could react, he smiled down at her and the discomfort was replaced by serenity.

After a few moments of silence, she asked, "Lord Gabriel, may I ask what brings you to Washington?"

Again, his penetrating gaze seared into her for a long moment before he finally answered. "I am here to..." he hesitated as if choosing the right words, "visit a relative. I heard that he was here, but I arrived too late to catch him."

They circled the dance floor. Victory glimpsed Laura in the arms of a senator as they swept past. Silently, she blessed their prep school teachers who had instructed them on the intricacies of ballroom dancing. At the time, she had thought that it was irrelevant, but it was worth every dull hour to be prepared for just this one dance.

"Lord Gabriel," she asked, "am I being too forward by asking the identity of your relative?"

He smiled down at her. Again, she felt slightly disoriented. "Not at all. I would appreciate it if you would call me Andrew. I hope it will not be assumed too forward of me to request that I might have the pleasure of calling you by your Christian name?"

It took a moment for her to realize the nature of his request. She smiled and nodded. He continued, "To answer your question, the relative I am searching for is Craven Maxwell."

She glanced up sharply, "Craven Maxwell?"

He frowned. His arm spasmodically tightened and pulled her against his chest as he asked, "Yes, Craven and I are actually half-brothers. Do you know him?"

"Doesn't everyone?" she answered rhetorically. "As a matter of fact, my friend Laura and I have just agreed to do some volunteer work at his campaign headquarters."

For the first time, the marquis appeared disconcerted. His eyes narrowed and his lips compressed. Victory felt chilled by the ferocity of his expression. She shifted slightly in his suddenly tight grip. As awareness returned, he smiled reassuringly and then relaxed. "Maybe I will see you there since I have urgent business to discuss with him. That is probably where I will catch up with him."

Victory was surprised. "Don't you know where he lives or have a phone number?"

"My brother values his privacy and guards it well. I have not had occasion to contact him in many years, so I have only outdated information."

When the music ended, she was about to suggest that he ask their hostess for Maxwell's contact information. Instead of releasing her, Andrew guided her over to one of the refreshment tables. As they sipped fruit punch and idly chatted, Mrs. Dumont joined them, as did Laura. After a few minutes, Mrs. Dumont declared that her niece had just arrived and was waiting to meet the marquis.

After they left, Laura turned to her friend. "I couldn't help but notice the rapport between you and the marquis. Are you going to see him again?"

Feeling suddenly deflated, she responded flatly, " I don't know. Nothing was arranged."

Laura's brows drew together, "You mean, you let a hunk like that get away?"

"I'm not that quick," she snapped.

"I think that was the idea when Mrs. Dumont whisked him away. You would have to be blind not to notice the attraction between the two of you. I think she has grand ideas of an English title for her niece."

Suddenly dispirited, Victory asked, "Are you ready to go?"

As they left, neither noticed the troubled turquoise gaze following their progress.

Chapter 3:
The Invitation

As the door opened, Victory glanced up from the telephone. One of the volunteers stepped into the room. Her eyes dropped back to the paper that she was filling out.

"Thank you for your time, Mrs. Robins, and don't forget to vote."

Dropping the receiver into the cradle, she checked her watch. Only one hour left in her first day as a campaign volunteer. Surprisingly, it was more interesting than she had expected. Sighing, she reluctantly acknowledged that she had been hoping to see Lord Gabriel, but her exciting companion from the previous evening hadn't materialized.

Her heart skipped a beat as the door opened again. Hope leapt into her face as she glanced up expectantly. Disappointment shadowed her eyes as the haggard campaign manager approached her desk.

Bill Rice had shown the ropes to the new recruits when they first arrived. Since they appeared capable of handling the barrage of telephone calls, pledges, and information, he left them unsupervised for most of the time. Occasionally, he bestowed superficial smiles and benevolent nods to indicate his approval.

"How's it going, girls?" he asked politely.

When Victory smiled and replied positively, the man quickly moved to the next row of volunteers.

At the adjacent desk, Laura yawned and leaned against the back of her swivel chair.

"Boy," she said, while stretching, which caused her white sweater to ride high on her rib cage, "I had no idea volunteering was such hard work."

Victory lifted one eyebrow. "You seemed quite enthusiastic last night," she commented dryly.

"True – and I still am. I'm tired but also pleased to be taking an active role in the campaign."

The door opened again. Victory glanced up sharply and then back at her friend.

Laura stared hard. "I don't think he's coming, Tory."

"Who?" she asked too quickly. She tried to ignore the sudden heat suffusing her face.

Laura pushed her long black ponytail behind her shoulder. Her gray eyes softened as she said quietly, "I've been watching you watch that door all day. It's now 4:30 and I doubt prince charming from last night's ball is going to show." She shrugged and then continued, "He probably caught up with his brother at home or he called him instead of coming by. How about seeing if we can get out a little early and grab a pizza?"

Victory smiled. Her friend knew that pizza was her favorite. Appreciating the gesture, she nodded. "He wasn't a prince, but a marquis," she corrected, "but I suppose you're right." Shrugging nonchalantly, she said, "Let's go."

The phone rang and she sighed. "Laura, let the boss know we're leaving," she instructed as she nodded towards Bill Rice, who was speaking with another volunteer, "and I'll take this last call?"

Laura nodded, stood, and stretched. Pulling her white wool sweater over her jeans, she started off. Victory courteously answered the callers' questions about campaign contributions and then hung up. Determined not to allow the phone to delay her again, she bent to retrieve her handbag. Stretching her arm, she groped blindly for a few moments and then peered under the desk. Searching the empty floor, she eventually spied her purse wedged under one of the far corners. Leaning forward, she strained towards the handle, but it was just beyond her grasp. Grunting, she edged closer. "Almost got it," she thought as she stretched her fingertips. Abruptly, her chair rolled and she lost her balance. Her face hit the side of a drawer as she toppled to the floor. Muttering as she rubbed her bruised cheek, she snatched the offending purse with a malicious jerk.

The door opened. Embarrassed, she scrambled up from the floor and banged her head in her haste. Grimacing, she rubbed her head and cheek. Her humiliation was surpassed by pain. The breath caught in her throat as strong hands gently caressed her face. Slowly, her eyes traveled up the plaid oxford shirt, past the column of a male throat, and over the lean hard face. Concern touched with humor emanated from the turquoise eyes as the marquis stood solicitously over her. He was even more handsome than she remembered. His jeans and oxford shirt combined with his rakish charm and slender physique gave him the look of a model out of GQ.

His penetrating gaze became pensive while a slight smile hovered at the corners of his sensual lips. As his gaze bore into her, she was incapable of breaking eye contact. Her heartbeat became erratic and her breathing quickened. She began to feel disoriented. Still, she could not look away. Satisfied with the inspection of her injuries, he straightened and leaned against the desk.

"Hello, again." The rich timbre of his voice was distracting. Surroundings faded as her attention was captured and held captive.

"Hello," she answered through dry lips.

"Can I be of assistance," the campaign manager interrupted deferentially. "Obviously," thought Mr. Rice, mentally rubbing his hands together, "this is a man of some prestige and importance. Despite the casual clothes, this man surely has money." He decided that it was better for him to handle this patron and not risk losing a potentially high contribution by leaving it in the hands of a novice.

The marquis turned towards the other man. Victory shook her head to restore her equilibrium.

"I'm Bill Rice," he said as he extended his hand, "the campaign manager."

Andrew studied the short balding man in his pressed shirt, tie, and dress slacks. The man cleared his throat. He obviously was uneasy under the marquis' scrutiny. Victory's respect for the little man grew as he stood straight without flinching while the turquoise eyes raked over him.

Apparently satisfied, the marquis nodded. "I am here to see Mr. Maxwell. Will you tell him Andrew Gabriel wishes to speak with him?"

Assuming that his request would be carried out, he turned his attention back to Victory. "Would you like to go out to dinner after I have finished my business with my brother?"

Distracted, she watched with amusement as Bill Rice's eyes widened. He swung around and almost collided with a desk in his haste. She guessed that the revelation of Craven Maxwell having siblings had come as a shock. Of course, not much was known about the private life of the vice presidential candidate, but she had assumed that his campaign manager would have biographic information. Then, the marquis' words registered. Her eyes snapped back to her companion.

With her mind still spinning, she looked disparagingly at her corduroys and light blue sweater. "I'm not exactly dressed to go out," she hedged.

"Neither am I," he reassured. "I realize this is a spur of the moment invitation, but I'd really like a chance to get to know you better. How does a pizza grab you? There's a small Italian restaurant I've been dying to try." At the mention of pizza, she groaned. "What's the matter?" he asked lightly, "You don't like pizza? We can go for hamburgers, instead."

She laughed. "It's not that. I love pizza. It's just that I already have a dinner date."

He frowned, studied her face intently for several seconds, and then asked soberly, "I know I am being presumptuous, but may I ask who has the pleasure?"

Warm heat flooded her face as her eyes dropped. "It's not really a date. My roommate and I are going to grab a bite."

His good humor was immediately restored. Victory wondered if she had misread his earlier expression. "Well, in that case..."

"In that case," finished Laura, approaching the desk, "I think you should go with the marquis."

Andrew smiled at the brunette. "I would not want to interrupt your plans. Victory and I can make other arrangements."

Laura waved her hand. "I insist. Besides," she said with her gray eyes twinkling, "I just received a dinner invitation of my own."

Victory flashed a grateful smile at her roommate. She was very fortunate to have such an understanding friend. Making a mental note to thank her later, she graciously accepted Andrew's invitation.

Mr. Rice came bustling towards them.

Authoritatively, he announced, "Mr. Gabriel, Mr. Maxwell will see you now."

Andrew nodded to the women. To Victory, he said, "I will see you in a few minutes." Then turning to Laura, "Miss Warner, it was a pleasure meeting you again."

Chapter 4:

The Bargain

Mr. Rice led the way down a long narrow corridor. Pausing at the last door, he opened it with a flourish and quickly closed it behind the marquis.

From behind his mahogany desk, Craven Maxwell stood while glaring at his visitor. Their eyes met, clashed, and then locked. Tension mounted and time seemed to stand still as supremacy was sought. Finally, Craven shrugged. His thin lips stretched to reveal a row of even white teeth.

Motioning towards a chair, he said, "Why don't you sit down, Andrew? Tell me what I have done to deserve a visit, at long last, from my dear brother."

Ignoring the sarcasm, Andrew sat. His eyes never left the onyx orbs. "Surely, Craven," he said levelly, "you could not have doubted that I would come to you sooner or later?"

Craven affected a comfortable pose in his chair, loosened his tie, and rolled up the sleeves of his white dress shirt. "No, I didn't doubt it, but ten years is a long time to wait. I was aware of your revival, of course. I thought that you would have sought me out at that time."

"I had other things to attend to," Andrew explained. "Being out of commission for such a long time left a lot of work to be done on the estate. You'd be surprised," he added wryly, "how much things can deteriorate over an extended period of time."

Craven leaned forward, "How about a drink while we enjoy our reunion?" Without waiting for a reply, he slid open a cabinet next to the desk and pulled out a bottle of reddish-brown liquid. Setting two crystal glasses on the desk, he poured and then handed one to the marquis. Andrew accepted the glass and cautiously sipped it.

Craven's brows lifted sardonically. "Afraid I'm trying to poison you?"

"If you could," Andrew laughed hollowly. "I wouldn't put it past you." Then, he soberly asked, "Craven, what are you doing?"

Craven leaned back. "That must be obvious even to you, brother. I am running for vice president of the United States. Doing quite a good job of it, too, I might add. Have you seen the latest polls? We are ten points ahead of our opponents. Are you proud of me, Andrew?"

He ignored the last comment, took another sip of his drink, and set it on the desk. "You know what you're doing is forbidden by the laws and customs of our people."

"I'm surprised at you, Andrew. You've always been such a strong advocate of integration with the diurnals."

"I advocate integration, not interference," he shot back. "In such a position of power, you would be able to influence the diurnals' laws, society, and their way of life. I doubt you would have their best interests at heart."

"I don't know about that. Have you read any literature about my political views? Mr. Callahan and I have a wide range of reforms that we have planned and this country is in desperate need of reform."

"Mr. Callahan may be sincere, but you aren't. I want you to withdraw from the race."

Craven idly twirled his glass while he gazed intently at the red liquid sliding up the sides. "I have no intention of withdrawing."

"Why not?"

Putting his drink aside, he shrugged. "A lot has changed while you were out of the picture. The human race has evolved emotionally. They have reached the point where they are not as superstitious about what they cannot explain. The religious fervor has died down. Their medical knowledge has expanded so that people with rare diseases are cured rather than persecuted. I believe the political climate is right for integration."

"I have a hard time believing your intentions are so noble. Yes, the diurnals have progressed far, but they have much further to go before they will accept something that could be considered a threat to their existence. It's also true that the religious fervor has died down, but there are still plenty of zealots ready to persecute any imagined evil. As far as medicine is concerned, do you really want to spend the rest of your life in a laboratory being poked and prodded while doctors and technicians analyze you? Besides, there are still many of our own kind who are opposed to being exposed."

"Perhaps, but they will learn to adapt along with the diurnals. Really, Andrew," he said in exasperated amusement, "anyone would think I was the one advocating integration."

Andrew thoughtfully gazed at him. He was sure that Craven was motivated by ambition and power. He searched the office for clues to his real purpose. The portraits of past presidents and serene countrysides offered no clues. "I can force you to concede."

Craven's lips twisted. "It might be interesting to see if you still could," he said congenially, "but I have no time to get involved in a power struggle with you, especially since there are other ways to protect my interests."

Craven pulled open another door of the cabinet and extracted a newspaper. Folding it back, he casually tossed it across the desk. Andrew glanced down without picking it up. The headline boldly glared back at him. It read, "Student Nurse Mutilated at Insane Asylum."

Snatching up the paper, he examined the date. He blanched as he skimmed over the story. Revulsion and anger tinged with remorse swept through him as he dropped it on the desk.

"That woman was alive when I left," he said through clenched teeth.

Steepling his fingers, Craven leaned back. "Suffice it to say, she wasn't after I left."

"What do you expect to do with that?" Andrew asked disdainfully.

"Well, I had considered using it as kind of a trump card."

"To turn me in if you couldn't overpower me?"

Craven nodded.

"That would do wonders for your campaign," he scoffed.

"I considered that. Fortunately, another more effective way to insure your cooperation has presented itself."

An image of Victory Parker flashed into Andrew's mind. He paled as he whispered hoarsely, "How did you know?"

"I knew the first time I saw her, which was by chance a couple of weeks ago. There was a haunting familiarity and the resemblance is striking. Don't you agree?" Savoring the moment, he slowly sipped his drink. There was such a strong resemblance that my curiosity was aroused. I did my homework and had her genealogy traced. The staff aides who did the research probably thought I was checking for a potential bride."

Andrew's lips tightened and his eyes narrowed. "I am warning you, Craven, stay away from her."

The ominous black eyes widened. "Jealous already? Are you worried that she might find me more appealing?" he taunted.

White-hot rage exploded through his brain. Andrew shot forward. Fury made him reckless. Missing his target by several inches, he drove his fist through a portrait.

Craven shook his head as he surveyed the damage. "Lincoln will never be the same." Before Andrew could begin another round, he continued, "I would be the last person to wish harm to that lovely young creature. All I need is your word that you will not interfere with what I am doing."

Andrew hesitated, withdrew a handkerchief, and wiped the blood from his knuckles. "I can't give you my word since I don't know what your plans are."

Again, the image assailed him. His stomach muscles convulsed. Reaching for his glass, he drained the contents and then slammed the glass down so hard that it shattered.

Craven shook his head. "It was such a nice set," he sighed as he watched the shards sprinkle onto the carpet.

A loud knocking sounded at the door. "Is everything all right, Mr. Maxwell?"

His eyes shifted towards the door and then back to his brother. He shrugged and explained to his sibling, "Security." He raised his voice, "Fine, John." His gaze hardened as he turned his attention back to Andrew. "I'm waiting for your word, brother," he asserted coldly.

Andrew closed his eyes. Trembling, he relived years of tormented loneliness. Now that happiness was within his grasp, was there any concern worthy of such a sacrifice? He remembered how Victory had looked minutes ago. She was vibrant and full of life while she spoke animatedly about going out for a pizza.

"You have my word that I will not interfere. Now, I need yours."

"Andrew," Craven said contemptuously, "you are a misguided fool. You spend your time agonizing over the fate of one diurnal when the whole race is beneath contempt."

Andrew stiffened. "I see. Now that you have my word, you no longer feel the need to keep up the pretense."

Craven's eyes burned. "I have done research," he proclaimed. "I found proof that we are superior. I've discovered ancient documents proving that the abilities we have today are only a mere fraction of our potential. You should work with me. Together, we can uncover the truth and right the wrongs of history."

Andrew shook his head. "You are the one who is misguided. We may be different, but we need to learn to live together. Your word, Craven."

Craven nodded. "As long as you don't interfere in my plans, no harm at my hands will come to the girl."

Chapter 5:

Domestic Crisis

Andrew walked back through the corridor. Pausing in the entrance, he slipped on his sports jacket. Silently, he watched Victory talking animatedly with her friend. Concern darkened his aqua eyes as he wondered about his decision. All that talk about research and discoveries, what did it mean? What was Craven really up to? His lust for power was leading him towards something other than just an altruistic desire to aid the plight of the country. Maybe he should investigate further before deciding on the role of objective observer.

Sensing his gaze upon her, Victory turned. She smiled warmly. He returned the gesture as he started forward. His misgivings were temporarily forgotten. He had made the right choice. The country would have to look out for itself because this woman was his destiny.

Victory stood and said to her friend, "Láura, I'll leave you the car."

A last wave to the brunette and they were out of the door.

"Where would you like to go?" Victory asked breathlessly? "If close proximity causes shortness of breath," she thought, "what would happen when they kissed?" The thought of ambulance attendants administering CPR while Andrew tried to explain the cause of the coronary brought a bubble of laughter rippling up her throat. She almost choked on her giggles. Andrew's immediate attentiveness caused her to laugh harder at the image of a death certificate showing that she choked to death at the thought of a kiss. She stared helplessly at the sensual lips and it was several seconds before she realized that she had missed his question.

"I'm sorry," she said as she gained control, "I didn't hear you."

He smiled, released her, and stepped back. "I was asking if you were all right?"

She nodded. Pulling her coat tighter, she replied, "Some of this crisp autumn air went down the wrong way."

"Strange," he mused while taking her arm, "I had the feeling I was somehow responsible for your breathing difficulties."

Embarrassed, she turned her hot cheeks into the wind.

"Since I have so recently arrived, I have not had an opportunity to do much sightseeing."

"If you like, I'll give you a guided tour on the way to dinner. My favorite pizza parlor is downtown near the Brooks Boutique." Searching the street, she asked, "Where's your car?"

Andrew took her arm and led her towards a silver Mercedes. "I gave Jack the night off," he explained while holding the door.

As they drove along Constitution Avenue, Victory took pleasure in her role as tour guide. They passed by beautifully illuminated landmarks, such as the National Museum of Natural History, the National Museum of American History, the Washington Monument, and the Lincoln Memorial, before they turned right onto 22nd Street. Then, the massive Department of State building loomed to their right and, in the distance to their left, they soon saw the picturesque John F. Kennedy Center for the Performing Arts. When they reached Pennsylvania Avenue, Victory motioned for him to turn right, as she pointed to the George Washington University Hospital where President Reagan was taken after the assassination attempt. After traveling for a few more blocks, she asked him to stop. The White House stood proudly in front of them. Its marble columns gleamed under the lights.

"Isn't it an awe-inspiring sight?" she said in a soft voice.

"Your people have a lot to be proud of," he said sincerely.

Victory frowned. "We did when the buildings were first built. I'm afraid we are used to resting on our laurels."

"What do you mean?"

Something in his voice caused her to glance sharply at his face. His turquoise eyes had turned dark aqua and the troubled look that she had noticed earlier had returned. She searched his face wanting desperately to sooth away the tension that she sensed.

"I believe this country still has the potential to be one of the world's greatest nations, but we are in a domestic crisis."

He started the motor as she continued. "Over the past few years, the internal structure of our class system has deteriorated. The middle class has virtually disappeared. Now, we have a few wealthy families who hold most of the political and financial power. Former white-collar workers are reduced to begging for handouts, mothers steal food to feed starving children, and fathers hang out under highways while holding signs saying, "Will work for food." Crime has skyrocketed and drug abuse has reached astronomical proportions. I personally think a lot of the drug use has to do with the pervasive feeling of hopelessness. People are convinced they can't do anything to improve their lot, so why not try to escape from reality?"

Andrew held the door as they entered the pizza shop. Their conversation was suspended until the hostess seated them. After ordering, Andrew resumed their discussion.

"How can the economy be so bad? What about our hostess and the millions of people like her? Aren't they considered middle class?"

Victory pulled off her jacket. Shaking her head at her companion, she explained. "People like our hostess haven't seen an increase in the minimum wage in twelve years. In the late 1990's, a law was passed because of the devastation of the economy. It made it legal for employers to hire laborers at minimum wage in order to avoid the mass bankruptcy that was rampaging throughout the country. These workers could not afford their own insurance and the employers were no longer providing benefits. So many people went on welfare that the system collapsed about eight years ago. Families found themselves homeless and millions found themselves without resources. The responsibility for providing aid to this new large group of poverty victims was placed on churches and other charitable organizations. When their resources dwindled, they called on large corporations and the wealthy to start towing the line. Unfortunately, it became apparent that most rich people are of the opinion that they don't need to be concerned with the plight of the common man."

While she paused to negotiate a strand of mozzarella, Andrew asked, "Do you believe that John Callahan and Craven Maxwell hold the key to the problems."

She hesitated. "As long as the incumbents are in power, I believe that things will only get worse. They have been in charge for the last twelve years and look what's happened. I do endorse John Callahan's proposals for improvements in the economy and in his philosophy that we must take care of our own people before we can afford to aid other countries. Your brother also has some interesting ideas on prison and mental health reforms."

At the mention of his brother, a shadow passed across his lean features. He asked, "Tell me about these programs."

"Well, it's not the programs themselves that are different; it's what happens afterward. Maxwell proposes lowering the recidivism by relocating the offenders and not putting them back into an environment that is conducive to crime. His idea is to give the offenders a second chance by providing them with a new identity in order to give them a fresh start. I believe he even proposes to loan them enough capital to pay for their first month's expenses while they are looking for employment. When they establish themselves, they will be responsible for paying the government back at a reduced interest rate. The idea is to give them a chance to procure employment without the prejudice of their previous records. Of course, this program will not be for hardened criminals with an extensive list of past crimes under their belts or for felons. I'm not sure about all of the details, but everything I've read so far makes the proposal sound very appealing."

Andrew stared into her eyes as he pondered what she had said. Reflections from the candle danced in her pupils as she gazed back. She squirmed self-consciously under the prolonged scrutiny, which made her think that she had dropped pizza sauce on her chin. The conversation had flowed more easily when they discussed politics.

"It sounds good on the surface," he finally conceded and then shifted his gaze to the last slice of pizza. "But the program seems like it would take many years to put in place."

Victory shrugged. "As long as they keep getting re-elected, he'll have all the time he needs."

He frowned. "But won't Callahan and Maxwell be retired in eight years?"

She stared back in confusion. Then, her face cleared and she smiled. Unable to resist, he put out a hand to caress her cheek. She captured his hand and held it against her face. "You have been out of touch for a while," she murmured. When he appeared startled, she dropped his hand and then hastened to explain. "The law was changed about twelve years ago. Now, as long as the incumbent gets re-elected, he can remain as the president indefinitely. The only way to get rid of an incumbent is for him to retire, get beaten, or die."

"I'll arm wrestle you for the last slice of garlic bread," he offered teasingly.

"You're on," she rejoined.

Half-expecting him to give in gracefully, she was surprised when he propped his arm on the table. Stubborn pride prompted her to do the same, although the outcome was a foregone conclusion. Studying the chorded forearm, she wondered if he would give her an advantage.

"Hey," she challenged, "how about a sporting chance?"

"Sounds reasonable," he agreed while eyeing the prize.

"We start from a position three-quarters in my favor."

He made a pretense of studying her arm, checking for muscle tone, and comparing it with his own before agreeing. By this time, she was laughing so hard that she wasn't sure if she could go through with the farce.

"Get serious," he warned. "I don't want you claiming foul play."

She sobered and placed her hand in his. The cool smooth feel of his fingers closing around hers caused her to forget the reason for the contact. However, the slight push on her arm as Andrew pressed the advantage refocused her attention. She had come within a hair's breath of the table when he flipped her arm over with such ease that she didn't realize what had happened.

As he began to slide the basket, she protested. "Hey, that wasn't fair."

He lifted his brows and she amended, "How did you do that? I didn't even feel anything."

Andrew smiled as he picked up his knife. "You're right. It wasn't fair. I forgot to tell you I work out. Do you want to split it?"

Andrew motioned for the check. He smiled at her. "That was some of the best pizza I've ever had."

"Really?" she asked in surprise and then with consternation, "Andrew, I'm so self-centered I completely forgot that you had a restaurant already in mind when we started."

Her companion chuckled. "I'd much rather discover your likes and dislikes. Besides, the food was great and I'm sure we will have an opportunity to try the other place."

She smiled and was warmed by the thought of future outings. "My dad and I used to come here whenever he came to town. It's strange that I haven't been able to face coming here without him, but, when you suggested pizza, it just seemed natural to come here."

He looked sharply at her, but said nothing as he held her jacket while she slipped it on. They walked outside into the brisk evening air. Victory paused for a moment to revel in its crispness. Andrew stepped to the Mercedes and bent to unlock the door.

A sudden gasp made him look back. Amazed, he saw Victory struggling with two teenage punks as they tried to snatch her purse. As his startled gaze took in the scene, Victory kicked one of the thugs, which caused him to release his grip. His partner snarled a curse as he raised his fist towards her face.

Andrew felt the blood pounding through his head as he stepped forward, but, before he could intervene, something pricked his side. Glancing to his left, he encountered the brooding face of another hood. Dressed in black leather, he held a switchblade to his ribs. Casting glances at both sides of the sidewalk, Andrew noted that the street was deserted.

Discerning his intention, the hood growled, "Hey, man, don't think someone is going to help you. My friends and I own this section of town. If you gimme your watch and wallet, I might call my pals off your girl."

Victory let out an enraged squeal of protest as the two thugs pushed her down to the sidewalk. The sound of tearing cloth galvanized him into action. Without glancing towards his assailant, he grabbed the kid's wrist and twisted it until the bone cracked. The knife clattered to the ground as the punk stared at his dangling hand for a moment before the nerve endings sent the first waves of pain screeching to his brain. He started to scream, but Andrew paid no attention. His gaze was fixed on the scene ahead.

He launched himself into the fray. With one hand, he lifted the heavier of the two muggers from Victory's body and tossed him through the air. The man collapsed like a rag doll as he slid down the wall of the pizza shop. Seeing his two comrades so easily beaten, the third assailant backed away.

White-hot fury possessed him. Blood lust raged through his veins. Sanity was lost amidst a red haze as he instinctively stalked his prey.

"Andrew," Victory gasped, as she started to rise.

Her voice restored his reason and he rushed to her side. Seeing their opportunity, the two thugs fled. Andrew seized Victory in a tight embrace.

"Are you all right," he asked when he could trust himself to speak.

"I think so," she replied. She tried to straighten her torn jacket. "But look at this mess," she exclaimed while indicating the strewn contents of her purse.

"This city you live in is not very safe," he remarked, as he picked up her lipstick and compact.

"I don't live in the city. I just work here. No one in their right mind lives here unless they're too poor to go elsewhere," she said, as she attempted to tie a knot in the broken purse strap.

"I can understand why," he dryly commented. While retrieving the purse's remaining contents, he noticed a paperback and moved it into the light. "What's this," he asked.

He read aloud, "Interview with the Vampire."

Victory laughed and held out her hand. "It's a old novel about vampires."

"Is there a darker side to Victory Parker that I should be wary of?" he queried mockingly with one brow raised.

She smiled for the first time since the attack. "Is that your polite way of enquiring if I am a vampire?" she countered. "I suppose this may sound strange, but I have always had a fascination for the subject. When I was a little girl, I used to watch all the old black and white movies. When I was older and the rest of my peers were reading romances, I preferred Stephen King and Ann Rice," she said, as she tapped the book.

Andrew paused while opening the door and gave her a searching look. "I don't think it's strange at all. Our interests are what make us unique. Just be careful which necks you bite. You never know what types of infections you might contract."

Standing on the landing of her townhouse, they stared at each other. The moon was as full as it was on the previous night. Its luminous rays cast silvery lights on Andrew's hair. His pale skin sparkled and his turquoise eyes glowed. "He's going to kiss me," Victory thought exultantly. She longed for those sensual lips – that could express emotions from grim determination to tender amusement – to claim hers. "What a fascinating and complex man he is," said a voice in the part of her mind that was not clouded by his overwhelming aura. "Alluring yet aloof, gentle but fierce when provoked." She desperately wanted to have his lips pressed against hers. She unconsciously moved closer into his arms.

Andrew leaned forward. She tilted her head. Surprise, confusion, and disappointment warred within her as she felt the light pressure of his lips on her forehead. A yearning for something that she couldn't quite name spread through her like liquid fire as she stared at him.

He caressed her hair and asked softly, "I know the evening turned out disastrous, but could I possibly convince you to go out with me again tomorrow?"

Seduced by the stroking of her hair, she murmured, "Where would you like to go?"

"I think I should like to visit your Museum of American History," he whispered, while nuzzling her ear.

Victory wasn't sure what he said, but it didn't matter. She agreed to be picked up the next afternoon.

Another brush of her temple and he was gone. Bemused, she stared at the departing Mercedes. Maybe courting rituals took longer in England, but she didn't want to be courted, she wanted to be kissed. Tomorrow, she decided, she would have to take the initiative. She closed the door against the suddenly frigid night air.

Chapter 6:
Deadly Seduction

The moon shone brightly over the cluttered city streets and littered alleys. The three leather-clad figures swaggered slightly as they passed the closed stores and warehouses. Intermittently, one of the group paused to hold his bandaged wrist, which protruded at an odd angle, while another pushed a bottle of Jack Daniels into his good hand.

"Here, Timmy, this will give you quite a kick on top of those drugs the hospital gave you."

Timmy took the bottle and tipped it to his lips. "Ah," he sighed, while wiping the back of his hand across his mouth. "Thanks, Fred." Then, he added, "Who'dda thought that skinny guy would have been so tough? Here," he said. He offered the bottle back to his companion. "You probably need this as much as I do."

"Yeah," Fred agreed. He gingerly rubbed his skull and massaged his ribs. "That guy must bench press or something," he agreed, as he took a large swallow of the fiery liquid, "'cause he sure was stronger than he looked."

"Did you see the way he looked when he came to help the bitch? Just like something out of a damn horror movie."

"Yeah," Timmy sneered, "I guess you got a good chance to look him over while you were backing away instead of helping us."

"That's right," agreed Fred, "If you'd helped us instead of looking after your own tail, it would have been three on one and we could have taken him, man."

"You're crazy," Joe argued hotly. "That guy could have torn all three of us apart without breaking a sweat."

"I think good old Joe was going to desert us, Fred," Timmy accused.

"I think you're right," Fred said as he took a threatening step towards the youth.

"You guys are nuts," yelled Joe. He began backing away from the menacing advance. Suddenly, Timmy smashed the empty bottle on the corner of a building. Flourishing the broken bottleneck, he charged the smaller teen. Outnumbered, Joe frantically groped for his knife. Finding his pocket empty, he realized that he had lost his weapon in the earlier fray. Fred flicked his switchblade out of his sleeve and the two advanced on their companion.

"I think our friend, here, needs a lesson in loyalty," Timmy jeered.

Suddenly, they charged. "Jack Daniels and empty wallets did not mix well," thought Joe, deciding to wait until tomorrow to try reason. Afraid of what his drunk and frustrated friends would do, he raced across the street, down the sidewalk, and around the corner. He cursed as he smashed into a pile of garbage cans. Slipping on spilled trash, he fell to one knee. Pain tore through his leg, but he straightened and kept running.

A few blocks later, he risked a glance over his shoulder. Finding the street deserted, he slowed to a jog, and then to a brisk walk. His knee ached, causing him to limp slightly as he headed home. Bending to examine his injury, he stared unhappily at the ripped jeans and the exposed torn skin of his left knee. His mom would have a fit when she saw his clothes and injury.

Straightening, he peered at his watch. It was late. He was way past curfew. So much for sneaking in unnoticed. His mother undoubtedly would be waiting with one baleful eye on the clock and the other fixed firmly on the front door. He could try to sneak in the back, but that damned squeaky screen door would give him away.

As he passed an abandoned warehouse, he caught a movement out of the corner of his eye. Poised for flight, he peered into the darkness. Better lose the guys before he worried about his mom. After all, his mom wasn't really going to kill him; he wasn't so sure about his buddies. He knew an army couldn't have stood between the blonde-haired man and his girl, but trying to convince Tim and Fred while they were stoned would be impossible. Better avoid them until they were sober.

He started to turn, but then paused. Detaching herself from the shadows was a girl who was not much older than he. Her dark hair hung in soft waves and her large velvet eyes caressed him. As she approached, he could tell that she was not much over five feet. Her features were dainty and perfectly formed. "A very well developed teen," he thought, as he admired her large breasts and rounded hips. She stopped in front of him and stared into his eyes. A slight smile curved her full red lips.

Lured by her beauty and seduced by her sensuality, he was captivated by her charms. A moment of panic ensued when he realized that he couldn't tear his gaze away from her deep brown eyes. The feeling passed as she continued to probe him. The soft velvet of her eyes reminded him of a mother deer. Last year, he had seen those beautiful animals at the zoo when his class had gone there on a field trip. "Her skin is almost as white as the underside of a deer's tail, too," he thought. He felt intoxicated by his arousal.

Her silver bangle bracelets tinkled softly as she placed a hand on his arm.

"Where are you going in such a hurry?" she asked in a low silky whisper.

"Home," he returned, but, when he realized that he was whispering, too, he cleared his throat and repeated, "Home."

"I don't think that's such a good idea," she said imploringly as she gazed up at him.

He swallowed past the lump in his throat. "Why not?"

She smiled sweetly and leaned closer to whisper conspiratorially, "Because I saw those guys chasing you. When they lost you, I overheard them say they were going to stake out your house so they could catch you when you went home."

As if searching for someone, she glanced down the deserted street. With her compelling gaze no longer fixed on him, Joe's eyes strayed downward. They passed the snowy column of her throat and delved into the deep v-neckline of her vest. She wore no blouse under the vest. Looking lower, he noticed skintight black leather pants with black ankle boots. Joe's eyes lifted to the exposed skin of her arms.

"Don't you get cold running around the city with no jacket?"

As if to emphasize his point, a strong autumn breeze blew and caused gooseflesh to rise on the alabaster skin.

"Why don't you share my jacket?" he asked, as he held open the side.

She snuggled close. Wherever she touched him, his skin tingled. An unaccustomed surge of protectiveness coupled with desire coursed through him. He was glad that his friends were preventing him from returning home.

"I know a place we can hang out while we wait for your buddies to give up," she offered. One hand slid down his chest, over the front of his pants, and firmly fondled his erection.

"Where?" he groaned.

She led him down the empty alley and around the corner of a large brick building. He waited impatiently while she produced a silver key and inserted it into the lock. Glancing up, he read, "Willow Grove Crematorium." Stepping into the building, he was disconcerted by the shelves containing urns of all shapes and sizes.

"You want to get laid in a crematorium?" he asked hesitantly.

She smiled and leaned closer to rub her hips sensually against his. "My daddy owns it and he is out of town. I know for a fact we won't be disturbed. And," she finished huskily as she removed his jacket and flicked her tongue across his lips, "there's a bed in the back room."

Lured by the promise in her eyes, he followed her behind the counter and through the door. The room was spacious, almost barren. She flipped on a switch that suddenly flooded the room with fluorescent light.

Her idea of a bed turned out to be a flat metal table. The tray of postmortem tools and intravenous bags provided him with a good idea of the usual usage for this room. He shuddered and swallowed hard as his eyes strayed cautiously around the room.

His gaze fastened on the huge furnace that took up half of one wall. A long-handled tray leaned against the iron grate like a beast waiting to be fed.

The girl chuckled at his expression. Embarrassed that he had let his fear show, he turned angrily towards her. The retort was forgotten as she wrapped her arms around his neck and pressed her lips to his. Anger and uneasiness melted into pools of desire as she seared a path of fiery kisses down his throat.

"You taste good," she whispered against his skin.

He shuddered as the dark head bent over him. He looked over her shoulder. Again his eyes fell on the furnace. He shivered involuntarily. "Do you really want to do it here," he asked, as he nervously glanced around the room. If she did, it would have to be on one of the metal tables or the floor. Personally, he preferred the floor.

A slight tugging on his torso caused him to look down. The girl was ripping the buttons off his shirt with her teeth. "What will my mother do when she sees this?" he asked thickly. His anxiety receded as heat spread through his loins.

"She will never know," responded the girl with a throaty chuckle. He frowned, but was unable to center on words as her hands began caressing his chest. She stroked downwards. Her long nails lightly grazed his skin and sent goosebumps down his spine. When her hands settled on his waistband, he groaned. The instant that the restraint of fabric was removed, his engorged mass thrust forward seeking release. Suddenly, his back pressed against the table. He jerked forward as the cold metal touched his skin, but, with the weight of the girl pressing into him, he succumbed to the slow warmth seeping through his limbs.

Disposing of her own garments, she settled his pliant body on the table. Sliding on top of him she brushed her hips back and forth against his. He could feel himself stiffening. More than anything else, he wanted to be inside her. Her mouth descended to reclaim his, as it demanded that he yield to the onslaught of her tongue. Sliding her lips along his body, she nibbled and teased her way down to his groin. Perspiration broke out on his forehead and, for a moment, he thought that he would lose control. As if sensing his limit, the girl suddenly straddled him and came down hard on top of his erection. He groaned. His mind was a hazy cloud of passion as she slid up and down while enveloping him in her velvet warmth. Again, the lights flickered on – and then out.

Her lips sought his, her tongue plundered, her hands stroked. Her fingers seemed to be everywhere. They were on his wrists and ankles. They sent little prickling sensations into his skin.

Joe's breathing quickened. Small moans of pleasure passed his lips while his stomach muscles tightened and his back arched. He was on the verge of the best climax that he had ever experienced. He was submerged in ecstasy. Any moment, he was going to explode. One more stroke and – now!

Abruptly, the movement ceased. Raw nerve endings tight with tension still strained futilely towards release. Disbelief gradually was replaced by reality as his brain finally registered the cool air instead of warm flesh. His breath still was coming in short gasps. Silently, he prayed that his partner was only changing positions and not her mind. A tightening across his chest jerked him back from the edge of ecstasy. His eyes snapped open. Darkness abruptly was replaced by the stark whiteness of fluorescent tubes. He blinked rapidly in order to adjust to the sudden brightness.

Confused blue eyes met triumphant brown ones. He tried to reach for her, but his arms were restrained. Looking down, he finally noticed the wide leather straps on his wrists, ankles, and chest. He also realized that there were syringes placed in several parts of his body. The syringes were attached to long tubes that fed into the intravenous bags that he had noticed earlier. "The bags are very large," he thought uneasily. As he watched, the blood began to flow through the syringe, up the tubes, and into the bags.

Annoyed, he jerked his attention back to the brunette. "Are you into bondage or some kind of kinky sex? I'm not sure how you managed this," he said, as he tried not to let his anger show, "but, if you untie me now, I'll forget the whole thing and we can part as friends."

Instead of answering, she turned her attention to the empty room. "Do you guys think you can handle this while I get cleaned up?"

Silently seething, Joe realized that he had picked up a fruitcake. For crying out loud, the bitch got off on talking to empty rooms! Straining his arm and leg muscles, he pulled against the restraints. He grimaced as the leather cut into his skin.

Eventually, he realized that brute strength wasn't going to accomplish anything. He forced himself to relax and think of another tactic. He was still at a loss to explain how the girl had managed to get him in such a vulnerable position. He wondered if bribery would work. He opened his mouth, but then snapped it shut. Shocked into silence, Joe watched in fascination as several shapes emerged from the shadows. Three men and one woman approached the table. The girl bent over and picked up her discarded clothing. She was totally at ease in her nudity. Straightening, she indicated the furnace.

"Cindy, would you be so good as to get the fire going? We wouldn't want our guest to catch a chill," she said, while exchanging a look of mysterious humor with the other woman.

Joe's unease mounted as she continued, "The rest of you must make sure our guest doesn't get lonely," she chuckled. "Thomas, I'm leaving you in special charge of this one," she threw over her shoulder as she headed towards a rear door.

Joe's anger evaporated. "Hey, where are you going?" he yelled as an insidious fear began gnawing at him. He watched the one called Cindy move towards the furnace. When she did not respond, he began screaming obscenities.

"Why not just knock him out and be done with it," asked one of the men.

The girl whirled so fast that her dark hair billowed like a black curtain. "Because," she said menacingly, "according to Daddy, it's the adrenalin produced by strong emotions that is the essential component to this process. You wouldn't want to disappoint Daddy, would you Walter?" she asked sweetly.

Walter quickly shook his head. "Besides," she said, as she glanced meaningfully from the boy on the table to the tall blonde man, "I'll bet Thomas can keep him quiet."

Joe didn't like the sound of that statement. Craning his neck, he sought the one called Thomas. One look at the handsome blonde caused numbing terror. He felt a loosening of his bladder and bowels as the bile rose in his throat. He had no awareness, however, as the others cleaned him. He was transfixed as he came face to face with his destiny.

The obscenities became pleas and then turned into prayers as Thomas slowly approached the table. Despite his horror, Joe was compelled to watch the man's deliberate progress. Dry heaves racked his body while perspiration drenched his clammy skin. When the bottle-green eyes bored into his, Joe felt as if he were being pricked by shards of glass.

Thomas took a roll of paper towels from the tray. He began to wipe away the sweat and was careful not to dislodge the syringes. Joe felt strange yet familiar stirrings. He had a deep conviction of the other man's intention. Dread mixed with desire as the man stared down at him. Tears slid out of the corners of his eyes as he belatedly regretted the impulse that had prompted him to flee from his friends.

The brunette chuckled softly. Sharing a last look with Thomas, she headed for the door. Thomas grinned back as he began unbuttoning his shirt.

Chapter 7:

Avenging Angel

"In the news today," announced the pretty blonde reporter, "the election battle has begun. Both candidates have hit the campaign trail with a vengeance." The newscast shifted to a scene of two men talking to a cheering crowd. "The incumbents," the reporter continued, as she flashed a bright smile, "spent the day touring California, while the challengers concentrated their efforts in the southeast." The station then broadcast a shot of a prominent man talking to cheering mobs, while an elegant and conservatively dressed figure smiled benignly in the background.

Laura clapped and whistled. "There are our men," she announced brightly.

Seated at the dining room table, Victory glanced up from the legal briefs that she had been studying. "If your enthusiasm could be translated into votes, they'd already be in the White House," she said with her eyes twinkling.

She suddenly sobered as she stared over her friend's head at the television. The anchor switched to the local news. The ravaged face of a middle-aged woman dominated the screen as she cried while speaking into the microphone.

"Well, we certainly couldn't have a better-looking vice president. Who wants to look at Sid Seymour's face for another four years?" She waited expectantly for her friend to rise to the bait and give the usual lecture about not electing officials for their looks. It was an old cozy argument and a slight source of exasperation to her roommate. For Laura, however, it seemed as good as any other system and it was better than deciding on the basis of party loyalty, as Victory did. So, whenever she couldn't decide politically between two candidates, she opted for the one who looked better. In that way, she at least would be insured of a pleasant face to look at for the term.

"Have you finally come around to my way of thinking, Tory," she teased when the silence continued, "or were you as charmed by Mr. Maxwell as I was?" Receiving no answer, she turned curiously towards her friend. Tory was staring fixedly at the television. Confused, Laura checked the screen.

"All I want is to find my son," the woman pleaded. "If anyone has any idea where he is, I need to know. I know the police believe he ran away, but I know my Joey. He didn't run away. He's missing or maybe kidnapped or lying somewhere hurt..." Her voice broke as she turned away from the camera.

During the interview, a picture of the missing teen was shown on one side of the screen. Victory's eyes were huge as she stared at the photo.

"This," commented the reporter in a detached voice, "makes the sixth resident missing in Washington in the past several months. Police are baffled by the disappearances, although, as we heard, they consider this latest disappearance a possible runaway and are unsure if it is related to the other cases. "

"Laura," Victory said in a strangled voice, "that kid is one of the hoods who attacked us last night."

Laura shot a disgusted look at the television and then hit the remote. "Maybe he did his mother a favor and really did run away," she spat.

Last night, when her roommate told the story to her, Laura had been concerned and outraged. She even had offered to drive Victory to the police station so that she could file a report. She wondered why Lord Gabriel hadn't settled the matter. Her softhearted friend, however, would have none of it. By the time that she had related the story, she had already invented dozens of excuses for the hoodlums. Everything from they were probably starving to they were homeless to they were victims of society. Finally exasperated, Laura had given up the hopeless task of getting Victory to prosecute and just was grateful that her roommate didn't make them adopt the kids.

Sensing her friend's distress, she leapt to her feet and put an arm around her shoulders. Victory sat tensely and stared at the blank screen for a few seconds. Eventually, she looked into her friend's anxious face and sighed.

"Maybe you were right. I should have gone to the police. If I had, they would have been out looking for the boy last night and this wouldn't have happened."

Laura frowned. "What do you mean?" she asked searching her friend's face. "According to the police, this is a case of another runaway. Do you know something else?"

Slowly, she shook her head. "No," she admitted.

"Tory, you've got to stop feeling guilty for things you have no control over. You had no way of knowing the kid would come up missing and you certainly shouldn't feel guilty after he tried to mug you. I shudder to think what could have happened to you last night. I certainly don't feel any sympathy for the punk and still think he did his mom a favor."

"Yes, but did the child really run away?" Victory thought. An image assailed her of the way that Andrew had looked when he started after the teens. There was fury in his face and his eyes. She shivered. Reality returned and she scolded herself. Was she thinking that the sophisticated aristocrat had dropped her off and then returned to stalk three youngsters through the city streets like an avenging angel? The idea was so ridiculous that she smiled. In order to spare her any further trauma, he probably had seen her safely home and then gone to the police. But, if he had, wouldn't the police have contacted her?

She answered soberly, "Even though nothing happened, being attacked like that was really scary. I'm just allowing the melodrama of the situation to influence my thoughts. Even so, I wouldn't wish any harm on those juveniles," she admonished sternly.

"Well, I would," Laura exclaimed vehemently. "If Andrew hadn't been there to scare them off, you could have been beaten, raped, or even killed as well as robbed."

Victory sighed and tried to push her misgivings aside.

"How long before Andrew arrives?" asked Laura. Her question brought Victory's thoughts back to the present.

Victory checked her Rolex. "About half an hour," she said. She stood up and headed towards the bedroom. "I'd better start getting ready."

Half of an hour later, the doorbell rang. "I'll get it," called out Laura, as she headed to the door.

Opening the door, she smiled brightly up into sparkling turquoise eyes. Standing on tiptoe, she grazed his cheek with her lips.

He raised an eyebrow and she explained, "That's for keeping my friend safe."

He nodded understandingly. "Have no worry on that score. She will always be safe with me."

She nodded soberly. From someone else, the boast would have been bravado or arrogance, but he made it a statement of fact. Lightening the mood, she asked, "How do you do it, Lord Gabriel?"

"Please," he protested, " call me Andrew. How do I do what?"

"Manage to look like a cross between a Greek god, Prince Charming, and the guy next door," she asked, while admiring his bottle-green turtleneck, jeans, and coffee-colored jacket.

He laughed and the sound reverberated through the apartment. "No wonder Victory is infatuated," she thought, "The man exudes sex appeal and charm with just the right touch of sincerity." Even though he easily was one of the most gorgeous men that she had ever seen, he did not seem pretentious. He possessed a special charisma that put those around him at ease. However, underneath the surface affability and gracious manners, there was undeniable strength and authority.

"Please sit down," she offered as she indicated the peach velour sofa. "Can I offer you something to drink while you wait?"

Andrew smiled and shook his head.

"I heard about what happened last night," she began.

Andrew's eyes darkened. Laura had a brief glimpse of the visage that had terrorized the teens. Clearing her throat, she began again. "I just wanted to say how much I admired the way you handled the situation. But I am confused about one thing. Why didn't you go straight to the police? I tried to get Tory to go later and she refused, but I think those delinquents should be arrested."

He considered what she had said for a moment. "You care for her a lot, don't you?"

She nodded. "We're more then friends. We've known each other practically our whole lives and are as close or closer than sisters. I can't bear the thought of Tory getting hurt," she finished and pointedly stared at him.

Andrew's gaze never wavered. "I also care and I saw no purpose in putting her through the additional trauma of filing a report when there was no serious damage. If possessions had been stolen or if she had been injured," his eyes darkened again, "the situation would have been handled differently."

The look in his eyes was reassuring, but she still was skeptical that he could care that deeply after such a short acquaintance. He probably felt responsible for Victory and seemed to be the type that would protect anyone in his charge.

Just then, Victory entered the room. She was wearing a yellow cable-knit sweater, designer jeans, and antique-white ankle boots. She smiled at Andrew. The intimate gesture was full of secrets that Laura couldn't fathom. Feeling like an intruder, she rose to allow privacy for the couple.

Victory's eyes lifted. She smiled at her roommate. "Do you have any special plans today?"

The marquis stood. Turning, he regarded Laura warmly. "You are perfectly welcome to come with us," he offered graciously.

Laura stood and began brushing out the folds of her skirt. "Thanks, but I'm going down to the campaign headquarters to volunteer for a little while."

"You certainly are dedicated," Andrew remarked dryly.

Victory laughed. "Laura is going to get John Callahan and Craven Maxwell elected single-handedly."

He glanced at her sharply, "Are you that attracted to my brother?"

Laura's face flushed. Was he implying that her political decision was shallowly based on Craven Maxwell's good looks? It was one thing to banter good-naturedly about it with her best friend, but it was quite another to be insulted by a stranger.

"I volunteer because I believe in their political platform – not because of a physical attraction for your brother," she said stiffly.

But Victory had detected the concern in Andrew's voice. Now, she stared at the marquis. "Andrew," she asked hesitantly because she remembered her initial uneasiness when she had been introduced to the politician, "is there any reason Laura shouldn't be interested in Craven?" she asked, while ignoring her friend's sharp glance. If he was married or even engaged, it was better for Laura to find out now.

He regarded the women and chose his words carefully. How could he warn them without breaking his word? Wasn't protecting Victory's friend part of his responsibility? They still were staring expectantly.

He turned to the brunette. "Be careful, Laura. My brother is a very ambitious man."

It was on the tip of her tongue to snap, " That is obvious since he is running for vice president," but a deep sadness came into the marquis' eyes as he gazed at her, so she checked her temper. Her anger dissipated as she realized that his concern was genuine.

The couple explored the Museum of American History and avidly examined the exhibits. Andrew was infatuated with the historical inventions. He gazed with rapt attention at the demonstration of the antique sewing machine, gasped in wonder at the original movie clips of Charlie Chaplin, and was fascinated by the first phonograph. Amused at his enthusiasm, Victory followed indulgently.

When he stopped at the television display for the fourth time, she finally asked, "Don't they have televisions in Cornwall?"

Andrew glanced up from his examination of the tubes and filaments. "Yes, but this is my first opportunity to examine the original forms of the inventions."

Afterwards, they stopped for dinner in Georgetown. Once seated on the open terrace, he requested that she tell him about herself.

"Isn't that the most difficult part about meeting someone new?" she asked, while making a face. "You always have the initial interview where your life is put on display for the other person. It kind of makes me feel like one of the exhibits in the museum."

Golden lights glinted off his hair as he shook his head. "Surely, it isn't that bad. I feel as though I already know you, but hearing of your life experiences would bring us closer," he prompted gently.

She laughed self-consciously. "All right, I will tell you the Victory Parker story, but I expect to hear yours, too."

He agreed. The waiter cleared their plates and they ordered coffee. During the interruption, she collected her thoughts.

"The Victory Parker story, narrated by Victory Parker." He chuckled as she continued. "I was born and raised near Philadelphia – in Bryn-mawr, to be exact. I grew up in a warm home with two loving parents until my mom died about ten years ago. Although he loved me very much, my dad was rather like the absent-minded professor. I went to private boarding schools, to college, and to law school. My dad, who was a very well-known psychiatrist, died about six months ago. He was very loving and we spent all our holidays together. I still miss him," she said sadly as she finished that part of her story. "Fortunately, he lived long enough to see me graduate from Harvard Law School. I think he was just about as proud of the accomplishment as I was. After graduation, I went into practice with a couple of partners. Recently, I built up enough clients to go out on my own."

He reached across the table to touch her hand. "Your dad must have been quite a man to inspire such love. I'm sure he would continue to be proud of his daughter if he were still with you. But you have skipped a very important piece of your history."

She took a sip of the strong brew. The sunset cast a golden orange glow over the surroundings. A fiery ray shone across Victory's face. Gold shimmered at her neck. Andrew blinked at the sudden reflection and put up a hand to shield his eyes.

"What's wrong?"

He leaned forward as he grasped her necklace in his hand. A small gold crucifix dangled from his fingers. "The reflection from your necklace was shining right in my eyes."

Victory looked down at the necklace. "My father gave me that on my last birthday before he died. I haven't taken it off since. Is it bothering you?"

"No, it's very beautiful," he said, while fingering the tiny cross. "Just let me move out of the line of its glare." He moved his chair next to hers. "That's better."

"Smooth maneuver," Victory thought. She, too, was pleased with the change in position. Disconcerted by his nearness, she became lost in the turquoise depths of his eyes. The marquis clasped her hand. He stroked her palm with his thumb, sending erotic sensations shooting up her arm.

"You were saying," he prompted.

"Oh, yes. I met Laura in first grade. When I started, I was new in the area and hadn't had a chance to make any friends. Laura was also new to the area. She was from Philadelphia, too, but from the north Philly section. In case you're not familiar with the city, that section is not such a good part of town. Ordinarily, people from the north side could not afford to send their children to a private boarding school, but," she looked at him with some amusement, "– this is going to sound really bizarre, but I swear it's true – Laura's parents won the state lottery and became millionaires overnight."

His eyes widened. "How extraordinary and fortunate for them."

She shook her head. "Laura didn't think so at the time, although I'm sure she would agree with you now. Anyway, the other kids in the school looked down on her because of her background. She was a loner and always tried to act as though she didn't care what the others thought. One day, I came across a group of older girls picking on her and I stood up for her."

The waiter delivered their check. She waited while Andrew paid the bill. They walked into the shopping district. As they window-shopped, he asked, "Did your support that day in the schoolyard cement the life-long friendship?"

"No," she said, while pulling her windswept hair from her face. "At the time, she didn't even thank me. For some reason, I just kept trying and eventually won her over. It was worth the effort. Laura is the best friend I've ever had. I believe we are even closer than sisters."

With his hands in his pockets, he leaned against a wall of a store. "I happen to know she feels the same way about you. True friendship is rare. You are both very lucky to have that bond. Don't ever let anything break it."

Without warning, he reached out and grabbed her by the waist. He pulled her into his arms. Unprepared for the move, Victory landed hard against his chest. He stole a brief kiss. She barely had time to register the tingling sensation before he abruptly released her. His eyes searched her face. As she gazed back, she realized that he was waiting for a reaction. Unsure of what he wanted, she smiled cautiously, while steadily holding his gaze. Seemingly satisfied, he took her hand as they started back towards the car.

"I found that story of how you met Laura very interesting, but that wasn't what I was referring to when I said you left something out."

"Oh?" she asked perplexed.

He shook his head. "I was referring to boyfriends."

"Oh," she said with a bit of embarrassment. "There haven't been any."

He looked at her skeptically and she amended, "No one special. Of course, I dated, but no man has kept my interest very long."

On the car ride back to her house, Andrew was quiet. Sensing his brooding mood, Victory decided to refrain from asking about his background. Instead, she kept her comments limited to descriptions of various landmarks. He showed some interest when they passed the Capitol building, but then lapsed back into silence.

"What is wrong with him," she wondered, as they pulled up to her townhouse. The lights were turned on and she caught a glimpse of

Laura passing the front window. There would be no opportunity for a private conversation inside. If she were going to discover what was bothering him, she would have to do it now.

She gathered her nerve, but, before she could say anything, he surprised her by announcing, "My business here is finished and I am going to be returning to England in a couple of days."

In dismay, Victory stared at him. Her heart sank. So, that was the problem. Now, she understood. They had just met and getting to know Andrew Gabriel was one of the most exciting events of her life. She was unprepared for the experience to end. But what could she do? He had come here for a specific purpose and, since it was finished, he had his own life to return to in Cornwall.

"I suppose you need to get back," she said flatly.

He intently stared at her. She sensed that he was suppressing intense emotions. Warily eyeing her, he said softly, "I would like you to come with me."

He tensed as if expecting to be rejected. Puzzled by his behavior yet elated, she clarified, "You want me to come for a visit?" She held her breath. She did not dare to believe that she had heard correctly.

He nodded, but his expression remained guarded.

Confused by his reaction, she asked cautiously, "For how long?"

He hesitated. It was too soon. "For as long as you like. Will you be able to travel on such short notice? When she hesitated, he continued, "I know we have known each other only for a few days, but I would hate for our acquaintanceship to end so soon and I'm not sure when I will be coming back to the States."

"I would love to come," she said recklessly. "Since I don't have any pressing cases at the moment, I won't have any problem getting away."

He exhaled and Victory smiled. "That's amazing," she thought, "He had actually been nervous!" Still smiling, she leaned across the seat to kiss him tenderly on the cheek. "Thank you for the invitation."

With his eyes glowing, he tentatively reached out a hand to stroke her hair. She nuzzled his palm with her cheek and kissed the inside of his hand. A thrill went through her as he softly groaned.

He leaned closer. His lips grazed her temple. "You must tell me if I ever do anything that frightens you."

"What a strange thing to say," she thought. But the thought was lost as his lips claimed hers in a kiss of such pent-up passion that she thought that she would faint from the onslaught of emotions that it provoked. Lost in waves of desire, she clung to him as he possessed her. His kiss promised ecstasy, eternity, and completion. In his arms were security, serenity, and the knowledge that her life had been spent waiting for this man. Nothing but this bond mattered. As she exploded, time ceased and shattered into a million fragments, only to be reconstructed again within his embrace.

Regretfully, he pulled back. He still was afraid to expose her to the depths of his desire. Several seconds passed before Victory drifted back to reality. When she opened her eyes, she found herself imprisoned in an iron grip. Oddly, she felt comforted rather than trapped by his strength. She smiled warmly into his questioning eyes. She was gratified when the expression changed from apprehension to relief.

She laid her head on his chest. "You will come to England with me?" he asked, as he stroked her hair.

The thought of his leaving without her made her nauseous. She knew that she had no other choice.

Chapter 8:

Dana's Secrets

Turbulent thoughts plagued Andrew, as he pulled into the driveway of his Bethesda mansion. "How ironic," he thought, as he stared at the whitewashed pillars glowing in the moonlight. He had bought the mansion with the intention of living in it with the woman whom he loved. Now, he would have to figure out how to convince her to relocate. Preferably, it would be in another country or even on his estate in Cornwall.

"How was he going to do it?" he mused, as he unlocked the front door. He hung up his jacket and strolled to the bar. Pulling out a bottle, he poured a generous amount of reddish-brown liquid into a glass and then headed for the second floor.

While crossing the large bedroom, he passed the four-poster bed and then threw open the French doors. He was still brooding when he stepped onto the balcony.

He stared at the twinkling lights of the city as if they could provide the solution to his problem. He sighed as he stared into the darkness. Now what? In Washington, Victory had a happy life, complete with friends and a budding political career. After listening to her impassioned speech about the injustices that had been suffered by citizens of her country, he realized how important that career was to her. Andrew frowned into the darkness. When had life become so complicated? His original intention had been to move here permanently and slowly become an intricate part of her life. The meeting with Craven had altered those plans. Now, instead of sharing her life, he had to convince her to give it up.

While swirling the contents of his glass, he wondered if he could think of an alternative. They could take their chances and stay, but he knew Craven well enough to know that it would be only a matter of time before something would shatter their fragile contract. It would be much better to retreat to Cornwall where he wouldn't be tempted to interfere and risk forfeiting Victory's safety.

He was so engrossed in his thoughts that it took several seconds to register the tinkling noise to his right. Abruptly turning, he peered into the darkness and was astonished. "Dana," he yelled exuberantly.

Rushing forward, the dark-haired girl threw herself into his waiting arms. Joyfully, he whirled her around several times while they both laughed.

Finally, he placed her back on the ground. "How did you get here? How did you know where I was? What have you been doing with yourself all this time?" After firing the questions in rapid succession, he smiled sheepishly, "I'm sorry. I don't know what happened to my manners. Would you like to come inside and have a drink?"

He pulled out the bottle and poured. Handing the glass to her, he stared while she sniffed the contents, made a face, and started to speak. Changing her mind, she downed the contents and returned the glass for a refill.

"You look wonderful," he remarked, as he admired her long wavy hair, glowing eyes, and lithe form under the dark-blue spandex dress.

"You look pretty good yourself," she returned, while sitting on the arm of his chair.

"How was Africa," he asked, as he linked fingers with her.

She was amused. "I went to Africa a very long time ago," she said. The silver bangle bracelets jingled as she moved her hands. "To answer your question, it was hot and full of bugs. The natives beating on their tom-toms gave me a headache."

Andrew laughed. "I am very happy you decided to visit."

"I'm actually in the States at my father's request." She emphasized the last word. "He needs my help with a project."

Andrew's interest peaked. "Can you tell me about it?"

Biting her lower lip, Dana looked away. "Only if you force me to. It would be bad news for me since Dad has no idea I'm here."

"How long do you think that will last," he asked ruefully.

She shrugged. "I can deal with his discovering that I came to visit you as long as I don't have to admit that I've disclosed his secrets."

"Very well," he said evenly. "I won't ask you to betray your father."

Smiling brightly at him, she leaned across the chair. "You should have realized I would come to you sooner or later," she said in a sultry whisper.

Sliding into his lap, she pulled his head down and kissed him forcefully on the lips. Her grip was strong and it was several seconds before he could pull free. He gently eased her off of his lap. Unprepared for the rejection, Dana hit the floor in an undignified heap.

"What was that all about," she asked plaintively. She stood and rearranged her dress over her voluptuous curves.

He remained silent and allowed her to read the answer in his thoughts. "So," she said, as her eyes narrowed, "you're in love with another woman." Then, she spat incredulously, "A diurnal?"

Retreating a step, she stared in shock. Then, she began rapidly pacing across the floor. "Who is she?" she demanded. If Andrew hadn't broken their connection so abruptly, she would already be on her way to eliminate the competition. "I'll tear her limb from limb. I'll cut off her head and use it for a lampshade. Better yet, I'll shrink it and use it for a necklace like the natives in Africa do. Did you ever see the process, Andrew? It's quite fascinating and involves..."

Jolting pain shot through her arm as Andrew jerked her around. The tirade died as she confronted the undisguised wrath on his face.

"Listen to me, Dana," he hissed, while shaking her so violently that she thought that her head would snap. "I am forbidding you from harming this woman. If any injury comes to her at your hands, you will have to answer to me. Is that understood?"

He ceased the shaking, but held her with an iron grip that was biting painfully into her skin. The shock of the sensation of physical pain and of Andrew's willingness to perpetrate it on her caused her anger and resentment to flare. She glared back at him. Eventually, the fury in her eyes wavered, flickered, and then died.

Submissively, she lowered her eyes. "Understood."

He released her and she hastily stepped back while rubbing her arms. Sending him a coquettish glance, she asked, "After all, how long can your interest in a diurnal last?" Then, she thought, "In another fifty or sixty years, she will be dead while I am waiting to console him. That's not a bad position." She brightened.

Now that his humor was restored, he laughed. "You're incorrigible," he said, as he ruffled her dark hair.

Chapter 9:
Dark Disclosures

Craven Maxwell sat hunched over the small desk in his Miami hotel room. He sifted through the papers scattered across the desk and occasionally copied a passage into his notebook. With his eyes glowing, he pulled one ancient document closer to the lamplight. His excitement escalated as he scrutinized the contents. After memorizing the details, he carefully laid the document aside and took more notes. "It must be the adrenalin produced by the fear," he mused, while rereading what he had written. Good. They were on the right track. He shuffled through more of the yellowed parchment and extracted several sheets. After more minutes of reading, his eyes narrowed. There was another essential component that had been overlooked. He shook his head to clear the cobwebs. Then, he reread the papers and hoped that he had been mistaken. Twenty minutes later, he sat back. He was exhausted and disgusted.

"If that's the secret of conversion, no wonder it remained a mystery," he mused, while staring out of the window. Coconut palms swayed in the breeze while stars twinkled in the inky sky. The act was so repulsive that it almost was inconceivable. Yet, if he was going to succeed, he had to disregard personal aversion to make use of these revelations.

Picking up his pen, he turned to a fresh page in his book. A loud knocking interrupted his labors. Cursing, he hastily shoved the papers into the drawer.

Tucking the black leather notebook into his jacket, he strode across the room and yanked open the door. A mask of congeniality slid across his face as he stood aside to allow the entrance of the visitor.

John Callahan stepped inside and pivoted to face him. "Did you see the news?" he questioned with his usual infectious enthusiasm.

Nodding peremptorily at the secret service agents, Craven closed the door. "No," he admitted, "I was doing some reading." He was sure that his reading was more important than anything that possibly could have been on the television, but he continued to appear interested.

Smiling broadly, Callahan announced, "Well, the polls have us ahead of our opponents by seven points."

Craven frowned, as he walked to the sofa. "The last polls I saw had us ahead by ten."

Callahan pulled the chair across from him and took out a cigarette. Lighting it, he took a long drag and exhaled the smoke before answering. "We were, but we must expect the gap to narrow as election day approaches."

Craven stared at the cigarette dangling from the other man's mouth. "Stupid diurnal. Your life span is already so short. Why hasten your own demise?" He gave a mental shrug. "Oh, well, all of it is academic, especially for this fool."

Aloud, he asked, "Do you think we will still pull through?"

The presidential candidate flashed a reproachful look at him. "That isn't positive thinking. Where's your confidence?"

For a split-second, the mask slipped and exposed Craven's contempt. The fleeting image flashed so fast that Callahan was certain that it was an illusion of the smoke. Sometimes, this vice presidential candidate of his made him quite uneasy. But, when the haze lifted, he saw only the young, bright, handsome, charming, and competent politician gazing back at him.

"Yes," he replied more seriously, "I think it will be closer than we thought, but we still will come out ahead."

He studied the end of his cigarette for a long moment and then ground it into the glass ashtray. "By the way, since I am updating you, the news had other comments about the election."

"Oh?"

Callahan nodded soberly. "The newscasters made a big deal out of the rising crime rate. Of course," he said grinning, "right now, that's in our favor. The media is digging the competition's grave by pointing out that DC has the nation's highest crime rate."

"Well, they have a point," Craven agreed. "That's why I have been working so hard on my reform packages. I want to assure the public that we have answers to that problem, at least. To which crimes were they referring specifically? Drugs? If so, I have a rehab program already outlined for our next conference."

Callahan waved a hand. "No, tonight's topic was mysterious disappearances and serial killing. It seems that there have been several people reported missing in DC during the past two years. The press wants to know why there haven't been any solutions to those cases."

The younger man tensed. "I thought there hadn't been any new cases in several months."

"Well, last night, there was another one that brought the entire issue under scrutiny again. The popular theory now is that there is a serial killer at-large. The media has portrayed the police as incompetent and the administration as lacking the ability to protect the people. That piece of propaganda will definitely swing votes."

"As long as the abductions remain unsolved."

Callahan thought that he detected sarcasm, but Craven's face was frozen into a mask of concerned interest. After the other man left, Craven stalked across the room and snatched up the phone. He punched in a code, let the phone ring three times, and then hung up. A few seconds later, the phone rang. Calmly picking up the receiver and speaking in a neutral tone, he asked for the identity of the caller.

"This is Walter."

"Well, Walter, I've just received a newsflash." He paused. The silence on the other end was almost palpable. "You do know, Walter, which news story I'm referring to."

The anxiety on the line was evident. Craven continued in a menacing snarl. "I thought it was understood that there were to be no more disappearances."

When there was no response, Craven exploded. "Are you there, Walter?"

"Yes," squeaked the frightened man.

"On whose authority did you take that boy last night?"

"Dana's"

"Tell her to call me the moment she arrives – and send me some supplies."

Victory bent low over the head of her sunny-yellow mare as they galloped over the tall grass. Glancing behind, she gasped in dismay. The midnight-black stallion was bearing down hard. Determinedly, she faced forward. She was relieved that the courtyard was only yards ahead. She dug in her heels and the gallant mare gave her final reserves in a desperate attempt to stay ahead. By the time that they reached the gate, the stallion was on her heels. Triumphantly, her mount sailed through the opening only bare inches ahead of the larger horse.

Delighted and breathless, Victory allowed a groom to help her to dismount and then lead the exhausted horse away. Jumping down beside her, Andrew swept her into his arms and whirled her around as she laughed.

Finally, he set her on the ground. "You would think," Victory said, while still laughing up at him, "that you had won the race."

His brilliant turquoise eyes reflected the rays of the setting sun as he gazed down at the beautiful woman. She was vibrantly alluring with her golden hair blowing in the coastal breeze and her cheeks rosy from her exertions. She was a perfect compliment to the imposing stone castle. Impulsively, his arms tightened and pulled her roughly against him. When their lips met, Victory was sure that the world stood still.

It was always that way, she reflected later as they sat down for dinner. A mere glance or the slightest touch would set her pulses racing. Nothing else mattered but the feel of him. His body communicated with a part of her that she hadn't known existed. The answering need had lain dormant and unrecognized until she met the marquis. Now, it was as though she had been blind all of her life and was experiencing the miracle of sight. Colors were brighter, edges more clearly defined, flora and fauna more vibrant, and the simplest task enhanced.

Immediately captivating her, Andrew smiled from across the table. "What would you like to do tomorrow?" he asked, as a servant placed roast mutton on their plates.

Victory considered. As we were riding, I noticed an outdoor flea market. That might be interesting. I would also like to explore the beaches."

Andrew raised his brows, as he carved his lamb. "Haven't you seen enough of the beaches?" he asked, amused. "You've been exploring them every day since you arrived."

"I love climbing cliffs and exploring beaches," she admitted, while sipping her wine. "We don't have any of them in Washington. If you are bored with the activity, we can do something else."

Andrew poured from a tall bottle. Sipping slowly, he considered the woman across from him. Her golden hair was piled high on her head and her long dress was cut in an old-fashioned style that blended well with the Victorian decor. He grew pensive. She had been there for a week, but he had not been able to think of a plausible way to convince her to stay. She enjoyed the daily excursions through the countryside, exploring the coast, and frequenting the inns. She was enchanted by the history of the Cornish coast and impressed by the cathedrals. She also had been won over by the friendly and charming residents. Still, he reflected, there was a world of difference between enjoying a vacation and relocating. Was it too soon to propose? Would the idea of marriage cause a premature departure or provide the incentive to stay?

"What is this stuff, anyway," Victory asked, while picking up the bottle.

Andrew immediately snapped out of his reverie.

"Oh," he said, as he waved his hand, "that is an electrolyte supplement."

"Like KM?"

"Similar."

"I know about KM. It's a potassium supplement. I never heard of this, though. What's it for?" she asked, while examining the label. "PS4" was scripted across the front, but there was no listing of ingredients.

"I'm not surprised that you have never heard of it since it is used only by a rare few. It's specially ordered. There is a hereditary lack of some basic enzymes in my hemoglobin. This liquid provides the missing elements."

"Hereditary? Your family suffers from this condition?"

He nodded.

"Can I try it?"

"You won't like it. It tastes worse than KM."

"I find it hard to imagine anything tasting worse than KM." Gingerly, she put the glass to her lips. The odor was noxious so she sipped the contents cautiously. "It's awful," she sputtered, while quickly placing it down and picking up her wine.

"I take it for the nutrients, not the taste," he remarked dryly.

The half-moon silhouetted the trees as it shone through the barren branches. The couple strolled around the estate. Glancing at the sapphire sky, Victory was awed by the scene. The moon cast an eerie glow across the stone edifice. She instantly was reminded of the old gothic horror movies that she had watched as a child. She smiled and was somehow comforted by the association. Melancholic yet content, she stared across the acres of deserted grasslands.

She looked up at her companion. "I really enjoy investigating your estate, but, during my wanderings, I sometimes get the strangest feeling that I am being watched. It has occurred to me that I might be trespassing on a neighbor's property.

"I have no neighbors."

She stopped and turned in surprise. "All this," she asked incredulously while waving a hand towards the plains, "is yours?"

Her eyes appeared large, luminous, and fathomless, as she gazed up at him. "Yes."

Doesn't any of it belong to Craven?"

"These estates were passed down from my father's side of the family. Craven and I are related through my mother. Why do you ask?"

She flushed and lowered her eyes. "Just curiosity."

He gently lifted her chin.

"It's silly. Earlier, when I was in the tower, I was viewing the landscape. I guess I got caught up in its beauty and found myself fantasizing." Encouraged by the silence, she continued. "You and I could stay here forever and, eventually, Laura and Craven would marry and join us."

He stiffened and dropped his hand. Embarrassed and hurt by his rejection, she pulled away. By sharing her dreams, she had known that she was risking rejection, but she still had been unprepared for the pain. What had she been thinking? They all had their lives to lead. Real life didn't fit into neat little packages. "I'm sorry. I didn't mean to be so personal or presumptuous."

Andrew could only stare. Euphoria embraced him as he realized that she had thought about a future with him, but it was eclipsed by the implications about his brother and her friend.

Suddenly, an owl's screech shattered the stillness. Victory jumped. The marquis placed a protective arm around her shoulders.

"I'm sorry. We don't have any owls in Washington."

At ease again, she plucked up her courage and asked, "Andrew, why did you tense up a minute ago?" He hesitated, so she took a steadying breath and plunged ahead. "I've seen similar reactions before. She stared at him. "They always seem to be related to your brother."

"What are you talking about?"

"You seem anxious, uncomfortable, and hostile."

"Very perceptive," he thought. He listened attentively while she continued.

"If there is something about your brother that could be detrimental to Laura, I wish you would tell me. If he is married or something else that will hurt her, I would rather she find out from me rather than from the media."

"Is your friend that involved?"

Victory nodded. "I think so. She told me before I left that she and Craven were dating. Once the campaign is over, she's expecting him to propose."

Andrew tensed while he fought to control the rage that swept through him. How dare Craven toy with the girl like that? Obviously, he was using Laura Warner as an additional guarantee against interference, as well as an unwitting spy. Troubled, he led Victory over to a stone bench and pulled her down next to him. He searched her face for a long moment and then sighed. "My brother is a very ambitious, powerful, and ruthless man. He is the type who will stop at nothing to obtain his goals and will use anyone in any way that he can to get what he wants."

"Sounds like your basic politician to me," she weakly joked. When she saw his serious expression, she sobered. "Those are pretty strong insinuations, but very vague and very general. What exactly are you trying to tell me?"

Closing his eyes, Andrew leaned back. How much did he dare to reveal? When he opened them, he was confronted by her concern.

"Many years ago, my father and Craven's father were rivals. You could say they ran for the same office. After a very bitter power struggle, my father eventually won. One day shortly after the election, my father was riding through a neighboring village when he met and fell in love with a local woman. The feeling was mutual and, eventually, they married. When Craven's father was introduced to the new bride, he became infatuated with her and attempted many times to seduce her away from her husband. My mother was deeply in love with my father and never wavered in her devotion. Eventually, she became pregnant and gave birth to a baby boy."

"You?" Victory interjected.

He nodded. "Yes, it was. However, my mother's family has a history of difficult childbirths and she almost died."

"Oh, how awful."

"Craven's father, consumed with jealousy and coveting the woman and child he thought should have been his, devised a scheme. He sent a messenger to lure my father from the castle with a false story of trouble in the furthest reaches of the estate. The problem was so serious it demanded his personal attention. Since my mother had made some improvement in her health, he felt he could leave long enough to settle the dispute.

Craven's father used the diversion to abduct my mother. He took her to an estate he had bought in Pennsylvania and continually raped her until she became pregnant."

Shocked, she asked, "What happened?"

"Traveling was difficult and it took several days for my father to get to the troubled area and several more for him to return. When he discovered the abduction, he scoured the country looking for them, but it was quite a while before he tracked them to America. By the time he arrived, it was too late. My mother, still weak from her first pregnancy, died while prematurely giving birth to a second son. My father, enraged and grief-stricken, burned down the mansion with Craven's father inside."

Victory gasped in horror, but the marquis, consumed by the past, didn't hear her.

"A servant dropped the infant from a second-story window of the inferno. Out of love for my mother, my father kept the child. Craven and I were raised together. It was apparent at an early age that Craven's character was similar to his father's. He was extremely competitive and constantly challenging me in order to prove his superiority. When he learned the story of our parent's tragedy, he became obsessed with hatred for my father. He eventually avenged his father by killing mine."

When Victory gasped, Andrew realized that he had gone too far. "I don't mean to insinuate that the man running for vice president of your country is a murderer. There is no evidence and I have only my personal conviction to support my allegations. Officially, my father's death was an accident and nothing has ever been proved to the contrary. After the inquiry, Craven left for the land of his birth. He and I have had an uneasy truce ever since."

"How can I stand by and watch while my friend dates someone who you suspect of murder?"

He raked a hand through his hair. "I have only my feelings to go by. Remember, according to the authorities, my father's case was an accident. I did not tell you this story so you would panic and alarm your friend unnecessarily." "If she does," he thought bleakly, "Laura will be in even more danger." Aloud, he continued, "I only want you to be wary and keep a close eye on the situation."

She looked at him with doubt in her eyes. "I don't know."

"Look at it this way: If I am wrong, you will be ruining their relationship and your friend's happiness for nothing. Craven will know where the idea came from and it will stir up trouble for all of us."

Reluctantly, she agreed. "But, if you ever find definitive proof, will you tell me?"

He agreed and they went indoors. On the way up to the second floor, Victory thought about what she had heard. Her mind still was assimilating the story, but she was uneasy. Parts of it didn't make sense. She didn't know exactly what it was, but knew that she eventually would unravel the mystery.

At her door, they paused. She wondered, as she had every night since arriving, if Andrew would enter the room with her. But, as on the previous occasions, he simply gave her a chaste kiss and continued walking to his own room. Disappointed and confused, Victory entered her room. Sitting at the vanity, she brushed her long golden hair. As she stared at her reflection, she wondered if something about her repelled him. In Washington, he had seemed to be overcoming his aversion to intimacy. She had hoped that being in his own home would have torn down the final barriers. Instead, their lovemaking was regressing.

She sighed and laid down her brush. In all of her previous experiences, she had never run across a man who was reluctant to have sex. "In fact," she thought ruefully, "I usually have more trouble discouraging my dates." She simply didn't have any experience in being the pursuer. Short of begging or throwing herself at him, she already had been so obvious that it was bordering on embarrassing. Placing her dressing gown at the foot of the bed, she pulled back the ivory lace quilt and climbed into the tall four-poster. If the status of this relationship didn't change soon, she would have to throw scruples to the wind.

Chapter 10:

The Villainous Vampire

Craven Maxwell straightened his tie as he stood in front of the full-length mirror. Turning to admire himself from different angles, he studied his reflection. Satisfied, he turned and picked up the bouquet from the side table. He was pleased with the progress of his plan. Since deciding to enter into a courtship with Laura Warner, he had the benefits of enjoying her charm and beauty as well as the bonus of keeping appraised of Andrew's movements. So far, he had kept to his word, but an additional trump card couldn't hurt. Another idea began to take shape. His reflection hardened. In addition to her use as a hostage, she would serve as the perfect alibi with the proper planning.

"Daddy, where are you going?"

Craven looked up to find Dana standing in the doorway. His eyes moved dispassionately over her wavy black hair, soft velvet eyes, and voluptuous curves covered by the black vest and leather pants.

He scowled as she approached. "I have a date," he said flatly.

Dana studied him in his elegant black suit and exclaimed, "With a diurnal? What is it that these women have that captivates you?"

Craven's eyes narrowed. As he probed her, Dana realized too late that she had slipped. Her father's face tightened as he glared at her.

Unable to bear the tension, she exclaimed, "All right, so I went to see Andrew. You know what he and I mean to each other. I had to see him."

He continued to observe her as she pleaded for understanding. "I didn't breathe a word about your plans."

Again, he probed her. Dana forced herself to relax and accept the invasion as he delved deep enough to ascertain the truth. Finally satisfied, he raised an eyebrow. "In the future, you might do well to remember that Andrew may be your downfall. As for the woman, my intentions are not quite the same as your former lover's. I will use her only as long as she serves my purpose." His onyx gaze sharpened. Dana's relief was replaced by trepidation. "I summoned you here because I wanted to make sure you understand my orders."

"What orders?" she asked, as she moved to sit at the dining room table.

"My orders regarding the termination of abductions."

Dana's eyes lowered. "I thought you would be pleased if I carried it off. Besides, we were running out of supplies."

Craven considered, as he gazed at the half-empty bottle on the table. "It would have been worth it if you had been undetected."

She looked up in surprise.

"Haven't you seen the news?"

She contemptuously curled her lip. "Why would I watch diurnals reporting about their mundane lives?"

Quick as a springing cat, Craven was on top of her. Grabbing her by the hair, he jerked her out of the chair. "You arrogant fool," he hissed. "Your indiscretions will bring the authorities down on our heads. Despite their weaknesses, the diurnals have many advantages that we are not ready to confront."

Releasing her hair, he backhanded her across the cheek. The blow knocked her across the room. Dana landed hard against an end table, which dislodged a lamp and sent it crashing to the floor. Stunned but unhurt, she stared at her father, as he nonchalantly straightened his tie.

Glancing over his shoulder as he headed out of the door, he said, "In the future, I hope you will heed my requests."

Victory awakened early in the morning with the urge to call her friend. Ever since Andrew's disclosures, she had been uneasy about her friend's relationship. Wanting reassurance, she went to the study to place a call to Washington. An excited Laura answered and, after asking about her trip, spoke animatedly about her upcoming date with Craven Maxwell. Only a few minutes into the conversation, the doorbell rang and Laura excused herself by explaining that Craven had arrived early for their theater date.

Now, as she sat tapping her fingers on the polished surface of the antique mahogany desk, she wondered if she should have tried to warn her friend. Despite Andrew's protests, she was sure that her roommate should be on guard. "But what can I do?" she wondered, while staring idly at the bookcase. If she were going to tell Laura, it would have to be in person. Otherwise, she probably wouldn't take her seriously. Even Victory had to admit that the story sounded incredulous. "To think, this man – who probably was going to be the next vice president and her best friend's lover – could be a murderer. Every time she thought of Laura with the man, she felt sick. Andrew's assertions of uncertainty were of little comfort. She was sure that if he had really believed in his brother's innocence and Laura's safety, he never would have related the story.

Idly, she scanned the rows of books as she considered a course of action. Suddenly, her gaze riveted on one of the volumes. Curious, she stood and approached the case. Standing in front of the book, she read the words on the binding aloud, "Vampires: Fact or Fiction."

"Strange," she thought, as she pulled the book off of the shelf. "Andrew knew that I am interested in vampires, yet he never indicated that he had books on the subject. It's pretty old," she reflected, while flipping through the yellowed pages. "An ancient ancestor probably acquired it. It is possible that Andrew is unaware of its existence."

Holding her discovery as securely as a newfound treasure, she stepped out of the study and was grateful for the distraction. She decided to take the volume to the beach and read while waiting for Andrew to rise. "He never gets up before noon," she thought dryly. Upon enquiry, she was informed that it was customary among the gentry to sleep during the day. Her own habit of waking early for work, accompanied by the disorientation of being in a different time zone, placed her on a different schedule. Now, she had something to do besides worrying while she waited.

Letting herself out of the castle, she started down the path towards the cliffs. Passing by wild flowers, she bent to sniff the heather. In the distance, she spied a lone horse and rider galloping across the meadow. She watched as she continued her trek towards the rocks. The owner's handling of the large stallion impressed her. She turned her attention back to the path as grass abruptly turned to sharp rock. "It would never do to drop Andrew's antique book into the roaring surf," she thought, as she cast a wary eye on the turbulent waves pounding the sand. She paused at an outcrop of jutting rocks. She decided that the rocks were high enough for her to enjoy Mother Nature without worrying about ruining the pages with salt water. She seated herself on one of the flatter stones.

Hours passed while Victory, sitting hunched on the outcrop, was absorbed by the text. Several pages from the end, she paused. On the opposite page was a portrait of a renowned vampire. According to the accompanying text, this Elizabethan overlord was one of the most infamous and cruel of his kind. His atrocities were limitless, his blood lust insatiable.

Curious, Victory turned the page to examine the picture of the ancient villain. The book fell from nerveless fingers as she shook with uncontrollable tremors. Her eyes became wide. Her hands continued to shake as she bent forward to retrieve the volume. She stared in horrified fascination. The black eyes in the portrait impaled her. The bared teeth mocked her while the face of Craven Maxwell stared back from the book.

"It's impossible," she rationally told herself as she continued to stare at the photo. The hair was cut differently and the clothing was of the Elizabethan period, but the face glaring maliciously back at her was that of the illustrious politician. She shook her head in disbelief while scanning the text.

"The villainous vampire, known as Raven, terrorized villagers along the Cornish coast for over two hundred years. Finally, in the mid 1600's, the infamous overlord was ousted from his position of power and driven from the land. Although his fate was unknown, it is believed that he eventually was destroyed since the evil overlord has never returned to plague the countryside. Also, reports of his misdeeds ceased after that period.

Victory sat for a long time staring at the sea. Unable to digest what she had read, she felt incapable of coping with the implications. Vampires, no matter how interesting she found the subject, simply didn't exist. Once that indisputable truth was established, what was left? She glanced again at the sinister visage. A shiver ran down her spine. She snapped the book shut. The only plausible explanation that she could come up with was that this barbaric overlord was Craven's ancestor. Could the traits of insanity, cruelty, and ruthless ambition, which she read about in the pages of the book, be passed on through heredity? Her father had told her that certain mental illnesses, such as schizophrenia and mood disorders, had genetic components. She realized that she was jumping to conclusions. She didn't know if those genes could affect future generations or, for that matter, if this man was related to Craven Maxwell. Does he pose a serious threat to Laura and the country? Surely, someone with a psychopathic personality couldn't have gone so far in the political arena. All politicians from mayors to presidents were subjected to merciless scrutiny of every aspect of their lives. It was inconceivable that someone who was campaigning to be the vice president could have had any serious defects that had gone undetected.

She was determined to confront Andrew with these revelations. Her concentration was interrupted by nearby shouting. Startled, she glanced around. Her mind was still caught up in the text. While she was reading, the sky had turned from pale blue to dull gray. The wind was whipping wildly, causing the waves to crash even more furiously against the rocks. She decided that she should start back to the castle. Andrew had warned her about the sudden storms that raged on the Atlantic. It appeared as if one might be brewing now. She stood and brushed off her pants. As she was about to ascend the slope, she paused. Again, a cry was carried on the wind. Hesitating, she scanned the surrounding cliffs, but saw nothing. She decided that it probably was a gull. Again came the cry. This time, it sounded very close. Victory peered over the edge of the outcrop where she had been sitting. Directly below was a girl of about twelve, who was excitedly running back and forth on the narrow band of beach. Her hands were cupped around her mouth and she was screaming something that Victory couldn't quite make out. She called to the girl, but the roaring of the ocean drowned her voice.

For a moment, Victory stood undecided. The tide seemed to be rising. The narrow strip of sand that the girl traveled was quickly shrinking. What's wrong with her? Surely, she could tell that this area was no place to be during an approaching squall. Victory's eyes searched the beach for the girl's parents. Surely, they would not have left the girl unchaperoned in such a dangerous area. To her dismay, the bluffs were deserted.

Again, she tried calling, but the wind whipped her words back at her. She stared down at the girl. Her red hair streamed behind her while her gestures became more frantic. Clutching the book under one arm, she carefully descended. Loose stones and gravel skidded down the path ahead of her. Slipping on the stones, she lost her footing several times.

At last, she reached the bottom and walked brusquely to the child.

A cold breeze blew against her cheeks. The dampness from the mist made her shiver. Her discomfort was increased by the scrapes that she had endured on her trek down the side of the cliff. By the time that she approached the girl, her mood had turned less charitable. Reaching her side, she grabbed the child's arm and spun her. Tears trickled down the girl's cheeks as she stared back with such anguish that Victory's sharp reprimand died on her lips.

"You should not be out here at a time like this," she admonished gently. "Where are your parents?"

Instead of answering the question, the girl sobbed as she threw herself into Victory's arms. "My dog, Sugar, is stuck out on the rocks and she can't get back in. The water is too high and I can't reach her. She'll drown!"

Victory peered about. In the veil of mist shrouding the landscape, she could barely glimpse the outcropping of rocks where the distraught child was pointing. She stared hard. After a few seconds, she glimpsed a white figure frantically prancing about on the rocks.

She turned back to the child and tried to sound calm. "What is your name?"

"Maggie," the girl wailed.

"Okay, Maggie, where are your parents?"

"They're back at the inn. They told me to stay inside, but, yesterday, we bought Sugar a new ball and she wanted to play. One time when I threw it, it rolled down here. Then, it bounced on those rocks. Sugar chased it, but she couldn't get it out of the crack. Now the tide is in and she's too small to swim back in that," she finished dismally as she watched the crashing surf.

"Well," thought Victory, glancing around once more in the vain hope that the parents had come and were looking for their missing child, "she's right about that. The white bundle of fluff out on the rocks appeared to be no more than a puppy – and a pretty frightened one, judging from it's frantic pacing.

"Dry your eyes Maggie. I will help you get your dog back."

Sniffing loudly, the girl obediently wiped her face with the end of her t-shirt. "I want you to hold my book for me while I go out to pick up Sugar."

She handed the book to Maggie and sat on the sand. Pulling off her hiking boots and woolen socks, she rolled up her pants. She then approached the water. The first wave crashed into her and made her sputter and shake. Well, what had she expected? It was November. She ground her teeth as a way of willing her body not to register the icy water as it swirled around her thighs. Suddenly, her leg was grazed by something hard. Relieved, she saw the buried portion of the jetty, which the dog must have used to wander out. Even though it now was buried beneath the tide, it still could be used as an anchor against the enraged waves that seemed determined to claim her.

A loud yelp came from overhead. Glancing up, she saw the dog, which was only a few feet above. Recognizing her as its savior, the little animal was whimpering pitifully and wagging its tail. Victory's heart went out to the puppy, as she lifted it from its precarious perch. Shivering from cold and fright, the animal burrowed into her jean jacket. Smiling down at the small ball of fluff, she stroked its head for a moment before retreating.

As she started forward, the sky suddenly burst open and torrents of water poured from above. Unable to see through the curtain of rain and ocean spray, Victory momentarily panicked. The waves buffeted them and tried to drag them backwards. Sensing more danger, the dog whined. Victory reached out with her right hand and grasped the outcrop of rocks. Using the jetty as a guide, she slowly retraced her steps to the beach. Looking through the rain, she thought that she could make out the girl's shape. A sudden flash of lightening lit up the sky. She thought that she glimpsed another figure with the child. It probably was one of her parents, but the darkness swallowed them. She again concentrated on reaching the shore.

As the water receded from the lower half of her body, she realized that only a few more steps should do it. Of course, in the deluge, it was difficult to tell where one body of water ended and the other began.

Ahead, she heard the girl yelling. She again peered through the rain. The dog, hearing the voice of its mistress, squirmed in her arms. She tried to keep a firm hold, but, suddenly, another flash of lightening and crack of thunder frightened the dog. The slippery animal wriggled free. Forgetting to keep her grip on the rocks, Victory hastily made a grab for the pet. As she started running after the puppy, she stepped off of an underwater ledge and suddenly plunged beneath the surf. She panicked and tried to retrace her steps, but the ocean, finally having captured her, was not about to relinquish its prize. It tossed her like a rag doll. Completely at the mercy of the tide, she felt herself being dragged out to sea. She desperately struggled against the current. Fighting fate, she flailed her arms until she finally struck the outcrop of rocks where the dog had been trapped. With gratitude and relief, she grasped the stone and was heedless of the sharp edges cutting into her skin.

The battle had not been won yet. The ocean, gearing up for the second round, battered her aching body and mercilessly pounded her. Saltwater sprayed into her eyes and stung the cuts on her legs and palms as she clung to the rocks. How would she ever get back now that it was high tide? She turned her head to gaze longingly at the shore. A wave crashed into the jetty and showered spray on her face. She turned her head and was caught off guard as another wall of water plowed into her. The ferocity of the blow snapped her head back against a sharp stone. Slowly, she sank into the sea.

Chapter 11:

Fierce Passion

"Good morning, Grayson," the Marquis of Penbrook said as he greeted his butler and headed towards the guest bedroom.

"Good morning, my lord," the butler returned. "If you're looking for the young lady, she's gone out."

Andrew turned to face the tall, soberly dressed man.

"Gone out?"

The butler nodded. "Yes, sir. A couple of hours ago, I saw the young lady heading towards the bluffs. She had a book in her hand."

"Oh," said the marquis, waving a hand, "she went to do some reading." He sauntered down the stairs into the kitchen. He had an idea brewing. "Lorraine," he announced to his French cook, "please pack me a lunch basket. Miss Parker has gone down to the beach and I plan to surprise her with a picnic."

The middle-aged French woman prepared the food eagerly. Her dark eyes twinkled as she considered the romantic implications.

While waiting for the basket, Andrew wandered into the den. Noticing the television shoved into a corner, he smiled. He remembered the way that he had been so engrossed in the original model at the Museum of American History. Only rarely had he looked at television in over five years because he considered most of the programming to be pure junk. Idly, he pushed the power button on the remote. A newscast came into view. "Today's news is tomorrow's history," he thought sardonically, as he changed the channel. He believed that anything worthy of remembering would be put into history books; the rest wasn't worth watching. He wondered if he should try to tune in an American broadcast to see if he could catch the status of his brother's campaign. "He might not get elected and there will be no cause for concern," he optimistically thought, but he soon recognized the futility of that hope.

His brother would not be attached to John Callahan's ticket if he did not stand the best chance.

The only thing that he was surprised about was that Craven had allowed himself to be relegated to the second-place position rather than that of the primary candidate. "I should be grateful for small blessings," he mused, but he could not reconcile the image of the Craven whom he knew and the Craven who was content to be second in any situation.

In the distance, the telephone rang. Seconds later, Grayson appeared proffering the instrument. Andrew paused, placed the remote on top of the television, and picked up the receiver.

"Hello, Andrew."

"Craven, I was just thinking about you," he said sarcastically.

"Are you and Miss Parker enjoying your vacation?"

The marquis gritted his teeth. "How did you know?"

A hollow laugh echoed through the line. "Didn't your girlfriend tell you I'm dating her roommate?"

"I want you to end the relationship."

"Tsk, tsk – and break the poor girl's heart? Andrew, do you think you have the monopoly on diurnals? I find this woman fascinating."

Andrew's eyes narrowed. "I will consider any harm to her as a breech of our contract."

Sudden tension crackled across the wire. "I'm calling to remind you of our agreement. Just because you are out of the country does not relinquish the obligation. Remember that as you ponder the plight of Miss Warner."

As he hung up the phone, Andrew considered the conversation. The last line had been ominous but opaque. Brooding over the brief dialogue, he stared blankly at the television screen. An image caught his attention and interrupted his thoughts. He paused with his finger poised on the remote. Quickly, he adjusted the volume.

"Today," announced the broadcaster, "Jordan Rush, the latest rising star in Parliament, announced his intention to run for prime minister."

The screen revealed a tall and strikingly handsome man with dark brown hair and jade green eyes. He was smiling into the camera. "It is my pleasure to announce my intention of becoming Britain's next prime minister."

The reporter came into view. "Lord Rush, Earl of Rockford, made this expected event official this morning. He is challenging the long reign of Prime Minister Lord George Hamilton. Lord Hamilton was unavailable for comment."

Stunned, Andrew stared blankly at the screen as the broadcast continued. Had his eyes and ears deceived him? Could that really have been Jordan announcing his intention to take a public office? "What would make him do such a thing?" he wondered as he thought about his long time companion. Icy fingers gripped his heart as he considered the implications of his agreement with Craven. Serious doubts assailed him. For the first time, he almost regretted his pledge. Buried deep in disturbing thoughts, it took several seconds for him to realize that the cook was hovering in the doorway. He smiled reassuringly at her.

"Is the basket all set, Lorraine?"

The cook shook her head. "That's why I came to seek you out. With all the rain, are you still going to have a picnic?"

Andrew turned to face one of the large rectangular windows. He barely could see through the torrent cascading in thick sheets across the panes. "Wow! We haven't seen a squall like that in a while. Has Miss Parker returned?"

The cook shook her head. Her eyes were uneasy as they met his.

His gaze sharpened. "She's probably lost her way in the storm. I'd better go check. Can you ask Grayson to dig up an umbrella for me?"

The cook agreed and bustled from the room.

Andrew headed towards the front door. Pausing to slip into fouled weather gear, he took the proffered umbrella as he pulled open the door.

The fierce wind sprayed water into his face. Despite his raincoat, he soon was soaked. With his heart beating erratically, he headed towards the cliffs. What if she had slipped on some wet stone and had fallen? As he neared the edge, the wind picked up and almost ripped the umbrella from his grasp. Deciding that the object was more of a hindrance than a help, he closed the apparatus and slung it over his arm.

Descending the steep path, he forced himself to go slowly while searching the shrubbery for any signs of a fallen hiker. Finally reaching the bottom, he stepped onto the sand. Behind him came a yell. Relieved, he turned and expected to see Victory taking shelter from the storm. Instead, a small girl in a drenched t-shirt and jeans stood under the overhanging rocks as she clutched a bedraggled white puppy in her arms.

He approached the weeping distraught child and bent down next to her. Both she and the dog were shivering. Slipping out of his raincoat, he fastened it around them while he asked, "What are you doing down here all alone?"

The girl gave him a grateful yet apprehensive look. "My dog and I were playing ball. Sugar got stuck on the rocks out there, " she pointed to a slight outcropping just visible above the rising tide. "The nice lady came and got her for me, but now she's stuck."

Panic replaced concern. He grabbed the child and started shaking her. She began crying again. The little dog growled at the threat to her mistress. Realizing what he was doing, Andrew forced his fingers to relax. Striving for control, he soothed the child.

"You must show me where the woman is stuck so I can help her. Can you do that?"

The girl nodded, placed the dog on the ground, and then started ahead of Andrew. At the water's edge, she stopped and pointed. Andrew's eyes narrowed as he attempted to peer through the shroud of mist and rain. Then, he saw her clinging tightly to a small protrusion of stones. As he watched, she turned. For a moment, he thought that she had seen him, but a wave smashed into her and drove her against the rocks. When the water receded, she was gone.

Terror gripped him as he dove into the surf. Swimming in powerful strokes, he sliced through the waves. He was heedless of the wind and surf that were trying to keep him from his goal. Gasping for breath, he reached the spot where she had vanished. Gulping air, he plunged under the waves. At first, he could distinguish nothing in the under-water gloom. Then, his vision cleared. He made out the shape of a woman being tossed about in the undertow. He grabbed her limp form and pulled her to the surface. Gasping for air, he broke the waves and began the arduous struggle back to the shore.

A light pierced the darkness as Victory struggled towards consciousness. She opened her eyes. The light danced, flickered, and finally shrank until it coalesced into the shape of a candle's flame. She was mesmerized as her eyes followed the light as it slowly withdrew. She struggled to shake off the shrouds of mist still clinging to her consciousness. Still groggy, she shook her head, but only became dizzy and fell through the black hole of oblivion.

Again, the light flickered. This time, it was accompanied by a faint sound. Her eyelids fluttered. She opened them to a darkness that was almost as complete as her dreams. Panic seized Victory and she immediately struggled into a seated position. Nausea gripped her and she slumped back against the pillows.

Her eyes scanned the darkness. Finally, she registered the dresser, vanity, paintings, and other objects scattered around her guest room. Her gaze eventually came to rest on a dark figure sitting in a chair next to the bed.

"Welcome back," said the marquis relieved.

"Have I been away?" she asked. She suddenly gripped the side of her head as a jolt of pain shot through her skull.

Andrew pulled her hand away when she began to probe the bandages. Slipping her hand into his, he said, "You could say so. You've been unconscious for several hours as a result of a nasty bump on the head. I assume that you have a concussion. Unfortunately, I have not been able to take you to the hospital for a thorough examination because the storm is too fierce and the electricity is out."

Despite the calm words, she could hear the anxiety in his voice. "But how did it happen?" she asked.

"You don't remember?" he asked anxiously.

She struggled to clear her mind of the cobwebs. Suddenly, she gasped. "Maggie! Is she all right?"

Stroking her hair, Andrew smiled. "Maggie and her dog are safely back at the inn with her parents. I sent Jack to drive her back as soon as we brought you home."

A shaft of lightening and crack of thunder drew her attention to the window. The rain still was cloaking the world with a wet blanket. For an instant, she thought that she glimpsed a figure in the darkness. She shivered convulsively as the memory of her ordeal came flooding back. Andrew moved to the bed, sat beside her, and pulled her against him.

"It's okay," he soothed as she wept. "It's all over now. You're safe with me," he crooned, while rocking her like a small child.

They sat that way for several minutes until Victory was lulled by the security of his embrace. Now that she was safe, the monotonous patter of the rain and the moaning of the wind were having a soothing effect. Victory laid her cheek against his warm chest. She could hear his heart beating. Suddenly overwhelmed by the need to revel in her renewed life, she raised her head to his and kissed his lips.

"I want you to make love to me," she whispered softly, as she searched his fathomless turquoise eyes.

Gently, he laid her back against the pillows. Kissing her lightly, he whispered, "I don't want to do anything to frighten you."

"I'll be more frightened if you don't," she said, as she stroked his cheek.

He captured her hand and pressed his lips to the inside of her palm. "I may become fierce in my passion."

Giving him a level look, she chuckled, "I think I can handle it."

He searched her face. His eyes rested on the bandages. "I'm not sure it is such a good idea in your condition."

She looked at him doubtfully and asked, "Andrew, are you sure my injury is the only reason? I'm beginning to think that you don't find me attractive."

"I would never want you to think that," he said huskily. His eyes turned a darker blue, as he used one finger to trace along her jaw line. As he began stroking her arms from her wrists upward, her breathing quickened. When he reached her shoulders, he gently pulled at the ties holding up her nightgown. The lacy fabric slipped down to her waist. His eyes probed hers for a long moment. Victory's heart raced at the fiery passion burning in their depths. Then, his gaze lowered. He consumed her exposed upper body with his eyes. She felt a tightening in her breasts as her nipples hardened under his gaze. His hands followed his line of vision. He cupped one breast in each hand as his thumbs lightly grazed the taunt peaks. His hands slid down her rib cage until they met the folds of her nightgown.

Pausing, he lifted his gaze back to her face. With her lids half-lowered, she stared back. The passion in his eyes reflected the glow in hers. Languorously, he slid the gown past her hips and down her legs. The material brought an erotic tingle as it slid along her sensitive skin. Completely exposed, she watched with anticipation as he stood to disrobe. Quickly divesting himself of the smoking jacket, shirt, and trousers, he was lying beside her in seconds. Leisurely, Victory perused the man beside her. His face was achingly handsome. In the soft glow from the fireplace, the planes and angles were cast into shadow. His eyes became dark aqua and his sensual lips curved in a slight smile as he waited for her to complete her inspection.

Victory's eyes lowered to the broad shoulders and muscled chest. As soft as down, a light matting of blonde hair spread across his broad chest. His upper torso gleamed in the firelight as the slight contractions of his chest muscles caused them to ripple under her probing fingers. Her gaze dropped lower to his smooth stomach, tapered hips, and long lean legs. Her examination paused at the proof of his arousal. Her eyes lifted to meet his.

Andrew's eyes crinkled at the corners, as he laughed softly. The sound flowed over her like a melody. "I hope this dispels any doubts you have about your attractiveness."

Pulling her into his arms, he held her tightly for a long moment against his lean frame. Tenderly, he kissed her hair, forehead, and each eyelid before taking possession of her lips. The kiss was gentle yet probing as he nipped at her lips and teased with his tongue. The kiss deepened, demanded, and then drew a primal response as their tongues intertwined. His hands began a sensual exploration of her body.

She was encased in a radiating warmth that spread from her center outward. Soon, it flowed through her entire body as it suffused her mind and brought her to heights of sensitivity that she never imagined. As if with a life of its own, her passion exploded, seized her body, and held it captive.

Sensing her desire kindled an answering spark in the marquis. His kiss deepened. His hands explored every inch of her body – sliding over her shoulders, her back, and her buttocks – and again moved upward to her breasts. Finally, his hand rested between her thighs. She moaned and arched against him as his fingers explored her inner warmth. Convulsively, her own hands came down to grip him and stroke him until he groaned.

Pushing her back, he showered her with kisses. His lips traced fiery paths down her throat and then returned to her mouth. Unable to restrain himself any longer, he leaned over and, with deliberate slowness, entered her. He slipped in only a fraction at a time while watching with pleasure as ecstasy transformed her face. Gently, he stroked in, then out – each time pushing a little further. As her breathing became more shallow, he quickened the pace until he was thrusting his entire length into her and driving harder with each stroke.

Suddenly, the stars collided and the world exploded. Victory arched her back while screaming his name as, with one final thrust, his life's juice poured into her. Clutching her close, he rode the rollercoaster of sensation. The world stood still and time had no meaning. His life was bliss; his destiny, this exquisite feeling of ecstasy. He was one with the woman and they were one with the universe. Together, they soared. They floated in space to that place where nothing mattered but their joy.

Descending through the clouds and drifting back to reality, he became aware of the sobs. Remorse gripped him. Lifting her face, he asked, "Did I hurt you?"

She blinked at him. Her eyes were wide and luminous with unshed tears. "No. It was just so glorious and so overwhelming. I've never experienced anything like that before."

Later, as they lay exhausted in each other's arms, she asked, "What is today's date?" He told her and she exclaimed, "The election is only a few days away. I need to go back and vote."

He was silent for a long time. Although letting her go back to a country that, at any day, could be in the grip of his ruthless half-brother was abhorrent, he could not think of a plausible reason to oppose it. Short of mental manipulation, he had little alternative but to let her go. Besides, since catching the broadcast about Jordan Rush, he had been determined to meet with his old friend to obtain an explanation about his sudden interest in politics. If his suspicions were correct, he would have to re-evaluate his promise to Craven. It certainly would be easier to deal with Jordan when he was free from distractions.

"I'll see to the arrangements tomorrow."

With great disappointment, Victory stiffened in his arms. She had hoped that he would protest her departure or offer to return with her. Reluctantly, she decided that the bond that their lovemaking had formed must have been one-sided. She tried to stifle the pain.

Thinking about the upcoming election reminded her of the portrait in the vampire book. "Whatever became of the book?" she asked in a cool voice.

Andrew frowned at the sudden aloofness. "Book?" he asked. He was perplexed.

"Yes," she continued, as she moved away and pulled on her robe. "I was reading a book when I went down to the beach. While rescuing the dog, I gave it to the little girl to hold for me."

"I don't know anything about it. Was it important? Maybe we can buy another one."

"It wasn't mine. I got it from your library."

"Then don't worry about it," he said, as he watched her closely.

"I'm not familiar with half of the books in that room and probably won't even miss it," he finished. He rolled out of bed and retrieved his smoking jacket.

She searched his face. "This one was about vampires."

He chuckled. "No wonder you're so distressed. Was it interesting?"

"Very," she said dryly, "especially the picture of your half-brother I saw in it."

His smile vanished. It was as if he had been turned to marble. The moon shone through the window and bathed him in an alabaster glow. "What do you mean?"

A chill swept down her spine as she looked into eyes that were as hard and lifeless as stone. She remembered the warning that he had given about frightening her. His present mood was much more intimidating than his lovemaking. Reliving the memory of being in his arms gave her the courage to continue.

She hesitantly explained, "I must have been mistaken. The man in the picture looked exactly like him, but his name was Raven. He was dressed in Elizabethan clothing and the book spoke about his reign of terror during the seventeenth century."

"Where is the book now?" he asked flatly.

Victory's uneasiness grew as Andrew continued to stand stark still while watching her as if her life hung on the response. She stood and tightened the sash of her robe. A wave of dizziness swept over her. She swayed slightly. Ignoring the impulse to climb back into bed, she leaned hard against the headboard.

Trying to appear casual, she shrugged. "I gave it to the girl to hold while I went for the dog. I suppose it's somewhere at the bottom of the Atlantic now."

He relaxed, his face broke free of the marble mask, and he smiled broadly. "Well," he said with relief, as he pulled her into his arms, "I'm sure that it was either an ancient relative or, more likely, someone who resembled my brother."

Victory smiled wanly. She wished that she could be as sure.

Chapter 12:

Craven's Victory

"Isn't this exciting?" asked Laura brightly. She jostled for a position next to her friend in front of the big screen television.

"I think we would have been better off watching the election results at home," replied Victory, as she surveyed the other occupants of the campaign headquarters. Dozens of tense and expectant campaigners sat or stood huddled around the oversized screen. They eagerly awaited the moment when they would hear that their candidates had 270 electoral votes. In anticipation of the victory, several had come equipped with streamers, noisemakers, and silly party hats. The group already had become overzealous with plenty of backslapping and cheering every time that a new state was added to their tally. Champagne flowed continuously as a steady stream of new arrivals constantly advanced into the room.

Victory delicately sipped her first glass of champagne and was sure that she was the only one in the room who still was sober. "Even Laura seems to be under the influence," she thought as she observed her friend's raucous cheering when their home state of Pennsylvania went to their side. "They should be having fun," she thought, "since most of the people in the room have worked hard during the past months. They have a right to enjoy the fruits of their labor." If it weren't for her concerns about Andrew and about her best friend's involvement with Craven Maxwell, she would be letting loose, too.

As if reading her thoughts, Laura turned to face her. "Did you speak to Andrew before you came?"

She lowered her glass. "Yes."

"And when is he coming back?"

"He's not sure," she admitted dully. "The business that he has to straighten out is taking longer than he thought. It seems that the person he needs to get in touch with is unreachable. At least, that's what he says."

Laura placed a hand on her arm. "You're not doubting him, are you?"

Victory stared into her glass. "I don't know what to think. We made love the night before I left," she admitted hesitantly. "Afterwards, when I mentioned having to come back, he didn't protest or even talk about wanting to come with me. He just calmly agreed to send me back."

"Well," said Laura, with her words slightly slurred, "he did say he had business to take care of."

"Yes, but what kind of business is the question. Oh, Laura, every time I ask him about his business, he gets so evasive that I'm beginning to wonder if he's not seeing someone else."

"You're in love with him, aren't you?" she asked, as she tried to focus on Victory's face.

Another loud cheer erupted from the crowd. It drowned out Victory's response, so she just nodded.

"Poor lamb," sympathized Laura, wrapping an arm around her shoulders. As she leaned closer, a man bumped against her arm. Laura's glass slipped and spattered its contents on Victory's dress before tumbling onto the carpet.

"Oh, Tory, I'm sorry," she cried. After throwing a fierce scowl at the retreating man's back, she inspected the damage. "We better try to get that out."

Victory nodded while following her to the bathroom. A few minutes later as they emerged into the hallway, she asked, "Do you think just putting water on it will be enough?"

"It will do until we get home," Laura assured her.

A door opened behind them. A melodious male voice stopped them. "Laura."

They turned in unison and saw an elegantly dressed Craven Maxwell hurrying towards them. A half dozen secret service men fanned out around him.

"Craven," Laura rejoined joyously, as she lightly kissed him on the cheek.

"Have I been gone that long?" he asked, while signaling for the men to disperse. He wrapped an arm around her waist.

Discreetly, Victory watched the agents slip unobtrusively into the crowd until she heard Laura asking, "When did you get here?"

He smiled down at her and said, "I just arrived."

"You look really sharp," she said, while admiring his tuxedo.

"This is my celebration outfit. When we are victorious, you and I will have our own private celebration."

"Speaking of victories, do you remember my friend, Victory Parker?"

"Yes, of course," he acknowledged, as he removed his hand from Laura's waist to shake hers. "Would the two of you care to watch the results from my office?" he asked, as he continued holding Victory's hand.

A tingling similar to a low-grade electric current coursed along her arm while he held her hand. Her mind went blank as the black eyes probed her. Laura laid a hand on his arm. With a final penetrating stare, he released her.

"We'd love to," Laura enthused.

"Yes, thank you," Victory gladly agreed. She felt claustrophobic at the thought of the crushing press of bodies in the main room.

"I don't mean to be rude," said Craven smoothly, "but it appears you have spilled something on your dress."

Chagrinned, she glanced down at her dress. "I'll join you in a minute," she said and turned towards the ladies' room.

"Don't bother," he said, as he took her arm. "I have some soda water in my office. That will take it right out."

Once inside, Craven made them comfortable, turned on the television, and offered them something to drink.

Laura eagerly accepted, but Victory, conscious of the drive home, refrained.

The politician walked over to a wooden cabinet and opened the door. Victory caught a glimpse of an unmarked bottle of reddish-brown liquid before he selected a bottle of wine. He poured the drink, pulled out a bottle of soda water and linen napkins, and settled himself on the loveseat next to Laura.

"May I say you ladies are looking quite beautiful this evening?" He smiled pensively down at Laura, who gazed back adoringly. "I like that color on you," he asserted, while running a finger lightly along one arm of the deep-rose silk dress. Then, his glance shifted to Victory. "Your dress is also quite becoming."

Wiping at the spots of champagne, she paused in her task long enough to bestow a sardonic glance in his direction.

"I'm sure it was quite lovely prior to the accident," he asserted diplomatically.

An enthusiastic reporter announced that only twenty more votes were needed to acknowledge Callahan and Maxwell as the winners. The incumbents needed fifty. It was still anybody's race.

Craven's attention strayed from the screen and returned to the woman across from him. "Are you still dating my brother?"

Victory paused. She was unwilling to disclose any private information, but felt compelled to respond. After all, what did it matter if Craven knew? It wasn't a secret and he was Andrew's brother. He was bound to find out sooner or later. "Maybe he already knows," she mused, while staring intensely at Laura.

"I was visiting Andrew at his home in Cornwall up until a few days ago. I left to come back and vote."

"Very patriotic," he said approvingly. He leaned against the back of the seat with one arm casually resting across the back. Laura leaned into his side and he dropped his hand to her shoulder. The proprietary gesture unnerved Victory. She felt as if Craven were demonstrating his hold over her roommate, but she dismissed the absurd notion.

"Did my brother return with you?" he asked disinterestedly as his eyes again flicked towards the television.

"No, he didn't," put in Laura indignantly. "Maybe you can shed some light on the matter, Craven. Does Andrew have any business associates in London?"

Victory was aghast at her friend's audacity and tried in vain to glare the other girl into silence.

The politician's eyes snapped back to her. Fear coiled around her like a boa constrictor. Craven thought for a long moment before answering. She thought that she detected a slight stiffening of posture. "Many," he answered. Leaning forward, he continued, "Maybe if you tell me the name," he said pleasantly, " I can be of more assistance."

Laura flashed a look of self-righteous vindication at her. The glance went unnoticed as Victory's gaze was caught and held by the mesmerizing onyx orbs. Entranced, she slowly shook her head.

"I'm sorry, but he didn't tell me who he was going to see. He said only that it was important and that he would join me after his business was finished."

"Are you sure you don't know the name?" he persisted. His eyes probed.

She suddenly felt lightheaded and slightly sick. Had she drunk more than she thought? "No, only that it was important."

"Important enough to risk sending his diurnal back unprotected," he thought suspiciously. He may regret that decision. "How long ago?" he asked in his silky and encouraging voice.

"He mentioned it several days ago, but, as of today, he still hadn't met with the party."

Satisfied, he leaned back again. "I wouldn't worry about another woman if that's what you're thinking. My brother is extremely loyal to those he cares about."

A loud cheer erupted from the other room. They quickly glanced at the screen. The election was over. "Hooray!" cheered Laura, jumping up excitedly.

Craven also stood and clasped her in his arms. "Thank you for your support," he said. He kissed her on the lips.

"Funny," thought Victory skeptically, "He doesn't seem very excited for a man who has just won the election. In fact, she realized that part of her uneasiness was due to an air of artificiality emanating from the politician. Then, he turned to her.

"Congratulations, Mr. Vice President," she volunteered, while holding out her hand.

"Thank you," he responded. "I will have to call John," he explained to Laura, "to see how he wants to handle the press. There will be the office party here to deal with, but, after all the necessities are over, you and I will have our own celebration. Will you wait here for me while I make my call?"

She nodded and then glanced perceptively at Victory.

Craven followed her gaze. "I would be honored if you would also stay, Victory."

As she started for the door, she shook her head. Being scrutinized by the politician had reminded her of the photo in the lost vampire book.

"Thank you, but no," she said uneasily. "I'm afraid I'm still suffering from jet lag and all the champagne is starting to give me a headache."

There was an awkward moment of silence that was broken by Laura. "While Tory was in England, she had an unfortunate accident that left her with a concussion."

Craven stared hard at the faint abrasion that still was swollen at her hairline. "Of course, you must go home if you are feeling ill. May I have one of my men escort you?" he offered solicitously.

She shook her head. "Congratulations, again. I'll see you when you get home," she said, while nodding at her friend. Mocking laughter echoed through her mind as she closed the door.

Chapter 13:

The Engagement

Nibbling a turkey sandwich, Victory sat at the kitchen table as she sifted through the mail. Bill. Bill. Bill. Aha! A coupon from her favorite department store. Smiling, she laid it aside in the "keep" pile, while gathering several other ads for the wastebasket. New clothes would be nice. Since Laura was dating the newly elected vice president, she would want to do some shopping. She separated the rest of the mail, while draining her glass of iced tea. On the verge of opening the newspaper, she paused. The front door creaked. A few seconds later, Laura appeared in the doorway. She was disheveled and her rose silk dress was wrinkled slightly.

"Good morning," she said. She pulled out a chair, fixed half-closed eyes on her friend, and stifled a yawn.

"Try 'Good afternoon'," Victory suggested, as she put the paper aside. "That must have been some party last night," she commented, while skeptically eyeing her friend. She still was uneasy whenever Laura spent lengthy periods with Craven Maxwell. Even though her intention had been to share Andrew's revelations with her roommate, the timing had never seemed right. After a few days, her fears seemed like part of another life: a fantasy full of castles, fairy tale princes, and romantic ideas. She began to doubt that any of it was real. As the days passed, so did her conviction that her concerns were justified.

"It certainly is – and last evening was fabulous!" the other girl agreed. Standing, she started the coffeemaker. After pouring a cup, she reseated herself and continued, "The volunteers were so riled up we never made it out of there. The last soul finally left around 3:00."

"I guess it would have been difficult to leave before the volunteers," she agreed. She secretly was relieved that they hadn't spent all of that time alone. "What did you do after they left?"

Laura airily waved her hand. Before she could give an accounting, Victory dropped the mail and grabbed her friend's hand. She stared in shock.

She slowly lifted her gaze to search her friend's glowing face.

Laura nodded at her friend's unspoken question. "He proposed right after you left. Oh, Tory, it was so romantic! He announced it on television during the victory speech."

Dazed, Victory could only nod.

She gazed in awe at the diamond, which was the size of a silver dollar. How many carats was the thing?

"Then, we went out to celebrate. I came back since I wanted to tell you before you saw it on television or in the newspaper."

Victory picked up the paper and opened it to the front page. The headline read: "Golden Boys Win It All." Below were two pictures. The first was of John Callahan giving his acceptance speech. Underneath was a photo of Craven slipping a diamond ring on an ecstatic Laura Warner's finger.

Oh, Tory," she cried, "Please say you'll be my maid of honor."

"Of course," she said numbly. " I am really happy for you if this is what you want."

Their eyes met and held. Theirs was a lifetime of intimacy providing unspoken understanding. "Tory, I know that you don't completely approve of Craven, but please try to like him for my sake."

Victory hugged her friend, but struggled to quiet her qualms. "All right," she conceded and was rewarded by her friend's sigh of relief. She was touched that her approval meant so much to Laura and vowed to try to be objective where her future husband was concerned. After all, she had no basis for her animosity. Inexplicable trepidation and hearsay allegations were hardly enough to condemn someone. If he could make her friend so happy, he had to have some good points. "When's the day?"

"Valentine's Day. Craven wants to wait until after the inauguration and thinks that day would be most appropriate. Isn't he romantic?"

"A smooth operator is more like it," she thought cynically. She could imagine the publicity that this kind of event would provoke. It was difficult to believe that the perspective groom wasn't going to capitalize on it.

She bent to retrieve her mail and tried not to show her true feelings. "Here is a letter from your mom," she said, as she handed it to her.

"I can't wait to tell her the news," she exclaimed excitedly, as she ripped open the envelope. "Can you imagine what Mom will say when she hears I am going to marry the vice president?"

Victory rustled the newspaper as she read the story. "They do get the news in Willow Grove, you know. I wouldn't be surprised if your mom called to lecture you for not telling her first. She's liable to be besieged by the local media." "For that matter, so will we," she mused silently, while watching her friend read her mom's letter. The gray eyes were troubled when she looked up from the page.

"Is everything all right?" she asked.

"I just can't believe it," Laura stated, after reviewing the letter. "According to my mom, my cousin, Ben, was arrested for embezzlement."

She reached across the table to squeeze her friend's hand. "If anyone in your family needs legal advice, I'm here for them," she said consolingly. Ben was Laura's favorite cousin. The three of them were about the same age and used to hang out together when they were children. She smiled fondly when she remembered the time that he had dumped one of the dead frogs from biology lab down her shirt. She had avenged herself by placing a cow's eye in his lunch box. The memory of the expression on his face when he opened his lunch almost made her laugh out loud. Shaking free of her reverie, she sobered.

"Thanks, but it appears that it's too late." Frowning, she continued to read, "According to this, he's already been tried and convicted. I don't understand this, Tory. Ben's always been so honest. My mom's explanation is very confusing. Obviously, she didn't understand the legal proceedings. From what I can gather, Ben was deep in gambling debts. He decided to go to some friends of a friend and borrow enough money to pay those debts. They charged astronomical interest rates. When it came time to pay them, Ben didn't have the money."

"Sounds like he got mixed up with some loan sharks."

Yes," she agreed and then sighed. "I don't understand it. Ben was never into those kinds of activities," she replied.

She put a comforting arm around Laura's shoulders. "It's been a long time and people change."

Laura stared at the letter and slowly began to shake her head. She sighed again. "It gets worse. When he couldn't come up with the money, the men threatened him, so he stole money from the company he was working for to pay them off. He got caught, pled guilty, and bargained for a reduced sentence of five years."

"Five years!" she exclaimed, "How much did he steal?"

Laura shook her head, "A lot. It's a shame, too, because I know Ben. In order for him to commit a crime, he must have been desperate. If only he had gone to my parents, they would have helped. Instead, he's going to prison." Her eyes brimmed, "Do you have any idea what happens in prisons?"

Victory did, but didn't want to provide details since reality undoubtedly was worse than her friend's imagination.

Suddenly, her face brightened. "I think I will ask Craven's advice," she stated, as she moved towards the phone.

"What can he do?" Victory asked doubtfully, "Provide a pardon?"

"I'll bet my cousin would be a prime candidate for Craven's new rehabilitation program. You know, the one where the criminals come out with their previous records expunged. My cousin is not a hardened criminal. If he committed a crime, I am sure he had his reasons," she staunchly defended. "He deserves rehabilitation and a chance to start over with a clean slate."

The prospect was appealing. Like Laura, she was inclined to give him the benefit of the doubt based on her knowledge of Ben's character. As she watched her best friend confidently dial the phone, she again wondered about the circumstances surrounding the case.

Chapter 14:
The Earl's Dilemma

"Damn," Andrew Gabriel exploded as he slammed the phone down and began pacing the floor of his London townhouse. This was the third time in as many weeks that he had received the same answer from both Jordan's home and office. The fact that he received similar explanations from both the butler and secretary only aggravated his annoyance. Frustrated, he raked his hand through his hair. Why did Jordan have to pick now to go on holiday? More importantly, where did he go and why was he being so reclusive? He considered visiting the office or home in person, but he doubted that it would do much good. Both parties were effusive when they discovered his identity, but were ignorant of any additional information. Obviously, Jordan did not wish to be disturbed.

When he left Tory at Heathrow, he had hoped that he would be joining her shortly. That prospect now was dwindling rapidly. At this rate, his business could drag out indefinitely. To make matters worse, he sensed an aloofness from Victory during their phone calls. That was not surprising since he had been evasive every time that she asked about his business. Deception was never his strong suit and he was sure that he had left the impression of doing something covert. That was true, but it was not what she suspected. Without a convincing explanation, how could he convince her that he wasn't seeing another woman?

He stopped in the center of the room. Desperately, he reached for his friend. Nothing. The sensation was like confronting a blank wall. Frustration at his helplessness tore through him as he confirmed his suspicions: Jordan's disappearance was deliberate. Andrew strode over to the window and parted the curtains. The misty rain condensed on the panes. The sky was a metallic gray. The somber weather suited his mood, as he stared disconsolately into the busy streets. People dashed through the rain, while sporting either umbrellas or raincoats. Cars sloshed along the wet roads and sprayed water as they charged through the puddles. A car splashed a young man waiting to cross the street. Andrew smiled as the angry young man shook his fist and yelled at the escaping vehicle.

Eyes still twinkling, he released the curtain and again faced the phone. As if on cue, the instrument rang. He snatched it up. "Hello," he said evenly.

"Andrew, is that you?"

The marquis let out a long sigh of relief. "Jordan, I didn't think you were ever coming back."

Jordan chuckled. "I could say the same thing about you."

Andrew laughed for the first time in three weeks. "It's good to hear your voice."

"Ditto."

He became more serious. "We have to talk."

"All right. How about lunch?"

"We can certainly do that, but it will be better if we talk first."

"I have an idea. Why not dine at my townhouse?"

"Okay. About half an hour?"

"Do you remember where it is?"

Andrew smiled, "If it's still in the same place. By the way, I just tried to reach you."

Jordan was contrite. "Sorry. My men didn't know where to reach me and, since I had no idea you would be searching..."

"Yes, I tried everything, but you were inaccessible."

"Like you said, we need to talk."

Thirty minutes later, the Rolls pulled up in front of the two-story brick townhouse. Andrew sat in the back seat and stared at his friend's home. It had been a long time since he had seen Jordan. He wondered if his former companion had changed. He smiled wryly. Probably not much. Staring at his reflection in a mirror, he wondered if time and experience had wrought changes on his countenance.

He approached the door. Before he could lift the knocker, the door was flung open. A tall, slender, dark-haired man with bright green eyes clasped his arm and almost yanked him off of his feet.

"Jordan," Andrew exclaimed, as he returned the embrace, "it is good to see you."

The green eyes twinkled merrily, but Andrew's intense scrutiny detected a soberness behind the superficial pleasure.

"Andrew, is it really you?" he asked, as he stepped back to arm's length.

He smiled. "In the flesh."

"It's been so long," Jordan remarked, as he closed the door and ushered him into the living room.

Andrew nodded as he surveyed the conservative but well-furnished room. The area was decorated in rich browns, tans, and creams. The plush carpeting and the drapes were a soft vanilla, while the furniture was upholstered in brown suede with tan throw pillows. The tables, chairs, and shelves were made of rich oak and a huge off-white marble fireplace took up one side of the room. On one case, Jordan had displayed knick-knacks and mementos from his travels. Approaching the case, Andrew lifted a small object.

Unfolding the painted silk fan, he said, "You still have this fan from Empress Kim?"

Jordan laughed, "That fan doesn't even begin to compare with your memento from her."

He continued his perusal, "And this," he said picking up a set of polished bagpipes. "Do you remember the foolish Scott who bet you his bagpipes that he could out play you?"

Jordan nodded, as he moved to an armchair by the fire. "Yes, I thought it was very unfair to take them since I had a rather long head start on his practicing."

Andrew's eyes crinkled at the memory. "Not half as unfair as when he challenged me to double-or-nothing to get it back."

Jordan smiled as he remembered. "Ah, yes. By the time you were through with him, he was kiltless, as well. Do you still have the trophy?"

Andrew sat across from him on the brown suede sofa. "Yes, as a matter of fact, I do. You and I had some good times traveling."

The other man concurred and then rose. Walking to a sideboard, he pulled out a bottle and two healthy drafts of reddish-brown liquid. Handing one to his companion, he sat while sipping the contents and watching the blonde beyond the rim of the glass.

Andrew leaned forward with his arms folded across his legs. "Jordan," he asked in a firm tone, "why are you running for prime minister?"

The understanding reflected in the turquoise eyes belied the harshness of his words. Jordan sensed that the answer was at least partially expected. "Why did you leave so much time between your revival and your contact?" he countered. Before he could answer, Jordan continued, "For several years after you came out of your self-imposed hibernation, I tried to contact you. Every time, I was met with a blank wall. No one I asked knew your whereabouts, so finally I stopped trying. The frustration you have been going through the past few weeks is a smaller scale of what I went through for several years."

The seeds of anguish planted in the green eyes softened the sting of his accusation. Andrew leaned back and sighed. Flinging one arm across the sofa, he stared at the fire while he sipped his drink. The rain that had been a steady drizzle began in earnest.

"It is true," he conceded, "that, even after my revival, I maintained isolation. The reason was entirely selfish and, if by doing so, I did you a disservice, I do apologize."

Jordan nodded his acquiescence. "Many years ago, Craven came to me with a plan. He would not tell me all the details – probably because he knew I would be opposed to them. He did tell me, however, that he planned to run for office in the United States and he wanted me to do the same here."

"Why you?" Andrew interrupted, "Surely, he would have been better off with one of his own followers."

"I pointed that out to him. He insisted that I was the best candidate because of my status, reputation, and popularity in this country. When I refused and pointed out our policy of non-interference, he laughed and stated that he was instituting his own policies. When I still objected..." his eyes dropped, "Well, once my attempts to contact you failed, I had no choice."

Andrew inhaled sharply. "He forced you?" he demanded. His eyes blazed. "How dare he?" he asked incredulously.

"Craven has dared a lot since you have been gone," he asserted quietly.

He contemplated these revelations and then asked with a calmness that belied his inner turmoil, "What are his plans?"

Jordan shook his head. "I don't know the details. Your return seems to have made a slight alteration in his plans. He originally planned to wait until he had everything in place and then run for president. Now, he fears your influence and has altered his course of action. His ultimate goal is to set our own people up as heads of the primary world countries. I," he said, while grimacing, "am not one of the chosen, so I am not privy to the details. Also," he added, "I don't know if this is relevant, but he has been doing a lot of research into our history."

The marquis' eyes narrowed as he gazed into the fire. He thought about how much he should confide. Finally, he said, "Altering his plans makes no sense since I gave him my word I would not interfere."

Jordan scoffed, "That agreement between the two of you was reached only recently. You agreed after Craven had already spent years putting everything in place. Besides, even without your direct interference, many of us would oppose Craven as soon as it was discovered that you were back in circulation. I am not the only malcontent who had to be forced to cooperate. Craven is well aware that many would turn to you at the slightest sign of encouragement. He has only a very small core group that is completely loyal. He also has a few who are being coerced and most of the others are neutral. If a serious conflict arises, the majority – who are not comfortable with the thought of being exposed – will abandon the cause and recede back into anonymity."

"And you have no idea how he is going to accomplish his goal," he asked with a sick feeling in his stomach? He also didn't know what relevance the research had, but stopping his brother's schemes was his top priority. He cursed himself for not questioning his brother about the research when he had the chance. Maybe if he had appeared more interested at the time, Craven would have been forthcoming.

"No, other than it will probably be soon. He's already placed porphyrians in the top leadership positions throughout most of the first-world countries." He rattled off a list that caused Andrew's stomach to tighten into knots.

"England and America are the final two on the list."

His blood ran cold as he considered the implications. "That would make sense." Extending his hand, he said, "Jordan, you have to resign."

Jordan clasped his hand as if clinging to a lifeline. "I can't," he said in a strangled whisper, "Craven has overruled my will. The only way I can refuse is if you forbid it."

He blanched. "You know how I feel about using influence."

The green eyes were steady. "Still, it's the only way." Unconvinced, Andrew wavered. Jordan continued more stridently, "You have the authority. If you are going to stop him, you can't be afraid to use it. Besides," he said more gently, "you wouldn't be forcing the issue. I am already opposed to interfering in diurnal politics."

Andrew stared long and hard into his friend's eyes. Finally, in a voice that was flat but firm, he stated, "Jordan Rush, I forbid you to run for the office of prime minister or to become involved in diurnal politics in any other way."

Rolling his eyes, Jordan mocked, "How many of those Lon Chaney movies have you been watching since you returned?" Suddenly, he sobered. "Have you been out so long you no longer possess the ability?"

Andrew cocked a brow. "Now, who is being melodramatic? If I hesitate, it is only out of fear of harming you," he said seriously.

Jordan opened his mouth to respond, but suddenly was speechless. His head pounded. The marquis' image expanded, contracted, and expanded again. Dizziness swept over him while black spots danced in front of his eyes. Sweat soaked his clothing while chills covered his skin. Violent tremors seized his body while a second wave of dizziness and nausea overcame him. Several minutes later, he propped his elbow on the floor and shook his head. Looking into the concerned face of his friend, he tried to smile.

"What happened," he asked weakly with a mouth as dry as cotton.

"You passed out."

Jordan groaned and pulled himself back into the chair.

Chagrinned, Andrew responded, "Sorry. The hold was stronger than I expected, but the influence is gone now." Picking up his wineglass, he toasted, "To your political retirement."

Jordan saluted, "I'll drink to that."

Chapter 15:

Race Against Time

Victory barged through the door of her townhouse and kicked her shoes off. Dropping her briefcase on a nearby table, she paused to listen. From the living room came the sounds of the 6:00 news. Entering the room, she found Laura slumped on the sofa. She had a blanket pulled up to her chin and a box of Kleenex at her side. The gray eyes flicked towards her as she approached. A wan smile wavered and then vanished in a fit of coughing.

Victory gently patted her friend's back until the coughing subsided. "You look worn out," Laura commented, while sniffling.

"I am," she admitted and flopped into a chair. I just finished defending a man accused of embezzling company funds to pay his bills."

"Sounds familiar."

Victory smiled wryly as she swept a hand through her golden hair. "It did remind me of your cousin's situation. Did you get any news?"

"Yes." She tried to stifle a sneeze. "Craven was sympathetic and agreed to intervene."

Victory wondered about the odd tone in her voice, "That was very good of him," she offered cautiously. "I'm going to make some soup. Would you like some?"

"No, thanks. I'm not hungry."

"You really are sick," she said. She was getting even more concerned about her friend.

Laura shrugged. Her eyes were dull. "I started to feel lousy halfway through the day and came home a couple of hours early."

"Do you need anything?"

Laura shook her head and Victory turned towards the kitchen. As she passed by the television, she paused. The London scenery reminded her of Andrew. Anything about England intrigued her and made her wonder when she and the British lord would be reunited.

"Britons were shocked today when Jordan Rush," the reporter stated while indicating a handsome dark-haired man in the background, "announced his resignation from the race for Prime Minister. A nomination he accepted only a few weeks ago." The reporter broadcasted with a note of professional confusion. "When asked the reason for his sudden change in plans, the Earl stated that family concerns prevented his running at this time. Queries about future political plans were ignored."

In an airport lounge at LaGuardia's International Airport, the Marquis of Penbrook sat tensely staring at the television while he stirred his cocktail. He lifted his glass towards the screen. "Right on schedule," he thought, while being both amused and annoyed. It wasn't Jordan's fault that his flight had been delayed and rerouted. He also couldn't blame him for becoming unavailable. Better that than having Craven discover the news prematurely. "Yes," he thought sardonically, "we planned everything so perfectly." He started to slip from the stool, but then slowly sank back down. The news had turned to national politics. He was fascinated as he stared at a smiling John Callahan who recited a portion of his victory speech. The president-elect then handed the microphone to Craven. Astonished, Andrew felt his stomach tighten as he watched his brother announce his engagement. He drained the contents of his glass and then slammed it so hard that the bartender jumped.

He checked his watch and realized that he was still on London time. Glancing at the wall clock, he cursed. He should have been back in Washington hours ago. Where was Craven now? Had he seen the news? What was he thinking? More importantly, what was he doing? Andrew tried again to contact him, but, as with Jordan, he encountered only blackness.

In his Bethesda mansion, Craven Maxwell sat and stared at the television. The London scenery vanished and was replaced by the city streets of the capital and then by the local news, but he didn't notice. Slowly, he squeezed the glass in his right hand until it shattered. Untroubled by the shards of crystal cutting his hand or the liquid drenching the carpet, he jerked upright and strode angrily to the phone. Placing the overseas call, he waited impatiently for the line to be connected.

"Hello," answered a voice tinged with a British accent.

"This is Craven," he ground out. Silence. Then he asked calmly, "What is the meaning of this?"

Jordan replied just as calmly, "If you saw the news, then you know."

"I ordered you to run for prime minister."

"And Andrew forbade it."

"Andrew," he said menacingly, "He broke his promise."

"I believe the terms of your agreement pertained to not interfering in your plans, not mine."

Craven's eyes narrowed. "So that is his justification. When did you see him?"

" I had lunch with him yesterday."

"How much did you tell him?"

"As much as I knew."

"Which fortunately wasn't much. " Then, he thought, "Andrew will pay for this interference." He said nothing else aloud. There was no sense in giving Jordan a chance to tip him off. "You realize you are no longer of use to me in that capacity."

Jordan breathed a sigh of relief. "I certainly hope not."

Craven growled, "However, you can still be useful. I want you to go to Andrew and stay with him while he is here. You will watch him for me and, when asked, provide reports on his activities. And Jordan," he added meaningfully, "I will be very annoyed if you are indiscreet regarding this assignment."

Jordan began to sweat. "I refuse to play that role," he said adamantly.

"You don't have a choice," he replied harshly and hung up.

Jordan rang the doorbell of Andrew's London townhouse. A tall distinguished man in pleated gray trousers and matching long-tailed jacket admitted him.

"Hello, Grayson."

The butler nodded. "Good day, my lord. "Lord Gabriel has already departed for the States."

"I am aware of that. I need his address in Washington."

"Very good, sir," said the man, who speculatively eyed him.

Jordan waited in the foyer while the elderly butler slowly ascended the spiral staircase. With trepidation and a heavy heart, he turned his back on the stairs and gazed out of the front window. Oblivious of the rain sweeping across the streets, he wondered how he could pull off such a deception and betray the man who was almost a brother.

As he waited, he wandered aimlessly down the hallway. Grayson seemed to be taking a long time. Could it be possible that Andrew had left in such a hurry that he had forgotten to leave it? Hope surged through the earl, who was in no hurry to begin his assignment.

Too nervous to stand, he turned and paced the length of the adjoining hallway. Portraits of ancestral Gabriels lined the paneled walls. He studied the pictures. Several bore a direct resemblance to the marquis. Jordan remembered Andrew's father and grandfather. They had been great leaders, kind to their loved ones, ruthless to their enemies. The next portrait showed a striking woman with hair as dark as a raven's wing and eyes the color of sapphires. She was smiling broadly at the artist. Her eyes glittered with happiness. Adorned in a long gown of red velvet, she held a large black cat in her lap. Stunned by the sheer beauty of the woman, he stared with fascination into her finely sculptured features. He was confident that he was looking at the only visual record of the last Marchioness of Penbrook.

Ready to retrace his steps, he suddenly stopped. A solitary portrait was partially concealed in shadow. Like a magnet, he was drawn towards the picture until he stood only inches away. The woman was in her early twenties and was as strikingly fair as the marchioness was dark. She also wore an adoring expression and broadcast a look of joy. The portrait lifted his spirits while the contagious love of life that was reflected in the face communicated with his soul. Entranced, he continued to stare at the portrait. Familiar with most of Andrew's past and present relatives, he was sure that this young lady was not a Penbrook.

Unable to delay any longer, he reluctantly turned back towards the foyer and walked towards the bottom of the stairs. Shortly, the butler reappeared and started his descent. Jordan's heart sank as he recognized the marquis' address book. Glancing down at the open page, he silently accepted the book. After he nodded, he scribbled the address on a slip of paper and tucked it into his pocket. He handed the address book back to the butler and allowed Grayson to usher him out of the door.

Confused, Jordan covertly observed his friend for a few moments.

Andrew appeared to be on a plane, but he should have been in Washington hours ago. "Craven called," he announced.

Andrew's hand froze on the page of the airline magazine. He snapped it shut and then carefully replaced the travel book in its pocket. Reclining in his chair, he closed his eyes.

Jordan was jolted by the fear emanating from his cousin. The intensity of the reaction seemed disproportionate to the situation. After all, Andrew had no need to feel intimidated.

His suspicion was confirmed by the marquis' next thoughts.

"What did he say?" he asked grimly.

The cab pulled up in front of Heathrow and the earl paled, which caused a porter to glance at him in alarm as he hastily divested him of his luggage. He ached with the need to warn his friend, but was forced to remain silent. Raking a hand through his chestnut hair, he thought quickly.

"He ranted and raved for a while, but then decided that I was of no further use to him in that capacity." His relief was evident as he reviewed the conversation.

Andrew agreed that Jordan's decision to leave the country was probably a wise idea. "By doing so, you won't be available for Craven's use if he thinks of an alternative plan."

Jordan winced. "What do you mean?"

"Did he threaten you?" he asked tensely.

Relieved to be able to tell the truth, Jordan vigorously shook his head. A woman sitting across the aisle eyed him warily, picked up her child, and moved closer to the gate.

Sensing the marquis' withdrawal, he ventured hesitantly, "Andrew, I'm coming to Washington."

Startled, Andrew sat up. "This is not a good time," he protested sharply, as the lights of the capital came into view. "I have other concerns that take priority and I can't afford to have any distractions."

"I'm already on my way. Besides, I may turn out to be an asset," he asserted with feigned confidence.

He sighed, "If you are eager enough to walk into the lion's den, that's your business. I could use the support," Andrew admitted with deep resignation. "Be forewarned. This is going to be no picnic. The stakes are high and the game is going to get rough."

Jordan broke contact as he walked towards the runway. He was unaware of the smile that the flight attendant bestowed on him as she settled him into his first-class accommodations. However, he did accept the cocktail with enthusiasm. "Let's not keep the other players waiting," he thought, as he drained the contents of the glass.

Chapter 16:

Forfeit

Dana stood at the second floor window of Willow Grove Crematorium. She watched distractedly as the first fluffy, white snowflakes of the year fell from the sky. Behind her, she could hear the slight rustling of fabric and muffled treads as the others entered the room. Focusing on the business at hand, she turned, walked to the head of the conference table, and took her seat. Thomas strode in, paused briefly, and took a seat further away. Their eyes met. He raised his brows as he glanced at the empty place beside her, but said nothing. "Good," she thought. As usual, she could rely on Thomas' loyalty.

She folded her hands on the table and waited for the others to be seated. Startled stares greeted her as she swept her gaze around the table. Walter opened his mouth, stared hard for a few seconds, and then snapped it shut.

"Good evening. There are several items to be discussed this evening, but the first order of business is the announcement that my father..." she emphasized the words as she studied their faces. Most appeared expectant until her glance rested on Jason. His blank stare caused a qualm of uneasiness. Refusing to let them sense her discomfort, she continued boldly, "has decided that it is too risky for him to be personally involved in the project at this level. From now on, I will be in charge of direct operations. Since contact from his daughter is unlikely to arouse suspicion, I will report to him and disseminate instructions from him." "A position that I reluctantly undertake," she thought, while eyeing Jason warily. He would have been the better choice, not just because of his experience and unquestioned authority, but also because she had been fighting the wanderlust that had plagued her. "There is no doubt that Daddy has sensed my restlessness and this responsibility is probably his way of keeping me bound to the project," she brooded. She allowed Jason to access this last thought.

She shrugged as she continued to eye Jason. The decision was made and that was an end to the matter. He inclined his head and she relaxed. "From now on, you will all answer to me. Any questions?"

Silence. She smiled briefly. "Good. Then let us proceed. Thomas, would you please give us your report."

The fair-haired man glanced around the table. He said, "Everything in the penal rehabilitation center is proceeding as planned. We should have our first set of successfully rehabilitated prisoners within the next few weeks. The transition is going smoothly and the staff is enthusiastically embracing the new administration's reforms." Grinning, he proclaimed, "At this point, we are ready to ingest our first group of reformees."

Chuckles reverberated around the table at his choice of words. Even Dana smiled slightly as she nodded for him to continue.

"Only ten for the first batch since it is a test group. They are scheduled to begin in about two weeks."

Dana steepled her fingers, "I assume you will be personally supervising the project?"

Green eyes sparkling, he nodded. "Every step of the way."

"Make certain that you choose only those inmates who have a minimal number of friends and family connections. After all, we don't want to raise suspicions by leaving a lot of loose ends in the way. There might be problems if loved ones try to find out information about their locations after they are released."

Thomas nodded. "We're very specific about our requirements."

A petite woman with dirty blonde hair and hazel eyes asked, "What kind of inmates are they: first-time offenders or hardened criminals?"

Thomas shrugged, "It doesn't matter for our purposes, but, if we use major offenders, it will be a harder sell to society. The voters will probably not approve of hardened criminals being given a second chance while they foot the bill."

Several of them nodded in agreement as Thomas finished his report. Dana's attention shifted to Walter. "How about in the drug treatment facilities?"

"Everything is progressing well. I think we should have our first group within twelve weeks."

Finally, she faced Jason. Silently, they glared. The air vibrated between them with tension and unspoken challenge. She lifted her chin slightly and his brooding expression softened.

"We have begun in about forty major cities," he replied to her unspoken question. I believe we should have the buildings constructed and operational by summer. Since it is the intention of the vice president to use the next few months to ascertain local effectiveness before incorporating his program nationally, I don't see any reason why we shouldn't be ready by then."

"What about the Marquis of Penbrook?"

Dana's eyes snapped to the face of a beautiful auburn-haired woman with eyes as large and dark as her own. "Did you have a question?" she asked coldly.

Not intimidated, the redhead glared back. Thoughts tumbled and clashed as past rivalries were revived. "That was a long time ago," Amanda thought, "A lot has changed since then."

"Yes," Dana mentally agreed guardedly.

"Well," said Amanda aloud, "we all know that Jordan has withdrawn from the race for prime minister. We are all aware that Jordan was never loyal to the cause, but the strength to defy Craven on the issue could have come from only one source." Several heads nodded in agreement. "I would like to know what is being done to prevent future interference."

Staring into the expectant faces gathered around the table, Dana wished that she knew the answer. A shiver raced down her spine at the thought of direct confrontation with the marquis. To cover her doubt, she pierced the other woman with a disdainful glare. "My father has the situation under control, but, if you prefer, I can explain your concerns and let him dispel your fears personally."

Amanda's defiance dissipated. With her eyes downcast, she mumbled uncomfortably, "I just wanted to be certain we wouldn't be jeopardized."

"Your concerns are noted." Abruptly, she rose. "This meeting is adjourned."

After the others had filed past, a hand settled on her shoulder. Lifting her eyes, she smiled weakly.

"Another headache?" Thomas asked softly.

She glanced around before answering.

"They've gone."

She nodded. Trust Thomas to pick up on her hidden thoughts.

"Do you have any idea what is causing them?"

She did, but was not about to explain.

"I just hope they don't become a hindrance."

She scowled. Her bracelets tinkled as she pushed him away. "Is it my position you covet under the guise of concern?"

"I covet something more than your position."

She resisted, but, if he distracted her from the pain, even for a little while, the diversion was welcomed.

As the white Rolls shrieked to a halt, Andrew catapulted through the door, up the steps, and into the foyer. He brushed past the startled butler, while tossing several orders over his shoulder as he raced up the stairs. Spying the housekeeper in the hallway, he paused.

"Is my guest settled?" he asked.

Fear tore through him when she frowned. He brushed past her and flung open the door – only to be confronted by the empty room. Desperately, he jerked open the closets and then yanked open the drawers. Empty. All empty.

"Martha," he bellowed.

Martha winced, dropped the coverlet on the bed, and hastened towards the master bedroom.

She hesitated at the doorway. Seldom had she seen her employer in such a state. "Is anything amiss, Lord Gabriel?"

The anguish on his face made her heart ache.

"Where's Jake?" he rasped.

The intense turquoise eyes bore into her. She felt slightly dizzy and disoriented. "He's not here," she said. She had to put a hand on the dresser to steady herself.

The marquis strode over to the phone. He jabbed the keypad and gripped the receiver so tightly that his knuckles turned white.

"Hello?"

"Jake, where the hell are you?"

"Following the girl."

"You weren't supposed to follow her. You were supposed to bring her here."

"Yeah," he coughed, "That might be a little difficult," he said, as he scanned the crowded shopping district.

"Why?" the marquis exploded.

He cleared his throat, "Because I lost her." He started to explain,

"She went into this crowded shopping area."

The marquis clicked the receiver and redialed. "Hi, Laura. It's Andrew. How are you?" He listened, nodded, and then replied, "Yes, you sound pretty bad. I hope you're better soon." He paused again and then asked casually, "Is Victory home?" He listened for a few more seconds and then asked with feigned calmness, "Have you seen my brother lately?"

"So, this Victory woman is the reason for your frenzy."

Andrew swung round to stare at his cousin. He ran a hand through his hair as he let out an explosive breath. "You sure arrived quickly." He held up a hand to forestall explanations. Then, he turned his attention back to the phone call. "Please have Victory call me as soon as she gets in." Jordan continued to gaze at him steadily. So, with a weak smile, he explained. "Jordan, my friend," he said, as he replaced the receiver, "I am trying to outrun the devil. Craven and I had an agreement that as long as I refrained from interfering in his plans, he would not interfere with my personal life."

The earl was shocked. "How could you make such a promise knowing what's at stake?" he asked incredulously.

Andrew made no response, but Jordan discerned the answer. "You're in love with her."

Andrew nodded curtly. "I chose Victory over Craven's plans."

"Are you sure you made the right choice? That's a lot to risk for the sake of one woman. I hate to be blunt," he continued doggedly, "but it's a huge chance to take, especially for a woman whose life will be over far before the long-term effects of Craven's schemes are realized."

Andrew paused. Jordan was his lifelong friend. It was important that he understand. "Yes," he said gravely, "this woman means more to me than anything else."

He stood still for a moment while allowing access to his thoughts. Jordan's eyes widened in dawning comprehension. "She's responsible for your revival."

He stared back bleakly. "For her sake, I bargained with the devil and, even though I cheated at the game, I'm not willing to forfeit. Do me a favor," he called, as he raced down the stairs, "Wait here for Jake in case he manages to find her."

"What did the woman, Laura, say?" he asked worriedly, as he followed the marquis down the stairs.

The rays of the setting sun cast a burnished glow on his golden hair and turned the strands into a fiery halo as he turned in the doorway. "She said Tory wasn't home from work yet. Craven is out of town, but expected back today. She is expecting Victory any minute. If I'm lucky, I will get there before Craven. If she calls while I'm gone, tell her I'm on my way," he tossed over his shoulder.

Sneezes and hacking coughs greeted Victory as she opened the front door. The whipping wind tried to rip the door from her grasp. Leaning hard, she finally pushed the latch into place. Quickly, she crossed to the sofa. Laura lay covered by a blanket, with her face flushed and eyes closed. Victory placed her wrist on her friend's forehead. Scorching heat burned her skin.

Wagging a stern finger at her friend, she admonished, "You need to go to a doctor."

Laura groaned. Slowly opening her eyes, she nodded. "Tomorrow," she croaked.

Taken aback by her friend's agreement, Victory was really alarmed. "And I am going to drive you there myself to make sure you go."

Laura threw a rebellious look at her and then closed her eyes.

"What will Craven think if he comes back from his trip and finds you have not been taking care of yourself?"

Laura considered. "Since he told me to take care of myself while he was away, he wouldn't be too thrilled, I guess." Suddenly, she blurted, "Oh, Tory, Andrew called a little while ago. He's back and wants you to call him."

Victory went numb. Standing stark still, she stared blindly out of the window for several moments. Shaking her head, she returned her attention to Laura. "I will when I get back. Right now, I'm going to get you some medicine," she asserted, as she pulled on her gloves. "I'll be back in a little while. Do you need anything before I leave?"

Glazed eyes stared feverishly back at her. Laura shook her head as she drifted off to sleep. Victory headed for the front door. "I think you should call him," Laura mumbled drowsily. "He sounded," she paused, "anxious."

Victory hesitated. Should she call? If he wanted to tell her that he had found someone else in England, the ordeal could wait until she returned. "I should only be gone for about half an hour. I'll leave the cellular on in case you need me."

Chapter 17:
The Conspiracy

The moon cast an eerie glow over the dingy tavern on the northwest side of town. The tall gaunt man stood in the doorway while scanning the dimly lit interior. Smoke made his eyes water while the stench of stale sweat mixed with alcohol made his nose twitch.

He narrowed his eyes. Snatches of conversation bombarded him. He found the press of humanity oppressive and repulsive. Contemptuously, he glared at the boisterous clusters of people as they sat, chattered, and drank in order to annihilate the pain and frustration of their mundane lives.

Abruptly, he was jostled as a rowdy group of college students pushed past. Caught off guard, he swayed slightly.

"Hey, man, are you a statue or what?"

Slowly, the man turned towards the belligerent voice. A youth of about twenty with the frame of a football player and the red face and bloodshot eyes of a drunk glared back with open hostility.

"Frank is on one of his Friday-night-fight binges," murmured one of the students to his girlfriend.

Frank was surprised to be at eye level with his opponent. At six feet four inches, not many men could look him in the eye. "Kind of scrawny, though," he thought. He was disappointed. After the fight that he had just had with Jenny, he needed a way to blow off steam. This guy didn't look like much of a challenge. "I can't back down now," Frank thought, as he glanced towards the expectant faces of his friends. His reputation was at stake.

He reached for the other man's collar. His hand froze in midair. Those eyes were like shards of glass piercing his brain. Suddenly, he turned and ran. He burst through doors and knocked people aside in his frenzied flight.

The other students looked at each other in bewilderment. Shrugging, they followed their friend. As they left the bar, one turned back to study the tall man. He stood, as before, like a hawk searching a field for its prey. Hastily, he followed his companions.

"Safe," Frank thought, as he collapsed to his knees in the parking lot. "Safe," he thought, as the vomit spewed onto the asphalt. Safe? He realized that he would never be safe again. As he laid his head against the cool metal of the car's door, tears of despair slid down his face.

Continuing his search, the gaunt man finally located his quarry. A small wiry man sporting a black turtleneck sweater was seated at a far table. Deep in shadow, he still was able to discern the cigarette dangling out of the corner of his mouth and his hands cupped around the frosted mug of ale. Slicing through the throng, he maneuvered his way to the table.

An elongated shadow fell across the hardwood table. The wiry man glanced up and sported a cocky grin that spread across his face. Their eyes locked. The grin froze. He shivered as the reptilian stare chilled his blood. Hastily withdrawing his hand, he lowered his arm and waved at the chair across from him in order to cover his confusion. Jason sat, but did not unbutton his dark overcoat or engage in idle conversation. The stony expression never wavered as he came directly to the point.

"You have been selected for three reasons: one, your reputation as the top in your field; two, your mercenary qualities; and three, your personal profile. Your profile suggests that you may have an added incentive for participating in the project. If any of these facts are inaccurate, please say so now and the transaction will be terminated." "...along with your life," he thought, as he coldly appraised his companion.

The man downed his drink, tugged on his Baltimore Orioles' cap, and ran his hand down his two-day razor stubble. "I would say that is an accurate assessment. Why don't you just tell me what you want and, depending on the circumstances, I can let you know what it will cost ya."

Jason's eyes bore into his and the other man knew genuine terror for the first time in his life. "Your assignment and the first half of your payment are inside," he said, as he indicated the briefcase that he had set by the chair. You will have 24 hours to decide whether or not to take the job. If not, give the briefcase back to the bartender tomorrow night. If you agree, meet me here tomorrow at the same time." He stood. "If you mention this to anyone or decide to skip out with the money, there will be dire consequences."

The wiry man blinked. When he reopened his eyes, he was alone. He stood, lifted the briefcase, and carried it to one of the upstairs rooms. A low whistle escaped his lips as he popped the latch and stared at the $100 bills banded in thick stacks covering the interior of the case. He pulled out one stack and thumbed through it as he listened with stupefied pleasure to the crackling of the new bills. Inside the briefcase was a pocket containing a newspaper clipping. The caption read, "Wonder Man Wins Election." Below was a picture of a smiling John Callahan waving to a cheering crowd as he gave his victory speech. Again, he whistled. Pulling out another Camel, he lit it and sat back. He looked from the clipping to the money several times. Making up his mind, he pulled out his lighter and held it under the clipping. A crooked smile curved his lips as the picture blackened and then turned to ash.

"Damn it," Andrew cursed, as he tried to maneuver the silver Mercedes through the rush-hour traffic. Being stuck for the past half-hour in a continuous onslaught of tangled cars and snail-paced traffic had almost shattered his nerves. While he waited impatiently for the police to clear the backup from an accident that was blocking the highway, he imagined all kinds of calamities. Why hadn't he had the foresight to insist that Jordan wait until he returned to Victory's side before resigning. He would have been better able to protect her. Instead, she was left vulnerable while he was trapped in a traffic jam. He pounded the steering wheel and then punched the redial on his cellular. Her line was still busy. Twenty minutes later, he finally passed by the obstruction. His tires squealed in protest as he peeled down the asphalt.

Laura rose to a sitting position on the sofa and frowned as the doorbell chimed again. "Victory must have forgotten her key," she assumed. Pushing aside the heavy wool blanket, she slowly stood up. A wave of dizziness overcame her and caused her to bump against the end table, which dislodged the phone. Maybe Victory had been right about the doctor. Leaning against the wall for support, she staggered towards the door.

Victory pushed her key into the lock. To her surprise, she easily could push it open. She was sure that she had closed it firmly behind her when she left. Confused, she stepped inside and firmly pushed it shut. The apartment was quiet and still. She cocked her head while listening intently. "Laura must be sleeping in her room," she thought, as she headed for the kitchen. As soon as she deposited the bag of groceries on the counter, she tugged off her coat, laid it across the back of a chair, and tiptoed to her best friend's room. She knocked softly on the closed bedroom door. She waited for several seconds, decided to forestall waking her friend, and headed back down the hall. She placed all of the soups except one into the cupboard and then extracted a bottle of cough syrup. "Chicken noodle soup and cherry cough syrup. What a combination!" she thought, while grimacing. After putting the soup on to heat, she shook the bottle as she headed purposefully towards Laura's bedroom. Squaring her shoulders, she knocked on the door and steeled herself for what lay ahead. Laura wasn't exactly cooperative when it came to medical treatment. Maybe she should have put the medicine in the soup. It would have been easier than the upcoming ordeal. With her cold, she probably wouldn't have noticed.

Pushing open the door, she sighed. Ever since their childhood, Laura had obstinately refused to seek medical assistance or take antidotes for illness. Victory always had to beg, bribe, and threaten her friend. Even when they were college students and Laura had strep throat, Victory was forced to trick her into going to the doctor. She still could remember Laura's consternation when they pulled up in front of the doctor's office instead of the movie theater.

Stunned, she just stood there while frowning at the Laura-less room. Turning, she retraced her steps down the hallway. As she searched each room, her concern mounted. Where was she? In her condition, she certainly couldn't have gone far. She began calling her name. Suddenly, she remembered the open front door. Could Laura have gone outside? She might have gone to check the mail and then felt too ill to make it back.

She stepped outside and looked around. Dusk was rapidly descending. She shivered and rubbed her hands over her arms. It was freezing. If Laura was outside, she had to find her before her cold turned into pneumonia.

Several pedestrians walked by and bicyclists sped past, but no sign of Laura. Briskly, she made her way to the mailbox, while keeping an eye out for her friend. Returning to the house, she wondered if her friend had gone out despite her health. That would account for the unlocked door, although Laura usually was more conscientious. The idea of her friend being too ill to go to work, lying half-conscious on the couch, and suddenly deciding to venture out didn't make sense.

She scooped up the medicine and headed towards the bathroom. Screeching car brakes caught her attention and she paused. She smiled when she saw the silver Mercedes through the bay window. Stepping towards the door, she slipped. She hit the wall hard and dropped the cough syrup. Straightening, she retrieved the bottle and frowned at the floor. A pool of tainted water was spreading across the tiles of the foyer near the bathroom. Her eyes followed the watery path until she encountered the closed bathroom door. She stepped onto the water-soaked carpet, while wondering if a pipe had broken.

Chapter 18:

Fatal Consequences

Unrelenting fear pursued Andrew like a demon, as he raced up the steps of the townhouse and jammed his finger against the bell while alternately banging on the door. No response. He knew that at least Laura was at home. Since she was sick, she probably was resting. Should he risk disturbing her, wait for Victory in the car, or try to find her?

Abruptly, an ear-piercing scream shattered the stillness. The sound ripped through him like a knife. "Victory!" his mind screeched. His control snapped. His veneer of calm sophistication was swallowed by unleashed pain, fury, and fear. With his head bent like a linebacker, he backed a few paces and then rammed the door with his shoulder. The wood splintered like dried kindling. Andrew pitched headlong into the foyer and instinctively hurled in the direction of the screams.

The fluorescent light cast Victory's profile in sharp relief as her features contorted with shock and horror. He plunged into the bathroom just as another scream tore from her. He seized her as he quickly scanned the area. Holding the hysterical woman in his arms, he tried to provide comfort while continuing to probe the room. She shook violently as racking sobs erupted through her body. He was thoroughly confused. He sensed no one but himself and the girl.

Fear finally faded and he exhaled loudly. He was so relieved that she was safe that it took him several seconds to assimilate his surroundings. "Since no one else is here, what was wrong?" he thought. "Could my arrival have interrupted an assault? Maybe someone had given her a fright before fleeing." Perplexed, he searched the room for the cause of her alarm. He probed again. Nothing. As his anxiety ebbed, he became aware of the water puddling at their feet. "Had Victory been planning a bath? If so, something had distracted her enough to allow the water to overflow." Now that his initial panic had subsided, he took a closer look. He frowned as he noticed the shower curtain that was drawn halfway across the bathtub. "That's strange," he thought, "Why would Victory have drawn the curtain if she were going to take a bath? Cradling her in one arm, he leaned towards the spigot. Victory stiffened. He opened his mouth and then stopped. The water overflowing the white tub was not clear, but was tinged a light pink.

Andrew closed his eyes to ward off the dread. "Blessed Mother of God," he prayed, as he tried to refute what he already knew. He slowly opened his eyes and reluctantly forced his head to turn. With mounting dread, he drew back the shower curtain. He blanched, as his arms convulsively tightened around Victory.

Laura Warner floated on a sacrificial alter of water. Her long black hair streamed like seaweed. Crimson pools of congealed blood contrasted sharply against her white robe. Her skin was translucent and her lips were almost white. Andrew leaned forward to check her pulse. Gingerly, he picked up one slim arm and turned it over. Fascination mixed with disgust as he studied the injury. Licking his suddenly dry lips, he dropped the arm as though it had scalded him.

It hit the water with a splash, sending little droplets cascading across the tub. Noticing the bloody razor on the side of the porcelain, he made the connection. As he led Victory from the bathroom, regret ripped through him.

Her glazed eyes finally focused on him. "Andrew," she cried brokenly, as she collapsed against him and sobbed hysterically.

Andrew held her close. He crooned softly while the haunting images flooded his mind. Pain and fear gripped his heart as he relived the last few minutes through the dead woman's eyes. Laura's fragility and vulnerability was a poignant ache in his heart, as he tried to provide consolation. Gently, he guided Victory to the sofa and dialed the police.

Leaving Victory on the sofa, he returned to the bathroom. Transfixed, he stood for a long time while staring at the corpse. A few hours ago, that drained lifeless body had been a vibrant and beautiful woman – a woman with her whole life ahead of her, a woman full of dreams for the future.

A low moan penetrated his thoughts. He returned to the living room. He cradled the sobbing woman while sirens droned in the distance.

Gradually, a blood-boiling rage began to replace his shock. What right did his brother have to wreak vengeance on this innocent? Retribution would be swift and just. He owed Laura that much

Outside, the shrieking sirens reached a deafening crescendo and then abruptly died. The night air seemed ominously silent with only Victory's muted sobs and sniffles disturbing the void. Pounding sounded at the door. Victory started. Disengaging himself, Andrew sighed and rose as the police rapped again.

Andrew admitted a tall dark-haired man wearing a trench coat who was accompanied by two burly police officers. The detective regarded the marquis sternly from behind thick wire-rimmed glasses. As he crossed the threshold, he flipped open his badge.

"I'm Detective Roberts," the man in the trench coat offered. "You called about a suspicious death?"

Andrew nodded, as he closed the door.

The detective inspected the splintered wood with raised brows and then pulled a notebook and pen from an inner pocket.

Victory sat numbly watching the uniformed men wandering through her home, as they poked into her belongings while going in and out of her bathroom. She felt numb and detached as if this were a television show and she was the audience. "Here comes Colombo she thought," as the detective in the trench coat spoke softly to one of the police officers, who nodded and then left. More people entered, including a stern-looking man carrying a doctor's bag. "And there goes Quincy," she thought and almost smiled as the medical examiner headed towards the bathroom.

With a concerned look on his face, Andrew headed towards her. Columbo grabbed his arm and they began speaking softly. Victory was distracted by the medical examiner as he re-entered the room and motioned to the detective. What was wrong with her? Laura was dead and she was playing "Guess the Profession of Strangers Who Come in to Look at the Corpse." Just a few hours ago, that corpse had been her best friend. Her mind shrieked denial, but there was no escaping reality. Her Laura, her best friend, the woman who had been like a sister to her since they were children was gone. A million pictures of Laura cascaded through her mind. She saw Laura as a young girl pretending to be tough so no one would see how much the taunts of the other girls really hurt. She remembered the double date with those two guys who had been such losers that she couldn't even remember their names. She pictured a proud Laura in her cap and gown when they graduated with top honors from law school. She reminisced about a happy Laura who had been so excited only a few weeks ago when she had become engaged to Craven Maxwell, vice president of the United States. Now, there was only a dead Laura, lying in an overflowing bathtub with her blood mixing with the water to form pink puddles on the floor.

Nausea overwhelmed her and she swallowed hard. "I think this is a nightmare," she asserted, while looking from Andrew to the detective. Andrew's face paled, but she didn't notice because she now was focusing on the police who were methodically checking the apartment for fingerprints and evidence. A visibly shaken young officer returned from the bathroom and beckoned to the detective.

As he turned, Andrew touched his arm. "Detective Roberts," he said in a low tone, "do you believe that this appears to be a suicide?"

The detective nodded impatiently, as he tried to pass.

"Then, why," Andrew persisted, while stepping in front of him, "are you acting as though you are conducting a murder investigation?"

"Is that what you think," he answered noncommittally.

Andrew glanced pointedly at the investigators who were examining the front door. "I need to know if my girlfriend is at risk."

The detective nodded and wearily sighed. "Do you know who is lying in the bathroom? Not your acquaintance, not your girlfriend's roommate, not the senator's aid, but the fiancée of the future vice president. That means lots of questions, secret service, FBI, and the need to rule out any potential risk to the new vice president."

Andrew tightly held Victory, while unchecked tears coursed down her cheeks. "I'm not dreaming, am I?" she asked, while searching his face.

He stared deeply into her eyes and tried to absorb her pain.

The detective wiped his forehead with a crumpled handkerchief and then dismissed the officer. He tensely approached the couple on the couch. He stood quietly for a long moment, while rubbing the back of his neck and looking towards the ceiling for divine intervention. "I'm going to need to know everything that happened," he stated grimly. "Down to the last detail. I don't know how long we can keep this from the press, but I don't want anything in the paper that I didn't know ahead of time."

Andrew frowned. "Is it absolutely necessary to go through this now, Detective Roberts? My girlfriend is devastated and suffering from grief and shock. You surely can get your information later."

Confused, Victory asked, "Newspapers?"

The detective removed his glasses, wiped them on the sleeve of his coat, and returned them to his face. He shook his head firmly. "I'm afraid I need to get a statement now while the facts are still fresh in Miss..."

"Parker," Andrew supplied.

"...in Miss Parker's mind. Yes, newspapers and probably television stations, too." Shock and pain shadowed her face and he softened. "The death of the vice president's fiancée is going to attract publicity, especially under these circumstances." He removed the small black notebook from his pocket, flipped it open, and then looked expectantly at Victory.

Tightly clutching Andrew's hand, she straightened her shoulders, as she gazed steadily at the detective. "I came home from the drugstore, where I had been purchasing some things for Laura's cold." Her voice faltered. The marquis squeezed her hand. Clearing her throat, she continued, "I discovered the door unlocked and slightly ajar when I came in. I closed it and then went to the kitchen to put away the things. When I looked in the living room, Laura wasn't on the couch, which is where she was when I left," she explained. She glanced down accusingly at the couch as if it were responsible for not keeping Laura safe within its cushions until she returned.

Her skin prickled. She looked up and caught Andrew gazing speculatively at her. Despondent, she still tried to smile. As he continued to study her, he squeezed her hand. His sober turquoise eyes turned deep aqua. She glanced nervously at the detective, as he scribbled on the pad.

He looked up and nodded. "Please go on."

Andrew stood, walked to the kitchen, and began searching the cupboards. He extracted a bottle of amber-colored liquid. Filling a shot glass with the brandy, he carried it to the couch. Victory's face was an ashen gray. As she sat with her arms tightly wrapped around herself, she shook her head at the detective. Andrew's heart went out to her. He pried one of her arms free and placed her cold stiff fingers around the glass.

"Drink this," he ordered, as he took her other hand.

Wide and uncomprehending blue eyes stared back. Slowly, she lifted the drink to her lips.

"Darling, I know it's difficult, but you must cooperate with the police."

She swallowed and grimaced. "I don't think I can bear to go through it again."

"I know," he said soothingly, as she drained the liquid, "but it's necessary. I'll be right here with you."

"Your boyfriend's right, Miss Parker," Roberts encouraged.

She stared at the marquis for a long moment. The reflected resolve poured courage into her flagging spirits. She turned resolutely to face her inquisitor. As she took up the story, Andrew again interlaced his fingers with hers. "I went to Laura's bedroom with the cough syrup, turned on the light, and saw she wasn't there. Then, I became confused, alarmed, and annoyed – all at the same time. Laura could affect people that way," she explained on a sob, but then regained her composure. "Anyway, I started checking to make sure she hadn't passed out. Then, I remembered the front door had been open, so I went back and checked outside. When I didn't find her, I assumed she had gone out and I returned to the house. I heard a car pull up. I looked through the window and saw Andrew. I was excited and ecstatic to see him and, for a moment, I forgot about my concern. I started towards the door and that's when I noticed the water."

By closing her eyes, she relived the experience of standing in the foyer with joy spreading through her like a warm blanket. As she sped towards the front door, she slipped, looked down in confusion, and was surprised by a spreading surge of water. Dread again clutched her heart as she recalled the long walk down the hallway and the opening of the bathroom door. Her mind rebelled and she dropped back against the cushions.

"The rest is as you found it when you arrived," she finished, looking helplessly at Andrew.

Detective Roberts frowned. With pen poised over his notes, he looked at Andrew. "And you, sir? I need a statement from you, also."

Andrew nodded.

"First," said the detective, turning to a new sheet, "your name." When he provided the information, the detective cocked a brow. "Do you also reside here?" he asked drolly.

Andrew glared. The detective's smile vanished. He cleared his throat and then brusquely asked for his address. The marquis provided his Cornwall and Washington addresses.

"All right," said Roberts, "let's start from when you arrived on the scene."

Andrew reflected. "I arrived about 45 minutes ago. I walked up the front steps and rang the bell. While I was waiting for the door to be answered, I heard screaming." As memories of those agonized seconds ticked through his mind, his gaze fixed on the shattered door. The screams had torn through his soul and no barrier could have kept him at bay. The detective also turned to examine the remnants of splintered wood. "Demolished," he observed dryly. "I haven't seen anything like that since my last action movie." Andrew shrugged.

"You're sure the door was completely intact when you arrived?"

"Intact and locked," he asserted, "That's why I had to break it."

"How did you do all that damage?" he asked, sizing up the marquis. "Not a bruise, scratch, cut, or smudge on his clothing to show for his assault on the solid wood," he thought, while removing his glasses and polishing them on his sleeve.

"I've taken some martial arts training," he said casually. "Once inside, I ran towards the sound of the screaming. It led me to the bathroom where I found Miss Parker and the deceased."

Another siren wailed. Andrew glanced through the window. Attendants in white were removing a stretcher from the rear of the ambulance. With her eyes closed, Victory was reclining against the back of the sofa. Leaning towards the detective, Andrew motioned towards the balcony. Roberts nodded his consent and Andrew led Victory onto the terrace.

In a few seconds, two men in white who were rolling a stretcher entered the house and headed towards the bathroom. Roberts gazed pensively through the sliding glass doors at the couple on the balcony. Lord Gabriel held his girlfriend tightly while she trembled violently. A commotion at the front door took his attention. He groaned, stood, and headed towards the door. The stretcher bearing the white-draped figure had made it as far as the stairs. The four attendants stood and stared at the new vice president as he climbed from the limousine.

Chapter 19:

Stalemate

Craven strode purposefully towards the stretcher, while leaving aides and secret service agents to follow in his wake. Before Roberts could stop him, he swept the sheet down and exposed the bloodless corpse.

Bulbs flashed and cameras rolled as the media hit their mark. Roberts scowled at the members of the press, who were bunched together like a pack of hungry wolves straining against the yellow tape. Despite his orders, the bright flashes continued to blind him. He hated the press and wished that the wolves had been kept at bay a while longer.

Roberts reverted his attention to the new vice president. He was as pale as the corpse. For a moment, Roberts was certain that the politician was going to drop. After a few moments, he reached out a pale hand to caress the girl's hair. Then, he pulled the sheet over her face and nodded at the attendants, who quickly scurried into the ambulance. New admiration and respect swept through the detective as he observed Craven Maxwell sparring with the press.

"Lord Gabriel, I assume you have some proof of your whereabouts during the time of the crime?"

Victory gasped in outrage, but Andrew calmly produced his airline tickets.

The other man grunted. "This still leaves a large block of time unaccounted for."

"You can't seriously suspect Andrew," Victory cried.

"Miss Parker," he replied, while turning narrowed eyes on her, "until proven otherwise, everyone is a suspect."

"I went from the airport to my house and settled my houseguest in. Jordan Rush, my houseguest, and my chauffer, Jack Collins, as well as my other servants will bear witness to my statement."

"There is no need to waste your time questioning the Marquis of Penbrook, Detective Roberts. I can serve as a character witness on my brother's behalf," Craven asserted, as he stepped into the room.

Roberts pulled his glasses off and once again wiped them on his sleeve. "Of course, Mr. Maxwell," he agreed, as he shot a disgruntled look at the marquis. "I had no idea Lord Gabriel was a relative."

Craven nodded curtly and turned to the couple on the sofa. "Victory," he said, as he extended his hand, "there are no words to express our mutual loss. I know how much you meant to Laura and you have my deepest sympathies. If there is anything I can do..."

Victory felt slightly nauseous as he continued to stare at her. For a moment, she thought that she was going to faint. As the sensation faded, she intercepted a strange look that Craven was exchanging with his brother. Andrew scowled back and nodded.

Turning his attention back to her, Craven finally released her hand. "You will understand if I take my leave. Please remember what I said."

He sighed heavily and quickly left the room. At the entrance, he paused for a moment with his shoulders slumped. He straightened as the light bulbs flashed and the microphones were thrust towards his face. Victory felt a twinge of pity as she realized his grief would have to be put on hold until he could gain privacy. Half of the occupants of the room seemed to disappear with him. She felt an oppressive weight being lifted as the last secret service man departed. Craven had tried to convince Laura that she also needed protection. If Laura had agreed with him, she still would be alive. Roberts turned his attention back to his notes.

Andrew tensed at the next question.

"Any speculation as to why she would want to kill herself?"

Victory shook her head.

"Do you know of anyone who might have wanted to harm the deceased?"

She shook her head.

One of the officers beckoned to the detective.

"Excuse me," said the detective.

Victory, pale and drawn, slumped against Andrew and leaned her head on his chest. A few moments later, Roberts emerged and beckoned to the marquis. Gently, he eased Victory against the back of the sofa. She gave no sign that she was aware that he had left.

Taking him by the arm, the detective led him out of earshot. Disgruntled, he admitted, "This is a strange case. The fact that the door was ajar would seem to indicate that the victim knew her assailant and let him in voluntarily. However," he continued, while casting a look in Victory's direction, "there is an abnormally small amount of blood at this crime scene."

Andrew's brows drew together. "You are sure this wasn't a suicide?"

The detective exhaled loudly. "It will be officially written up as a suicide unless we find something more concrete than my gut instinct. But it will probably be publicized as an accident for political reasons. My gut feeling is that the open door and the lack of a note suggest other possibilities. Do you know of anyone who would have wished her harm?"

The marquis stared at the man. "Detective Roberts, I did not know Miss Warner well, but, from the knowledge I did have of her, I find your suggestion highly unlikely. Under the circumstances, I cannot allow Miss Parker to remain here." "Not that she would wish to," he added silently. "I hope there are no objections if I take her to my home."

"As long as I can reach her if I have any more questions."

Andrew led a despondent Victory up the stairs of his mansion. Entering the guest room, he lowered her onto the four-poster and covered her with the blanket. The sleeping pills that he had found in her medicine chest were beginning to take effect. Her eyes fluttered, jerked open, sought his, and then drifted until they closed. Once her breathing deepened, Andrew retreated. He padded along the hallway and stopped at another guest room. Knocking softly, he entered.

Closing the book that he had been reading, the Earl of Rockford looked up as his host entered. In a jade green lounging jacket that matched his eyes, he was the picture of aristocratic elegance. He watched as the marquis took the other armchair in the room and sat while staring into space. The tension and deep distress were almost palpable. Sensing his friend's distress, he rose and walked over to his nightstand. He allowed a few moments for Andrew to gather his thoughts while he pulled a bottle from the cupboard. He poured a glass of the reddish-brown liquid and carried it to the marquis.

Andrew took the proffered drink and continued to sit, while staring into the glass as though he could discern the answer to his problems in the liquid. Finally, he drained the contents, placed the empty glass on the table, and faced his companion.

"Laura Warner is dead," he said, as the color returned to his face.

Jordan's eyes widened. "Victory returned from the store to find her lifelong friend's body floating in the bathtub with her wrists slit."

Solemnly, the other man nodded. "Craven?"

"Yes."

"How?"

"Officially, suicide."

The earl stared hard at his friend. "There's more."

The marquis stared back bleakly. "The police are considering the possibility of murder."

Jordan sipped his drink. Finally, he said, "It isn't like Craven to be sloppy. If he left loose ends, he had a good reason."

Andrew stood, walked over to the fireplace, and stared into the flickering flames for several seconds before answering. "He wanted the killer to get caught."

Jordan frowned. "That doesn't make sense. Even if he had one of the others do it, the risk would be too great."

The marquis turned towards him. Jordan inwardly cringed as the dark aqua of his eyes revealed his distress. "Neither Craven nor any of his followers will be suspected as the perpetrator."

"Then, who will the police suspect?"

"Victory."

Jordan inhaled sharply. "That's too diabolical even for him."

"Apparently not," he said dryly.

"Why would he do such a thing?"

Andrew laughed hollowly. "Two good reasons: to derive sadistic satisfaction and to make his point. I think it is time to pay my brother a visit. I'm leaving Victory in your care. I gave her some sleeping pills, so she should sleep through the night. Make sure she is not disturbed by any unwelcome visitors."

Jordan hesitated. Craven's direct orders had only pertained to spying on Andrew. There had been no mention of the girl, but what if that changed? He confided his misgivings and again the turquoise eyes turned aqua.

Andrew warily entered Craven's mansion. Feeling the ominous weight of his brother's presence, he allowed his telepathic sense to guide him to the study. Craven sat alone in the darkened room. He was staring into the fireplace. Slowly, he advanced and took the opposite seat. The silence hung thickly until Craven turned his onyx eyes, glowing with embers reflected from the fireplace, on him.

"Why?" Andrew asked.

Craven shrugged, "Why not?"

Andrew longed to knock the insolence off of his brother's face. Instead, he said quietly, "Because killing people is both immoral and illegal."

Craven stared back impassively. "Unlike you, I consider diurnals nothing more than a means to an end. As for the legality, you were the one who prevented justice from prevailing."

Faced with the detached objectivity, Andrew's composure snapped. "How could you murder someone you were personally involved with?"

He laughed, "I didn't kill her, but the girl serves better purposes by being dead than by being alive. Even you must admit it was an effective reminder of the consequences of breaking our agreement."

"You bastard," Andrew hissed. Grabbing his brother by the lapels, he shook him in a grip that would have snapped a normal man's neck. "You had no right to kill that woman. Not only have you murdered an innocent, but you also have caused Victory great emotional pain. You did all of that just for the sake of making a point?"

As he shook off his grip, Craven scornfully looked at him. "First of all, I have the right to do whatever I choose. Need I remind you that I am the new vice president? I only need to give the word to have you removed, barred from my presence, taken into custody, or even have your visa revoked." Andrew glared and he continued smoothly, "We had an agreement, which you chose not to honor."

Andrew eyed him furiously, as he strove for control. "Our agreement was that I would not interfere in your political plans in this country. You never mentioned foreign affairs."

"Well," said Craven smoothly, "I agreed not to harm only Victory. That understanding did not cover anyone that she was connected with."

"By killing Laura, you have hurt her emotionally."

"And, by pulling Jordan from the race, you have hurt my plans abroad."

"Your plans are going to put our people at risk."

"To the contrary, I am going to be their salvation. You are the one who is harming them with your antiquated ideas of assimilation."

"That murder is going to cause alarm bells to start clamoring in their already-superstitious minds."

"Unsolved crimes are a regular part of any big city. After a couple of weeks, this one will start to take a back seat to others."

Andrew glowered unsatisfied. "I think it's about time you and I reached an understanding. I can no longer sanction your plans and I am forbidding you to proceed any further."

"What of Victory?" he scoffed. "Are you willing to sacrifice her to appease your conscience?"

"I don't plan on making any sacrifices."

"Then think again."

Andrew drew a revolver from his pocket. "As the acknowledged leader of our people, I have decided that you are a danger to society and need to be terminated."

He laughed. "You may be able to pull that with the others, but not me. Remember that we have the same blood coursing through our veins. I don't have to subjugate myself to anyone, including you, brother," he snarled maliciously.

Andrew raised the gun towards Craven's head. Their eyes locked. For several minutes, a battle of wills ensued. The veins stood out on Andrew's neck. The sweat poured from Craven's brow. Andrew's body shook. Craven's lips trembled. Andrew's gun arm rose fractionally and his finger tightened convulsively on the trigger.

Suddenly, the fire poker launched itself at his head. Sensing the intention at the last moment, he was too late. The iron crashed into his skull and knocked the gun out of his hand. Flipping through the air several times, it landed in the middle of the burning logs.

"I think we have reached an impasse," Craven mused, as he picked up the poker to push the revolver out of the flames. "As you can see, I have become stronger since our last conflict. In the future, I think you should consider your position before you start making threats."

The marquis advanced menacingly towards his brother. Suddenly, the study door burst open and admitted several armed men.

"Ease up, gentlemen," said Craven smiling reassuringly. He turned to the marquis. "They've been edgy all day."

Jordan studied the sleeping woman. "She is a beauty," he conceded, as he gazed at the heart shaped-face framed by long golden hair. Mesmerized by the rise and fall of her chest, he again wondered at the fragility of these diurnals. During his life span, he also had formed attachments to various people, so he could partially understand Andrew's feelings for the woman. However, he had never lost sight of the fact that their impact was fleeting and he had never allowed one to influence him to this extreme. He walked around the bed. Yes, she was beautiful, but Andrew, with his good looks, charm, and wealth, could have any woman of his own kind or of the diurnals. Yet, inexplicably, his cousin was not only impressed but obsessed with this particular female.

The shrilling of the phone interrupted his reverie. He snatched it up, while glancing quickly at the girl. Her brow creased as she stirred restlessly. Jordan tensed and then relaxed when she settled.

"Hello," he murmured.

"Where's Andrew?" Craven demanded tersely.

Jordan stiffened. As he looked at the bed, he knew that his face betrayed his guilt. He fervently wished that he could hang up. "Isn't he with you?"

"He was, but that was over an hour ago."

"Well, he hasn't returned."

"Where's the woman?"

Jordan's eyes darkened as he again studied the sleeping woman. Will she be the next innocent to fall victim to this monster? He closed his eyes to blot out the picture of guileless serenity that she presented. The image was imprinted on the inside of his lids. It was replaced by the image of Andrew's trusting features when he asked Jordan to watch over his love.

"Well?" came the harsh command.

He considered lying, but knew that it was only a matter of time before Craven discovered the truth. "She is here. She's trying to recover from the ordeal you put her through."

"Are you forming attachments to diurnals, as well?"

He glanced at the bed. "Just in this one's case, but only because of her importance to Andrew."

"Good," Jordan," he added ominously, "There may come a time when I will need you to perform certain tasks and I don't expect to have any hesitation. Is that understood?"

"Perfectly."

Chapter 20:

Willow Grove Confessions

Victory peeped around the study door. Andrew sat in one of the high wing-backed chairs facing the fireplace. As she approached, she noticed that he was absorbed in the daily newspaper. She took the seat next to his. Ever since he had brought her into his home, he had seemed preoccupied. He also had done his best to spare her from the publicity that had been provoked by the case. He had become adept at handling the press and had kept her clear of any adverse media. Today was no exception. Realizing that she had entered the room, he quickly folded the paper and tucked it under his arm.

She smiled wanly. "Eventually, I will run across a newspaper or a newscast."

He nodded solemnly. "But not yet."

Tears gathered in the corners of her eyes. "Is it still that bad?" He hesitated and she conceded, "Never mind. I don't want to know."

Absently nodding, he stared into the fire. She wondered if he were thinking about home. Was his prolonged visit to the states interfering with his affairs back in England? Recently, she had caught him staring at her – or into his drink – or, sometimes, even into space. She knew Andrew. He would never admit that caring for her was causing a hardship for him. Unable to summon the strength to pull herself out of her own misery, she hadn't paid close attention to his change of attitude. Now, as she studied the lean chiseled profile, she felt ashamed of her own self-centeredness. She had lost her best friend, it was true, but Laura was gone. Andrew was still here and he obviously had a problem.

She moved over to perch on the arm of his chair. As she linked her hand through his, he looked up. She was gratified to see the warm glow in his eyes. "I spoke to Laura's mom," she said with her voice shaking slightly, "The authorities have released the body and the funeral is scheduled for the day after tomorrow."

"The day after the inauguration. I suppose Craven will attend," he mused contemptuously.

She swallowed past the lump in her throat. "I would think so."

"Where will the services be held?"

"Willow Grove. It's a small town in Pennsylvania. That's where Laura was born."

Andrew's face took on a strange expression, but the look was so fleeting that she thought that she imagined it.

"Would the family consider it an intrusion if I attended the service?"

She smiled softly. "I've already asked," she said, as she leaned her cheek against his hair, "Mrs. Warner assured me it would be all right."

Victory hesitated. She wanted to find out what was causing his strange mood, but a wave of grief overwhelmed her. The thought of coping with any more turmoil twisted her stomach into knots. The door opened. The Earl of Rockford spared her from the conflict with her conscience.

He smiled at them and said, "Would you two care to join me for lunch? As much as I enjoy your cooks excellent meals, Andrew, I can't possibly finish the spread she has prepared all by myself."

"I don't know, cousin," Andrew joked, "Ever since you arrived, you have been putting quite a dent in the pantry."

Jordan laughed and Victory was suffused by a warm glow as she observed the play. For the first time in days, Andrew's good nature seemed to surface.

"I was really thinking of Victory," Jordan scoffed, "She is becoming a stick figure right before our eyes. Come on, love," he insisted, as he took her arm, "Cook doesn't like it if her meals go unappreciated."

She smiled up at him, as he propelled her along. Even though she had known the earl for only a few days, he seemed more like a big brother than a stranger. His easy-going manner, genuine warmth, and sincere concern for Andrew had endeared him to her, while his care and sensitivity to her situation had cemented the spontaneous spark of friendship. Theirs was a friendship that had flourished since their introduction.

"Well, introduction might not be quite the right word," she reflected.

She had been sleeping in the giant four-poster in Andrew's bedroom. At first, after waking from her drug-induced slumber, she had been disoriented and frightened. Never having been upstairs in Andrew's Bethesda mansion, she had not realized where she was, so she panicked. Her fear escalated when an unfamiliar form detached from the shadows. The image of Laura lying bloody in the bathtub assailed her and she was sure that she was about to become the night's second victim. She struggled to a sitting position and opened her mouth to scream. Before she could utter a sound, the man placed a hand over her mouth.

"There's no need to wake the servants. You're safe." Gathering her into his protective embrace, he had tried to provide comfort. His kind words and light touch had not penetrated past her terror. Desperate to free herself, she had kicked, punched, scratched, and even tore at him with her teeth. He patiently had endured it all, while holding her loosely but firmly in an iron grip. His face had borne an expression of tolerant compassion that eventually calmed her.

Finally exhausted, Victory's struggles ceased. With blood trickling from several scratches and a bruise already forming on his right cheek, he had asked quietly, "Do you feel better now?"

She eyed him warily while trying to decide whether to attempt a scream or to ask his name.

As if discerning her intention, he said loudly, "Andrew, I am not doing well as a punching bag. Please let her know it's all right before she gears up for round two."

As she slumped against the headboard, relief flooded through her. Andrew stepped forward and said dryly, "Jordan, I think this is the first time I ever saw a woman who was unwilling to stay in your arms." Then, he added soberly, "Thanks for your restraint. Victory has been through a lot and she is overwrought."

Jordan looked understandingly at her. Shrugging, he said, "I'll heal."

A slow flush slid up her cheeks. "I'm sorry. I had a nightmare. It seemed so real that I thought you were part of it."

The compassion that she saw reflected in the jade eyes had won her instant affection. Now, she watched benignly as the two men talked together.

"Victory and I are going to Pennsylvania for the funeral. Laura is being buried at the family plot in Willow Grove."

Jordan was stunned. "Willow Grove?"

The marquis nodded as he handed him a folded sheet of paper. "I have compiled a list of those who I think can be easily persuaded to abandon Craven's project. While he is occupied playing the bereaved fiancé, I would like you to sound them out."

Jordan looked doubtful. "I don't think Craven is going to take very kindly to that."

The marquis rubbed his jaw. "I'll deal with Craven. At least for now, you might be more successful with those who are not close at hand. I was thinking in particular of Alexander in Germany and Pierre in France. Do you know anyone who might be privileged to the details of his plans?"

"His daughter," he responded bitterly.

"Dana," he mused. He wondered about the intensity of his friend's response. "I can get the information from her if necessary, but I would prefer for her to provide it voluntarily."

He shook his head. "Not likely. She's pretty much in charge and answers directly to Craven. The stakes are too high and the punishment too severe for her to betray him voluntarily."

Andrew drove the rented car through the countryside. After the ordeal of the funeral, he needed to retreat. The drive had a two-fold purpose. He knew that Victory had been devastated all over again by the burial ceremony and he did not believe that it would be in her best interest to go back to the house. He had explained the situation to Mrs. Warner, who was concerned for the woman whom she regarded as a second daughter. Victory had been unresponsive when he took charge of escorting her from the cemetery. And she had not resisted when they did not return to the house.

Craven's performance had been difficult to bear. Standing forlorn and aloof, he was the perfect picture of a bereaved fiancé. His solemn condolences had seemed genuine when he offered them to the grieving parents. The feigned sincerity that he projected when speaking to Victory had sparked a cord of fury that Andrew had barely controlled. He had considered having words with his brother, but the secret service and the media had kept him in check.

He turned off of the paved road and followed a dirt track, as it bent and curved. Ahead lay his second reason for making this journey. Turning off the motor, he stared ahead at the two-story brick and stone building partially concealed by an enormous willow tree. As far as he knew, this spot had been deserted except for a block of charred earth. Of course, that had been a long time ago. Now, it appeared that someone else had settled here and had restored the area. "Progress is good," he thought, while reaching for the ignition. This was a part of the past that should be buried and forgotten. How coincidental that Craven's fiancée should be from this place.

Victory opened her purse, extracted a handkerchief, and wiped her eyes. She glanced disinterestedly out of the car window. "Oh," she said, as she leaned her head against the headrest. "So, this is where they originated. It makes sense."

Concerned and confused, he asked politely, "What do you mean?" At least, she was taking an interest in something. Her complete and continued apathy had started to alarm him.

Victory waved a negligent hand at a sign by the side of the road that he had overlooked. "The crematorium," she said, "Because of the name, I should have figured that this was where they originated. I wonder if Laura knows... " She trailed off and then closed her eyes, as tears slid down her cheeks.

Andrew hardly heard her as he stared in shock at the sign. "Willow Grove Crematorium," he thought wildly. Was this some sort of sick joke or simply a coincidence? Alerted, he gazed speculatively at the unobtrusive building. An idea took root. Then, it blossomed. Only Craven would have the audacity to build a crematorium as some kind of macabre shrine on the spot where his parents had burned to death.

His mind abruptly snapped back to Victory's last words. Trepidation tore through him as he faced her. "Why did you say that you should have figured out this is where they originated?" he asked tensely.

Startled out of her misery, she leaned forward. "Well, because the name is Willow Grove Crematoriums, I suppose it should have dawned on me that the founders would have been from Willow Grove."

He gripped the steering wheel hard. "Are you trying to tell me there are more of these places?" he asked.

Her gaze sharpened. His tone was making her uneasy. Her concern was reinforced by the dark aqua of his eyes. Hesitantly, she nodded. "I don't know how many there are or if it's a national chain, but there is at least one in Washington and I recall another in Boston. I used to pass it everyday on my way to law school," she added. Alarmed, she watched as Andrew's body jerked spasmodically. Throwing open the car door, he bolted towards the building. He stopped at the entrance and stared at a plaque next to the door.

Victory unfastened her seat belt. With one hand on the door handle, she paused. Andrew was already striding back to the car. Alarmed, she watched in confusion as he lowered his head onto the steering wheel. After a moment, he raised his head and turned on the ignition. As they sped down the country road, gravel and dirt sprayed into the air. They hit the underside of the car like tiny missiles.

Unable to endure his strange behavior and tense expression, she ventured, "Andrew, what is wrong?"

He shot her a quick glance. "I need to get back to Washington."

"Now?"

Yes, now," he confirmed.

"I would at least like to say goodbye to the Warners before I leave."

He gave her a curious sideways look, but said nothing. The ominous silence continued until they reached the hotel. Once inside the suite, he turned to her. Raking his hand through his hair, he motioned for her to sit on one of the leather sofas.

Taking a seat opposite, he sat and deliberated for so long that Victory began to get annoyed. Just as she was about to demand an explanation, he spoke. As he began his narrative, her eyes focused on his sensual lips, which stirred the first passion that she had felt in weeks. Guilt overwhelmed her as grief reasserted its grip.

He leaned towards her and then reached across the coffee table to take her hands in his. "Victory," he began earnestly, "I love you. It was my intention to ask you to marry me after you had some time to recover."

A shaft of joy pierced the darkness! For a moment, she basked in its glow. Then, realization struck. "Was?" she asked with an obvious tremor.

Andrew searched her face, squeezed her hand, and sat back. Sighing regretfully, he nodded, "I have some things to tell you. Things I would have preferred to explain over a period of time. Time I could have used to allow you to know and understand me better."

Victory was undaunted. She loved this man and nothing that he could say would alter her feelings. She was forestalled from telling him so by his upraised hand.

"Please wait until I've finished before you decide. Although my dearest desire is to have you return my feelings, you need to be apprised of all the facts."

"So apprise me," she said jauntily. She was eager to get the confessions finished. Then, she reconsidered. "He might want to tell me that he is divorced and has a nasty ex-wife hovering in the background. He might have a child – or several children. Or maybe," she thought with her mind rebelling, "he is already married and can't offer me an honorable relationship." Tightly controlling her conjectures, she nodded for him to proceed.

Andrew warily eyed her. He was aware that her attitude had changed from benevolent unconcern to suspicious aloofness. He wondered what could have been the cause. "Not that it matters," he thought despondently. Nothing that she could be imagining could be even close to the truth. Abruptly, he stood and walked over to the mahogany bar. He poured two stiff drinks. Using the task as an excuse to study her, he memorized every detail of her elegant face and graceful form. Stopping beside Victory, he handed the glass to her.

"What is it?" she asked. She wrinkled her nose when she sniffed the contents.

"Jack Daniels," he said, as he resumed his seat.

She examined the glass. "This looks like enough liquor to drop a horse. If I drink all this, I'll never know what you said."

He didn't respond. Instead, he upended his glass that contained twice the amount of hers. Placing his glass aside, he said, "I am returning to Washington this evening – alone." She started to protest, but he continued, "Hear me out." Taking a deep breath, he plunged ahead, "I am not who you think I am, Victory."

"Do you mean you're not really Andrew Gabriel, Marquis of Penbrook?"

He shook his head. His eyes locked on hers. A premonition of dread settled in the pit of her stomach. He restated, "I am the marquis, but I am not what you think I am."

She reached for the drink, while she waited for him to explain. "I am a porphyrian." She was totally puzzled. He rushed on, "We are a subspecies or race, if you prefer, whose main genetic makeup differs from humans in that we manifest a rare condition called porphyria. This condition is caused by a lack of certain enzymes in the blood's hemoglobin."

"That's why you drink that awful-tasting liquid. Right?" she asked tentatively. She recalled how he had told her about drinking it to replenish electrolytes that were lacking in his system. "But you couldn't think I would be so shallow as to reject you because of a rare blood disorder?"

The corners of his lips lifted slightly. "No, but there's more. Some of the other characteristics unique to my people are intense sensitivity to sunlight, receding gums, and, in some cases, neurological damage. Our women are more prone to suffer and are especially vulnerable during pregnancy when they can not partake of the drink."

Victory shifted nervously. "I'm not sure I am following you. You claim that you have a rare genetic disorder called porphyria. I've heard of it, although, right now, I can't remember in what context. What I don't understand," she said puzzled, "is why you believe having this disease classifies you as a subspecies or why you think it would alter my feelings. Unless," she said with her eyes widening, "you're concerned about the affect on potential children."

Andrew lifted agonized eyes to meet hers. "The answer to both your questions is the main characteristic of porphyria. One of my ancestors was responsible for inventing the PS4. However, prior to the utilization of the drink, our people were plagued by an insatiable need to derive the enzymes we needed by drinking blood."

Chapter 21:

Subspecies

The glass dropped from Victory's suddenly nerveless fingers. Rolling several feet, it left a yellowish brown trail on the snowy carpet. She stared in shock. Now, she remembered where she had seen the term. Porphyria was in a book that she had read. The book in Andrew's Cornwall library. The one that she had lost while trying to rescue the dog. The one with Craven's likeness in it. The one about vampires that Andrew had not wanted her to read. The room tilted. She felt lightheaded. As the dizziness passed, she stared at him in astonishment.

"There's more," he said doggedly.

"How much more could there be?" she wondered, as she listened in fascinated horror.

"There are other differences that I don't believe stem from a mere enzyme deficiency. These differences support the theory that, somewhere along our evolutionary history, our people split off from the main branch. We appear to live longer then diurnals, which is the name my people gave to the people who are active during the day. We also have about five to ten times their physical strength."

"That isn't difficult to believe," she thought with the part of her mind that still was functioning rationally. She remembered the splintered door of the townhouse and the way he had thrown the muggers around on the night that they had been attacked.

"In addition," he finished, "my people have a telepathic link that allows us to communicate without words. A very few have the skill of mental manipulation."

When he lapsed into silence, she asked incredulously, "Is that all?"

"What do you mean?"

"Well, " she said caustically, "I think you left a few things out. For instance, what about your aversion to running water, garlic, and crosses?

Or," she added with her voice becoming shriller, "what about your lack of reflection in mirrors or the fact that you have to lie in a coffin of interred earth – and you forgot to mention the best part, the part that you can be killed only by a stake through the heart."

"Don't be ridiculous. Those are fairytales made up by movie studios," he snapped.

"Don't be ridiculous," she echoed indignantly, as sparks shot from her eyes and bright color stained her cheeks. "You sit there and tell me a story out of a Bram Stoker novel and you tell me not to be ridiculous. If you wanted an excuse to get out of our relationship, you could have told me something much less dramatic – like you were married or that you just didn't care for me. There is no need to go into some insane story about being some sort of modern-day vampire."

She stood up and stalked towards the bedroom door. "I will pack and get out as soon as possible," she thought. "Of all the excuses for breaking off a relationship that I have heard in my day, this one takes the cake. The man should get an Oscar for this performance. Well, the sooner I put this episode behind me, the quicker I can start over. Not only have I lost my best friend, but I no longer have the love of my life." Her shoulders slumped, but she continued resolutely towards the door.

Abruptly, her progress was cut short as an iron grip encircled her. She resisted, but it was no use. She slowly turned to confront him.

"I realize this sounds like a delusion of a sick mind, but the least you could do is hear me out before you pass judgment. Have I ever lied to you before?" he asked when she continued to stare.

"There's always a first time," she thought, but refrained from speaking the thought aloud. She exhaled, while bleakly searching his desperately demanding turquoise eyes. His gaze was so compelling that she allowed herself to be led back to the sofa. Sensing her urge to flee, he sank down next to her and firmly held her hands.

"In the early days of our history, our people were viewed as supernatural beings," he conceded, "because of a lack of communication and unsophisticated cultures steeped in superstitions. Our need for the enzymes that our bodies lacked drove some of the deviant and mentally unbalanced of our kind to slake their thirst by slaying humans. Even though they represented a minute portion of the population, our people as a whole were labeled as bloodthirsty demons. For centuries, we were persecuted, hunted, and indiscriminately destroyed. The diurnals never stopped to consider that not all of the porphyrians were guilty. Nor did they realize that the few who went on bloodthirsty rampages were as misrepresentative of our kind as the serial killers in your own species. Fear and suspiciousness of what they didn't understand motivated them to attempt genocide – and they very nearly succeeded. Those who survived did it by learning to integrate into your society by camouflaging their true nature." His eyes took on a faraway haunted look as he continued. "As I mentioned, one of my ancestors eventually invented this enzyme supplement, which, by the way, contains only the blood of several animals, none of which is domestic. We have internally purged our psychopaths and, for the past several centuries, have lived in peaceful coexistence with diurnals. The main ingredient to our successful assimilation into your society," he explained, as he released her hands, "has been our anonymity. I am taking a monumental risk by telling you all of this. Not only," he said with a wry smile, "because you will think I am mad, but because there is always the potential for a resurgence of the panic that could lead to the extermination of my people."

Victory stood and walked over to the window. Parting the heavy velvet drapes, she looked out at the dreary January day. "Life was so simple a few weeks ago," she reflected. Now, a new year was underway and she wondered what lay ahead. She could feel Andrew's eyes boring into her back, but she couldn't force herself to face him.

While watching a car pass through the slush on the road in front of the hotel, she thought, "If I'm not mistaken, Valentine's day is only a couple of weeks away. It's the day that Laura would have been married." Her heart constricted, as she watched two boys throwing snowballs at each other. On the other side of the road, an elderly woman in a long red coat walked a poodle sporting a red sweater.

She continued to gaze out of the window even though she knew that Andrew was waiting expectantly. "What does he want?" she wondered wildly, as she attempted to assimilate the details of his story. Did he really expect her to believe that he was a supernatural being, a legend, or creature out of folklore?

In order to avoid grappling with the main issue, her mind grasped at something that Andrew had said. Finally turning, she was taken aback momentarily by the look of despair, anxiety, and affection hovering in his turquoise eyes. They might be able to get some sort of help. Her heart constricted even more. She wished that her father were still alive to advise her. "My father," she thought wistfully, "would have thrived on a case like this." A memory flickered in the back of her mind, but she pushed it aside in favor of the more pressing concerns.

"If you didn't feel that this was the right time to bring the matter up, why did you do it?" she challenged.

Andrew's face tightened and he suddenly appeared haggard. Momentarily lowering his head, he reluctantly confessed, "Because I think your safety is in jeopardy." She gasped. His eyes searched her stunned face. "That's why I need to go back alone. I don't have a clear picture of what is going on, but I will tell you as much as I know and then you can make an informed decision."

Victory slowly walked over and sank onto the bed.

"I originally came to this country to investigate my brother's activities. After I met you, I entered into an agreement with my brother. The agreement was that I would stay out of his business affairs. In exchange, he would not interfere in my personal life."

"Why should the two of you have to make such an arrangement?" she asked skeptically.

"It's a rather long and complicated story. It all boils down to my brother's past actions. When I returned and found him running for vice president, I was certain he was up to some sort of corrupt scheme." He paused and waited for comments, but she remained silent. "Everything went well until our trip to England," he continued. "One day, I saw Jordan on television and he was campaigning for the office of Prime Minister. Because of our ability to influence diurnals, we are prohibited from procuring any status in your society. To see Jordan flagrantly violating our customs caused me grave concern."

Her eyes widened, "Are you trying to tell me Jordan is also one of these porphyrians?"

He nodded.

"And I suppose it goes without saying that Craven is also?"

"Yes."

"Exactly how many of these porphyrians are there?"

His heart sank as he realized that she was trying to humor him. "About 2,000." Suddenly, he realized the futility of continuing. It didn't matter what he said. He would never convince her. If he were in her place, he probably would be thinking about having him committed.

He stood, gazed at her sadly, and then headed for the door.

"Where are you going?"

"For a walk to consider what I should do to salvage this mess," he said, while slipping into his jacket.

"Please don't go," she pleaded. She was surprised at her own desperation. How could she allow someone in his condition to go walking through the streets? If she could get him to finish his story, she and he might be able to determine the best way to proceed.

He searched her face and then returned to the chair. "After you went back to the States, I visited Jordan and confronted him with what I had seen. Up until that time, I had only my own misgivings to prompt me not to trust Craven's sudden interest in promoting a beneficial society for diurnals. Jordan told me that Craven had some sort of plan for killing the president after they were elected and then setting himself up as the head of this country. He also wanted to have porphyrians established in as many other key positions in foreign countries as possible. Unfortunately, Jordan did not know enough details for me to counter Craven's plans, but I was able to prevent him from using Jordan as a tool. Craven was not very pleased and considered it to be a breech of our agreement."

She waited for him to finish, but, when he hesitated, she prompted, "Is that all?" Expectantly, she waited, as he sat down beside her and once again took her hands.

"I believe Craven is responsible for Laura's death."

Chapter 22:

Accusations

Mortified, Victory jerked away from him, but Andrew persisted, "I don't have any proof. I would never make such an allegation if I weren't so concerned for your safety."

Pain seared through her and she forgot her intentions to humor his ravings. "I am really beginning to wonder about you. This is the second time you've accused Craven of murder without any proof. In England, I took your story at face value because I trusted you. But, after I returned, I never saw Craven treat Laura with anything but love, respect, and kindness. Damn it, Andrew, they were engaged to be married. Having her killed makes no sense."

"Everything you say is true. Unless you know him well, it doesn't make any sense. Please listen to me," he pleaded. "To my brother, diurnals are completely expendable. Laura meant nothing more to him than a way to keep track of me. Her death meant nothing more than a warning for me to back off."

"You're beginning to sound paranoid."

He grabbed her by the shoulders. "You've got to take me seriously. Craven killed your friend and he poses a serious threat to your safety."

Impotent rage at being deprived of her best friend whirled like a tornado in her brain. Ever since she had found Laura's lifeless body floating in the tub, she had needed to lay blame. Now, she finally had a target.

Pulling free, she stormed to the phone. "Yes, operator, can you please put me through to the Washington, DC, police department?"

Andrew sprang at her and immediately snatched the phone. "What are you doing?" he asked, after slamming the receiver.

"If Craven has anything to do with my best friend's death, then I'm going to see he pays."

"Are you insane?"

"That's rich! You're the one spinning stories out of a horror novel and you ask me if I have a mental problem!"

"If you can stay calm for a moment, I will explain." She glowered at him. "What are you going to tell the police? That you think the vice president killed your girlfriend? You have no proof. Even if you did, I still couldn't let you make the call."

Indignantly, she asked, "Why not?"

"Because you would be the one at risk, not him. First of all, he supposedly wasn't even in town when it occurred. It also would be very easy for him to point out how distraught you are. He would play the concerned friend and even recommend that you get professional help. He might even offer his own personal assistance. Besides, if Craven was investigated, it could have devastating repercussions for my people."

Enraged, she asked, "So, you think that the murdering of people by these porphyrians should be sanctioned?"

"No. I'm asking you to let me handle the situation. My people have moral guidelines and murder is just as reprehensible among my species as it is yours."

Deflated, she sat down on the bed and began shaking her head. What did it matter? This latest story about Craven killing Laura was just another aspect of his psychosis. She now realized that her emotions almost had persuaded her to accept his explanation. She realized the futility of trying to reason with him. He was so far gone that she didn't know if even a psychiatrist could help.

"You don't believe any of this, do you?"

She studied his worried exasperated tense features and regretfully shook her head.

"I'm sorry, but you have to admit it is a bit out of the ordinary," she said in an enormous understating of her misgivings. "Maybe some therapy?" she suggested tentatively.

"You think I'm crazy," he said flatly. "If only there were a way to prove it to you," he frantically exclaimed.

How?" she asked aloud and then thought, "If I act like I'm going along and his proof failed, he would be more amenable to counseling."

"I don't know," he snapped irritably, "It's not as if we can wait around fifty or sixty years to see if I age."

"You did say you were allergic to the sun," she volunteered helpfully.

He shook his head. "No good. During the past decade, I've been desensitizing myself to the sun's rays. Now, I would have to be exposed for several days without a break for it to have an adverse effect."

"You could lift something heavy," she offered brightly.

He scanned the room. "I don't think that is going to be enough to convince you or you would already believe me."

Her shoulders slumped. He was right and her facade was not fooling him. Something that he had said was still nagging at the back of her mind, but, when she tried to make the connection, it eluded her.

"You could always shoot me with a silver bullet," he offered dryly.

"I believe you have your monsters mixed up. Silver bullets are only for werewolves."

"It's just as well because it wouldn't have worked."

"Are you trying to tell me that you are immune to bullets?" she asked incredulously.

He studied her for a long moment and then answered slowly and deliberately, "Because of slight differences in our internal organ structure, it would be difficult to kill a porphyrian by gunshot."

"Oh, great!" she said sarcastically, "Why don't we just go out and use you for target practice?"

"That would solve the problem," he agreed blandly.

"No, it wouldn't," she said heatedly. "I was being sarcastic."

"Well, I wasn't," he replied impatiently, "If that's what it takes to convince you, then so be it."

He rose and headed for the door. When she did not follow, he glared at her with a gaze that was half challenge and half accusatory.

"I'm not willing to take the risk," she said softly. "I know you believe what you are saying, but I can't bear the thought of plowing bullets through you just to determine whether or not you're right."

"We need to come up with some way for you to believe me or our relationship as well as your safety will be in jeopardy."

"Well," she said doubtfully, "what about the telepathy? Couldn't I think of something and you tell me what it is?"

Andrew returned to his seat and sighed wearily. Closing his eyes, he said, "It's not that simple. I said porphyrians can communicate telepathically with each other. When it comes to diurnals, the term 'mind control' is more accurate."

"Mind control?"

"Yes, most porphyrians possess the ability to mentally nudge diurnals. We can influence them into performing actions as if they were their own ideas. For instance, if you were considering whether you should wear a black or red dress and I had a preference, I could actually nudge your decision towards my desire. A few porphyrians possess a more potent power. With it, they actually can impose their wills on the minds of diurnals. A very rare few also have the ability to supersede their wills on their own kind. There is a difference, however. When their wills are focused on their own, the receivers are aware of the influence. When their wills are aimed at diurnals, their control can be accomplished without the receivers' knowledge."

Chills ran down her spine as she contemplated this information. What a powerful and dangerous delusional system he possessed. He really believed that he could control people's thoughts! She gazed at him as he massaged the back of his neck. Every inch of his body bespoke tension and frustration. He seemed genuinely concerned and desperate. Never before had she known him to exaggerate or fabricate. Could any of these wild tales be true? Not even for one minute did she believe the story about a subspecies, but could there be a cult that had developed hypnotism to such a degree that they were capable of imposing their will on others?

"Can you do it to me?"

His eyes snapped open. "I could, but I won't," he said vehemently.

"Why not? It might convince me that at least part of what you say has some validity."

He shook his head. "It might and it might not, but we are not going to find out."

"Why not," she asked. She was highly annoyed. She was giving him a chance to prove himself and he was refusing. Her hopes plummeted as she reaffirmed her opinion of his mental state.

"Because the process is tantamount to mental rape," he said harshly and then more calmly added, "Putting that ethical dilemma aside, if I influenced you to do something, you would never trust me again. Every time you made a decision, especially one regarding me, you would wonder if you had been influenced. It would always stand between us. After a while, it would tear us apart."

"How do I know you are not already doing it?"

He raised his brows. "Do you think we would be having this conversation if I were?"

"If you expect me to believe your story, you're going to have to come up with more tangible proof," she insisted.

He walked over to stare out of the window. He stood there so long that she thought that he considered the matter closed. Then, he turned and slumped against the wall. "All right," he said flatly, as he gazed levelly at her. "I can see there is no other way to convince you. If it were just a case of having you think I was insane, I might have just walked away." He closed his eyes, but not before Victory glimpsed the intense pain. "Unfortunately, leaving and allowing you to think you were lucky to escape marrying a lunatic won't solve the problem. I need you to believe my story for your own sake." He finished his explanation as he studied her in detail in order to memorize her features. Once this demonstration was over, she probably would shun him as a freak or some sort of monster, but she at least would have the full knowledge of what she was up against. In knowledge lay caution and perhaps a degree of security, he hoped.

Resolutely, he faced her. The resignation that she detected made her feel uneasy. She tilted her chin defiantly, but said in a gentle voice, "I want you to promise me something."

He nodded hesitantly.

"If this experiment doesn't work, I want you to agree to see a psychiatrist."

He smiled wryly and agreed. His quick acceptance of her condition surprised her. This indication of how deeply he was affected made her uneasy.

"Well," he asked, "what kind of test shall it be? We have to agree on the terms ahead of time so that there can be no mistake about the results."

Victory nervously thought about it. Now that the moment was at hand, she was not so eager to proceed. This was going to be difficult on him, so she tried to think of something that would be conclusive yet uncomplicated.

"I would recommend," he said watching her, "something out of the ordinary, but nothing that would be embarrassing."

She agreed and began scanning the room. Suddenly, an image of the boys playing in the snow imprinted on her mind. "Does it have to be simple or can the task be complicated?"

"What do you have in mind?"

"I thought maybe something like my going outside and throwing snowballs at the window. That is certainly something I would not do."

His mouth curved. "Even porphyrians have limits. Once you left my line of vision, the contact would weaken. After a couple of minutes, it would break. I would have to go outside with you and stay in pretty close proximity."

She thought about his suggestion for a moment. She was unsure if she wanted to take a chance on going outside where she might have to contend with his delusions in public. Hurriedly, she cast about for another solution.

"Well, how about if you get me to open the window and make a snowball with the snow on the ledge?"

He glanced at the window. A couple of inches of white powder skimmed the surface of the ledge. He nodded. It would suffice. "I must give a word of caution. If you sense what is going on, which has happened in some rare instances, don't resist. The attempt would be futile and would result in pain and possible neurological damage."

She quelled her nerves and nodded. Sitting back in her chair, she waited. Without another word, Andrew pushed away from the wall and walked to the other side of the room. He sat on the corner of the bed. Victory was reminded of their time in England. Heat suffused her face and she looked away. Her eyes strayed to the window. Would she actually feel a compulsion to exercise the demonstration or would they sit in silence for an extended period until one of them called off the charade.

Impatiently, she stood. It was a mistake not to have a prescribed time period since they could go on for hours in a stalemate. She pushed aside the curtains and looked out. The boys still were engaged in their snowball fight, but the elderly woman and her poodle had vanished. Pushing open the window, she leaned out into the brisk air. Inhaling deeply, she sighed contentedly as the tingle of crisp clean air filled her lungs. Glancing down at the powdery film that hid the ledge, she traced patterns in it with her finger. Wistfully, she recalled her childhood when she had been carefree and able to indulge in frivolities such as snowball fights. "Maybe," she thought, "Andrew and I should try something like that to break the tension." Feeling in a lighthearted mood for the first time since Laura's death, she packed the white powder between her hands and shaped it into a ball.

Lifting the snowball into her cupped palm, she turned to throw it at Andrew. Suddenly, she froze. Her hand quivered. Her arm trembled. Her whole body shook. She tried to turn her hand over in order to drop the ball back on the sill, but it was as if her hand were in a vise. Despite the chill air, she began to sweat. By shear will, she prevented herself from turning with the ball in her hand. Her mind screamed to her hand to do its will, but to no avail. Inch by inch, she inexorably turned into the room. A scream of mental anguish built inside of her head. She groaned. Something broke and, instantly, she was free. As if a dam suddenly had broken loose, her hand squeezed convulsively and smashed the ball. She screamed and then collapsed to the floor.

Chapter 23:
Divided Loyalties

The Earl of Rockford leaned over the balcony of Andrew's Bethesda mansion. He stared at the barren trees stretching their bare branches towards the inky starlit sky. Turning his back on the scenery, he faced the house.

"Dana, don't you believe in using the front door?" he asked dryly.

Dana laughed as she emerged from the shadows. "I think this is much more dramatic. Don't you?"

His breath caught as he drank in her dark beauty. "You always did have a flair for the sensational," he returned, as he eyed her billowing gray gown and matching cape. "Where did you get that costume?"

"I've been around," she said, while sliding her arms provocatively around his neck.

"Well, it doesn't look very warm," he replied harshly and pulled free. "You'd better come inside."

Dutifully, she followed him and then perched on the arm of his chair. After allowing him to get settled, she slid into his lap. Disgusted, he jerked upright and she spilled onto the floor. "Is flirting all you know how to do?"

Unabashed, she tipped her head to one side. "If you're not interested, then why did you summon me?"

"Because I'd hoped you'd changed. Because you and I need to talk."

Her eyes narrowed. "About what?" she asked suspiciously.

"About what your father is up to."

She stood, shook out her garments, and shrugged. "You know what my father is up to."

He gritted his teeth. "I only know as much as he feels it's safe for me to know."

"That's true," she admitted without rancor. Then, she laughed, "and you expect me to tell you the rest?"

179

Ignoring her comment, he started to pace. "I know he is going to try to have the president assassinated so he can take over, but I don't know the details."

"And what would you do if you did? Tell them to Andrew?" she sneered.

Again, he ignored the interruption. "I have been forced into a role that is loathsome to me. Do you have any idea how much it hurts to betray Andrew?"

Unable to endure the pain in his eyes, she inspected the paintings on the wall.

"I found out the truth about Craven's rehab programs." She spun to face him as he continued. "I had a very difficult time reconciling the Craven I know with the benevolent rehabilitator he is trying to portray. Once I discovered that Thomas is in charge, my suspicions were confirmed. You're planning to use this new rehab program as a front to massacre diurnals. And I'll bet it's part of the research Craven has been doing."

Her eyes widened and she bit her lip. "So, I hit a nerve," Jordan thought.

"Do you honestly think I could tell you anything even if I wanted to? I know you are in Andrew's confidence and I can't take the risk of having what I tell you get back to him. Besides," she added, as she regained her composure, "I'm not so sure Daddy's wrong."

"Explain it to me," he pressed, as he reached out to take her in his arms.

Her breathing quickened and, for a second, she relaxed against him, but then she jerked out of his embrace. "Do you think I am so easily fooled?" she asked angrily.

"Dana, we have to do something before this goes too far and not even Andrew can set it right."

In less than an hour, Dana sat across from her father in his study. Seated behind his desk in a large leather swivel chair, he regarded her coolly. "Your report is thorough," he said, as he glanced down at his notebook. "But," he continued, while studying her intently, "you are holding back something. What is it?"

Dana looked away. She had detailed the arrangements for the assassination and reported the progress of their other projects. "Am I allowed no privacy, even in my personal life?"

"Not if it impairs your judgment and compromises our goal," he replied to her unspoken question. "Jason has made the contact. The man has agreed to take on the assignment. Our own personnel are being inconspicuously transplanted into key positions in the rehab facilities and we are getting ready to make the most monumental move to benefit our species in history. I will not tolerate any possibility of sabotage."

Dana shifted nervously. "I doubt Jordan's misgivings could constitute sabotage. He will continue to follow orders as long as they are not countermanded."

Craven leaned back in his chair, as his black eyes bored into her. He raised his brows and she flinched.

"Jordan is probing," she admitted reluctantly. "He is trying to determine the details of the assassination and it is my opinion that he is planning a strategy to discover the details of the project."

Craven leaned forward to make notes in his book. Looking at her levelly, he stated, "Jordan will have to be watched more closely. When he becomes more of a liability than an asset, he will have to be eliminated."

Dana's expression was impassive. "Perhaps," she agreed evenly.

He studied her intently for a moment and then dismissed her. Slowly, he reread his last entry. Fingering the pages of the black leather notebook, he shook his head. It was taxing to remain out of the mainstream, but he had to endure it for only a few more days. Soon, he wouldn't be just in the mainstream. He would be the head of it.

Andrew and Jordan watched the drama unfolding on a large screen television. The president was broadcasting live. He explained that the vice president would be on a short leave due to the recent personal tragedy. He stated that, although the recent death was tragic, he did not feel that either his safety or that of the vice president was impaired.

Andrew turned to his companion, "Well, he's got that half-right he said bitterly.

Jordan glanced at him sharply. Ever since returning from Laura Warner's funeral, the marquis' mental state had seemed precarious. His decreased attention span, inability to concentrate, and lack of motivation were troubling. The one thing that they didn't need right now was for Andrew to retreat again.

He had been concerned when Victory had not returned with the marquis and he feared the worst. His enquiry had been met with a cryptic response and then the matter had been dropped. A few days later, Jordan had been relieved when he was unable to satisfy Craven's curiosity. Livid at the loss of his bargaining chip, Craven had demanded that Jordan discover her location. He gained immense gratification in being able to refuse.

Now, he wondered if protecting Victory from Craven was the only reason for her absence. Andrew had been melancholy and lethargic since returning from his trip. In fact, Andrew was starting to show signs of the same despondency that he had demonstrated prior to his last hibernation. He was abruptly snatched from his reflections by his cousin's voice.

"We're running out of time."

Jordan nodded as he glanced again at the president's placid features. "I can't get anything out of Dana and I doubt any of the others have the information. But this would be the perfect time for the assassination since Craven has a built-in alibi."

Andrew sighed. "I suppose I will have to probe Dana," he reluctantly decided. "Were your other endeavors successful?"

Jordan raised his eyebrows. "Obviously, you haven't been keeping up with the news. A few days ago, a news bulletin was telecast. It announced that the car of the Prime Minister of France exploded when he started the ignition. The blaze was so intense they doubt there will even be enough remains for dental records. Several terrorist groups have already stepped forward to take credit."

Andrew nodded. "And Alexander?"

Instead of replying, Jordan turned up the volume of the television. The news had switched from domestic to international. In the background was a river with several men conferring on the bank. Further out, a boat could be seen. In the foreground, a correspondent was reporting. "As of this evening, rescue attempts for the German Chancellor had proven unsuccessful."

Jordan switched off the set. "Early this morning, it was reported that the chancellor was out for a pleasure ride in his new Mercedes. He was driving in excess of 120 miles per hour when he had a head-on collision with a logging truck. His car spun out of control and plunged into the river. As you saw, retrieval efforts have been unsuccessful."

Chapter 24: Quest for Answers

Victory sat idly in the window seat. "As she absentmindedly sipped her coffee, she was oblivious to the surrounding scenery. She turned into the room and allowed her gaze to wander. The cozy room with its wicker furniture and throw rugs certainly gave no indication of the extreme wealth of the owners. The simple wood cottage reminded her of a house in a fairy tale, complete with latticed windowpanes and flower boxes under the sills. Looking through the beveled glass, she realized that the day was promising a hint of spring. Puffy white clouds speckled the dazzlingly bright blue sky. Despite her melancholy mood, she smiled when a sparrow lighted on a nearby oak branch. Suddenly restless, she had a compelling desire to escape the confines of the house. She walked over and placed her cup in the sink. Slipping on her wool coat and gloves, she let herself out.

The brisk breeze tainted the hint of spring. She quickened her pace in order to stay warm. She wandered aimlessly through the woods in back of the house and was grateful that the Warners had no close neighbors. Casual conversation with other pedestrians was not an inviting prospect while she was trying to put the events of the past few weeks into perspective.

Three weeks ago, she had sought refuge on the Warners' doorstep in order to escape from the man whom she had thought was the love of her life. She was sure that the events just after the funeral were a part of a stress-induced psychosis. A break from reality was the only explanation of the distorted memories plaguing her tortured mind.

She paused as she approached a large willow tree. The image

evoked a half-buried memory. "I must have suffered some sort of nervous breakdown," she decided, while pulling up her collar. A stark visage of Andrew staring with a mixture of shock and horror at the Willow Grove Crematorium flashed into her mind and then vanished beyond her grasp. Suddenly, she turned back to the house and headed to the garage.

Thirty minutes later, she stood on the steps of the deserted building. "Of course, they wouldn't be open on Sunday," she chided herself. What had possessed her to come out here? Was it some misguided hope that the key to Andrew's delusions was concealed behind the bricks? With shoulders slumping, she leaned her head against the glass door. Was it Andrew's sanity that she really was concerned about – or her own? Just imagine: He concocted an ancient species of people who drank blood and hypnotized humans. How preposterous! But, just like he claimed, it had worked hadn't it?

The memories after the demonstration had been worse. Each flashback had been like getting a low-grade electric shock. Each shock brought back long-forgotten memories of her dad bragging about one of his most-interesting patients. One particular patient lacked solar tolerance and never seemed to age. He had broken through solid steel bars in order to escape from the sanitarium. This very dangerous patient had mutilated a student nurse because she had caught him trying to escape.

Her father had revealed one aspect of the grizzly death that had never made it into the papers. An abnormally small amount of blood had been left in the victim's body. She shuddered as the wind tore at her clothes and whipped her face. What did it mean? Years ago, did her father actually have some sort of alien in his facility?

Past merged with present as she recalled the day when Detective Roberts had been speaking softly to Andrew in her living room. Unchecked tears rolled down her cheeks and spattered onto the bricks as the detective's words mirrored her father's and echoed through her mind.

And what of the demonstration in the hotel room? How did he manage such a feat? Even though her memory of the incident was blessedly hazy, she clearly remembered his ravings about being some sort of renegade blood-drinking subspecies. "Stop trying to avoid the truth," she berated. Andrew had tried his best to convince her that he was a vampire. He may have called it by another name, but that didn't change what he had tried to prove. "Even more frightening was the fact that I had almost credited his delusions – or at least part of his story," she amended. After the experiment with the snowball, she had been gripped by searing pain shooting through her head. The pain had escalated until she thought that her head was going to explode. Then, it ceased so abruptly that she had fainted. When she had awakened, she was lying on the bed with Andrew solicitously hovering over her. Shame flooded through her as she remembered her hysteria. She had jerked upright, while screaming for him to get away from her. When he complied, she had run for the door. Primal fear and unconscious survival instinct drove her as she bolted out of the hotel and across the street.

She would have died if it hadn't been for Andrew's persistence. He had followed with the intent of protecting her from the danger that he had insisted was her fate. She had glanced over her shoulder and had panicked when he was behind by only a few steps. Screeching tires and a blaring horn had snapped her attention back to the road. The front grill of a car had been bearing down on her. She had known that the vehicle was going too fast to stop on the icy street. She had frozen. Within inches of the fender, she had felt herself being grabbed and hauled against a hard object. When she had realized that she was safe in Andrew's arms, she broke down and sobbed.

The loss of her best friend, her shattered relationship, and the trauma in the hotel room had been too much. Completely devastated, she had wept all of the way to the Warner's house. He had wanted to come with her in order to insure her safety, but she had refused and ridiculously had kept her destination a secret. After a last futile attempt to get her to talk to him, he had left.

Laura's parents, deep in their own grief, had tried to console her as much as they could. Never probing, they had allowed her to take all of the time and solace that she desperately needed in order to wade through her own sorrow. She had been sure that they had suspected that there was more to her depression than the death of their daughter, but, having regarded her as one of their own since childhood, they had respected her privacy.

Now that the initial shock had faded, she tried to make sense of the situation. She lifted her head from the door and stared blankly at the wall. No matter how she tried, she couldn't accept the explanation. Her mind skidded away from the issue every time that she tried to apply logic. Suddenly, her gaze sharpened and the plaque that she unconsciously was staring at came into focus. Andrew had read this plaque right before returning to the car and insisting on telling her his story. Had this engraving triggered something?

She read the inscription, blinked, and then read it again.

"Dedicated to the memory of Crystal and Raven Maxwell, 1615."

Her memory shifted and she again was sitting on the outcrop of rocks and reading the vampire book from Andrew's library. A chill went through her when she remembered the story of how Andrew's father had burned the house of his wife's abductor to the ground. Craven's father had been killed during that attack.

Before being interrupted by the little girl, the last passage that she had read in the vampire book was about a vampire named Raven. Was there a connection? How did the pieces fit? She reread the inscription, "1615." Something didn't make sense. Either the inscription was wrong or she grossly had misinterpreted Andrew's story or... Suddenly, she remembered Andrew's words in the hotel. He had mentioned an extended lifespan. She frowned at the inscription that became another piece of the puzzle that didn't fit.

If this building were dedicated to the memory of Craven's parents, it would mean that they had died almost 400 years ago. That was inconceivable. Her mind veered away from that prospect, only to be confronted by another unwelcome intrusion. What kind of a man would build a crematorium as a shrine on the location where his parents had burned to death? The crematoriums were a national chain. Did the vice president own all of them? She closed her eyes and was plagued by the uneasy feelings that she had whenever she was in close proximity to Craven Maxwell. All of a sudden, the idea that he was involved in subversive activities didn't seem so far fetched.

"Hello," Jordan answered as he lifted the receiver.

"Have you made any progress locating the woman?" demanded a cold voice.

"No," Jordan answered complacently. He was relieved that he had been unable to comply with the demand. "I've made several enquiries, but Andrew is guarding his thoughts."

Craven swore, "Damn it! Locating her is crucial."

"I'd say I'm sorry, but I'm not. I happen to like Victory Parker and have no desire to help you find her."

"Nonetheless," he replied implacably, "you will continue as ordered and, if you find out anything, notify me immediately. What else is the Marquis of Penbrook up to?"

"Moping through the mansion as if he's lost his best friend."

"I thought you were his best friend," he said mockingly.

"Not any more," he replied bleakly.

"I know all about Peter and Alexander," Craven continued smoothly. "An investigation is underway regarding the details. It's true that they were not my most loyal supporters, but I doubt they would have defied me on their own. How coincidental that Andrew should find my two weakest links."

That night, Jordan drove into Georgetown. He wandered among the shops, while trying not to think about what was happening at the house. As soon as Andrew had voiced his plan to elicit information from Craven's daughter, Jordan had argued that his presence might be a distraction. Andrew had not agreed and requested that he remain. Jordan finally had confessed that his feelings for the girl might cause him to interfere with the process.

Of course, that hadn't been the only reason. He also had been worried that Dana might tip off Andrew about his duel role, especially if she had a reason to feel that he was aiding Andrew. He realized that she might reveal information either purposefully or inadvertently. If Andrew probed deep enough, he would know everything that Dana knew, including Jordan's duplicity. However, if she had no reason to connect him with the situation, she would be more inclined to keep his secret.

Dana threw open the French doors and casually strolled into the mansion. Walking into the living room, she was surprised to find Andrew sitting alone at the bar. Joining him, she stood silently and studied him for a long moment. He was thinner and his face was drawn with a troubled look in his turquoise eyes.

"Andrew, what is wrong?" she asked, while slipping her arms around his waist.

He returned the embrace and tightly held her. Not for the world would he harm this young woman who was almost like his own child. His lips twisted at the irony. It was for the sake of the world that he was taking this action.

"Your father killed a diurnal," he said flatly.

She stepped back, as she stared at him levelly.

"The woman was Victory's best friend."

Dana's eyes shifted to the window.

"You know my agreement to keep out of your father's affairs extended only as long as Victory remained unharmed."

Her eyes challenged him. "She has not been harmed."

"Yes, she has – indirectly."

"And you have indirectly interfered in my father's plans. It seems to me as if you are at a stalemate."

Sweat trickled down his neck as he approached one of the windows. Opening it, he said with his back turned, "I think the time has come for you to tell me exactly what your father is up to."

He heard the gasp. Turning, he found her staring at him in horror. "I can't."

Resolutely, he strode towards her. "You can and you will," he said with finality.

"Do you know what Daddy will do to me if he finds out I've betrayed him?"

He thoughtfully studied her, "Not much when he realizes you had no choice."

She tightly clasped her hands together to keep them from shaking. She said pleadingly, "You don't know what you're asking. He has commanded me to remain silent."

"Come here, Dana," he ordered, as he gazed steadily into her eyes.

As the turquoise eyes bore into her, she felt as though she were being impaled on twin spikes of steel. Her legs moved on their own volition as she realized that she really didn't have a choice. At any time, this man could have forced her compliance. The fact that he hadn't exercised that privilege previously filled her with respect. Unfortunately, fear surpassed admiration. She dashed for the door. He caught her easily. Lifting her in his arms, he carried her back into the room.

Chapter 25:

Betrayal

Distractedly, Victory let herself back into the house. Mrs. Warner sat at the dining room table and beckoned as she passed. Victory approached reluctantly. She wished that she could have reached the privacy of her room so that she could sort through her disturbing revelations. A fresh wave of grief washed over her as she sat across from Laura's mother. Mrs. Warner's features were so similar to Laura's that it was almost like stabbing a knife into an open wound. She considered the possibility that she would be better able to recuperate at home.

Mrs. Warner smiled slightly. "I have just received a letter from my nephew, Ben," she said, while affecting a cheeriness that Victory knew that she didn't feel. "It appears that he is going to be released from prison in a few days." Victory's face clouded with confusion. The other woman continued, "He is singing the praises of the rehab program that Laura got him involved in. He says he has sent a letter to her with more details. He also mentions wanting to visit Laura to thank her in person when he is released." Her eyes misted and she said in a choked voice, "I guess I will have to write him and tell him what happened."

Victory nodded her agreement, as she clasped the other woman's hand in hers. After a few seconds, she stood. The germ of an idea began to take shape and she said, "Why not let me do that for you?"

Mrs. Warner's eyes shone with gratitude. "Are you sure you're up to it?"

She wasn't sure, but she nodded.

On her flight back to Washington, she read the report that the head nurse from St. Mary's had provided. Mrs. Brown always had had a soft spot for her, so Victory easily had managed to persuade her to send a copy of the papers about the doctor's most infamous patient. Her father, she realized as she sifted through the sheets, had been very close to publishing a study on the subject. Victory frowned as she read. She sat back and steepled her hands. She should be feeling something – like shock, revulsion, fear, or even elation – at Andrew's vindication, but, right now, she was just numb.

She stared at the file in her lap. This information would be useful in formulating her plan. If Craven was really involved in a plot to take over the government, then maybe Ben had gleaned something from the rehabilitation program. That was the vice president's pet project. It was the one that he had stressed throughout the campaign. She realized that she was grasping at straws, but it was a start. She briefly considered the possibility of co-conspirators. As in any new administration, a whole host of new personnel had been assigned to positions of power. She had to admit that she did not know much about any of them, which, in itself, was suspicious. Being in the political field should have acquainted her with most of the rising stars.

She sighed as she returned the file to her purse. Whether she was on a wild-goose chase or not, she was obligated to meet with Ben. Most likely, he would not be able to tell her anything of relevance, but she needed to let him know about Laura.

As the taxi pulled up outside of her townhouse, she looked around nervously. Maybe it hadn't been such a good idea to return home. But where else could she have gone? Andrew's mansion? Not while she was still unresolved. She paid the driver and then followed him as he piled her suitcases on the porch. After the cab pulled away, she stared at the door for a long time until she realized what was wrong. The entire structure had been replaced. The splintered wood was gone. Instead, a solid oak frame confronted her.

With fingers trembling, she inserted her key and turned the lock. Stepping inside, she pulled her cases in and firmly closed the door. Leaning against the frame for several seconds, she finally got up the courage to venture further. Slowly, she approached the bathroom. Was it wise to confront the murder scene or should she avoid the room? Squaring her shoulders, she stepped into the room. It had been cleaned meticulously. "Probably Andrew's handiwork," she thought wistfully. He surely had been responsible for the front door, as well. Realizing that she was avoiding the tub, she turned to face the structure. She gasped. The tub was gone and in its place was a shiny new brass bathtub, complete with shower attachments. Even the towels had been replaced. Startled by the unexpected thoughtfulness, Victory sat on the edge of the tub while unchecked tears of regret rolled down her cheeks.

Silently, Jordan approached the lone figure on the balcony. Standing next to his cousin, he stared out into the darkness. Acknowledging his presence, Andrew turned. Jordan was stunned by the blazing fury in the turquoise eyes. A shiver ran down his spine as Andrew continued to glare. Had Dana been compelled to betray him after all? Several seconds ticked by. Finally unable to stand the suspense, he broke the silence.

"Were you able to find out anything?"

The question had been foolish, but Andrew nodded curtly. "It's worse than I thought."

Jordan's blood ran cold, but he forced himself to keep his gaze level.

After another pause, Andrew leaned against the railing and spoke in a voice filled with contempt. "Craven is mad." Jordan stiffened and he pushed on. "Yes, I mean he's gone insane, just as our people did before the invention of the drink. According to Dana," he grimaced, "Craven has an intricate plan that he has been developing for years. He has been doing research on the bloody history of our race. Somehow, he has managed to discover documents that indicate that our abilities at one time were much more potent and diversified. After a prolonged examination, he has come to the conclusion that our downfall is a direct result of a deprivation in our diet. He believes that the missing ingredient is human blood."

"Vampirism," Jordan groaned, "After all this time, I didn't think there were any left who credited the story, much less wanted to be involved in the practice."

Andrew stared into the garden with narrowed eyes. "Unfortunately, that is not the case. In addition to Dana and him, there are several other hardcore followers."

"But what has this got to do with his taking over the country? I would think," Jordan speculated, "that engaging in that kind of practice would induce him to stay out of the spotlight."

Somewhere a dog bayed at the moon. The two men listened attentively to the eerie song. As the cry died, Andrew continued his revelations. "As we already know, Craven is planning the assassination of the president. I'm sure he convinced John Callahan to take him on as a running mate. I'm just as sure that he nudged the appointment of his conspirators to key political positions."

Jordan's eyes widened in alarm. "And, by having Callahan appoint them, he can have his key people in place without bringing scrutiny to himself for re-appointments after the assassination."

Andrew smiled wryly and briefly covered his eyes with his hand. "Yes, the venomous vipers. With those men in office, Craven can pretty much do almost anything he wants. But, to get back to the point, the assassination is set for tomorrow. The president will be heading from the White House to the airport. He'll be on his way to an Arab/Israeli peace conference. A man will attempt to kill him somewhere on route."

"Didn't she know specifically where?"

Andrew shook his head. "Craven is very cagey. He's aware that any of his co-conspirators, including Dana, could be probed. He hasn't provided any one of them with the complete details. That's his own system of checks and balances," he finished sardonically.

Andrew paused to stare into the night. Just as Jordan was going to prompt him he continued. "Only Jason, who has been making the arrangements with the man, knows the location of the assassination details. After the assassination, Craven will become the president. The rehab programs will launch on a national scale and the ex-convicts will supposedly be successfully rehabilitated. In actuality, whenever an ex-con comes out of a center, they will receive new identification papers, a new start, and an escort to death. His group has purchased several crematoriums where they take the prisoners, supposedly for debriefing or, as they call it, an "exiting interview." In reality, they have a process for extracting blood that they have been using instead of the drink. This would account for Craven's increased strength at our last meeting," he reflected.

"What happens to the human?" an appalled Jordan asked.

Andrew shrugged. "After the blood is drained, they dispose of the body in the incinerator." Jordan gulped, but Andrew seemed not to notice. "The goal of this grisly plot is to make a new species of porphyrian who are stronger, more powerful, and more dominate over humans. Most of the diurnals are to be used as a food supply, while the others are enslaved."

"Craven actually thinks he can accomplish something that monstrous? He is insane," Jordan exclaimed incredulously. If the diurnals get wind of this, it could set off a panic that would result in the genocide of our people."

"That and the risk to the diurnals are the reasons why he and his followers must be stopped."

Jordan was appalled and wished fervently that he weren't being forced to participate in the demented scheme.

"Dana told me one more thing," he said in a deceptively calm tone.

"What is that?"

He looked Jordan squarely in the face, "She told me you are a spy."

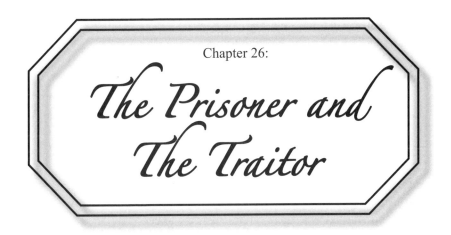

Chapter 26:

The Prisoner and The Traitor

Victory waited impatiently to be connected with Ben Warner. At first, the prison personnel refused to put her through. Prison regulations were rigid and all contact between inmates and outsiders was restricted. After considering her problem, inspiration struck. She quickly redialed. When the operator came on the line, she claimed to be Ben's attorney. Her guilt about the deception was surpassed by her confusion and frustration. As she waited anxiously for the connection, she reflected upon the unusual procedure that was required by the prison.

Hopefully, Ben wouldn't say anything to tip them off. She had a strange feeling that he was not being allowed to communicate with her for a reason. The sense of paranoia was potent, but she attempted to curb her rampant suspicions. After several long minutes, a deep voice resonated through the line.

"Hello."

"Hello, Ben," she said cautiously. She was not sure if the lines were being monitored. "This is Victory Parker, your cousin Laura's friend."

His voice warmed. "Victory, it's been a long time. How are you?"

"I've been better. There's been a lot happening lately and I'd like to arrange a time to talk to you."

"What types of things?" he asked warily.

"Are your phone calls monitored?" she countered.

"Sometimes," he admitted. "They don't think we know, but, sometimes, they are not very careful and we can hear a click on the line."

"Then, I would prefer to wait until we can talk in private."

"Well, your timing couldn't be better. I'm scheduled for release tomorrow."

"I know. Can I meet you? I can pick you up and, after we talk, I can drop you off wherever you want to go."

"Sounds fine. I have to attend some sort of exiting interview first thing in the morning, but, after that, I will be free. Will you be bringing Laura?"

Victory hesitated. "No, she won't be able to come."

"Oh." He sounded disappointed. "I'd like a chance to thank her for getting me into this program. I was told that they have strict criteria for the participants that I didn't meet, so I'm being given this chance only because I'm related to the vice president's fiancée."

"I'm sorry," she said awkwardly, "but she's not available."

A short silence followed and then she asked, "What kind of interview?" She also wanted to ask about the criteria, but, realizing that the phones might be monitored, she decided to wait until they met in person.

He laughed. "They call it 'an exiting interview.' I think it is supposed to be some sort of evaluation of their program. It's new and I guess they are looking for feedback to justify it to the voters. At that time, I suppose I'll be getting my new identity."

Victory thought that she detected some resentment, but decided to wait until she saw him in person to discuss it further.

Andrew glared at his cousin and felt like he had been kicked in the stomach. He contemplated the tall handsome man before him and regretted the confidences of the past few weeks. How long had he been betraying him? It certainly was for the entire time that he had been here. Now that he thought about it, the whole episode seemed contrived. He had been blind to the obvious. Always the fool for his trusted companions, he unwittingly had been feeding information to Jordan for Craven's benefit. Pain and fury sliced through him as he turned his back and walked into the house.

Self-loathing kept Jordan from defending himself as he followed. He was sickened by the look of pain that he saw in Andrew's eyes. How could he explain the compulsion that he had been made to endure? He should have struggled harder, but, in the end, it would have been no use. Andrew knew that, but, at the moment, Jordan doubted that he was thinking clearly.

"Andrew," he began hesitantly, "you know I would never harm you or yours voluntarily."

A strangled cry of rage was torn from Andrew's throat as he whirled on him. Jordan inhaled sharply as he took an involuntary step backwards. Unleashed fury shot from the turquoise eyes as Andrew asked in a steely voice, "What reason could there possibly be to justify your treachery? After all that you and I have been through together, after a lifetime of trust, after all the shared confidences, after I entrusted you with the care of the woman I love..." He broke off suddenly. His eyes narrowed ominously. "So, that's why you've been trying to pry Victory's location out of me. You were going to report her whereabouts to Craven. I trusted you and you've been conspiring to betray me! This whole escapade has been nothing more than a ruse for you to turn over the bargaining chip that Craven needs to keep me under control."

Jordan started to protest. He wanted to explain that he had no choice. He wanted to make Andrew understand the guilt and self-contempt that he had felt during the past weeks. A fist crashed into his jaw. Jordan lunged to the side, but he could not avoid the blow. Andrew was on top of him and was pummeling him.

The two grappled. They turned and thrashed around the room. Furniture overturned and glass shattered. Twisting away from the marquis' murderous grasp, he broke off a leg of a chair and smashed it across his adversary's head. Andrew shook off the blow as if batting away an irritating insect. In desperation, Jordan grabbed a burning log from the fireplace and held it aloft between himself and the marquis.

Watching the log warily, Andrew stood and glowered just out of reach. While he had his attention, Jordan quickly explained.

Trying to catch his breath, he gingerly rubbed his jaw. "When you came to me in England and prevented me from aiding Craven with his plans, I was honestly relieved. I had every intention of fading out of sight for a while. I had considered offering to come back and help you, but I was worried that Craven would get to me and force me to help him again." He stared at the other man silently while pleading for understanding. "Unlike you, Craven has no scruples preventing him from using either his own kind or diurnals to get his needs met."

Andrew suspiciously stared back at him. Jordan glanced at the log. The flames were rapidly consuming it and he knew that his defense was dwindling.

"Unfortunately, Craven got to me before I had a chance to disappear. He ordered me to track your movements and report to him. Later, he told me to keep track of Victory in case he needed collateral. It made me heartsick, but I did it because I had no other choice. You could have put an end to the deception anytime you chose," he added bitterly, "but, because of your high morals, you would have me branded as a traitor for being manipulated rather than risk offending your own sense of misguided morality."

Andrew's eyes flicked to the log. Jordan realized that the wood had burned almost to his hand. Flinging it back into the fireplace, he glared defensively back at his cousin. "Andrew, the stakes are too high for you to stand by your old dogma. You are going to have to reconsider the consequences and alter your tactics if you want to challenge Craven. I am offering you an opportunity to read me and see for yourself that I speak the truth."

A tense silence ensued while green eyes clashed with blue and then drowned in their depths. Finally, Andrew's face relaxed. "You're right," he conceded, while holding out his hand. Jordan reached out, but added, "This isn't over. You are going to have to overrule Craven's dominance or risk this happening again."

Andrew grimaced, but reluctantly agreed.

Victory turned the car off of the main road and drove down the driveway of the new rehabilitation facility. It's pristine white walls contrasted starkly against the bright blue sky. A high barbed-wire fence clearly marked the perimeter of the grounds. Several hundred yards of clearing surrounded the structure and a forest of pine trees provided a scenic backdrop.

Heading for the main gate, she drove past the outer concrete walls. She had arranged to meet Ben as he left the facility. He had some final preparations and some paperwork to finish. When he emerged, he would be a new man, complete with new identification documents and ready to embark on a new life. She shivered. Part of the program required that, once released, the inmates must agree to sever all of their ties with their previous lives. Persons caught violating that stipulation were immediately remanded to the prison system that would enforce extremely severe penalties. She wasn't sure that she could have agreed to that deal even for a clean slate and Uncle Sam's help in getting re-established.

She glanced at her watch. She was over an hour early. She intentionally had planned to arrive ahead of schedule in case the phones had been monitored and whoever was in charge tried to avoid her. Even though she had no reason for her conjectures, she couldn't shake the feeling that prisoners having contact with outsiders would be avoided if possible. While she waited, she listened to the radio. The love ballad reminded her of Andrew. Frustrated, she turned it off.

Hearing a car motor, she glanced up. Even though she had half-expected it, she was surprised to see a car approach the front gate. The unmarked police car pulled up, papers were exchanged, and the barrier arm was lifted. As it passed, she recognized the passenger as Laura's cousin. Distressed by the disruption to their plans, she considered the implications. Either Ben had reconsidered their meeting and arranged to leave early to avoid her or the phone line was monitored after all. She remembered the difficulty that she had encountered during the previous day when she contacted him. If that were the case, then why would anyone object to their meeting? Was it that imperative for the reformed convicts not to have any dealings with people from their past? That made sense, considering what Laura had told her about the program. But even the government would have to take into consideration that they would have families and loved ones whom they would contact after being released. Filled with vague uneasiness, she followed the car at a discreet distance.

She slammed on the brakes as she rounded the next bend. Perplexed, she watched as the unmarked police car pulled alongside another vehicle. The driver of the first car consulted briefly with a young woman and then spoke with Ben. When she passed documents to the driver, Victory assumed that the woman was a government agent. After again consulting with Ben, he got into the other car. The first car did a u-turn and retraced its route. Victory momentarily panicked as the car approached, but the driver didn't even glance in her direction as he passed.

Confused, she watched as the car driven by the young woman retreated. Originally, she had planned to follow the police car and pick up Ben from wherever they left him. She had assumed that they simply were providing him with transportation from the premises. Did this new development mean that they were not finished with the rehab process? In addition to Ben and the woman, she had noticed two men in business suits. The taillights receded, but she still hesitated. Should she continue on her original course? What kind of trouble could she get into for interfering with the process? She had the feeling that she would not be welcomed. Could she be disbarred for intruding upon the vice president's pet project? Maybe she should go home and wait for Ben to contact her. If he forgot or received strict instructions to the contrary, what would happen then? An image of Andrew's desperate face convinced her to pursue her original impulse, so she put the car into gear.

Chapter 27:
Lamb to the Slaughter

Jordan walked cautiously into the office. He was sure that his nervousness would be detected, thus putting Craven instantly on guard. He licked dry lips and opened the door. Craven was seated behind the desk and was writing in his notebook. He did not look up as Jordan entered, but motioned to a chair with a wave of his hand. Jordan shifted uncomfortably. After several seconds, he finally looked up. Coolly examining the earl, he questioned, "Since you requested a personal contact, I assume that you have information of relevance."

Jordan nodded. "I've discovered the location of the woman and I didn't want to risk being overheard on the phone. He finished quietly and then curiously looked around at the walls. They were studded with pictures of people in various scenes. They all focused on an urn except for one picture that depicted a group assembled on the deck of a ship. The group was tipping a container over the water while ashes spread across the waves.

Craven cocked a brow. "Charming pictures, aren't they? They lend a sense of authenticity. Don't you agree?" Not waiting for a response, he continued, "All right. Tell me about the woman."

Jordan looked levelly at him. "Andrew confided that he sent Victory to his Cornwall estate. He said she would remain there only for another couple of days because he was worried that you would find a way to penetrate his defenses."

"His concern is certainly justified." Craven stood and Jordan followed suit. "Your information confirms what I already suspected. Since it is impossible for me to leave the country at such a crucial time, let us go downstairs and discuss the matter with the others. I am sure a couple of them will be obliging enough to escort Miss Parker home."

Jordan inwardly winced. He hoped that this meeting would last long enough for Andrew to get into position.

Each minute seemed to slip by quicker than the last as the Marquis of Penbrook anxiously checked his watch. He climbed into the back seat of the Rolls. "To the White House," he ordered. The chauffeur's wide eyes and raised brows confronted him in the rear view mirror. "And don't spare the gas."

As the car moved away from the curb, he leaned against the leather upholstery and wondered what he was going to do after he reached his destination. Dana had told him that the assassin would be waiting with a high-powered rifle in a building somewhere on route. But where? The possibilities were limitless. He stared out of the window and was oblivious to the distractions of the inner city. If he had been able to retrieve the details, he wouldn't need to go to the White House. He simply could have surprised the assassin in his hiding place.

Nervously, he again checked his watch. Callahan was scheduled to depart for Geneva within the hour. "He is going to be late," the marquis thought grimly. Once in Callahan's presence, he was certain that he could gain an audience. "After all," he thought sardonically, "wasn't he the brother of the second in command?" Getting to speak with John Callahan was going to be the easy part. Establishing the validity of his claim would be another matter. How could he convince the man that his life was at risk without exposing the full truth to him? Supposedly, the secret service had examined and approved the route. Craven had the secret service in his back pocket, but the president didn't know. Callahan was like a lamb being led to the slaughter. Andrew admitted that he would be skeptical of the allegations if he were in the president's place.

Again, he checked his watch. By now, Jordan was helping Craven plan Victory's abduction from his Cornwall estate. He shuddered. Thank goodness that she was safely far from the unfolding drama. Hopefully, forming a strategy to obtain Victory would keep Craven distracted long enough for Andrew to disrupt the assassination. He still would need to convince Callahan that the person responsible for Laura Warner's death was going to make an attempt on his life. Grimacing, he thought, "That much is certainly true."

Even though he had probed Dana thoroughly, an escape plan for the assassin had not been revealed. Andrew was left with the distinct impression that the man was meant to be the scapegoat for both crimes. He reviewed the method that Dana had imparted about how they were going to insure the assassin's cooperation. He assumed that the man knew nothing about Laura's death. Certainly, he was ignorant about fellow conspirators. To ensure this point, they had given an additional command to the man in order to convince him that he was a lone perpetrator acting out of vengeance. Placed in the assassin's mind was a completely fabricated story about how John Callahan, while governor of Florida, had sentenced his father to the electric chair. As a result, the family had been forced into abject poverty. Eventually, his mother had died after years of working three jobs in a valiant effort to provide for the children.

"A touching story," Andrew admitted wryly, as they passed by the Potomac River. He wondered if the man's parents were still alive. As they neared Pennsylvania Avenue, the traffic became congested. A crowd of demonstrators blocked the street and crossed in front of the Rolls. Looking ahead, Andrew noticed that the entire next two blocks seemed to be full of pedestrians. Silently, he cursed his lack of foresight in checking the news for any demonstrations scheduled near the White House. He considered traveling the rest of the way on foot, but he knew that he would never be able to move quickly through the milling crowds that were picketing and protesting. Sighing heavily, he leaned against the seat and prayed.

Victory watched as the car halted in front of the Willow Grove Crematorium. The brunette alighted from the car and guided Ben towards the building. He halted, studied the building, and then shook his head. He turned towards the woman and the two spoke for several seconds. Obviously satisfied with her explanation, he relaxed and allowed himself to be escorted inside.

The two men, whom Victory assumed were agents, paused as they got out of the car. They exchanged words as they glanced in her direction. She frowned as she allowed her gaze to sweep along the buildings on either side of the street. Lifting a piece of paper, she frowned again and continued to drift slowly down the street. Still affecting the pose of a lost traveler, she passed by them. When she glanced in her rearview mirror, the men had disappeared.

Turning the next corner, she pulled into the alley behind the building. Parking the car a couple of blocks away, she quietly walked to the crematorium. A sense of foreboding gripped her as she wondered why they had brought Ben to this location. In all of her experience as an attorney, she had never heard of a "exiting interview" taking place in anywhere other than in a government institution. A crematorium was absolutely absurd. How was all of it connected? What did all of it mean? And what, if anything, did the vice president have to do with it? She shivered as she remembered the inscription on the building in Pennsylvania.

Cautiously, she crossed to the other side of the street. Ducking between two warehouses, she surveyed the crematorium from the safety of the shadows. The back of the building was composed of solid concrete with one forbidding-looking metal door. Scanning both sides of the street, she was relieved to find them deserted. Crossing to the back of the building, she tried the door. Locked. She took a few steps back and glanced up. There were windows, but they were several feet above. Cupping her chin in her hands, she considered her predicament. Reason dictated that she should stop acting like she was in the middle of an espionage movie and that she should go back to her car and wait for Ben to emerge. She shivered. The late afternoon air was cold and the chill already was penetrating her clothing.

She turned towards the direction of her car, took a couple of steps, and then froze. Voices were emanating from somewhere nearby. They were faint at first, but, as she continued to listen, the voices became more distinct. Glancing around, she spotted an open basement window just below street level. Bending, she peered through the opening. Stacks of packing crates obstructed her view, but she clearly could hear the occupants of the room.

"I don't understand," said a confused male voice that she recognized as Ben's, "why we have to have our meeting in a crematorium."

Ben involuntarily shivered as he looked around the room. A large furnace dominated the room and metal tables were placed at intervals along the walls. Beyond the tables lay various trays with paraphernalia that he assumed was used on the corpses before cremation. He wrinkled his nose at the pungent odor, as he turned towards his companion to protest. She indicated a door and he gratefully followed her into a small conference room.

He rubbed his hands together and blew on them. It was freezing and he wondered if someone had forgotten to pay the electric bill. He noticed that the others seemed to be comfortable, as they took their seats around the table.

As if reading his mind, the young woman said, "Don't worry. You won't be here long enough to freeze."

She motioned for him to sit at one end of the table. She surprised him by sitting adjacent rather than across from him. As he eyed the conspicuously empty chair, it dawned on him that another party would be conducting the interview. He shifted nervously in his seat. Since leaving the center, he had felt like part of a spy movie: covertly leaving the facility ahead of schedule, being escorted by the police, rendez-vousing with secret service agents for his exiting interview, and then winding up in a crematorium.

The woman and two men did not conform to his idea of what feds should look like. However, he had to admit that his knowledge came only from what he had read and seen on television. The woman was beautiful. She had long wavy dark hair and big velvety brown eyes. She wore a pair of jeans interspersed with snakeskin and decorated with chains. Her jean jacket matched her pants and was buttoned so low that most of her cleavage was revealed. The men appeared more in character with dark business suits and ties. Even so, they gave him the chills with their malevolent stares and brooding faces. If it hadn't been for the identifications, he would never have believed in their authenticity.

Dana noticed his nervousness and explained. "Mr. Warner, you will need to have a physical examination before you are allowed to proceed. After that part of the process is over, you will be provided with your new identification papers."

He nodded and asked tensely, "Why the examination?"

"Because we have to determine any distinguishing marks and other signs so that the government can keep them on record for identification purposes. As you know, your previous identification records were expunged from the computers. Distinguishing physical characteristics are going to be the only way of knowing who you were prior to your incarceration."

"Why not use my records from the exam I had when I entered the facility?" he questioned skeptically.

She smiled apologetically, "Unfortunately, there was a mix up and those records were expunged with the rest."

"Damned government can't get anything right," he muttered, as he relaxed in his chair. "I have to tell you," he continued, "I'm not on board with the idea of severing all ties with my family. I have people on the outside who I want to stay in contact with."

Dana studied him. The corners of her mouth lifted as she said, "Don't worry, Mr. Warner. In your case, I think we can make an exception."

He glanced around the room. "Which one of you is the doctor?" he asked with lifted brows.

"Would you believe I am," she asked guilelessly.

He started to laugh, but, catching a movement out of the corner of his eye, he turned to face his assailant, but it was too late. The man gave him a light touch behind the ear and he unconsciously slumped forward.

"Good job, Thomas."

"What was the purpose of the story?" Thomas asked, as he slung the body onto the table.

She shrugged, "I was practicing. You never know when a good story might come in handy. I was also trying to stall. I didn't know if Daddy wanted to question him."

Victory wondered who the woman's father was, as she removed her shoes and dropped through the window. From the heavy thud and the way that they were talking, she assumed that Ben was unconscious or dead. After peering around the boxes, she stared in horror at the trio gathered around the metal table. Ben lay motionless. She was sure that they had killed him until she heard the man's next words.

"I didn't hit him very hard. He'll revive in a few minutes."

"Good. We don't want him to miss all the fun."

Victory wondered at the cryptic remark. Being positive that something awful was about to happen to Laura's cousin, she turned to leave in the same way that she had come. She would find the first available phone and call the police. Could she trust the police? After all, hadn't the police just handed Ben over to these people? In fact, this whole program was part of the federal prison system. Who would believe her story and act quickly enough to help Ben? "Andrew," she thought wildly, "Andrew will help me." She had to get out undetected and call Andrew.

Stealthily retracing her steps, she approached the window. She stared up in dismay at the eight-foot high sill. It hadn't seemed that far on the way in. Extending her arms, she jumped. Her fingers grabbed for the sill, but she slipped and landed hard. Pain shot through her right ankle. She leaned her back against the wall as she thought about her predicament. She stared at the rows of boxes. No good. They were too highly stacked and too tightly packed. Pulling out even one would cause the entire wall of boxes to crash. The only alternative was the door. Somehow, she would have to sneak past the room's occupants while remaining undetected.

If she could make it that far, she could access the phone in the front office. Remaining undetected would be difficult, but, if she could maneuver around the perimeter of the basement, she should be able to reach the door without being noticed. She peered around the crates. The large medicine cabinet that was standing about ten feet away looked plausible for her next safe haven. She looked back at the porphyrians and froze in horror. Her eyes widened in shock and she gasped. Ben was strapped to the table with plungers protruding from several points on his body. Red fluid ran through the tubing and into glass bottles. She thought that it looked like an inverted transfusion. Almost gagging, she realized that these monsters were draining his blood.

Ben's life depended on how quickly she could get help. She silently slid along the wall while keeping one eye on the door and the other on the group around the table. The door was only a few feet away. Sliding next to the jam, she slowly reached for the knob, while still keeping one wary eye on the activity at the table. Ben regained consciousness and groaned weakly. Victory flinched at his scream of anguish.

The elevator doors slid open. Craven and Jordan stepped into the basement. As they strode towards the double doors at the end of the hall, Craven turned to his companion. "Are you sure about your infor-mation? This is a critical time for me and I would hate to send one of my valuable assistants on a wild-goose chase."

Jordan attempted to maintain a relaxed pose. "To the best of my knowledge," he shrugged, "I don't have any reason to suppose Andrew would lie to me."

Craven nodded and reached for the doorknob. They paused as a loud wailing assailed them. Jordan blanched, but Craven appeared only annoyed, as he scowled and then threw open the door.

Chapter 28:
Captured

The reprimand died in Craven's throat as he stared at the blonde in the doorway. Victory tried to lunge past, but, quick as a striking snake, Craven snatched her hair and hauled her hard against him.

Furiously, he turned on Jordan, "Are we in England," he asked, while harshly shaking Victory, "or have you been lying to me, Jordan?"

Numb with shock, Victory could only stare from one man to the other. She could hardly believe that Jordan, the man whom she had come to trust as a friend, was a part of this. And Craven? Even though she knew about the vice president's involvement, actually being confronted by his treachery was too much to bear. Desperately, she tried to break away, but her captor inexorably pulled her head back until her neck was bent far over his arm. One look into the onyx orbs convinced her of the futility of trying to break free. The commotion at the door caught the attention of the others.

"Here," Craven snarled as he thrust Victory towards Walter, "Hold her while I deal with this traitor."

As Walter grabbed for her, Jordan lifted a piece of metal piping and pounced. He smashed Walter across the temple. Dazed, he slumped to the floor. "Run!" Jordan yelled at Victory. Since Craven blocked the exit, she dodged back to the way that she had come in. The dark-haired woman loomed ahead and Victory was sure that she would catch her, but, to her surprise, she let her pass. Her eyes were glued to the scene that was unfolding between Craven and Jordan. Visible ahead was a metal door with a red "EXIT" sign illuminated above it. Hoping that it was open from this side, she dove for it. Just as she hit the door, she was tackled from behind. The door flew open. She and the porphyrian spilled into the alley. Grabbing her by the hair, he dragged her back to the building.

Inside, she twisted around to examine her captor. What she saw made her blood run cold. The man holding her was an extremely handsome man of about thirty with blonde hair and green eyes. His rugged features were stern and, when they made eye contact, she looked away quickly. His eyes were the most malevolent that she had ever seen. Looking into them had been like staring into a bottomless pit. Not only that, but also the way that he was using unnecessary force to subdue her indicated that he was the type who enjoyed inflicting pain.

Thomas dragged her to the table and she winced. Ben was unconscious again or dead. The porphyrians already were removing the needles from his arteries. Victory gulped as she considered her fate. Desperately, she glanced at Jordan. He was engaged in a battle of wills with Craven so she knew that she was on her own.

Two of the porphyrians picked up Ben's lifeless body and placed it on a long tray with a handle. As Victory watched in fascinated horror, one of the men opened the door of the furnace and the dark-haired woman slid the tray into the roaring flames. Tipping the tray slightly, she eased the body into the fire and then nodded for the man to close the door. Victory watched transfixed as the flames licked at the flesh and spread to Ben's hair and clothes. As she watched, his eyes opened. Sickened, she realized that he still was alive. Bile rose in her throat as she turned away from the grizzly scene.

"Don't close the furnace," said Craven in a conversational tone, "We have more fuel for the fire." Turning back to Jordan, he said pleasantly, "You have been a real disappointment to me, Jordan. Unfortunately, I can't take the risk of you causing me any more trouble. Thomas, "he said to the man who was strapping Victory to the metal table, "I have other plans for Miss Parker." He grinned ominously, "She is going to assist me with an experiment in a little while. First, we must attend to the Earl of Rockford."

He stared hard at Jordan for a moment and then nodded. As if of his own accord Jordan, moved inexorably towards the furnace. The room's occupants stared in shock. They had never seen one porphyrian being terminated by another. Jordan reached the opening and hesitated. Sweat poured from his skin and his face contorted as he tried valiantly to resist Craven's command.

Victory's mental barriers collapsed as she finally accepted the truth. A shrill scream broke from her as Jordan lifted his leg towards the flames. She screamed and screamed until her lungs burned. Craven grabbed her and shook her so hard that her teeth snapped together. "You may have succeeded in breaking my concentration, but you can't prevent the inevitable."

Tears rolled down her face as she glanced in Jordan's direction. He was slumped against the wall and was staring vacantly into the room. He seemingly was incapable of moving from his position.

"However," Craven continued in the same conversational tone, "if the proceedings disturb you so much, then you don't have to watch."

Before she could react, he slipped his hand behind her ear and she collapsed onto the table. As he turned back to Jordan, a metal tray flew at him from the side. The tray smashed against his temple. It knocked him off balance and he crashed into the wall.

Jordan shook his head as he threw off the bands of control. Casting a grateful glance at Dana, he ran for the door. Receiving no orders, the others stood dazed as he escaped. Running to the car in which he and Craven had arrived, he tore open the door and dove into the driver's seat. Grateful that he had done the driving, he pulled out the key and started the ignition. "Where is Andrew?" he wondered, as he wildly careened around the corner. Approaching the White House, he decided to turn the car in that direction. Could Andrew catch his thoughts with Craven's influence so close? He'd better try. At that moment, another thought intercepted his own.

"Craven," he whispered, as he swerved to avoid two pedestrians. The car spun as he fought for control of his thoughts. It was no use. After a few moments, he pulled the car to the side of the street. A few pedestrians curiously looked at him, but no one interfered as he reached into the glove compartment. Opening the drawer, he fumbled until he grasped the gun. While firmly holding it, he flicked the safety open and slowly guided the gun towards his head.

Andrew drummed his fingers impatiently against the back seat. For the better part of an hour, the limo steadily had been inching its way through the streets that were crowded with protesters. The majestic White House was still many blocks away. Andrew checked his watch. He exhaled his frustration. They barely had moved in the past twenty minutes. Deciding to attempt the rest of his journey on foot, he directed

Jack to pull over. Complying, the chauffer angled towards the curb. Abruptly, the marquis was thrown hard against the seat.

"Andrew!"

The anguished cry drove into him like a cannon ball. "Jack," he barked into the speaker, "turn off here and head down this side street. Burn rubber!"

The image of Jordan trembling in a car as he fought for control of a gun assailed him. Exploring the image, he found no one else in the car. "Jordan," he ordered, "don't do it!"

"Craven," the other man thought.

Andrew understood. Taking his mind from the image of Jordan in the car, he hurled the full force of his fury at his brother.

"Craven, release him!" he ordered, as Jordan's car came into view. For a split second, he caught the image of a startled Craven in what appeared to be an examining room. He was holding someone in his arms and, as the force of Andrew's fury hit him, he was driven back against the wall. Being quick to recover, he threw up a mental barrier that effectively blocked Andrew's thoughts. The last glimpse that he had was of the triumphant look in his brother's eyes. His blood ran cold as he realized that the woman in Craven's arms was Victory.

Chapter 29:
The Assassination

Andrew wrenched open the car door. Jordan leaned listlessly against the seat with the gun in his lap. The strain of combating Craven had been too much for him. Andrew placed a reassuring hand on his shoulder. Slowly, Jordan's eyes opened. The anguish that he saw only increased his trepidation. His heart froze as he listened.

"Craven has Victory," the earl whispered weakly.

"I know. What happened?"

"I'm not sure," he groaned, as he allowed Andrew to help him from the car. Still shaky, he leaned heavily on his cousin. "All I know is that everything was going as we planned. Craven believed that you had sent Victory to England. He didn't decide to go himself, though," he grimaced, as he remembered the hitch in their plan. "I was racking my brains trying to think of a plausible way to convince him to go himself." Then, we opened the door and found Victory standing on the other side as though she were head of some damn welcoming committee. Craven immediately suspected complicity and tried to force me into a furnace." Andrew grimaced as Jordan continued. "I tried to provide a distraction so Victory could escape, but Thomas caught her. I would be little more than ashes if it hadn't been for Dana. She distracted her father long enough for me to make it to the car. Even then, if you hadn't intervened when you did, I would still be..." He trailed off, as sirens wailed and tires screeched. Suddenly, several police cars and unmarked vehicles came careening around the corner. As they disappeared in the opposite direction, Andrew's face hardened. He was silent, as he returned to the car. While the two men settled in the back seat, Jack confirmed their fears.

"The radio just reported that the president's been shot," he announced when he lowered the partition.

Andrew nodded curtly and the divider rolled up. Turning to Jordan, he asked bleakly, "Where do you think he's taken her?"

Jordan shook his head, as he regretfully looked out of the window. "It would appear that we've failed at both parts of our plan," he thought, as he stared at the crowds that already were hurrying towards the scene. The traffic, which had been bad a few minutes ago, was now completely impenetrable. Then, he noticed the ambulance that had its lights flashing while weaving through the traffic.

"Think there's any hope?" he asked nodding towards the vehicle.

Andrew faced him. Jordan winced at the raw pain reflected in the turquoise eyes. He decided to be honest. Sighing heavily, he said, "No, I don't know where he took her. However, since he will need to remain accessible during the crisis, I don't think he would have time to take her very far. She might still be at the crematorium." He forced himself to continue. "I don't think he's killed her, yet. He said he had plans for her."

The marquis blanched. "What sort of plans?" he asked tersely.

The earl studied his friend's face for a long time before answering. His jaw muscles tensed and his brows drew together. Andrew's expression slowly changed. His eyes darkened while still blazing with an inner determination and fury. Chills raced down Jordan's spine.

He answered hesitantly, "Well, he did say that she wasn't to be harmed because he had special plans for her. She was going to help him with some sort of experiment." Then, his eyes widened. "In all the excitement, I forgot to tell you I found out what part the crematoriums play in Craven's plans."

Andrew's expression was thoughtful. Jordan paused. He was unsure if his companion still was paying attention. "I'm listening," he said in a hollow voice.

"Well," he said uneasily, "if I am correct, Craven is having the participants of his rehabilitation programs sent to the crematorium for an exiting interview. After all of their identification records have been expunged, his core conspirators drain their blood and store it. The dehydrated bodies are fed into the furnace. I think," he finished with a grimace, "they are using the blood for nourishment."

Victory struggled up through the thick layer of mist that was covering her like a heavy blanket. Awareness slowly penetrated her senses. Her lids lifted, but everything was black. Her limbs felt like lead and her throat was parched. Licking dry lips, she tried to think. Ropes cut into her wrists and a barrier prevented her from extending her legs. Craning her neck, she cried out as her head hit metal. She finally became aware of the vibrating pulse of an engine. The ride was punctuated by an occasional jolt as she was jostled by a bump or pothole. A car trunk.

She had been tied and thrown into a car trunk. She began to panic. A scream welled up in her stomach and then traveled up her throat. "Now was not the time to get claustrophobic," she decided, as she slowly exhaled.

She groaned as she relived the moments leading to her capture. Rocking back and forth, she strained against the bonds. Instead of loosening, they seemed tighter. Exhausted, she subsided. She consoled herself. Eventually, there would be an opportunity to escape. When it came, she would need her strength and wits to take advantage of the situation.

The smooth ride abruptly turned jarringly bumpy. Victory was pitched from one side of the trunk to the other as the car rolled over what seemed like a continuous line of potholes. The vehicle stopped abruptly. With a final thump, Victory landed on her back. "What now," she wondered, while trying to regain control of her racing heart.

The car's door slammed. Keys were jangled, scraped, and then ground into the trunk's lock. Victory blinked at the sudden brightness as the hood was lifted. She squinted into the rays of the setting sun until she finally was able to focus on the face of her captor.

A pair of malicious green eyes glared back at her. Her eyes widened as she recognized the man who had foiled her escape. Victory shivered. She actually would have preferred Craven's company. The man roughly seized her under her arms and dragged her from the compartment. Victory's cramped muscled screamed in protest as she was placed on her feet. Pins and needles prickled through her numbed limbs and her legs collapsed beneath her. For several seconds, the man scowled at her. Then, he lifted and carried her towards a building.

She stiffened in the stranger's arms when she recognized the structure. "Why are you taking me here," she asked, as she struggled against her bonds. An ominous silence prevailed and was accompanied by a tightening of his arms around her ribs. Having the breath squeezed out of her convinced Victory to remain still as they approached the Willow Grove Crematorium.

She momentarily closed her eyes and briefly wondered how the man would open the door. Standing her on her feet, he propped her against the door while leaning hard against her. As an additional precaution, he wrapped her hair around his hand. Producing a small silver key, he unlocked the door and yanked her through the entrance. The prolonged silence was becoming unbearable. Victory's fear evaporated into angry frustration.

"What are you going to do with me," she demanded, as she was pulled through the outer office. Resisting the tug on her hair, she dug her heels into the carpet. She was tired of being led around like a dog on a leash. She wanted answers.

In response to her resistance, the porphyrian viciously jerked her hair. Tears stung her eyes as she hung suspended by the strength of his hold on her strands. She turned to glare rebelliously at the man as he propelled her through the front office. It was difficult to retain her anger in the face of her precarious position, so she lapsed into morose silence.

They reached a door that was marked "Crematorium." Victory shuddered as a vision of flames engulfing Ben's body flashed through her mind. "Maybe," she thought hopefully, "this is the opportunity I've been waiting for." Presumably, the porphyrian would have to release her in order to navigate down the stairs. Maybe, she could push him into the basement. She doubted that it would do him any real harm, but she would have a few moments for a head start. Then, what? How could she escape with her hands still bound? Her speculations were cut short as the man lifted her, threw her over his shoulder, and started down the stairs without flicking the light.

She tensed when he paused at the door. Instead of setting her down, the man simply kicked the door open with such force that it crashed against the wall. He passed through without even breaking stride. Victory's heart fluttered and her stomach tightened when she realized that the room was set up to mirror its counterpart in Washington. Her only solace was Craven's last words instructing that she was not to be harmed. Her mind refused to dwell on the rest of his statement.

The silent stranger unceremoniously dumped her on the concrete floor next to the wall that was facing the furnace. Victory stared at the steel contraption. Its open door gaped like a hungry mouth waiting to be fed. Thomas glanced at her and noticed the direction of her glassy-eyed stare. When he chuckled at her discomfort, Victory's earlier annoyance returned. She was at a loss for words, so she watched silently as the man bent down and reached behind her. She stiffened as he untied the bindings around her wrists. She still felt too weak to stand, so she sat in a stupor as she observed his every move.

He pulled her arms from behind her back in a gesture of solicitude. Abruptly, he pulled her arm taught and, in a flurry of movement, he snapped a handcuff around her wrist. Momentarily startled, Victory stared in shock at the shackle. Her eyes followed the length of chain to where it connected to the metal pipes leading to the furnace. The porphyrian leaned forward to secure the clasp. Victory pulled back violently against the metal. Annoyed at her resistance, Thomas struck her hard across the face. She saw stars and her senses reeled as the blow sent her head crashing against the concrete. Before she could recover, her arm had been secured.

He stood and brushed his hands together as if trying to wipe off dirt. Staring down thoughtfully, he studied her. Then, he spoke for the first time.

"What does Andrew see in your kind," he asked rhetorically. Victory didn't think that he wanted an answer so she didn't bother to reply.

"For that matter," he continued, while shaking his head, "I am at a loss to see what beneficial purpose could be served by sparing you." At the alarm in her eyes, he smiled sadistically. "You have nothing to fear from me, diurnal. That is, you have nothing to fear as long as you behave yourself. My orders are to watch and guard until Craven arrives. Besides," he offered, as he walked towards the stairs, "I believe it will be very interesting to see exactly what sort of experiment he has in mind."

The last comment sent the recently banished terror resurging through her veins. Thomas, noting her reaction, laughed again. "Maybe I will be able to have a little fun after all," he mused. "You seem very susceptible to suggestive statements and it is clear you have an active imagination. Yes," he said with emphasis, "this could turn out to be quite entertaining. After all, Craven said only the body was to remain unharmed. He said nothing about your mental condition."

A lead brick settled in her stomach. Looking into those cold and calculating green eyes brought to mind all of the worst terrors that she had ever imagined. Dread settled over her. She was relieved when the man turned back to the stairs.

When he reappeared a few minutes later, he was carrying a chair and portable radio. Leaning the chair against the furnace, he took up a position directly in front of her and then switched on the radio. Immediately, the tense voice of the news reporter could be heard. "A very sad and tragic day for the country. The president, who was shot by an assassin earlier today, was pronounced dead on arrival at the hospital. The assassin, whose identity is still a mystery, shot himself before he could be captured."

There was a brief pause. Victory stared at the porphyrian in shocked horror. His face was impassive, but she detected a light of triumph reflected in his eyes. The reporter again began to speak, which caught her attention. "I believe the vice president is ready to make a statement. We now take you live to the White House where Rebecca Hughes has more on the situation. Rebecca?"

Chapter 30:

President Maxwell

"Yes, Henry. President Callahan was shot around 2:00 this afternoon and was pronounced dead at 4:17. We are still waiting for details about the assassin. Currently, Vice President Maxwell is in the Oval Office. He is going to speak to the nation and..." she hesitated, nodded, and then resumed, "He's about to start now."

"Can you believe his nerve?" Jordan asked with disgust, while watching the portable television in the back of the limo. Craven was stationed behind the president's desk in the Oval Office. "Callahan's body isn't even cold and he's already set himself in his place."

Receiving no response, he glanced at his cousin. Andrew sat absolutely still. His gaze was fixed on the image on the small television screen. Jordan tore himself away from the image long enough to check their progress towards the crematorium and then gave his attention back to the screen.

As the camera came in for a close up of the vice president's sad but composed features, Jordan had a sudden urge to lash out at the screen.

"This is a very sad day for all of us," stated the vice president. His face reflected solemn dignity. Jordan felt a fresh wave of disgust. "Due to the tragedy, I will keep my statement brief. At 2:10 this afternoon, President Callahan was shot and killed while leaving the White House on his way to Geneva. His assassin, still unidentified, committed suicide before he could be questioned. At this time, that is all that is known about the assassination." He paused for a moment and then stared earnestly into the camera. "John Callahan was a good, honest, and wise man. He was a sincere leader who was full of integrity and hope

219

for the nation's future. Although no one can possibly fill his shoes, I hope to follow in his footsteps." His manner then turned stern. "A full investigation will be conducted into the death of President Callahan and any conspirators will be brought to justice. I have every intention of upholding the president's policies and plans for the country. I will have more detailed information at a later time. Until then, God bless America."

Jordan turned to Andrew. "A bit mellow dramatic, don't you think?"

Andrew shrugged. "Do you think he will be tied up long enough for us to search the crematorium and his house?"

Jordan glanced back at the television. The scene had switched to news correspondents commenting on the speech. When one of the commentators mentioned the swearing-in ceremony, Jordan turned up the volume. "The advancement of Vice President Maxwell to the office of president will be completed as soon as possible. Reports are circulating that the ceremony will occur within the next couple of hours, but it will not be broadcast publicly. The immediate need is to make a smooth transition and to provide the country with an official leader."

Jordan turned down the volume and grimaced. "I guess that will make it official." Redirecting his attention to Andrew's last question, he said, "Your guess is as good as mine. I don't see that we have any choice."

Andrew's eyes flashed. "I would rather strangle the information out of him."

Jordan shook his head. "Craven Maxwell is now the most well-protected man in the world. With his fiancée dead for only a few weeks and the presidential assassination, I doubt he will be allowed to go to the bathroom unguarded." Andrew glared and Jordan continued in an exasperated tone, "You're talking about laying hands on the president of the United States! You'll be arrested if you even look cross-eyed at Craven. After today, he's going to be surrounded by secret service men so thick that his own shadow won't be able to get near him."

Andrew nodded as the car halted outside of the crematorium. They alighted and approached the front door. Andrew pulled on the handle and, to his surprise, it opened. He frowned as he entered. Surely, if Victory were here, there would be more precautions against intrusion. He eased his way through the darkened offices so that he would not make any noise that would alert the occupants. Turning, he motioned for Jordan to precede him. Since the other man had been in the building earlier that day, he knew where they had to go.

Jordan led the way to the elevator. He was about to push the call button when Andrew stopped him. "Someone might hear the chime," he cautioned. He pointed towards the stairs. Jordan nodded.

They slowly crept down one flight and pushed the metal door open just a crack when they reached the bottom. Detecting nothing in the eerie darkness, Jordan slid the door open wide enough to slither through. Andrew followed. They remained flat against the wall for several seconds. Finally, deciding that they were alone, they stepped forward.

Their hasty search of the room revealed that it was empty. A more thorough examination revealed traces of blood on the examination table and still-warm ashes in the furnace.

"Looks like they were in a hurry to leave and didn't do their normally thorough job of cleaning up," reported Jordan.

A stray beam of afternoon sunlight glittered off a small object on the floor. Andrew walked over to pick it up. His hand shook as he examined the small golden crucifix. A wave of pain swallowed him. It was several seconds before he could speak. His companion's hand on his arm finally penetrated the haze of pain. He glanced from the crucifix to his friend and then out of the back door.

"Is that Victory's?"

Andrew could only nod as he continued to stare.

"We're not going to find her here. We might as well go on to Craven's house," he suggested gently.

"Why?" asked Andrew bleakly, "She won't be there, either."

"Probably not," he agreed, "but there might be a clue to her whereabouts."

Andrew nodded and, after pocketing the crucifix, he followed his cousin outside.

Tears clouded her vision and her throat constricted as Victory continued to listen to the news report. When Craven Maxwell's silky baritone began broadcasting, she lost control. With her outrage overriding her common sense, she glared at the porphyrian, who was listening so intently to the radio that he had ceased paying the slightest attention to her.

"Craven Maxwell was behind the assassination of President Callahan, wasn't he?" she demanded furiously.

He paid no attention to her outburst and she grew even angrier.

Andrew had been telling the truth. Craven was capable of all of the crimes that the marquis had alleged. How dare he kill the president! Obviously, he dared a great deal. If she had heeded Andrew's warnings, she wouldn't be in this predicament. Craven Maxwell had betrayed and destroyed everything that she held dear. Vengeance swelled in her heart while the blood boiled in her veins. She must get free, go to Andrew, ask him to forgive her for doubting him, and help him to make a stand against his brother.

Noticing what appeared to be a double-headed metal prong, she snatched it from the floor and drove it point first into the porphyrian's back. The man slumped to the floor. Quickly, she thrust her hand into the pocket where he had put the key to her handcuffs. An iron band encircled her hand as she pulled it from the man's pocket. With eyes wide, she stared in disbelief at the man as he reached behind him and pulled the prong from his back.

The green eyes lit with surprise. Surprise was quickly replaced by anger and then humor, but no pain, Victory noticed despairingly. Was it possible that she had not thrown the prong hard enough? She watched incredulously as the man yanked the protruding handle from his body. A third of the handle was plastered with blood. Droplets sprinkled the cement and sprayed the air as Thomas threw the metal instrument aside. She swallowed hard as she looked from the prong to the man in the chair. The porphyrian's face was a malevolent mask as he gazed back at her. Cold chills ran down her spine. She swallowed convulsively and regretted the impulsive act.

"So, diurnal, you enjoy violence?"

Victory continued to stare. She was so shocked that he was unharmed that his words didn't register. He should be dead or severely injured at least. Remembering Andrew's words about the differences in porphyrian anatomy, she paled. Thomas appeared even more amused at her reaction.

"I see that you are finally grasping the reality of your predicament. Well, I'm afraid you learned this lesson a little too late."

He leaned back in his chair. Relief flooded through her as she realized that he simply was baiting her. Abruptly, she was engulfed in flames. She gasped in alarm as flickering pillars of red and orange sprang up all around her. Jumping to her feet, she backed against the wall while trying to avoid the sudden onslaught of heat. Victory was petrified as she tried to peer through the dense cloud of smoke and fire in order to see her tormentor. Her skin singed and her eyes watered. She coughed and tried to gulp in air, but the smoke filled her throat and burned her lungs. Slowly, she sank to the ground. Just when she thought that she would pass out, the fire vanished. Victory sat up, leaned against the wall, and gulped fresh air.

The room suddenly was plunged into darkness. The hair rose on the back of her neck as a man's voice echoed eerily ahead of her.

"That was just a small demonstration to put you in the mood. The real fun is just starting."

Victory shuddered, as she strained her eyes in the direction of the voice, but the blackness was too complete. "This porphyrian is playing with my mind," she reasoned, as she remembered Andrew's demonstration in the hotel room. She desperately clung to that thought as the slithery voice continued to echo around her.

Abruptly, the light returned. She blinked rapidly at the sudden brightness. Her relief was cut short as her eyes focused on the creature before her. Her eyes widened and her mouth dropped open as a scream tore from her throat. She watched in awestruck horror as the thing approached. Caught somewhere between a reptile, a rodent, and a human, the thing stood upright and appeared to have two arms and two legs. The creature had glowing red eyes and a head shaped like a toad, except for the nose and mouth. The snout was that of a dragon. When it spoke, a long forked tongue snaked out from between protruding fangs. The entire body was scaly with a set of greenish-black leathery wings on its back. The creature had claws in the place of hands and feet and it dragged a long hairless tail.

Revulsion and terror held her in an iron grip. Her sanity broke. As the creature advanced, she covered her face with her hands and screamed. Straining against her bonds, she moved as far out of reach as her chain would allow. She became numb with fear. She watched the creature advance, while it flicked its tongue and targeted her with a baleful amphibian eye. Petrified, she shrank against the wall as the thing backed her into a corner. "It's only a hallucination created by the porphyrian! It's only a hallucination. It's not real. It's not real!" her mind screamed.

Victory shook violently as the creature grasped her arms and scratched deep furrows into her skin. Its tongue flicked her face and she tried to turn towards the wall. One claw grasped her chin and held her in place. Its tongue felt like wet sandpaper as it coursed down her cheek. She gagged as the tongue slithered across her lips.

"What's the matter, bitch?" the thing rasped in her ear, "Don't you want to play anymore?"

Victory almost choked at the foul-smelling breath. The part of her brain that still was functioning rationally wondered about the intricacies of this hallucination. A tearing sound jerked her back into focus and she realized that the creature had ripped her blouse down the front. Gooseflesh rose on her exposed skin and she shuddered in revulsion as the claws grasped at her breasts. Bile rose in her throat as she wrenched from his grasp. Lashing out, she kicked at what she hoped was the most vulnerable spot. Then, after collecting the loose chains, she attempted to smash them into its face. The image vanished. Thomas reclined in his chair and studied her with his half-closed lids. Quickly glancing down, Victory gasped as she discovered that her skin and clothing were free of injury. Drained of tension, she sank onto the concrete. Her respite was brief. Lazily, the porphyrian stood and stretched. She watched him warily and cringed against the wall as he approached. Towering over her, he contemplated his next move. Victory wondered if this were another illusion. "Not that it matters," she reflected dismally. Again, he tightly grabbed her hair and yanked her against him. Illusion or not, the pain was certainly real. Releasing her hair, he tore open her blouse. She gasped as his hands moved down her flesh and caught in the fabric of her jeans. The ripping of the cloth brought her back to her senses and she understood his intention. Wrenching out of his grasp, she moved as far away as her bonds would allow, but her efforts to avoid him seemed only to heighten his excitement. She desperately lashed out and struck him across the face with her chain as her knee connected with his groin.

The breath rushed between his clenched teeth as he doubled over. "Well, that part of his anatomy is comparable," she thought with relief. Her reprieve was brief. As the porphyrian straightened, he pierced her with a venomous glare.

"Still in the mood to play? And I thought you had learned your lesson."

She clamped her hands tightly across her tattered blouse, but she was no match for his brute strength as he wrenched the fabric out of her grasp. Ripping his fingers downward, he tore off blouse and bra in a single motion. Continuing his downward thrust, he placed his hands on either side of her hips and jerked the material downward. He bore down hard, roughly pressed her onto the cement, and spread her legs as he unfastened his pants. Even as he entered her, the image changed again. She quickly closed her eyes to avoid the visual onslaught. Prickly hair scraped across her skin. She kept her eyes firmly shut for as long as she could. Finally, morbid curiosity forced her to look. Eight eyes and two mandibles greeted her incredulous stare. The furry body rubbed against her skin and her flesh crawled. In mounting revulsion, she realized that, despite the illusionary image, this time the porphyrian really was raping her. A wave of disgust and loathing washed over her as the alien's life juice poured into her. She screamed until she was hoarse.

Abruptly, she was liberated. She watched as the porphyrian regained his natural form, sailed through the air, and landed heavily against the far wall. Relief at being rescued quickly dissolved into despair as the ominous form of Craven Maxwell towered above her.

Chapter 31:
Captive Conquest

"Sorry. I'm not your knight in shining armor," Craven said sardonically before turning his attention to the prone man.

"I asked you to guard her, not torture her."

Thomas sat up and rubbed the back of his head. "She is unharmed."

Craven cast a critical eye over her. Victory attempted to regain her composure, as she sat huddled in the corner. Shivering, she tried to cover her exposed skin with the remnants of her clothing. Craven strode over and pried her body open. He inspected her as though she were a prized animal that he was buying at the county fair. Satisfied, he turned back to Thomas.

"She appears all right physically, but what about her mental condition? I hope you have not been up to your usual tricks. I want this one cognizant during my experiment."

Victory shuddered at the renewed reference to using her as a laboratory animal. Then, she focused on the chastened porphyrian. Whatever Craven intended could not be as awful as being at the mercy of that perverted creature. Despite his earlier denial, Victory considered Craven Maxwell to be her savior at this moment in time. Of course, she would have preferred Count Dracula himself to playing cat-and-mouse with that green-eyed monster.

"I think," said Craven, fingering her tattered blouse, "you should visit my daughter and get some garments for our guest. After all," he said, while smiling at her, "it would never do for her to get sick."

Victory found it difficult to take much comfort in Craven's interest in her health.

"And, Thomas," he said to the retreating porphyrian, "be careful. I am sure that Andrew and Jordan are in earnest search by now."

Her heart leapt with hope. Seeing the light in her eyes, he cruelly added, "Not that it will help you. In a couple of days, it won't matter if they find you or not."

Jordan walked into the study of Craven's home. Andrew glanced at him. He shook his head. The marquis turned back to his examination of the desk. He slammed the last drawer closed and stood up.

"Nothing!" he spat bitterly, "The man either does not keep any personal records or must keep them with him."

Jordan flopped into an armchair. "I know he keeps at least one black leather-bound journal. I've seen him writing in it."

Andrew stared at him. "You're right. I've seen it, too. Since he took the time to hide it, I guess it must contain valuable information." He turned to gaze out of the window for a moment. The street still was deserted and there was no sign that the president was returning. "However," he said, as he turned to face his companion, "we are obviously wasting our time here. Craven is not holding Victory anywhere locally. That would be too easy."

"Besides, every moment we spend here is increasing our chance of detection," agreed Jordan.

Andrew's face grew fierce. "At this point, I would welcome a confrontation. I would like to get my hands on any of the conspirators and wring their necks. I would especially love to lay hands on my brother right about now. I can assure you that his grandiose schemes would die a quick death."

"You're sure he isn't at the White House?"

Andrew shook his head. "I nudged one of the secret service men. He obligingly had a call of nature while I entered the president's residential quarters. My dear brother was nowhere inside."

The door opened and admitted a man in a business suit who was carrying a sheath of papers. Startled, the man looked from Andrew to Jordan and then back again. Andrew stood behind Craven's desk. The man opened his mouth, but Andrew shook his head and held out his hand. Placing the papers on the desk, the man silently turned and left. Andrew picked up the stack, sifted through the papers, and let them slip back onto the desk in a scattered heap. He glanced wearily at Jordan, who asked, "Are you taxing yourself? After all, that must be about the fiftieth person you've had to mentally manipulate in the past two hours."

"This place is like Grand Central Station," he agreed. Noting the concern, he waved his hand. "It doesn't take any effort other than reconciling myself to the fact that I've had to lower my ethics to Craven's standards. That's the only way to level the playing field."

"Well," said Jordan after a moment's reflection, "doesn't Craven have a winter home in Miami? Maybe he has Victory stashed away there."

Moving around the desk, he strode towards the door. "Let's face it," he spat out savagely, "Craven has holdings scattered all over the country and abroad. He could have had one of his accomplices take her anywhere by now. While you and I have been chasing our tails, Victory could be dead."

They walked outside and paused next to the limousine. "Do you think we should proceed on that assumption?" Jordan asked hesitantly.

The look of steely determination on his cousin's face sent a chill down his spine. "No. I am going to continue the search until I either find Victory, proof of what happened to her, or my brother. When I do, I am going to do what I should have done originally: take care of him before he has a chance to harm anyone else."

Victory groaned as she shifted her position on the cold cement. The single bulb hanging from the light in the center of the room provided only dim illumination. The ill-fitting clothing that Thomas had thrust at her a few minutes ago barely kept out the chill. To her relief, Craven had dismissed the other porphyrian after he had delivered the clothing.

Giving instructions for Thomas to return later, Craven settled himself in the vacated chair and began studying a black leather-bound notebook. He read several pages and then stared at her intensely. Victory shifted uncomfortably under the probing stare, but met his gaze defiantly. Craven finally put the book aside and said teasingly, "Really, Victory, you must do something about your wardrobe. No one would believe you are a socialite or attorney in that outfit. It's unfortunate that Thomas couldn't locate my daughter in order to obtain more attractive apparel, but don't worry. I will make sure that you are suitably attired when we leave."

If this was his idea of a joke, she wasn't amused, but she did gain a modicum of hope from his words. Would he really allow her to leave or was he simply trying to pacify her into complying?

The onyx eyes stared with their usual repellent intensity. She shivered despite the oversized wool sweater and men's corduroys that she had been given. Those eyes and that false smile disconcerted her. Why had Laura found him so compelling?

"Did you kill Laura?" she shot at him.

"Yes," he replied evenly.

"Why?"

Instead of answering, he countered with a question of his own. "Are you in love with my brother?"

Despite the pain wrenching at her heart and the fury blazing through her soul, a tell-tale blush stained her cheeks. "You bastard," she hissed and dove for him. The jerk of her bonds brought her up short and she landed hard on the floor.

Craven smiled and didn't seem to take offense. He stood, removed his suit jacket, and meticulously laid it across the chair. Taking a key from the pocket of his pants, he advanced towards her. Surprised, she watched as he leaned over her and unlocked the handcuff. Rubbing her chafed wrists, she warily glared up at him.

Craven offered his hand for assistance, but she chose to lean against the wall as she stood up. He beckoned for her to follow him as he climbed the stairs. They walked down a long corridor. Producing another key, he opened the door to an office and allowed her to precede him as they entered. Cozy furnishings in soft colors gave the impression of serenity and familiarity. Craven sat on the sofa, while patting the seat beside him. She opted for an armchair on the other side of the coffee table. He shrugged. His relaxed pose and conversational tone made it clear that he had no fear of any attempt to escape. Reluctantly, Victory forced her tense muscles to relax. The temptation to flee was overwhelming, but she knew that Craven would never have released her if he had not been confident in his ability to keep her as a prisoner. No, her best plan lay in trying to appear passive for the time being until she could catch him off guard.

"I'm glad you have such a high regard for my brother," he went on conversationally, "It makes my final revenge that much sweeter."

Startled out of her reverie, she asked, "Revenge?"

He nodded soberly, as he penetrated her with his probing eyes. "Yes, the revenge you and I will perpetrate on Andrew."

Her eyes widened and she stood up. He caught her arm. His fingers made her flesh crawl, but she replied firmly, "I am not going to be any part of your plans, especially if you intend to harm Andrew."

He shook his head and jerked her down beside him. "Andrew will be sorry that he ever interfered. Not that it will do him any good. By the time we are done here, you will belong to me body and soul. There won't be anything my dear brother will be able to do about it. I will even predict," he said sadistically, "that seeing the woman he loves beholden to me will be enough to drive him insane. Then, sweet Victory," he sighed, as one finger traced her cheek, "I will have everything: my revenge, control of the United States, the secrets to the mysterious past of my people, and – oh, yes – you."

Victory frowned. She found it difficult to concentrate while he was so close. Her stomach muscles tightened as she asked tensely, "Why did you kill Laura?"

He groaned wearily and stood up. "Technically, I didn't, but such complicated discussions should not be contemplated on an empty stomach. I have your favorite, I believe," he said as he offered her a paper plate with two slices of pizza. "Laura mentioned you were especially fond of anchovies."

Victory took the plate and laid it aside. His callousness was making her sick. Craven quickly devoured the food. After several seconds, she began nibbling on a slice. She would need the energy to keep her wits about her. Who knew if he planned on feeding her again.

Reading the question in her eyes, he offered, "You don't understand. Let me explain," he said. Victory gazed deeply into the onyx eyes and wondered what she had ever found so disturbing. "You see, sweet Victory," he murmured huskily, "Laura served a better purpose for me dead than alive. Her death provided several benefits. I am really rather indebted to her. She allowed me to teach Andrew a lesson, her funeral provided me with an alibi during the time of the president's assassination, and her death gave me the spontaneous sympathy and support of the people."

"But you just said you didn't kill her."

"That's right."

She frowned.

"You, sweet Victory, actually killed Laura. Unfortunately, Andrew did such a thorough job in blocking the incident from your memory that you will just have to take my word for it."

Victory slapped him. The sound reverberated into stillness. Although a red handprint marred the pale face, the president remained unmoved. His lack of emotion infuriated her and she grabbed his tie. She jerked as hard as she could and twisted the fabric in her clenched fists.

"Liar!" she screamed as tears blurred her vision. She shook her friend's murderer while screaming obscenities until she collapsed into incoherent sobs. The man continued to stare at her with bland complacency.

Raising her tear-stained face, she stared at him. He was observing her with the same objectivity towards her outburst as he had shown towards the killing of his fiancée.

"I hate you," she said dully through the ache in her throat.

"I'm sure you do," he said dispassionately. "Now, I will explain my experiment and its relevance to you. In my travels abroad, I have discovered ancient documents. They indicate that, in our ancient history, my people were much more powerful. They had, shall we say, 'enhanced' skills. We were capable of mental and physical accomplishments that make our present abilities seem paltry by comparison."

Victory inhaled the intoxicating aroma of his cologne and watched the sensual movement of his lips. She wondered why she had never noticed them before. His head bent lower and she moaned as his lips grazed her ear.

"Through my diligent research, I have ascertained why our powers have been diluted. One of our own, probably one of Andrew's ancestors," he sneered, "decided that, instead of feeding off of humans, we should try to peacefully coexist. It seems the porphyrians were in danger of extinction by superstitious diurnals. Instead of securing a way to be free of their threat, they developed an alternative source of nourishment," he said contemptuously. "They mixed the blood of a few animals, added a few minerals and vitamin supplements, and concocted that vile potion we've been drinking for the past millennium. But, my pet, I've discovered the truth. The way to unleash our full potential is by draining the blood that pours through your veins."

Delving deeply into her eyes, he paused. His gaze seemed to permeate her entire being and dampen her will. Lethargic desire stole over her. She watched in fascinated dread as his lips descended. The kiss was savage yet seductive, repellent and appealing. As he prolonged the exquisite torture, her resistance and resolve melted. By the time that his mouth released hers to trace a fiery trail down her throat, she had abandoned any idea of escape. "Now that you are a more willing assistant, would you like to know the details of the experiment?"

"Yes," she whispered breathlessly despite the inner voice urging her to refuse.

"I have read," he murmured, while unfastening her sweater, "During the time of our people's greatest glory, they had developed a ritual for indoctrinating their victims into vampirism. I am very interested to find out if there is any truth behind the myth."

Victory's mind whirled. All of her knowledge about the subject assailed her. Her numbed mind sought for the reference. If she correctly remembered her ancient folklore, the only way for a vampire to convert and gain complete control of his victim was to..."

"No," she screamed, as his mouth reclaimed hers. Her protests fell to whimpers and eventually subsided to moans of pleasure as Craven kissed his way down her throat. Sliding the sweater off of her shoulders, he glided his hands down her smooth skin. Gently, he pushed her back against the sofa until he leaned over her. Her breath came in short ragged gasps as his mouth closed over a breast. He slowly unfastened her pants and slid them down her legs. Methodically, he stroked her skin. He was touching and rubbing until she was a mass of sensitized nerve endings. She was shameless as she moved against him. She ached for release. Gently, he opened her thighs and began probing her with his fingers. Her hips arched and she strained against his hand. Time after time, she thought that she would explode from pent-up passion, only to be pulled back from the edge. He paused long enough for her to regain her senses and then began the tantalizing process all over again. He sat back and pulled her by the legs until her buttocks rested across his lap. Using one hand to manually manipulate her, he used the other to pull her wrist towards his mouth. Confused, she watched as his thumb caressed the erratic pulse. Dreadful anticipation swept through her as his lips descended. Suddenly, he extracted a razor from his pocket, slashed it across her vein, and covered the wound with his mouth. Just as she was about to snatch her hand away, a new sensation began to pulsate through her body. Her sensitive skin screamed for release as shafts of arousal pierced her. Craven's fingers continued to massage her tenderly and she groaned. Panting and moaning, she pleaded for him to allow her release. She was a prisoner of her own need. With one final stroke and a long drawn pull on her wrist, she climaxed. The sensation seemed painfully prolonged yet exquisite. Spasms shook her body and cries wrenched from her throat. She landed hard on Craven's lap. Reality pierced the haze of arousal. He was still fully dressed. Not only that, but he was not even aroused. Shame flooded through her as a flush stained her cheeks. She was lightheaded and dizzy, but managed to roll onto the floor. She sat huddled while tears of revulsion and self-loathing rolled down her cheeks.

Chapter 32:
Detection

Andrew wandered aimlessly through his Bethesda mansion. He was despondent as he walked through the French doors onto the balcony. Spring was thawing the snow from the rooftops and turning the ground into slush. Patches of green grass and mud emerged from under the retreating white blanket, but Andrew was completely oblivious to nature's rebirth. Leaning against the rail, he stood with his shoulders slumped. It had been over a week since Craven had taken Victory. He was no closer to solving the mystery of her whereabouts than he had been when Jordan had first given him the news.

During the first few days, they searched all of the logical hiding places. After that, they looked in the not-so-obvious ones. Each night, Andrew and Jordan stationed themselves outside of the White House and waited for Craven to emerge.

He never did. However, during the day, he was always present for interviews, conferences, and executive duties. Discouraged and bewildered, Andrew finally had been persuaded by Jordan's entreaties to lay the problem aside in favor of the larger picture.

Andrew was in full agreement that Craven could not be allowed to continue as this country's leader. He already had corrupted the system by appointing Jason Sade as attorney general. With Jason as the head of the criminal justice system, the nation really was going to be in dire straights. The information that Jordan had provided did not leave much room for speculation regarding Craven's plans for the country. At this rate, it would not be long before his schemes were realized.

Sadly, he shook his head. After all of the time that it had taken for his people to assimilate into society, a few throwbacks were going to jeopardize the entire race. Not if he could help it. Perhaps, he had lost his love, but he would be damned if he were going to leave the fate of his people and the diurnals in the hands of his delusional brother. He grimaced at the thought of putting Jordan's idea into action, but, after careful consideration, it seemed to be the only alternative.

A sound caused Andrew to turn. Jordan was making his way up the stairs while shouldering two large duffle bags that he had slung over his shoulders.

As he dropped the bags to the floor, their eyes locked.

"Is that everything?" Andrew asked flatly, as he nodded towards the bags.

Jordan nodded. The two men faced each other for a few seconds before Jordan spoke. "Andrew, I don't like this any more than you do," he said, as he shifted uncomfortably under the inscrutable turquoise gaze, "however, I don't see any alternatives."

Andrew fell back against the wall and closed his eyes. He had been wrestling with the problem for two days. "Neither do I," he admitted wearily. "Have you been able to contact Dana?"

"I have not been able to make contact with her since the day at the crematorium. I'm worried. She really put herself at risk by defying Craven on my behalf. I wouldn't assume that being his daughter would protect her from his wrath."

"More likely, it would make him twice as furious at her betrayal," Andrew thought, but refrained from burdening his friend with his speculation. "Well," he said with finality, "we'd better get started."

Jordan agreed, picked up one of the duffle bags, and handed it to his cousin.

In the car, Jordan turned to face the marquis. "Have you considered the possibility that he is holding her in the building?"

Andrew accelerated as he guided the car through the busy highway traffic. Turning onto the exit ramp, he said, "I considered the possibility, but, if what you said about his not wanting to kill her is true, it doesn't make much sense. If she is being held there, we will find out soon enough."

Thomas yawned and stretched as he leaned forward in the chair. He eyed the semiconscious figure with disgust. What Craven wanted with the half-dead diurnal was totally beyond his comprehension. She had been something pleasant to look at when they had first taken her, but her looks had dissipated severely during the past three days. The healthy skin had taken on a pasty pallor and the resilient flesh had become emaciated. "Of course, these are the natural side effects of someone who has been drained of two thirds of their blood," he thought, as he walked over to nudge the woman with his boot.

The eyelids fluttered, the tiny blue veins fluctuated, but the eyes remained closed. He viewed the rest of the face with interest. The sockets appeared sunken and the black circles seemed to be painted into place. Her cheekbones were predominant in her shrunken face and her lips were drained of color.

Thomas rolled his eyes. She was not a pretty sight. Certainly, she didn't appear in any condition to jump up, break her bonds, and run away. He regretfully shook his head. On the first day, she had been so much fun to torture. It had been like playing cat and mouse. What an adversary. Defiant bravado on the outside and tender submission inside. Such a contrasting blend of emotions. The mental manipulation had been almost as stimulating as the physical arousal. He probed but gained no response. This one had about had it. Still, his orders were to watch her and he knew better than to cross Craven.

His eyes slipped to the nearby examination table. On the polished metal surface were two black leather-bound notebooks. Craven had left strict instructions that they were not to be disturbed. Thomas suspected that they held the secrets to the mysterious night rituals that he was never allowed to witness. Temptation burned through him as he stared at the journals. "It couldn't hurt if I read the contents," he thought, "Eventually, Craven might require my assistance and I could serve much better if I were already informed. Besides," he reasoned, "I definitely need to get a diversion from this boring task with this sorry specimen. Too bad," he lamented, while shaking his head. She had been so entertaining. Even yesterday, she had been conversational. A sudden thought struck him and he bent down. Taking her wrist, he frowned. Gauze was taped halfway up her arm. Pulling the bandage away, he stared curiously at the wounds. Puzzled, he checked the other arm. The pulse was slight and erratic, but it did exist.

For a moment, he contemplated summoning Craven. The woman was near death and, if his plans were contingent on her being alive, he might not get a chance to complete them. He stared at the books. He would call Craven right after he read the notes.

His fingers tingled as he picked up the first volume. A dragon's head in gold and green had been embossed on the cover. His excitement mounted as he guessed that he was about to discover material of great import.

A loud groan caused him to glance across the room. The girl was crying out in her sleep. She tossed restlessly on the cot. The handcuffs clinked as she moved on the bed. Thomas cocked his head. Had he detected another sound beyond the groaning victim? He listened intently. Suddenly, he shot to his feet. Above him, the floorboards were creaking ever so slightly as if someone was treading delicately in an attempt to avoid detection. Could it be Craven coming earlier than usual? "What luck," he thought, while staring at the books in consternation.

Reluctantly, he placed the books back on the table. Returning to his chair, he paused. Why would Craven or anyone else in their group be sneaking around? Tentatively, he sought for the source of the disturbance. An image of two men in one of the upper rooms imprinted on his mind.

Jordan blinked and began shaking his head. "Thomas is here."

Andrew frowned. "Where?"

He again shook his head. "I'm not sure. Maybe in the building, maybe outside. He threw up a wall before I could get a fix."

Since Andrew and Jordan thought that the building would be empty, they hadn't expended the energy that was necessary to camouflage their presence. That was a colossal oversight.

Andrew concentrated. "He's got up a wall all right. If he initiated the contact, he's detected us."

Jordan stared at his friend. "That means he knows we're in the building."

Andrew nodded grimly. "I think the best place for the explosive is near the furnace in the basement."

Jordan nodded, as he glanced at the duffle bag. "You know we will have to kill him."

Andrew's jaw hardened. "Quickly, if we are going to prevent him from broadcasting our intent."

Craven Maxwell steepled his fingers under his chin, as he reclined in the leather swivel chair. Easing back from the massive oak desk, he studied the man across from him. A slow smile crept across his austere features. He had been wise to appoint Jason Sade as attorney general.

The tall lanky man with the dark hair and ominous deep green eyes stared unflinchingly back. In his dark business suit, he gave the impression of being a mortician rather than a politician, but Craven was completely satisfied with his service.

The president's dark eyes were alight with satisfaction. "Are plans in place for an expansion of the new rehabilitation centers across the country?"

Jason nodded soberly. "I have overseen the plans personally and will go to several facilities to deal with the final arrangements. I will leave one member of our team in charge at each facility. They should be operational inside of six months. "Then," he said, with his thin lips curving, "we should be ready to proceed. At that rate, we should have a continuous supply of..." he paused, "nutrients within a year."

"Are you sure there will be no way to trace the prisoners?"

"We have been very selective in choosing the candidates. Only those devoid of personal ties and cumbersome family connections have been allowed into the program. Their new identities will be classified information. The files will be available only to you, me, and, of course, the vice president since I assume it will be his responsibility to oversee the project. Do you have any idea who will be nominated?"

Craven started to nod, but then stopped. His eyes widened and he stiffened. He stood and brought the meeting to an abrupt end. "Jason, everything sounds fine the way you have planned it. If you will excuse me, I am needed elsewhere."

The attorney general stood and bowed slightly. This was a custom of his that was left over from another time. "Can I be of any further assistance?" he enquired somberly.

Craven shook his head. "Not right now. If I need you, I will let you know."

After the other porphyrian had retired, Craven placed two phone calls and then hastily left the office.

Thomas steeled himself for the mental reprimand. As soon as he had learned that it was Andrew and Jordan who were invading the building, he had alerted his commander-in-chief. Although he was not responsible for the intrusion, he had no doubt that he would be held accountable if they succeeded.

As he glanced at the woman, he wondered how they had discovered her location. Seconds passed before he realized that his mental message had been received with only surprise and apprehension. Quick orders echoed like gunshots in his head. Gather the girl and the books. Then rendezvous with the president at the crematorium in Washington.

He strode over to the diurnal. After checking her vital signs, he frowned. Her pulse was still erratic and weak. He was certain that Craven had overdone the draining. If she died on the way, he was sure to get the blame. However, if they remained and the girl was taken, Craven's wrath would be too awful to contemplate.

He glanced at the table. The other directive regarding the books had been even more imperative. No chance was to be taken that they might fall into Andrew's hands. Craven had been quite definite when he stressed that those books were even more important than the diurnal. Striding over to the table, he scooped them up and securely placed them in his inner pocket. Bending over the sleeping figure, he considered his predicament. Since Craven had planned to come back for the diurnal, he had not left the keys. As another floorboard creaked, he quickly pried the chains from the wall. The links stretched in protest, but yielded as he tugged. Rolling her into the blanket, he tossed the burden over his shoulder. "Not the most brilliant of disguises," he reflected, especially with the chains hanging. He considered removing them, but then decided that it would take too long. Besides, Craven might need them in the other building – not that this dilapidated woman presented much of a threat in her present condition. If the president's theory were accurate, that would change shortly. The irony of the situation struck him and he chuckled. He could imagine the picture that he would present to any curious onlookers. Any diurnals who questioned him would wish that they hadn't.

He started to climb the stairs, but then paused. He cursed under his breath. He had hoped to depart before the other two made it this far. Now, his acute hearing detected the stealthy steps of his adversaries on the floorboards overhead. Hastily, he turned back into the room. Hiding Victory behind the furnace, he set the dials. A flash followed by shooting flames leapt from the interior. He stepped back. He instinctively knew that this encounter would be fatal. Not everyone who entered this basement would leave. His survival depended on killing his prince and his twin.

Chapter 33:

Discoveries

Jordan nodded his agreement. "The furnace is in the basement." He led the way to the elevator and pushed the bottom button. As the elevator started its climb, Andrew touched his arm.

"Don't you think it will be rather risky to go down this way? Thomas knows we are here and we don't want to be trapped like a pair of sitting ducks."

Jordan grimaced as he imagined the two of them exposed and vulnerable when the elevator doors slid open. He nodded and then led the way to the back stairs. They crept down as silently as possible, but the wooden stairs made an occasional creak that announced their presence. Jordan knew that Thomas' sensitive ears would detect their descent if he were anywhere near the stairway. He broke out in a cold sweat. Talking about killing Thomas had been easy while it was an abstract concept. Now that the moment was at hand, he wasn't sure that he could do it.

Sensing his companion's distress, Andrew gripped his arm to forestall his entry through the door marked "Crematorium." Relieved, Jordan stepped aside and allowed the marquis to pass. He paused. He listened. He heard nothing beyond the thick panel of wood, yet he sensed another presence. He pulled the dagger from its sheath beneath his jacket and cautiously opened the door.

Andrew stepped into the semi-darkness and instantly was hurled through the air. He landed hard on the concrete. The force of the impact knocked the dagger from his grasp and the air from his lungs. He lay winded for a moment and then sat up. By the glow from the furnace, he could see Jordan struggling with another figure on the landing. As he watched, the two smashed into the railing, splintered the wood, and then crashed to the floor.

Andrew retrieved the knife and started towards the combatants. Out of the corner of his eye, he caught a glimpse of a blanket with a chain protruding from under it. The rest of the object was hidden behind the furnace. Andrew stepped around the structure, bent over the blanket, and lifted the edge. He gasped in shock. Victory lay under the cover. She was battered, bruised, and as pale as a corpse. As he stared, the blood pounded in his ears as a roar of outrage ripped from his throat.

Hatred burned through him as his lust for vengeance robbed him of reason. He charged across the room towards the perpetrator of the crimes against his beloved. Thomas and Jordan were still struggling. They stood with arms locked in combat beside the door of the inferno. As he approached, Jordan's gaze swung towards him. He froze as the turquoise eyes impaled him on twin spikes of rage. Taking advantage of his twin's lapse, Thomas smashed Jordan's head against the steel wall.

Thomas watched with satisfaction as Jordan crumpled to the floor. A noise from behind alerted him to Andrew's presence. He swung around to confront his assailant. Andrew grabbed him by the hair, snapped his neck back, and slashed the blade across his throat.

The smell of burnt flesh finally penetrated Andrew's rage. In a daze, he stared at the severed head in his hand. The memory of how Victory had looked a few moments ago flashed through his mind. Fury seized him again. Andrew shook the grizzly trophy back and forth. Blood dripped from the open neck and sizzled as it hit the flames. The eyes stared back in shock. Disgusted, he threw Thomas' head into the furnace. He watched dispassionately as the flames engulfed the head. At his feet, the body lay in an expanding pool of blood. Stepping around it, he bent over his friend.

Jordan groaned and opened his eyes. Andrew smiled with relief. A blow that would have crushed a normal man's skull had only dazed the porphyrian.

"I found Victory," he cried out, as he rushed to the back of the furnace. A glimmer of the earlier emotion returned to his eyes and made Jordan shiver.

"Is she alive?"

"I don't know." Andrew's jaws tightened and his eyes dulled. Taking a deep breath, he knelt by his love, pulled back the blanket, gently lifted her head, and lovingly embraced it in his arms. Her ravaged face tore at his heart. He stared at it while trying to detect any sign of life. Finally, a slight flicker from beneath her closed lids rewarded his patience. Exhaling, he felt her throat. His fingers grazed abrasions on her smooth skin. He leaned closer. Two small oval lesions punctured her smooth white skin over the jugular. Studying Victory's face more closely, he registered her extreme pallor, darkness under her eyes, and her colorless lips. Pulling on her upper lip, he discovered that her gums were almost white. A suspicion that was too incredible to believe began to form.

"Search him," Andrew ordered tersely, "and let me know if there is a key."

"Key?"

"Yes. Victory is handcuffed."

Jordan looked at him with trepidation as he began the search. "The last thing I remember is seeing you with a look of demented fury on your face. Andrew, you looked as though you were going to rip someone apart with your bare hands."

"I did," said Andrew grimly, while gesturing towards Thomas' decapitated body and the violent splashes of blood on the floor and walls.

Jordan looked at the grotesque sight and turned pale. In all of the commotion, he had not noticed the grim scene located only a few feet away.

As he continued his search, he glanced at the chains and whistled. "It looks like they didn't want to take any chances on her getting away," he said. Then, he became perplexed. "But why such strong bonds? Certainly common rope would have sufficed – unless Craven was trying to anticipate your finding her. He surely couldn't expect these chains to stop you." He inserted two fingers into one of the links and exerted pressure until the metal pried apart. The broken link fell onto the floor with a clink. If he attempted to do the same for the locked metal bands around her wrists, he might have injured her.

"Andrew," he said, "there is no key."

Andrew cradled Victory's head in his lap. His hands smoothed her tangled and matted hair. His eyes were fixed and slightly glazed as Jordan waved his hand in front of his face. He blinked.

"Thank goodness!" exclaimed Jordan. "For a moment, I thought I'd lost you."

Andrew tilted his head and asked, "Thomas didn't have a key?"

"No," he responded, as he studied Victory's bound wrists.

Andrew studied the handcuffs for several seconds. Finally determining the spot where he thought the metal would be most likely to give, he inserted two fingers from each hand and pulled. He was amazed at how much room there was between Victory's wrist and the metal. Renewed anger swept through him when he realized how thin she had become. His rage added renewed strength and the metal stretched under his grip. As soon as the opening was wide enough, he slipped her arm through. He repeated the process for the other arm. He was appalled by the bandages on Victory's wrists. He rubbed her hands gently. He was unnerved to feel how cold they were. Checking for a pulse, he frowned.

Jordan also stared at Victory's bandaged wrists. Slowly, he shook his head. "While I was looking for the key, I found these two notebooks," he said as he held up two black leather-bound volumes. "They look like the ones I've seen Craven writing in."

Momentarily distracted, Andrew glanced at the books. "Yes," he agreed. "Why don't you have a look?"

Jordan opened the first one as Andrew turned back to Victory. Her pulse was very faint and erratic. It abruptly wavered, paused, and then resumed. His frown deepened. She obviously was suffering from an extreme deprivation of blood, along with probable exposure and starvation, too.

"Oh, my God!" Jordan exclaimed.

Andrew looked up. "What's the matter?"

The earl gaped at him while clutching the book with trembling hands. He exhaled deeply and ran a shaky hand through his hair. "I glanced through them. The first one is full of appointments, mainly with the porphyrians in the conspiracy. From the little that I skimmed, I'm sure that there must be a lot of evidence implicating Craven in the plot to kill the president and his diabolical plans for the diurnals."

"Good," said Andrew bitterly, while holding out his hand for the volume.

Jordan hesitated and then passed the first one to him. "You're not going to believe the contents of the other," he asserted, "I can't even begin to describe the horror that I glimpsed as I skimmed through it. You will have to read it yourself."

"What I am more interested in now is how we can help Victory."

Studying the woman, Jordan nodded his head. "I don't think we have a choice. She needs to go to the nearest hospital."

"Ordinarily, I'd agree with you, but I'm not sure how far we are from the nearest hospital. She won't last much longer and besides there will be a demand for some sort of explanation."

Jordan examined the prone figure. In an oversized sweater and men's trousers, she resembled a street person more than a high-powered attorney. Andrew was right. Her injuries and condition would arouse suspicion. "I think you should read the second book. It will give you an idea of what is going on."

Andrew opened his mouth to protest, but Jordan forestalled him. Placing a hand on his shoulder he said emphatically, "Read it."

Andrew scowled. "I don't have time to read about Craven's rantings," he insisted tersely, as he lifted Victory in his arms.

The earl removed the journal from his pocket. His fingers traced the imprinted dragon on the cover and then he opened the volume. The pages were full of Craven's small and precise handwriting. He began to read aloud the details of the research that the evil prince had conducted.

Andrew's stomach contracted as Jordan read. With his mind reeling, he continued to listen. He hardly could believe what he was hearing. He thought about the number of times that he had caught Craven making notes in this book and had never suspected the true nature of the journal. As Jordan continued to flip through the pages, his incredulity turned to horror.

"Towards the end of the notebook," continued Jordan, "his objective note taking changes to personal observations. According to this journal, Craven determined that the ancestral porphyrians used human blood for nourishment. It appears that he concluded from his research that this was the source of the supernatural abilities that the porphyrians were purported to possess." His revulsion mounted as it became clear that Craven had begun testing this theory by changing his diet to human blood several weeks ago.

He glanced at Jordan. "You can keep reading while we ride," he said, as he headed towards the stairs. The earl shook his head and blocked Andrew's path.

"What are you doing?" the marquis demanded angrily.

"You can't take her to the hospital."

"Watch me," he challenged.

"According to the journal..."

"We don't have time for this now. Can't you see Victory's dying? If you're so concerned about the damn book, you can read it on the way to the hospital."

Andrew shouldered past the earl and started up the stairs.

"If you take her to the hospital, she'll die."

Andrew halted abruptly and slowly turned back to face him.

"It gets worse," he said grimly.

Andrew returned to the basement. After gently laying Victory on the metal table, he turned to his cousin and held his hand out for the journal. Leaving it open at the proper page, Jordan handed it to his friend. Then, he went to stand beside Victory, as Andrew applied his attention to the book. After a few seconds, he looked up. "I can't believe it," he said slowly. Victory stirred and he glanced down. Studying her features, he suddenly was filled with despair. He set the book down and looked at his friend.

"The man is obviously insane. I'm afraid there is no hope. According to the notes, he has drained large quantities of her blood during the past two nights. He was going to complete the process tonight." He shook his head, slipped his arms under Victory, and then stood up.

"What are you doing?" asked the earl anxiously.

"I'm going to take her to the hospital. She will probably die, but I have to make the attempt."

Jordan shook his head. "Are you insane?"

Andrew glared at him and he said more softly, "I'm sorry, but think about it for a second. First of all, you said yourself there would be a lot of questions to be answered and explanations to be given. Are you prepared for that? Besides," he added, while looking at the girl in Andrew's arms, "I agree that she won't last long enough to make the trip."

As if to give credence to his prediction, Victory's breathing became ragged and more labored. Her erratic pulse fluttered. Then, it stopped. Apprehensively, Andrew held his breath until it resumed. "I can't just let her die," he said bleakly."

"I'm not suggesting you do, but the hospital's not the answer."

Andrew carried the limp form back to the table. Carefully laying her on the metal surface, he turned to Jordan. "What suggestion do you have?" he asked sharply, as he raked his hand through his hair in frustration.

"You're not going to like it."

"I'm listening."

Jordan drew a steadying breath before walking over to the implement tray next to the metal table. "I think your only alternative," he said, while picking up a syringe, "is to complete the process Craven started."

Chapter 34:

Blood Bond

Andrew was shocked. "Now, who's insane?"

"Hear me out. According to the notes, after draining her blood, he planned to replenish the supply with his own. You can do that. If it works, you will save her life. If not, we'll try the hospital." Staring at the girl, he thought, "Providing she lives that long," and then added aloud, "According to the notes, the two blood types are incompatible. Her remaining blood will have to be drained at the same time as the infusion."

Staring down at Victory, he gently stroked her hair as he contemplated his options. Her breathing had become more labored and shallow. Her pale skin and sunken features gave her the appearance of a corpse. He frowned. He should have taken her to the hospital right away and to hell with the explanations. Now, it was too late. She would die and he would be alone again. How would he survive the heartache and loneliness?

Jordan walked over and laid a hand on his arm. "You've got nothing to lose. You can't hurt her. Would you be able to forgive yourself for not trying every alternative while you had a chance?"

He shook his head. Those notes were the ramblings of a mad man, someone who obviously had lost touch with reality during a hopeless search for self-aggrandizement. He gazed at the small oblong blemishes on her throat. He was appalled at the idea of completing the heinous procedure, but the alternative was unacceptable. She stopped breathing again. Holding his breath, he prayed. After an eternity, she groaned. The small sound galvanized him into action. He desperately began searching the room.

"What are you looking for?"

Andrew didn't pause in his search. "The rest of the equipment for the transfusion. If he was siphoning blood, he must have tubing and a pump around here somewhere."

Jordan joined in the search. After several minutes, they returned to the examining table with the necessary equipment.

"I don't think they've gotten around to using this building for their diabolical activities," said the earl, as he wiped the dust from the IV." The IV was the intravenous apparatus that was used for transfusions. "We don't have any way to sterilize this stuff," he complained.

Victory's breathing ceased. Once more, Andrew held his breath while he waited for the erratic pulse to start. After several seconds, he turned stricken eyes on his friend.

"Any other ideas?"

Jordan glanced from the dusty equipment to the girl. Bending over her, he performed resuscitation compressions on her chest until he heard the marquis' sigh of relief.

"She's breathing again, but for how long?"

Jordan shook his head. "No guarantees. We'll have to go ahead and worry about infection later."

Andrew's gaze fixed on the bandages wrapped around one slender wrist. "You know what to do," he answered, while studying the face of his beloved.

"Fortunately, I've had some training in this procedure."

While the earl set up the IV, Andrew strode across the basement, pulled a gurney from the corner, and rolled it next to the table. Lying on it, he extended his arm.

The earl inserted the needle into the marquis' arm. Checking the tubing, he said warily, "We don't know how her body will react to your blood. If you feel lightheaded or nauseous, let me know. It may be necessary for me to give you some of mine."

Andrew smiled wryly. "Well, at least we know that we're compatible and I ..."

"Andrew. Andrew!"

The marquis blinked and then groggily shook his head. I must have dozed off," he said thickly.

"Dozed," the earl scoffed. "You passed out from severe blood loss. You were supposed to let me know," he chided.

Andrew propped himself on one elbow, while ignoring the dizziness. He stared hard at his friend. "Did it work?"

As he nodded, Jordan unrolled his sleeve. "Look for yourself."

Hesitantly, he faced the table. The color already was returning to

Victory's skin and her breathing was deep and even. Relief swept through him and he exhaled sharply. As he continued to study her, his joy gave way to nervous tension. Frowning, he turned back to his friend.

"Why hasn't she regained consciousness?"

The earl averted his eyes as he fiddled with the equipment, but the force of Andrew's gaze compelled him to answer. "She's been through a terrible ordeal and she's in shock. I still don't know if her system will accept or reject your blood." He shrugged helplessly, "To be honest, I don't know if she will fully recover, but she's alive and stable."

Anxiety gripped him as he frowned at his friend. "What..." Andrew stopped short as Jordan gasped. Jordan put his hand on his own temple.

"What is it?" the marquis asked with heartfelt concern.

"Craven," he groaned. "He's been trying to read me for a while. Fortunately, he is out of range. However," he said, as he smiled weakly, "we should leave before he realizes what happened."

Craven paced the floor of the Washington crematorium. He stopped, checked his watch, and then resumed his pacing. Thomas should have been here by now. Something obviously had gone wrong. He stalked over to the window and glared out at the city streets. If Andrew took possession of his journals, the results could be disastrous. In frustration, he pounded his fist into his palm.

His eyes suddenly widened and then narrowed to slits. His breath hissed from between clenched teeth. So, the prince actually had killed one of his own for the sake of this diurnal. That fact certainly would not sit well with even his staunchest supporters. He walked over to his desk and sat down. Drumming his fingers against the wood, he considered his options. Even though he had to assume that Andrew had the books as well as the girl, he still might be able to salvage something from this situation. He stared at the phone for quite a while and then lifted the receiver. Jason Sade slowly replaced the receiver. A rare smile touched his thin lips as he contemplated the president's latest plan. It would be easy enough to carry out if Andrew cooperated. He shrugged. Andrew was a sentimental fool and, as a matter of course, would go along with the arrangement. His predictability would be his vulnerability. He frowned as he leafed through his appointment book. After he checked his schedule, he penciled in the required appointment. He stared hard at what he had written, while tapping the pencil against the paper.

Dana's hand shook as she replaced the receiver. She closed her eyes, while still trying to assimilate the shock of Thomas' death. Again, she reviewed the conversation. Her father's voice had thrown her completely off guard. "So much for seclusion and safety," she thought wryly. He probably had known her location for the entire time. Shivering, she realized that the bond between them was too strong for her to retreat. Her sanctuary was only at Craven's discretion. He had made it perfectly clear that he expected complete compliance and loyalty. He emphasized that there would be dire consequences for further transgressions.

Confused, she carefully contemplated her father's proposal. Despite her growing unease, she was unable to disregard a direct command. Jordan's imminent peril had forced her to confront her feelings. They had been lucky last time, but would fortune prevail again? Not with Craven on his guard.

Sighing heavily, she walked onto the terrace of Jordan's Palm Beach home. She stared absently at the palm trees swaying gently in the breeze. Would Jordan ever forgive her for the part that she had played in all of this? She sadly shook her head. She probably would never know. Her instincts warned that they were headed for disaster. Still, she had no choice except to attend the meeting.

Chapter 35:
The Transformation

Andrew gazed steadily into Victory's face as he lowered his head to her neck. His stomach clenched and the bile rose in his throat, but he forced himself to continue. Propping one arm behind her head, he slightly lifted her. The oblong marks became mournful eyes accusing him with their sorrowful stare. He pressed his lips against the skin covering the jugular vein. Her skin was warm, but he still couldn't detect a pulse. Restraining his revulsion, he opened his mouth and pressed his canines into the wounds.

Nothing happened. Had he expected a scene out of a gothic horror movie? Convulsively inhaling, he felt relief that was tinged with regret. He almost gagged when a spurt of warm liquid entered his mouth. He swallowed by reflex. The blood trickled down his throat and left a tingly sensation. His eyes opened wide in surprise and then glazed in unexpected ecstasy. The taste was sweet like honey with a slightly metallic aftertaste. Instinctively, his mouth opened wider to allow easier passage. He lost himself for a few moments while reveling in the erotic sensations as the bloody nectar passed his lips, swept down his throat, and infused his body.

Andrew had never felt so vibrantly alive. The blood seeped into each part of his body, revitalized it, and made it tingle. He felt aroused yet controlled as his body was gaining strength, power, and vitality. He was on the edge of orgasm. His mind expanded to encompass the room, then the building, then the vast world beyond. He was able to focus either on the entire world or pinpoint his senses on the tiniest activity. He became one with his victim. His whole being cleaved to her as her life force sustained him and invigorated him in a way that he had never imagined. He felt a closeness, a bonding that time, distance, and even death could not break.

Someone tugged at his arm. He shoved the distraction away like batting an irritating insect. The irritator returned and was pulling, tugging, and yelling incomprehensible words. What was he trying to tell him? It wasn't important. Nothing mattered but the taste of the blood. Abruptly, the flow trickled and then stopped.

After several seconds, he lifted his bewildered gaze from Victory's throat. The Earl of Rockford glared accusingly at him.

"You were supposed to stop before draining all of it." Andrew glanced guiltily down at the corpse. The earl shoved him aside. He felt her pulse. Green eyes pinned him to the spot as he said harshly, "You've killed her!"

His eyes flew open and he jerked upright. Sweat trickled down his face as his body went rigid. Glancing across to the bed, he exhaled. He leaned back in his chair and took a couple of steadying breaths. The constant vigil finally was taking its toll. No wonder he had dozed. He walked to the adjoining bathroom and splashed cold water on his face, which removed the last remnants of the nightmare.

Re-entering the bedroom, he returned to the side of the bed. Stroking the soft skin of her face brought back so many memories. Shame flooded through him as he recalled the nightmare. His hand dropped. Abruptly, he fled the room.

He soon returned with Jordan. Flicking the light switch, they stared down at the sleeping figure. Andrew willed Victory to open her eyes. Despair darkened his eyes as he wondered if his imagination had played a trick on him. Then, he saw it. It was the barest movement of her right hand on the blanket. Again, the slight tremor stirred the fabric. His eyes sought Jordan's. The earl nodded. Andrew closed his eyes in relief. Maybe, just maybe. He sank onto the bed and cradled Victory in his arms. The light brush of her breath against his skin comforted him as he pulled her closer.

He watched Jordan walk over to the fireplace and stare into the flames. Her lips felt good against his skin. He savored the feel of her lips pressing against his throat. He stiffened slightly as the sharp teeth sank into his flesh and then lost awareness of everything except the sensations.

Erotic sensations swept through his body as he floated on a tide of bliss that was striving towards nirvana. The mounting excitement of sexual arousal combined with a languorous drowsiness. His life force was pleasantly slipping away and the temptation to surrender to the promise of eternal peace was overpowering. He sank slowly as he slid into a soft, light haze of comfort. His arousal rose and ebbed, which provided a tantalizing backdrop as he entered oblivion.

Suddenly, the pressure on his throat was gone. He slowly was being dragged back to consciousness. The lethargy waned and desolation swept over him. For centuries, he had longed for peace, eternal rest, and, now that it was just within his grasp, he was being denied. Resentfully, he glared at his companion. Annoyance subsided as he became aware of the scene. He lay sprawled across the bed. Above him was a demented woman struggling violently with the Earl of Rockford. Propping himself on one elbow, he shook off the lethargy and focused on the struggle.

Victory – her face tinged with a pink flush and blood dripping from her mouth – was thrashing and clawing at the earl. Teeth gnashed and eyes blazed as she attacked. She looked like a possessed demon right out of a horror movie. The sound of cloth tearing heralded the parting of Jordan's sports jacket and shirt.

Andrew sat bolt upright and stared in amazement. Victory had torn through the jacket, shirt, and skin. A bright scarlet line appeared across the earl's chest. Victory's eyes gleamed. Her tongue flicked across her bloodstained lips and her attack became more frenzied as she tried to reach the wound.

"Could you provide a little assistance, old chap?" asked Jordan, as he glanced ironically at the marquis. "I am beginning to regret the removal of the chains."

Andrew stood unsteadily and lunged for the woman just as she became free of the earl's grip. He caught her around the waist. The force of the impact sent them sprawling back onto the bed. Deprived of her quarry, Victory unleashed her fury on her captor. She twisted in his arms and then brought her hands up to slash at his face. Andrew turned aside just as her nails whizzed past his ear. Jordan approached from behind and grasped her in a bear hug. Before she could attack again, the two men imprisoned her writhing body facedown on the bed.

Andrew used his body weight and strength to hold Victory down while Jordan dashed across the room to snatch the sashes from the drapes. A sharp pain in Andrew's arm astounded him as he realized that she had fastened her teeth into his wrist. Jordan appeared to be having difficulty with the wildly flailing legs and the ever-increasing strength of the captive.

Andrew tried to keep his thoughts focused on the task, but lethargy rapidly replaced the blood being drained from his body. He slowly opened his mouth to speak. The effort was almost too much for him. "Jordan," he croaked in a strangled whisper, "Could you try picking up the pace a little?"

Jordan glanced up. Realizing the marquis' predicament, he gave the knot a final tug and lunged towards the top of the bed. Yanking a bunch of the woman's hair, he pulled her head away from Andrew. Dazed, the marquis lifted himself from the prone figure. He shook his head, took a few steps back, and leaned against a wall. He studied Victory. His eyes gleamed with despair that gradually was replaced by grim determination.

"What have I done?" he asked softly, while wiping a hand across his face to shut out the aberration.

Jordan joined him. "You did what you had to. No one could have predicted this would happen."

Andrew stared at his friend for several seconds and then slowly shook his head. "I should have realized the risk from reading Craven's notes." He stared bleakly at the figure writhing on the bed. "Instead of saving her life, I've changed her into some sort of demented creature. I certainly can't take her to any hospital in that condition."

Jordan laid a hand on his arm. "No, but you have saved her from death – or worse. We don't know what Craven was planning."

Andrew slowly nodded. "That's true, but I doubt I did her a favor by saving her life. Instead of giving way to my own selfish desire to keep her with me, I should have let her go," he said with his voice full of self-reproach. "Is she now condemned to spend the rest of her life like that?"

Again Jordan touched his arm. Sensing his intention, he said urgently, "Wait. Maybe she'll come out of it."

Andrew shot a skeptical glance at him. The earl's gaze shifted uncomfortably. Watching Victory's struggles tore at his heart. "Maybe this is some sort of transition phase," he offered hopefully.

Andrew closed his eyes. When he opened them, his gaze fell on the cut. "She really sliced into you, didn't she?"

He glanced down ruefully. "It's nothing but a scratch. See? It's healing already. If she hadn't caught me off guard, it would never have happened. I was completely unprepared for the sudden surge of energy and strength. You should have seen it, Andrew. It was incredible. One second, she was lying over you and, the next, she was springing at me." He finished and looked at the bed in awe.

Andrew started to reply, but a shrill waling split the air. They were both at her side in a second. Victory's mouth opened and allowed another piercing shriek to pass between her lips. She arched and squirmed on the bed as her eyes began to roll up. Strange guttural sounds rose from her throat. Immediately, Andrew pulled her across the bed.

"She's seizing!" shouted Jordan, as he grabbed her other arm.

"But why?" asked Andrew, whose face suddenly was drained by fear.

"I don't know," Jordan replied. "Maybe her human internal organs are rejecting your porphyrian blood. I think she's going to be sick and I don't want her to choke on her own vomit. Roll her over. Roll her over!"

Freeing the woman, they managed to turn her onto her stomach. Then, they slid her head off of the edge of the four-poster just as the contents of her stomach spewed on the wooden floor. The vomit was mixed with blood. After several more dry heaves, Victory's body went limp. Gently, Andrew turned her over. She had fainted.

Jordan sent an ironic look to his friend. "What a time to send the servants on holiday."

He smiled wanly. "I could never have explained this," he gestured towards the limp figure, "to my housekeeper."

Jordan walked into the bathroom and returned with damp towels. Wiping the floor, he spared one for Andrew, who applied it to her flushed face. Straightening, he observed while the marquis put a hand on her forehead.

"How is she?"

Andrew smoothed the sweat-soaked hair from her forehead. "Unconscious with a high fever."

Jordan studied the serious expression on his friend's face. "What do you want to do?"

The marquis frowned as he studied the unconscious figure. Her breathing was strong and steady, but perspiration beaded her forehead. Every few seconds, a slight tremor ran through her body. A low moan escaped her parted lips. His face registered concern and determination as he faced the earl.

"I think we will have to take turns watching over her until her condition changes."

He nodded solemnly. "And then?"

Andrew winced, but his voice was steady as he said, "We will watch her for a few days. If she doesn't improve, I'll release her."

He nodded curtly. Compassion darkened his jade-green eyes. "Do you want me to take the first watch?"

Andrew gazed at Victory. Her makeshift clothing, which had been sagging on her emaciated body only a few hours ago, was now completely filled out. Miraculously, her limbs were again full and well defined. Her bosom and hips were rounded and well shaped. Her skin, despite the perspiration, had a glow and her hair had a new luster under the superficial dust. The sight lifted his flagging spirits and he tried to gain hope. Drained and exhausted, he smiled gratefully and then nodded.

Jordan took the seat by the bed as Andrew started towards the door. Opening the door, he paused. "Will you be all right alone?"

The earl glanced down at the sleeping figure and then into his friend's worried eyes. Masking his doubts, he smiled and waved away the marquis. As the door closed, he said a silent prayer.

Several hours later, the fresh and alert marquis reappeared. Gazing down at the sleeping figure, Andrew found it difficult to imagine her as the frenzied creature of a few hours ago. The only blemish on the innocent face was the trickle of dried blood from her lips to her chin. "My porphyrian blood," he thought. Once again, he reviled himself for his mistake.

He settled her on the four-poster and then walked into the adjoining bathroom. Turning on the tap, he called over his shoulder, "Jordan, could you go to my room and get some of Victory's things? There should be a clean nightgown in the drawer and her brush is on the dresser."

When Jordan returned, he held her inert body upright while the marquis disrobed her.

"Do you need any help with the bathing?"

Andrew smiled for the first time since discovering Victory in the crematorium. "I don't think so," he said. He imagined how Victory would react if she discovered that she had been bathed by the earl.

"If it becomes a problem, I'll call you."

He carried her into the bathroom. Setting her gently in the tub, he propped her against the back. He paused to make sure that she would not slide before he began lathering. As he washed, he noticed the subtle but unmistakable changes. Her skin had acquired a faint luminescent gleam that paled to alabaster. Her hair had taken on a golden sparkle and her eyes, which always had been a bright blue, were shocking in their intensity.

His breath caught. Her eyes were open and staring at him. He thought that he detected recognition and lucidity, but he remained wary. "Victory," he questioned cautiously, "can you understand me?"

He perceived a slight nod before her body was racked with contractions. She clutched her stomach and groaned while her body shook. Quickly rinsing the shampoo from her hair, he wrapped her in a towel. She lunged towards the toilet and began vomiting a combination of blood and sputum. When her stomach finally emptied again, she was wracked by a second wave of dry heaving. For several seconds, he watched helplessly while she struggled for control. Finally finished, she collapsed unconscious onto the floor.

Tears glistened on his cheeks as Andrew gently toweled her hair. He slipped her into the nightgown and carried her back to the bedroom.

Jordan was waiting. His face was full of concern.

"I was about to go in the bathroom when I heard the wailing start up again."

Andrew's eyes never left Victory's face. Her rapid breathing had subsided from sharp gasps to a steady rhythm. "She regained consciousness for a couple of minutes, but the sickness overpowered her before she could do much of anything except throw up."

"You're lucky that's all she did."

Andrew turned. "I think she was lucid for a moment."

He reached out with trembling fingers to stroke her hair. Abruptly, he withdrew his hand and walked towards the fireplace. Jordan had built a fire while he had been in the bathroom. Now, the blaze provided warmth to the chilly room. The flames cast a rosy glow on his face and danced reflectively in his eyes. He stared transfixed for several seconds as if trying to decipher a puzzle. Finally, he extracted one of the leather-bound notebooks and began ripping the pages. He cast them into the fire and allowed the greedy flames to engulf them. He studied the outer shell with its dragon emblem for several seconds and then tossed it into the fire. He watched in fascination as the flames slowly enveloped the dragon. They were curling the wings, singeing the tail, and burning through the eyes.

Jordan's voice snapped him out of his reverie.

"Why did you do that?"

"Because I had to."

"Which one was it?"

The marquis finally turned his back to the flames and leaned against the mantle. "The research log."

Anticipating the answer, Jordan nodded.

"I don't want that information to fall into the wrong hands and have porphyrians trying to kill diurnals for their nutrients. I also don't want anyone else to get ideas about conducting conversion experiments."

"He was right," said the earl softly.

"Unfortunately for him," responded Andrew. His face took on a distant look.

Jordan began to reply, but a loud knock interrupted him. He frowned as he glanced at the marquis. "I thought the servants were gone."

"They should be," he replied, as he strode across the room and jerked open the door. A disgruntled butler confronted him. "Grayson, I left orders not to be disturbed," he said sharply.

"Excuse me, sir," said the butler, evidencing no expression as he observed the scene, "but there is a Detective Roberts downstairs. He is quite insistent about seeing you."

Chapter 36:

Entrapment

"Correction, there is a Detective Roberts upstairs who insists on see-ing you," boomed a loud voice as the detective plowed into the room.

The butler blustered at the lack of protocol. In England, people knew how to conduct themselves upon entering others' residences. Especially when entering an aristocratic establishment. He sniffed disapprovingly. "I would offer to call the authorities, sir" he offered apologetically to the marquis, "but it appears they have no better manners then the common-ers." He sniffed again, while staring hard at the detective.

"Would you like me to have him removed?" he asked disdainfully.

The marquis waved a hand. Bestowing a final baleful glance at the intruder, the butler withdrew.

"Grayson," the marquis called as the door began to close.

"Sir?"

"You're on holiday. Remember?"

The butler appeared disgruntled. Opening his mouth to protest, he looked from the marquis to the earl and then back to the marquis. He nodded reluctantly and departed.

While untying his trench coat, the detective strode into the room. He stopped short at the foot of the bed and stared at the occupant. After several seconds, he turned to the marquis. He surveyed him from head to foot before slowly shaking his head.

"I guess you never know," he said dryly.

Ignoring the comment, Andrew asked, "Would you mind telling me what this is about, detective? As you can see," he said, while indicating the bed, "my fiancée is ill and I am anxious to get back to her care."

The detective's face was as hard as granite when he grated, "You're as cool as a cucumber. I have to hand it to you. Are you getting rid

261

of this one, too?"

"What are you talking about?" asked Andrew, who was beginning to lose patience. The day had been long and fraught with emotional tension. All that he wanted to do now was to relax, get a drink, and keep vigil by Victory's bed. He had no tolerance for playing word games with a fool who looked like a carbon copy of Columbo.

"I'm talking about murder, Lord Gabriel. More precisely, your murder of Laura Warner."

"You're insane."

"Am I?"

Andrew sighed wearily. "I didn't kill Laura. What makes you think that I did?" he asked. His voice reflected his tiredness.

"Well, for starters, the fingerprints on the razor the victim used match your prints on the door and the telephone. Secondly, I have uncovered evidence that suggests you were having an affair with both Miss Warner and Miss Parker at the same time."

"That's ridiculous! Even if I had done something as despicable as that, would that make me a murderer?"

Roberts shrugged. "It would give you a motive if Miss Warner threatened to tell her friend about your infidelity." After all, Miss Parker is an heiress and quite a catch."

Andrew shrugged. "So was Miss Warner. I could have acquired considerable wealth, if that was my goal, by marrying her."

"True, but, if Miss Warner was angered because of your relations with Miss Parker, she might have threatened to expose your unfaithfulness and your scheme. Then, you would lose Miss Parker and probably Miss Warner, too."

Andrew recognized the futility of arguing. Turning towards the earl, he said, "Would you stay with Victory while I'm gone?"

He nodded at the marquis and pulled a chair towards the bed. "What if Craven comes looking for her?" he asked silently.

"He won't. Since she has bonded with me, she's of no use to him."

Jordan looked startled, but kept his thoughts silent. "Have you forgotten Craven's lust for revenge?"

"Do the best you can. I won't be gone long."

"Who's he?" the detective demanded sharply.

Andrew turned to face him. The detective's heartbeat quickened under the ominous glare. "He is Jordan Rush, my personal friend and hers, too. Since my fiancée is so ill, I will not leave her unattended."

The detective briefly studied Jordan. Suddenly his brows lifted. "Aren't you the guy who was running for British prime minister a few months ago?"

Jordan nodded and Roberts hesitated. He studied Andrew with new interest. "All right, but I'm going to leave my officers in the front and in the back of this house. If you decide to leave, they will follow you."

Satisfied, Andrew preceded the detective as they walked downstairs.

Jordan walked into the adjoining bathroom and re-soaked the washcloth in cold water. Walking back to the bed, he felt the extremely hot flesh and then placed the cloth on her forehead. He frowned as he tried to guess the degree of the temperature. He returned to the bathroom to rifle through the medicine chest for several minutes. Then, he remembered that Andrew would have no need for such a mundane device as a thermometer. Retracing his steps, he sat beside the patient, took her hand as Andrew had done a few minutes ago, and prepared to wait out the long night.

A scratching sounded at the window. He tensed and then flinched as he stood to face someone who had jumped onto the balcony. A half-smile curved his lips, as he hurried towards the pane to admit the lone figure.

"It's about time," said Dana with annoyance, "I've been poking at that window for twenty minutes."

"Why didn't you let me know you were there?"

"And risk broadcasting the news to Andrew? In case you hadn't noticed, I've been keeping a low profile lately."

"I noticed and, by the way, thank you." Jordan said, as he grinned broadly down at the petite brunette while he embraced her. "What's with the get-up?" he asked with surprise at her jeans and t-shirt. "The outfit makes you look like a teenager."

"Do you like it?" she queried, while turning gracefully, "It's my new image: the sweet and innocent look."

"You haven't been innocent since the day you were born," he said. His grin took the sting from the words. "You saved my life. I know how difficult it was to defy your father."

"Yes, it was," she agreed earnestly, "but I'd do it again if I had to."

Jordan's green eyes glittered as he pulled her close. Their lips met and they clung together as though each were a life raft that provided protection for each other from the raging storm. Reluctantly, they pulled apart. Dana opened her mouth to speak, but a low groan from the bed caught their attention.

Shocked, Dana glanced from the earl to the bed and then back. "How is she?" she asked, as she examined Victory with interest.

Jordan joined her. He shrugged. "I doubt she'll live. Converting to porphyrian blood is too much of a shock for her system."

"I tried to tell my father that it wouldn't work. But he is obsessed with the ancient myths and legends. He really believes that they hold the key to liberating our people from what he considers to be the chains of humanity." She shook her head. "I used to believe in him. I believed that his way was right, but now...," she said while glancing back at the bed, "I think he's gone over the edge. Do you know that he is talking about making a trip to Romania to search for the remains of Vlad Tsepish?"

Jordan held her close, "I think you should stay with me."

She raised her eyes to his. "That was why I came. I also came to warn you and Andrew," she paused as she realized that he was not on the premises and then continued, "about the meeting. Father has scheduled one for tomorrow night." She looked around with interest. "Where is Andrew? I'm surprised that anything could pry him away from his diurnal's side, especially while she is in such a fragile condition."

"Andrew has been accused of Laura Warner's death and is at the police station trying to clear himself. I hope you were discrete in coming here. There are guards in the front and the back of the house."

Dana waived her hand dismissively, "The ones in the back are out for the count."

He raised his brows.

"Asleep," she amended quickly.

"Perfect. Now, tell me everything you know about this meeting," he urged.

Ten minutes later, she was on the verge of catapulting from the balcony when she paused. A low moaning had begun issuing from the figure on the bed. The noise quickly escalated into a crescendo of anguished screams that were so terrible that Dana had to cover her ears. The wailing continued at the high pitch. The intensity of the sound pierced her eardrums and threatened to imbed itself in her brain. She swayed and pitched forward into the night. Strong arms encircled her and pulled her back inside.

"What's wrong with her?" she yelled in Jordan's ear.

Jordan squinted through the haze of pain. His head felt like it was going to split. He slowly made his way towards the bed, but the shrieking was like a force field that kept him at bay. He turned to Dana and shook his head as he gestured towards the balcony. She nodded in agreement.

Before they could move, the door was thrown open and Andrew rushed into the room. Hurrying to the bedside, he concentrated all of his energy on the figure. The air palpitated with the aura that his authority and power produced. The noise abruptly ceased. Gingerly, Jordan and Dana lowered their hands from their ears, as they stared at the bed.

Victory's body swelled. At first, the degree of increase barely was discernable, but, suddenly, her body inflated like a balloon. As quickly as it bloated, it shrank. It shriveled until she appeared to be no more than sticks covered by skin. Her tongue protruded and her eyes rolled up into her skull. Her entire body suddenly went rigid and then sagged as if boneless. Her eyes focused and rested on Andrew. She opened her mouth as if to speak, while lifting one hand towards the marquis. Bending forward he took it. Victory's mouth curved slightly. Then, her hand slipped, her eyes became glassy, and a long sigh like the whispering of the wind escaped her lips.

Jordan approached and put a comforting hand on his friend's arm. The marquis leaned forward and closed her eyelids, as a sob wrenched from his throat. This time, he was not dreaming nor was his imagination deluding him.

"Is she dead?" asked Dana, who still was confused by the rapid turn of events.

Andrew nodded, as Jordan turned to gaze at her. "Why don't you go now? I will stay and explain what you told me. Besides, your father will miss you soon."

She started to protest, but thought better of it. He was right. Craven would notice her absence and her visit would not be viewed favorably. Reluctantly, she walked to the open veranda. She glanced back once and then faded into the shadows.

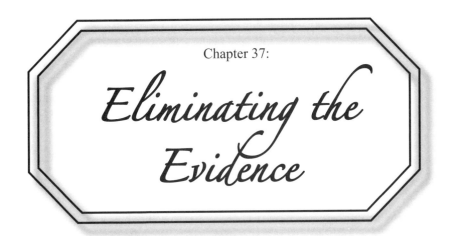

Chapter 37:

Eliminating the Evidence

Andrew laid his palm against Victory's forehead. "Still too warm," he thought, as he collapsed into the bedside chair. His troubled gaze roamed restlessly over her as he considered how to break the fever. Jordan placed another compress against her brow. "I'm afraid all we can do is wait," he said tiredly.

The marquis nodded, as he linked his fingers with the unconscious figure on the bed. Allowing privacy for his cousin, the earl strode to the French doors and stared out at the recently vacated veranda. They shared the silence for several minutes with each immersed in their own thoughts until a soft knock at the door intruded.

The butler, carrying a silver tray with two crystal glasses and a decanter, opened the door. Setting the tray on the dresser, he poured the contents of the decanter into the glasses, handed one to each, and then withdrew. As the door closed, Andrew raised his glass. He silently saluted his companion and drained the contents. He leaned forward and refilled his glass. Sipping the second glass more slowly, he stared broodingly into the fireplace. "Craven was right," he again reluctantly admitted to himself, "so he and his followers must be eliminated."

"Do you think she bought it?"

Andrew was ripped from his reverie by the sound of his friend's voice. Turning slowly, he smiled sadly. "Didn't you?"

Jordan looked at the bed and back. "Yes, but why did you do it?"

He lifted one hand to cover his eyes and then slowly lowered it. Shrugging, he responded, "I had a sudden inspiration. While I was at the police station being interrogated by our diligent Detective Roberts, I had time to think. If Victory survives the transition, she will be bonded to me. That doesn't necessarily mean she will be safe. Unfamiliar with her new abilities and vulnerabilities, she would be easy prey. After using her to validate his theory, Craven would consider her expendable. I am quite sure Craven would rather see her dead than allow his plans to play a part in my future happiness. It's ironic that he kidnapped her with the intention of the ultimate revenge and, instead, provided me with the ultimate gift. He chuckled hollowly. "Anyway, since his original plan for revenge failed, he is liable to go for a backup."

"Backup?" asked a confused Jordan.

Andrew nodded. "Originally, his intention was to have her bound to him by infusing her with his blood. I'm sure he thought having the woman I love beholden to him would drive me mad. Now, she is no longer of use to him in that capacity. If Victory survives, that will be enough proof to validate his research. She then is expendable and what better revenge than to destroy her?"

"So you staged her death."

"I had been planning it all the way home, but the opportunity was coincidental. I had no idea that Dana would be here when I returned and the shrieks were authentic expressions of intense pain. I had to expend a great deal of power to ease her suffering."

Jordan inhaled sharply. "Since you were already broadcasting such an enormous amount of energy, Dana couldn't detect when you switched over to illusion."

"Right," he agreed. "Even if she did detect my influence, she would assume I was trying to use my strength to support Victory's struggle for life."

Jordan lifted his glass, "Bravo, old chap. I'm sure when her father asks her about the condition of his test subject, which he will undoubtedly do, she will be able to report sincerely that she has expired. Even if she were willing to try to hide the truth, Craven would have delved deeply enough to decipher it. It's much safer for Dana if she actually believes what she is saying. What about your meeting with the detective?"

He made a dismissive gesture. "His theory had more holes than a slice of Swiss cheese. He's under a lot of pressure since the assassination. He's convinced the murders are related and that there is a plot to kill the new president, too."

"And he's right."

"Yes," said Andrew wearily, "right conclusion, wrong premise."

Craven Maxwell sat alone in his dark study. As he stared into the fireplace, he sipped a glass full of a dark viscous fluid. The dying embers did little to dispel the chill in the large room, but they did offer solace to the porphyrian.

"Come in," he commanded silently to the figure in the doorway.

Still unsure of her welcome, his daughter advanced hesitantly until she stood before him. Ignoring her, he continued to gaze into the embers. He finally looked up and motioned for her to be seated. Poised for flight, she perched on the chair that was directly in front of him. The dying fire cast shadows across her face and, for a moment, the visage of her mother haunted him.

"What did you find out?" he demanded sharply.

She was unnerved by the harsh tone, but was not surprised that he knew where she had been. Since the incident in the basement, he had been tracking her movements. Annoyance flared as she confronted the fact that he had spied on her most intimate moments and she was powerless to prevent it.

"You knew where I was. Why didn't you just stick around and check the status for yourself?"

Craven's eyes bore into her, as he lowered his glass to the side table. One eyebrow rose. He continued to stare at her. The onyx orbs impaled her. Feeling like an insect caught under a microscope, she shifted restlessly beneath the prolonged scrutiny. She finally dropped her gaze to the embers.

Satisfied, he picked up his drink and leaned back in his chair. His daughter's defiance was beginning to annoy him. "Still," he thought, "I need her for purposes such as this." From long distances, Craven was unable to read the thoughts of others, especially when they were shielded, but he could examine his daughter's thoughts from almost everywhere.

"That diurnal is dead," she stated flatly.

Craven jerked as though an electric jolt had shot through him. He probed her mind and received the mental images of the scene. His amazement grew as he realized Andrew's presence.

"What was he doing there?" he demanded in a harsh whisper.

Dana's brow furrowed. "You tried to have Andrew framed for the murder of the other diurnal," she whispered in amazement. "Jordan said Andrew had been taken to the police station for questioning. Either they believed his protestations or he influenced them to let him go."

He was silent for a long time. He had counted on Andrew's scrupulous respect for diurnal law to keep him out of the way until after the meeting. His early release might mean trouble. Absently, he dismissed his daughter. There was no sense in allowing her to know too much about his plans and risk having them find their way back to his enemies.

After she departed, he picked up the phone and dialed. The conversation that followed was brief but explicit. The attorney general confirmed the president's suspicions. Craven decided that the need for the meeting was immediate. He left the arrangements in Jason's hands. As he headed for the door, he decided which of his secret service agents to take with him. He thought that it was better to leave one of the porphyrians with the two remaining diurnals. Conners and Peters were starting to scrutinize his affairs a little too closely. They were causing only a minor irritation that he could settle after he dealt with the Marquis of Penbrook.

Detective Roberts glanced up from the book. The clock on his office wall read, "11:15 p.m." He rubbed his aching eyes and glared menacingly at the fluorescent lights. He returned his attention to the pages of the journal. The cramped black handwritten words became spiders chasing flies across the page. He shook his head.

Reaching for his Styrofoam cup, he gulped the cold brew. Grimacing, he wondered what the police psychiatrist would have to say about his hallucinations. He probably would tell him that it was some sort of deep-rooted sexual fantasy caused by his mother. Roberts preferred to think that it meant that he was working too hard.

The phone rang, shattering the stillness of the deserted office. Roberts yawned as he picked up the receiver. "Yes?"

"Detective Roberts, this is Oliver Wayne."

The detective stifled another yawn as he recognized the handwriting expert whom he had called. Was it three hours since he released the marquis? He carefully chose his next words. Although he had worked with the handwriting expert on several occasions, this assignment was extremely delicate.

"Thanks for getting back to me, Wayne. I'm going to need your assistance."

"It must be pretty important for you to call this late."

Roberts leaned back in his chair. He tugged on his necktie and pushed up his shirtsleeves before answering. "It sure is," he asserted, while looking at the black leather-bound journal. "If the handwriting in this notebook is authentic, I may have the crime of the decade."

Wayne whistled. "That serious?"

"Yes. If this pans out, the case will immediately go out of my jurisdiction and into the hands of the FBI."

"In that case, do you want me to come over now?"

"I would appreciate it."

Roberts replaced the receiver. He frowned as he noticed a light switch on in the outer office. Footsteps echoed on the linoleum. A moment later, a tall lanky figure filled the entrance.

The detective immediately stood and extended his hand to the advancing man. The attorney general clasped it briefly and then sat down. Roberts involuntarily shuddered as he stared into the deep green eyes. Relieved to break eye contact, he excused himself to adjust the thermostat.

When he returned, he had an expression of polite respect fixed firmly in place. "What can I do for you, Mr. Sade?"

Jason Sade silently studied him. Roberts had the uncomfortable feeling that one of the spiders from the journal had escaped the confines of its pages.

"It has recently been brought to my attention that you have come into possession of certain documents that might be of assistance in the investigation of the late president's assassination."

Roberts's eyes snapped from the man's face to the journal and back. Following his gaze, the porphyrian leaned closer.

"Due to the sensitive nature of the material, the documents must be handled very delicately. It is imperative that all of the evidence in this case must be handed over immediately. I have already cleared the request through your police chief," he added. He provided the necessary paperwork when he saw that Roberts was about to protest. "He agreed that this case was not within the jurisdiction of the local police."

Roberts sifted through the forms. His jaw muscles tensed. Everything appeared to be in order. Although irritated and uneasy about releasing the journal, he didn't appear to have much choice. "Would you mind indulging me while I call my superior? It's just as a formality, of course," he said, as he smiled to hide the frustration.

He thought that he caught a brief glimpse of hostility in the cold green gaze, but it quickly was masked. Jason waved a hand at the phone and then leaned back to wait. Roberts dialed and waited for several seconds before the phone was picked up.

"Hello," answered a groggy voice.

Roberts cleared his throat. "Chief, it's Roberts. The attorney general is here to pick up some documents on a case I'm investigating. I just want to confirm clearance for releasing them."

He held the phone away from his ear as the orders were barked at him. Hanging up, he eyed the attorney general. "Well," he said, "it looks as though I have clearance. You guys are certainly on top of things. I just received the journal a few hours ago."

Sade stood and tucked the notebook into his inside pocket. Nodding curtly, he strode from the office.

Roberts stared through the doorway for a long time after he left. He was baffled. A few minutes later, Oliver Wayne appeared in his doorway. Shaking himself back to awareness, he apologized for dragging the expert out of bed. He decided to stop for a drink on the way home, so he cut off the light and walked Wayne to his car.

Chapter 38:

The Murder of Justice

Jordan flicked through the television channels. Occasionally, he glanced up from the screen, but Victory's condition remained unchanged. He checked his watch. "We need to be leaving soon," he thought aloud, while gazing down at the sleeping figure. Leaving her shouldn't be a problem since Craven thought that she was dead. He wondered how Andrew's butler would control her if she regained consciousness. She would have to be bound and the door would need to be locked. The butler would have to be given strict orders to admit no one.

Again, he glanced anxiously at his watch. They would have to hurry if they wanted to have everything in place tonight. He hesitated with his finger on the off button. Leaning closer, he turned up the volume.

As Andrew slipped silently into the room, he asked hesitantly, "Isn't that the detective who took you in?"

Andrew rubbed his eyes and then peered at the screen. The interviewee was the chief of the DC Metropolitan Police Department, but the small square on the upper right corner of the screen portrayed a typical picture of Detective Roberts with his tie slightly askew and wearing a trench coat. Frowning, the marquis focused on the dialogue. According to the news report, Roberts had been mugged and murdered as he was heading towards a neighborhood pub. His wallet and jewelry were missing, but, since the pub was a local hangout for cops, one of the patrons was able to identify the body. Roberts had no local family.

Andrew clicked off the television and stared at the darkened screen. He sat, closed his eyes, and massaged his temples.

Jordan studied his friend with concern. "Do you think they will try to connect you with this?"

Wearily, he shook his head. "No, but I am responsible."

Jordan skeptically eyed him. "You didn't do it?"

He shook his head. "But I made it necessary for them to kill him."

"I thought they were using him as a tool to persecute you."

"Yes, but without considering the consequences for Detective Roberts' safety, I turned the tables by giving him the book."

The earl exhaled. "It could be coincidence."

Andrew gazed at him. "A few hours after receiving evidence implicating Craven in the murder of the former president? My only excuse for the oversight is I was distracted by my concern for Victory. Still, I wonder how they found out so soon." He frowned. "I thought the information would get out eventually, but only after it was entrenched in the system. By then, so many people would have been aware of the contents of the journal that it would be impossible to cover up.

Jordan shifted uncomfortably and then whispered. "Dana!"

He nodded. "When she reported, she must have told her father I was here. He obviously figured out that, if I was no longer being detained, the police must have had a good reason for letting me go."

"He knows you wouldn't use your influence, so his logical assumption would be that the police must have attained some type of evidence that cleared you. I'll bet he didn't expect you to provide the book to the diurnals."

Since they were teenagers, Craven had known about Andrew's diligence for respecting the laws of diurnal society. Furthermore, he was quite familiar with Andrew's abhorrence of using his unique abilities to take unfair advantage.

Jordan continued, "The mugger was probably a porphyrian. It makes little difference," he added.

Andrew glanced at him sharply.

"Well, at some point, the book would have been turned over to the FBI for evidence and would have eventually found its way to Jason Sade."

"Yes," he agreed "but, by that time, there would have been too many people involved for them all to be eliminated."

Jordan gave him a strange look. "The attorney general has the authority to confiscate any material pertaining to a federal investigation."

Andrew's eyes closed and lips thinned. "I had no idea. I might as well have signed the poor man's death warrant."

Jordan cleared his throat. "We need to get started if you want everything in place tonight."

Andrew said nothing, but, within moments, the butler appeared. "Grayson, Lord Rush and I are going out. I need you to keep careful watch on Miss Parker. At the slightest change in her condition, contact me."

Grayson nodded and climbed the stairs. Andrew walked to the closet and handed a jacket to Jordan. Slipping into another, he stooped to retrieve the large duffle bag.

Wasn't it Darwin who proposed the theory of the "survival of the fittest?" thought Craven Maxwell, as he studied the inscrutable faces of the group assembled around the conference table. How ironic it is that this diurnal's theory would be implemented by a superior species in order to bring about the extinction of Darwin's own race.

He sat at the head of the rectangular table with porphyrians along the length of both sides. Jason was directly opposite him, while Dana sat at his right. The thought of evolutionary justice brought the barest twitch to the thin lips as he ticked off his mental agenda. He stared hard at his daughter. Should anything happen to him, she was his acknowledged heir and would take his place as leader. His gaze swept past her to Walter, a coward but loyal to the cause. His eyes shifted to the empty chair on his left. The void seemed to mock him. He would have to settle with his brother on that score. "I was very fond of Thomas," he thought broodingly. He recognized him as a kindred spirit. He had relied on the porphyrian to act as a steadying influence for his wayward daughter. Eventually, he would have encouraged a permanent union, but, now, Thomas was gone.

His glance passed over the expectant faces of his nineteen core conspirators. As his glance rested on Jason, he felt a genuine smile spread across his face. Here was someone upon whom he could rely. He looked from his newly appointed attorney general to his daughter. Dana was not particularly fond of Jason, but she would adjust. The sooner that she was settled with someone who could curb her impulsiveness the better.

Aware that he held their rapt attention, Craven opened the meeting. "As you all know, a recent change in events has altered our plans. I had been conducting an extraordinary experiment on a diurnal. If the experiment had been successful, the potential would have been unlimited. Unfortunately, Andrew and Jordan interfered and killed Thomas in the process." There was a collective gasp. He paused to allow the shock to settle. "Our adversaries also obtained some valuable information regarding the experiment, the research I have been conducting, and our...," he glanced knowingly at Jason, "involvement in political affairs."

A sharp gasp emanated from Cynthia and Walter opened his mouth as though he wanted to speak. Craven glared them into silence. "The vital documents were recovered," he announced to the relief of the assembly. "However, we are faced with the problem of future interference from the Marquis of Penbrook and the Earl of Rockford. I do not tolerate interference!" he bellowed, while slamming his fist on the table. "Therefore," he continued evenly, "I am entertaining suggestions about how the problems can be eliminated."

With narrowed eyes, he searched the faces of his followers. Psychically sensing dissention, he wanted to weed out the traitor. If necessary, he would make an example of the weakling. His gaze fastened on Dana. Fury boiled inside him and a red flush spread across his pale cheeks. How dare his own daughter attempt to undermine his authority by mentally broadcasting doubts? In a blast of anger, he silently ordered her to leave the room. He speculated about her motives as he watched her retreat. Turning, he caught Jason's eye and nodded. The other porphyrian glanced at Dana and nodded. Craven smiled.

Softly clicking the door behind her, Dana dejectedly wandered through the deserted building. She felt like she was being torn apart. She owed her undivided loyalty, devotion, and respect to her father and the cause, but her treacherous heart constricted in agony whenever she considered harming Jordan Rush. She couldn't reconcile the idea of hurting Andrew, either, no matter how much of a threat he was to the project. Sighing heavily, she wandered towards the front of the building. A walk in the brisk spring air might help to clear her mind.

She pushed the glass doors and strolled to the sidewalk. Following the road, she headed away from the building and towards the main highway. Life had been a lot simpler when she believed that her father was right. "Being in control of my feelings helped, too," she admitted ruefully. Damn the Earl of Rockford! It was his fault that she was plagued with these doubts. Jordan and his cursed idealism. Damn the marquis, too. The absolute love and devotion that he showed for his diurnal made her long for something that she hadn't known she was missing. She relived the horrible moment when she almost lost Jordan forever in the fire of the furnace. At that moment, she knew that she would have sacrificed herself to prevent his suffering.

She rubbed her arms and watched dispassionately as a group of school children in uniforms ran past. Now, she understood what Andrew experienced with his diurnal. She tensed as she reentered the building. How could she shield her thoughts? Did she want to? Were her father's plans the right ones for her people? If not, should she continue to provide her support? Craven would never forgive her. She shuddered at the prospect of his wrath.

Andrew straightened from his position behind the furnace. Making final adjustments to the explosives, he covered the box with strewn clutter and turned to his companion. Jordan was guarding the doorway. His face was tense and his body taught. He joined him. Touching his arm, he asked, "Is that it?"

"Yes."

"Are you sure they have not detected us? Craven and Jason are usually very observant."

Andrew appeared weary and despondent. Jordan wondered if the strain of screening their presence and purpose from the other porphyrians in the building was too much for him.

Andrew answered his unspoken question. "No, it's actually been easy to deceive them. They are so caught up in their debate about how they are going to terminate us that they don't realize we've beaten them to the punch."

Jordan searched his friend's face until he finally understood his anguish. "You're doing the right thing. That group represents the heart of the conspiracy. They're mad. They've developed a taste for human blood and want to revive vampirism. The diurnals will retaliate. You are preventing the spreading of a cancerous growth that eventually will lead to the extinction of our race."

"I know." He smiled weakly and gathered the empty duffle bag. "Let's go."

They made their way up the stairs and out of the front door. The meeting was in a back room on the second floor. Andrew would be able to sense any porphyrian who left the room, so stealth was unnecessary.

Turbulent thoughts whirled like cyclones in Dana's mind as she approached the conference room. With her hand on the knob, she hesitated. If she reentered, her father would know that she was unresolved. Right now, he was too busy in the meeting to focus on her thoughts. Turning away, she headed towards the front of the building. She walked to the window and gazed down at the street. Two men emerged from the building and stood on the pavement while conversing.

Jordan glanced back at the building and gasped. Wide brown eyes registered shock as the figure stared back at him. "Dana," he whispered shakily. He turned and glared accusingly at Andrew. "I thought you said she had left the building."

Andrew glanced up. "She did. She returned and was heading back towards the conference room when I last checked."

"Why didn't you stop her?" Jordan was outraged.

Troubled turquoise eyes shot an intent look at him. "I'm not sure we can trust her. As far as Craven is concerned, she is an open book. The reason she is looking out the window instead of sitting at the conference table is because she knows he will discern her divided loyalties. She loves you, but she is still under her father's influence. And," he finished softly, "despite her misgivings, she loves him. If she's alerted, there is a good chance she will sound an alarm."

"Then, she's probably already alerted him to our presence and getting her out won't make any difference."

Andrew sadly stared at him. "All she knows is we're here, not why. She hasn't alerted Craven to our presence and doesn't intend to, but, if you become insistent that she leave the building, she's liable to get suspicious. If Craven finds out we're here, he will assume the worst. He and the others might escape. We can't take that chance." Jordan appeared unconvinced and he continued implacably, "Rebelling against her father is one thing; letting him die is another. I'm not willing to risk it."

Jordan glared at him. "If it were Victory in there, would you let her die?" Without waiting for a response, he dashed towards the building.

"Jordan, it's not safe. You only have three minutes before the place blows."

Chapter 39:

The Confligration

Jordan crashed through the door. Glass shattered. He was sure that the noise would alert the others, but he was beyond caring. He heard Andrew calling and realized that he was following. Afraid that he would use his influence to stop him, he ran faster.

Dana turned from the window as the door opened. Jason stepped in and softly closed the door behind him. She had never trusted this man so she watched warily as he stepped over to a machine that was leaning against the adjacent wall. Her brows drew together as he flicked switches and set dials on some sort of device resembling a clothespress.

She stepped away from the window to distract him so that he would not see the scene below. "What were they doing here, anyway?" she wondered, while walking towards Jason.

"What is that?" she asked curiously.

"A tanning bed."

"Are you planning to catch some rays?" she enquired lightly. She wondered if this was part of her father's plan for dealing with Andrew.

He ignored her question. "Your father sent me to talk to you," he said, as he turned to her, "He's concerned that your lack of support might cause dissention." His grasp was cold and hard as he wrapped his fingers around her wrist and yanked her towards him. Inwardly cringing at his touch, she refused to give ground. "That is exactly the reason why I didn't go back. I am sure the others would have sensed my ambivalence. I thought I would take a few private moments to collect myself," she added pointedly.

Jason gripped the front of her dress and yanked. A gasp escaped her lips as the material parted and was peeled off. Outraged, she glared at him in shock and then with mounting anger. "What do you think you're doing?" she enquired, while coldly wrenching free. She raised her hand to deliver a stinging blow, but her arm froze. With her mind reeling, she fought to regain control. Her eyes widened and her face paled. "Father, please don't."

Jason stripped the rest of her clothing and placed her suddenly compliant body onto the table. Instantly, her skin began to itch as though a million fire ants were biting into her flesh. Unable to move, she stared into the ultraviolet rays. The light seared her, singed her skin, burned her nerve endings, and boiled her blood. An agonized scream welled in her throat, but she swallowed hard. She'd be damned if she was going to allow him that satisfaction.

Jason's eyes narrowed. "I think in about five minutes, you will be more amenable."

She defiantly glared back, but soon had to close her eyes against the searing heat. He chuckled. "Not nearly so arrogant now, are you?" Bending over her, he spread her legs. Again, she tried to resist, but her mind locked. So, rape was part of the punishment. She groaned.

"Yes," he said, as he confirmed her fear. "If it's any consolation, not by me." Confusion was replaced by revulsion as he explained.

"Your father has decided to procure the integrity of the line." Their eyes met and locked. She stared so hard that her eyes watered and stung, but she still refused to look away. Finally, Jason dropped his gaze.

Amazed but satisfied, Dana started to tell the porphyrian where he could put his ideas. Abruptly, the door burst open and a frenzied Jordan Rush charged into the room. Startled, both porphyrians stared at the intruder. Dana was the first to recover.

"He's alerted father and he's sending reinforcements."

Jordan gaped at the scene and then turned murderous jade eyes on his foe. Pulling his revolver with its attached silencer from his pocket, he shot the other porphyrian between the eyes.

Dana winced as he helped her out of the machine. Gasping in an effort to breath, she implored, "Jordan, you've got to get out of here. I can hold them off for a few minutes, but your life is in grave danger."

Ignoring the warning, he slipped his jacket over her raw skin. She winced. He stared furiously at the figure on the floor and wished that he could kill him again. Grasping her wrist, he dragged her towards the door. "I'm not leaving without you."

Dana pulled back. Are you crazy? They will be after you in a heartbeat if you take me. Allow me to buy you some time and I'll join you later."

Jordan's eyes narrowed. Dana glanced over her shoulder. Walter was casually strolling across the room. He had been ordered to check up on Dana and Jason, but, because of the silencer, the group had not heard the shots. "You know, Jordan," he said coldly, "you've saved us a lot of trouble. Now, instead of wasting time on planning how to eliminate you, we can focus on Andrew."

Hurling Dana towards the open door, Jordan turned to face his adversary. The earl lifted his arm and aimed the revolver. Before he could pull the trigger, the gun was torn from his grasp.

Walter lifted his own gun and aimed it at the earl's head. Dana screamed as she launched herself in front of Jordan. A crash sounded behind Walter as a body smashed into his back causing the bullet to be knocked astray. Before Walter could react, Andrew plunged the dagger deep into his back. Walter grunted and tried to maneuver, but the marquis deftly sliced his throat with a force that decapitated his victim.

Andrew turned to face them. His expression was grim. Silently, they maneuvered their way along the hallway and past the conference room. As they passed, the door opened and Craven confronted them.

"Gate crashers," he said mockingly. "Won't you come in and join the party? After all, it is in your honor."

"How long?" Jordan asked silently.

"One minute," Andrew returned. "If we try to leave, they will come after us and some will escape."

Jordan nodded his understanding. Together, they entered the room.

"You know, brother," Craven said with a voice as smooth as silk, "you are not being a very good uncle. That's twice that you have deprived Dana of suitors."

Jordan's face flushed. Dana opened her mouth to protest, but one look at her father silenced her.

Andrew moved further into the crowded room. The hostility in the faces surrounding him was palpable. There was something else about their faces: a fullness, a flush on their cheeks, a brightness in their eyes, an agitation in their movements. Walking over to stare out of the far window, he finally spoke.

"How long have they been drinking blood?" he demanded quietly.

"About a month and you can see the difference already."

"Yes," Andrew replied sarcastically, as he moved away from the window. "They already look like freaks and are wound up as tight as wires ready to snap."

"Your concern is touching, but I can control them."

"That remains to be seen. What are your intentions?"

Craven's eyes followed him like a predator stalking prey. Andrew stopped and glared around him. The faces were hostile but uncertain. He knew that they would not initiate an attack, but, at the first provocation from their leader, they would be quick to follow.

"My intentions," he scoffed, "after I rid myself of my current problems," he said while glaring first at the marquis and then at Jordan and Dana who were huddled at the far side of the room, "I will go to work on making this country the largest base of porphyrian sustenance the world has ever seen. My long-term goal is to be announced after my research has been completed. Too bad you won't be around to witness it."

As if on cue, the occupants of the room formed two groups. One group surrounded Andrew while the other lunged at the earl. Crouching low, Andrew catapulted into the air and hurtled through the skylight. Shattered glass rained onto the confused porphyrians. Using the distraction, Jordan slipped from the grasping hands and dove through the window as the building exploded. He desperately tried to grab Dana, but the building shifted, shook, and began to collapse. Dana stared imploringly at her father, "I swear I didn't know," she wailed.

As a second explosion shook the earth, flames shot through the floor and engulfed the room. Craven compelled his daughter towards him as he stood defiantly in the center of the inferno. A murderous rage lit his onyx eyes. Jordan's fingers grazed something as he was propelled through the air. Hair! "Bless Dana's long hair!" he thought as he clutched the strands.

BUILDING THE BRIDGE

The blonde sat on the balcony with the moonlight glittering off her golden hair. She leaned forward. Amazement again washed over her as she stared at the gold band encircling the third finger of her left hand. She still couldn't believe that she and Andrew were married. She reflected on the past few weeks, as she gazed at the ocean. Her eyes pierced the inky black water, as it crashed against the Cornish coast and sent foam and spray high into the air. While the breakers reverberated through her head, the moisture infiltrated her pores and the tangy salt burned her nostrils. She wondered if she would ever get used to her heightened senses. Andrew had explained all of the aspects of her condition as soon as she had recovered enough to comprehend. He explained that her heightened sensitivity at times would be uncomfortable until she learned to filter out unnecessary sensory input. He also had explained her need to stay out of the sun, her pale complexion, her prolonged lifespan, and her dependence on the drink. Explaining the necessity of giving up her career and relocating was a bit more difficult, but Andrew logically had pointed out that, until she had built up a tolerance to the sun and adapted ways to cover her lack of aging, it was unfeasible to continue her former life.

Victory frowned as she again looked down at her hand. Andrew had explained that marriage was against the custom of his people. It wasn't forbidden, but porphyrians had such an extended lifespan that choosing a single mate to spend one's life with was ridiculous and almost impossible. In addition, marriage was detrimental to the race. According to Andrew, the men outnumbered the women by four to one.

During pregnancy, the symptoms of porphyria became more severe and most women didn't live through childbirth.

"Then, why the commitment?"

"Because," a voice inside her head answered, "I love you so completely that I am certain my feelings will last an eternity or as much of that time as we have left.

Victory was unnerved slightly. The telepathy was one aspect that she never thought that she would accept. "Until I learn to guard my thoughts, I'm an open book for anyone who cares to read."

"An open book with lots of pretty pictures," Andrew said, as he joined her. Planting a kiss on her cheek, he handed a glass of reddish brown liquid to her. He spoke out loud since he knew that Victory was more comfortable in that mode. She leaned her head against his chest. "What will become of us, Andrew?"

He looked into her eyes and his turquoise gaze lost some of its humor. "I think we have taken the next step towards unification between the two species. I don't mean it will happen overnight, but, gradually, you and I will work together to unite our people. Eventually, you will realize your dream of becoming a Supreme Court justice and continue to stamp out bias and bigotry. I will plant the seeds of integration and weed out any future Craven Maxwells. When the time is right, the unification of our societies can be achieved. "In the meantime," he continued, as his eyes darkened, "I think it's time you and I considered some unification of our own."

The Author's Notes

Porphyria is the name of an actual blood disease that has a lack of certain enzymes in the hemoglobin of red blood cells. Symptoms such as lightened skin pigment, photophobia, and receding gums also can be aspects of the illness.

In creating this work of fiction, I took certain liberties in adapting this disorder to the storyline. For example, heightened senses, enhanced strength, and telepathic abilities are not part of the real disease. Contrary to the characters in my book, people suffering from porphyria usually have shortened rather than lengthened life spans. According to my research, those afflicted with this disease in ancient times were thought to be exhibiting signs of vampirism, especially in small villages and rural areas where superstitions ran rampant.

I have been interested in vampires, werewolves, mummies, and other classic monsters since I was a child. As I grew up, some of my favorite times were sp ent in front of the television while watching old movie classics starring Lon Chaney, Boris Karloff, and, of course, Bela Lagosi. I enjoy the gothic and mysterious as opposed to the typical slasher movies and that is what keeps vampires near and dear to my heart.

Going blind at the age of nineteen did nothing to deter my interest in movie monsters or in writing about them. I experienced difficult and challenging times with many temporary setbacks. For a while, I was filled with doubts about my ability to persevere. The guidance and support of those around me along with my own determination enabled me to enter the world of creative fiction.

I thoroughly enjoyed writing this first book of the Vampire Royalty series and I hope that you experience the same pleasure while reading it. – VH

For single copies or bulk purchases of
this and other books by
Valerie Hoffman:

Send your payment to:
American Legacy Books
PO Box 1393
Washington, DC 20013

or call:
202-737-7827
(1-888-331-2665)

or order online:
www.AmericanLegacyBooks.com/bookstore

One book: $9.95
plus postage and handling: $3.95
The total is: $13.90

If you are ordering by mail within the United States, please add $11.20 for each additional book ordered at the same time. (This price already includes $1.25 for postage and handling.) For the mailing costs for non-USA deliveries, please call 202-737-7827 or send an email that includes the name of your country to: orders@AmericanLegacyBooks.com.

Please allow two to four weeks for delivery within the United States.

American Express, MasterCard, VISA, and Discover credit/debit cards are accepted when you call the telephone number above or order online. For payment by check or money order, please mail to the address above.

Please call or email to learn if the price or postage has changed.